## THE MISSING FLAMINGO

Where in tarnation could the flamingo be?

She peered into the woods. A few yards away stood a clump of bushes beneath a stand of trees. Was that a bit of pink she saw?

She stopped in front of the bushes. Sure enough, there was her flamingo. Its pink head was sticking up about an inch through the foliage. She reached for the flamingo, then stopped.

What was that smell?

Geeze Louise, it stank something awful, like someone had been using these bushes for an outhouse. There was some other smell which seemed familiar, but she couldn't quite place it. Holding her breath, Wanda Nell reached for the flamingo again and tugged.

It didn't give much. That was strange, Wanda Nell thought. She tugged again. This time she could hear and feel something move in the bushes.

With one hand on the flamingo, and the other hand pushing some of the foliage aside, Wanda Nell looked down. Then she wished she hadn't.

She let go of the flamingo and stumbled backwards. She was trying not to vomit. She couldn't erase that picture from her mind.

Someone had killed Bobby Ray Culpepper, driving the metal legs of her flamingo through his neck, pinning him to the ground.

A Trailer Park Mystery

# Flamingo Fatale

## Jimmie Ruth Evans

BERKLEY PRIME CRIME, NEW YORK

**THE BERKLEY PUBLISHING GROUP**
**Published by the Penguin Group**
**Penguin Group (USA) Inc.**
**375 Hudson Street, New York, New York 10014, USA**
Penguin Group (Canada), 90 Eglinton Avenue East, Suite 700, Toronto, Ontario M4P 2Y3, Canada
(a division of Pearson Penguin Canada Inc.)
Penguin Books Ltd., 80 Strand, London WC2R 0RL, England
Penguin Group Ireland, 25 St. Stephen's Green, Dublin 2, Ireland (a division of Penguin Books Ltd.)
Penguin Group (Australia), 250 Camberwell Road, Camberwell, Victoria 3124, Australia
(a division of Pearson Australia Group Pty. Ltd.)
Penguin Books India Pvt. Ltd., 11 Community Centre, Panchsheel Park, New Delhi—110 017, India
Penguin Group (NZ), 67 Apollo Drive, Rosedale, North Shore 0632, New Zealand
(a division of Pearson New Zealand Ltd.)
Penguin Books (South Africa) (Pty.) Ltd., 24 Sturdee Avenue, Rosebank, Johannesburg 2196,
South Africa

Penguin Books Ltd., Registered Offices: 80 Strand, London WC2R 0RL, England

This is a work of fiction. Names, characters, places, and incidents either are the product of the author's imagination or are used fictitiously, and any resemblance to actual persons, living or dead, business establishments, events, or locales is entirely coincidental. The publisher does not have any control over and does not assume any responsibility for author or third-party websites or their content.

PUBLISHER'S NOTE: The recipes contained in this book are to be followed exactly as written. The publisher is not responsible for your specific health or allergy needs that may require medical supervision. The publisher is not responsible for any adverse reactions to the recipes contained in this book.

FLAMINGO FATALE

A Berkley Prime Crime Book / published by arrangement with the author

PRINTING HISTORY
Berkley Prime Crime mass-market edition / July 2005

Copyright © 2005 by Dean James.
Cover art by Paul Slater.
Cover design by Judith Lagerman.
Interior text design by Kristin del Rosario.

ISBN: 978-0-425-20398-9

BERKLEY® PRIME CRIME
Berkley Prime Crime Books are published by The Berkley Publishing Group,
a division of Penguin Group (USA) Inc.,
375 Hudson Street, New York, New York 10014.
The name BERKLEY PRIME CRIME and the BERKLEY PRIME CRIME design are trademarks belonging to Penguin Group (USA) Inc.

PRINTED IN THE UNITED STATES OF AMERICA

10  9  8  7  6  5  4  3  2

*For Carolyn Haines,*
*whose support and encouragement*
*have made a tremendous amount of difference.*

One who never turned his back but marched breast forward,
  Never doubted clouds would break,
Never dreamed, though right were worsted, wrong would
  triumph,
Held we fall to rise, are baffled to fight better,
                    Sleep to wake.

—Robert Browning, Epilogue to *Asolando*

# Acknowledgments

First thanks must go to my agent, the irrepressible Nancy Yost, who asked the important question, "Why hasn't anyone written a trailer park detective?" This book is the result, and I can't thank Nancy enough for the inspiration.

Natalee Rosenstein, my editor at Berkley for over a decade, has been unfailingly patient, encouraging, and supportive, and I owe her tremendous thanks for the many opportunities she has given me. Thanks also to her former assistant, Esther Strauss, for patiently answering my questions. It's a great pleasure being part of the Berkley Prime Crime family.

My uncle the judge, Henry Lackey, cheerfully and helpfully answers my questions about legal procedure in Mississippi. Any errors are mine, not his!

My very dear friends Tejas Englesmith (thanks for the flamingos!), Julie Wray Herman, and Patricia Orr have never flagged in their support, and having their broad shoulders to lean on sustains me each and every day.

# One

Wanda Nell Culpepper set the pot of hot coffee down so she wouldn't be tempted to throw it right in Fayetta Sutton's face. It would have been a pleasure to wipe away that nasty smirk and hear her howl like the witch she was, but Wanda Nell just couldn't do it. Now, if her best friend Mayrene Lancaster had been there, she would have grabbed the pot out of Wanda Nell's hand and done it for her. But Mayrene was at home, getting ready for a hot date.

Wanda Nell looked Fayetta straight in the face and lied. "I couldn't care less if Bobby Ray Culpepper has dragged his sorry behind all the way back here to Tullahoma. The day I divorced that loser was the best day of my life."

"It sure was the best day of *his* life," Fayetta cooed, as she pretended to wipe down the counter. She and Bobby Ray had been hot and heavy at one point, and she still acted like he couldn't get enough of her whenever he came back to town. "He musta gotten awful tired of such a tight-assed woman."

"Why, Fayetta," Wanda Nell said, her voice sweet as sugar icing, "I had no idea. You know a good dose of Ex-lax will fix you right up." She turned and walked away, smiling a little at the sniggers from a couple of the bubbas sitting at the counter.

"She done got you good, Fayetta," said Junior Farley. He was laughing so hard his big belly must have been shaking like Jell-O in an earthquake, but Wanda Nell didn't turn around to look. She just kept walking.

She went around the edge of the counter and on into the back dining room. The crowd tonight had been sparse, and she had only a couple of tables left back there. One table wanted their tea glasses topped up and a to-go box. By the time Wanda Nell had taken care of them, she had cooled off and was fussing at herself for letting Fayetta get to her. That heifer delighted in needling her, and Wanda Nell resolved, for the thousandth time, that she wasn't going to fall into the trap ever again.

Wanda Nell eyed her other customer. He had been sitting there for going on three hours now, most of the time just staring off into space. Every once in a while he stopped and scribbled something on a notepad. He had long since finished his dinner, and Wanda Nell had approached him a few times to refill his tea glass. He was so caught up in what he was thinking about he hardly noticed her, so she attended to his tea and left him in peace.

Now, as she watched, he put his pen down with a sigh and stared at his empty glass. Picking up the pitcher, Wanda Nell walked over to his table. "Another refill?" she asked, trying not to grin.

He pushed his glasses up his nose as he focused on her. "Oh, no thank you, I guess I've had enough by now." He looked at his watch. "Guess I also lost track of time. Y'all must be getting ready to close soon."

"You've got a while yet," Wanda Nell assured him, staring at him as discreetly as she could. She knew who he was, though she wasn't certain whether he remembered her. His name was Jack Pemberton, and he was her daughter Juliet's English teacher at Tullahoma County High School.

"Thanks," he said. Then he smiled shyly, and Wanda Nell couldn't help but smile back. He was so cute, in a professory kind of way, with his round, rimless glasses, boyish, brown locks hanging down across his forehead, and thin, intelligent face. He was also about Wanda Nell's age, fortyish, and his wedding-ring finger was bare.

"You're Juliet Culpepper's mother, aren't you?" Jack Pemberton said, still smiling.

"Yes." Wanda Nell's smile widened. Her youngest child was the light of her life. "Wanda Nell Culpepper," she said. "I met you back in the fall at one of those parent-teacher nights."

"I remember," Jack Pemberton said, and the tone of his voice warmed Wanda Nell for a moment. He sure had nice eyes, she thought.

"Jack Pemberton," he said, standing up and offering her his hand. Wanda Nell took it and enjoyed the warmth of it as he clasped her hand.

"I remember," Wanda Nell said, "and Juliet wouldn't let me forget, that's for sure. Now, don't you dare tell her I told you this, but she's always talking about what Mr. Pemberton says. You get quoted a lot around our house."

Jack Pemberton stood awkwardly, a light flush rising in his cheeks. "Juliet is my best student, Mrs. Culpepper. I wish I had a hundred more like her."

"Thank you," Wanda Nell said, a little flustered by his earnestness. She pulled his check out of her uniform pocket and put it on the table.

Almost absentmindedly, he picked it up. "Guess I'd better be going," he said. "This was my first time to eat here in the evening. I'm still finding my way around Tullahoma." He paused. "It was very good."

"Thank you," Wanda Nell said, waiting. He couldn't seem to make up his mind to start walking toward the front of the restaurant or to say something else.

"Nice to see you again," Pemberton said, his legs finally working and moving him away from the table. He was a few paces away when he paused and looked back for a moment. "I guess I might start eating here more often." He gave her a nervous smile, then almost ran toward the cash register.

Turning away to hide a pleased grin, Wanda Nell bent over and began to clear the table. He had left her a big tip, she was glad to see. He was a bit on the shy side, but he sure was nice. She wouldn't mind seeing him again. Humming a little, she finished with the table.

Glancing at her watch, she saw it was a few minutes past nine now, and the Kountry Kitchen closed at ten. Business had been so slow tonight, maybe Melvin would let her leave a little early. That way she'd have time to run home, check on the girls and the baby, and have a quick shower before she had to clock in at Budget Mart. She needed something to perk her up, and she reckoned a shower would just about do it.

Wanda Nell cleared her last two tables in the front dining room, gratefully sliding the generous tips into her pocket. She was trying to make an extra payment every other month on the trailer, and she was getting close to having enough for one.

When Wanda Nell finished, Fayetta was near the cash register, talking to one of the good ol' boys who hung around her like flies around a cow patty. Wanda Nell couldn't repress a grin at the image. She pushed through the door into the kitchen and looked around for Melvin.

"Out back smoking," said Elray, the dishwasher, jerking his dark head to one side.

"Thanks, Elray," Wanda Nell said. After waving at Lurene, the cook, she grabbed a bit of fried chicken off a plate, wrapped it in a napkin, and stuffed it in her pocket.

She walked down the short hall to the back door of the restaurant and stopped in the open doorway, sniffing appreciatively. Ever since the baby came, she had given up smoking, and it was darn hard not to backslide. When she was around other smokers, she enjoyed every minute, getting a little buzz from the secondhand smoke.

Before she could say anything, she felt the brush of something warm and smooth against her legs. She bent down and rubbed the stray cat on the head. "Hey, there, fella, how are you tonight?" She pulled the chicken from her pocket and started tearing it apart for the cat, now almost dancing with excitement at her feet.

Melvin Arbuckle turned to watch her and the cat. "Why don't you just take him on home with you, 'stead of keeping him hanging around the back door all the time?"

"I guess one of these days I will," Wanda Nell said, sighing. Strays always seemed to find her, but she didn't need one more body dependent on her at the moment. Maybe if she held out a little longer she could find somebody to adopt this little guy. Once he realized there was no more chicken he trotted off into the bushes a few feet away.

"Slow night, wasn't it?" Melvin said, watching her through the smoke drifting from his nose and mouth.

"Yeah," said Wanda Nell, leaning up against the door frame and gazing up into the night sky. The April breeze was soft and cool on this beautiful evening, and she let the calmness wash over her.

"Reckon you wanna leave early and run home."

"Yeah, if you don't mind."

Melvin shrugged. "Don't matter to me none, but Fayetta ain't gonna thank you for having to close up."

"Uh-huh," Wanda Nell said. "Like she won't be all over you, rubbing up against you like a cat in heat the whole time." She kept her tone light.

Melvin grinned as the smoke drifted out of his nose. "Girl's gotta have something to compensate her for you bailing out."

"Don't flatter yourself," Wanda Nell said. "That girl goes after anything in pants that even looks like it's male." She shook her head. "Why you put up with her carrying on, I'll never know."

"Since you won't have nothing to do with me," Melvin said, his voice taking on a slight edge, "I don't think you need to be worrying about who I take up with."

Wanda Nell tensed. Now was not the time to get into that old argument again. Melvin was a good-looking man, and a lot of women in Tullahoma would have been downright happy to go with him. Wanda Nell liked him, and he had always been a good friend to her. That was just the point—no use letting sex get in the way between them.

"We've been over this before, Melvin," she said, trying to keep an edge out of her voice.

"I know, I know," Melvin said with resignation. He turned and flicked his cigarette butt through the air and into the Dumpster.

"You're gonna set that thing on fire one of these days," Wanda Nell said.

Melvin just grunted, his back still to her. She almost reached out to touch him but held back.

"So you don't mind if I head on out?"

"Naw," Melvin said without turning. "Get on outta here, and I'll see you tomorrow."

"Thanks, Melvin," she said. "I appreciate it."

Before her boss could change his mind, Wanda Nell grabbed her purse out of the small storeroom where she stashed it and her change of clothes. Melvin had gone back into the kitchen, so she left by the back door. Melvin could explain to Fayetta that she had left.

As she unlocked the door to her dusty red Cavalier, she glanced around the parking lot. Only a few cars were left, and the streets around the restaurant were quiet. Not much action this late on a Wednesday night in Tullahoma, Mississippi. Wanda Nell nosed the car out onto the highway and headed east toward the lake.

One good thing about a small town like Tullahoma, she reflected, was that, even though it had grown a lot in recent years because of several new factories, it still took only about ten minutes to get from one end of town to the other in any direction.

Three minutes later she turned off the highway onto the reservoir road and wound her way through the gentle hills for nearly two miles before reaching the turnoff for the Kozy Kove Trailer Park. Wanda Nell had lived there for five years, and she liked the trailer park's proximity to the beach at the lake. She also enjoyed the woods around the trailer park, because she could step out of her front door and only a few strides later be out under the trees. Whenever she needed a quiet moment, she went for a walk in the woods. And lately, with the baby so active and Miranda being so difficult, she needed those walks even more. The silence and solitude of the woods helped her make it through the long, tiring days when it seemed like everybody she knew needed something from her.

Wanda Nell sighed heavily as she pulled her car into the little carport attached to her double-wide trailer. Juliet's light was still on, even though it was a school night and she was supposed to be in bed at nine. She was reading, Wanda

Nell guessed as she heaved herself and purse and clothes from the car. She didn't have the heart to fuss at her, because Juliet was such a bright girl. She was the one who was really going to make something of herself. Wanda Nell held tight to that thought. The light went off as she watched.

She walked around the car toward the front door of the trailer, and as she got closer she could hear music and laughter coming from inside. She frowned. She hoped it was just Miranda listening to the TV, and not some no-account boy she had invited over.

Miranda's high-pitched giggle hit her as she opened the door. She stood there, angry and startled, though she realized she shouldn't be in the least surprised.

"What the hell are you doing here, Bobby Ray?" she said, stepping inside and pulling the door shut with a thump. She did not need this. She was tired, and she still had her shift at Budget Mart to get through. She did not need to hassle with her ex-husband right now.

Bobby Ray Culpepper's lazy, sexy grin taunted her as he stood up from the couch, where he had been sitting with his middle child. "Hey there, Sugar Booger." He knew how Wanda Nell detested that particular endearment. "You know I had to come by and see my girls and my new grandbaby."

"Well, I hope to god Lavon is in his crib and asleep by now," Wanda Nell said, fixing Miranda with a stare. Her daughter squirmed a little and refused to meet her eyes.

"Now, don't go picking on Randa the minute you walk in the door," Bobby Ray said, his voice jovial. "I just know she's a good little mother."

Suppressing the urge to ask him how the hell he would know, this being the first time he had been around since Lavon had entered the world fourteen months ago, Wanda Nell ignored him. Her eyes swept around the living room, and as she had expected, Miranda hadn't lifted a finger all afternoon to do the cleaning she had been told to do. How she had raised such a slob for a daughter, Wanda Nell didn't know. She was getting real tired of trying to make Miranda pitch in and help, instead of letting her mother and sister do everything around the house.

Miranda rightly interpreted the annoyed look on her mother's face. "I fell asleep this afternoon, Mama," she whined. "Lavon just about wore me out last night, and I was so tired I couldn't do anything but lay here on the couch." She brightened. "And then Daddy showed up a little while ago, and we've been talking."

Miranda always had some excuse as to why she couldn't get even the simplest job done. Wanda Nell had threatened more than once to kick her and the baby out of the trailer, but it hadn't done any good. Miranda knew her mama was too softhearted to do such a mean thing.

"I promise I'll clean up tomorrow," Miranda said.

Wanda Nell sighed, tired of the fuss and bother Miranda created. Miranda's promises were about as reliable as her father's. She was Bobby Ray all over again, and that was not a good thing.

But, thank the Lord, she wasn't as bad as her older brother. Wanda Nell had no idea where T.J. was at the moment, but no doubt he was in some kind of trouble. Miranda at least she could keep an eye on.

"I'd ask you to sit and visit for awhile," Wanda Nell addressed her ex, keeping her voice as even and calm as she could, "but I got to get ready for my shift at Budget Mart, and I'd appreciate it if you'd let the girls get to bed now." She hadn't heard a peep from Juliet's room, but she was probably at the door, listening. The girl barely knew her father, since he had lit out eleven years ago when she was only three. The few times he did come around, Juliet wouldn't have much to do with him. She didn't take easily to strangers.

"How's that working out for you, Wanda Nell?" Bobby Ray asked. He almost looked like he really cared, but Wanda Nell knew better.

"Just fine," she said shortly. "I can't wait to get there every night after my shift at the Kountry Kitchen so I can start restocking those shelves. I just about pop from the excitement."

"Yeah, well . . . " Bobby Ray's voice tapered off. He never had known how to handle Wanda Nell's sarcasm. He turned to look down at Miranda. "Sorry, Randa, but your old daddy has to get going, I guess. But I'll be seeing you again, real soon. I'm aiming to stick around awhile."

Wanda Nell took a good look at him. He was as handsome as ever, his hair thick and dark, with just the tiniest touch of gray at the temples. His face was lean and tanned, though he had the beginnings of a serious beer belly creeping over his belt. He was wearing what looked like brandnew cowboy boots, and expensive ones at that. Whenever he got his hands on some money, he never could hold on to it for more than five minutes. He was always spending it on something that didn't do nobody but him a bit of good. He sure hadn't spent it on his wife and children.

Bobby Ray turned back to Wanda Nell, and she would have sworn that, for a moment, she saw regret in his face. But it was quickly gone. He reached into the pocket of his worn jeans and pulled out a wad of bills so thick that Wanda Nell's eyes nearly popped out of her head.

"Bobby Ray! Where on earth did you get that kind of money?"

He smiled at her. "Don't you worry 'bout that, sugar. There's gonna be plenty more where this came from." He peeled off several bills and dropped them into Miranda's lap. They were hundred-dollar bills, Wanda Nell noted with shock.

Wanda Nell took three steps closer, so that she was only inches away from him. "What the hell have you gotten yourself into, Bobby Ray?" She knew too much about to him to expect that it was anything legitimate.

"It's none of your goddamn business," he said, anger flaring in his face. "Now you back off, and don't mess with me." His hand curled into a fist.

"You wouldn't dare hit me, Bobby Ray." She stood her ground. That was one thing he had never done, thank the Lord. He might have treated her like dirt, but he had never hit her.

He shifted uneasily. "Don't bet on it," he said, but his words lacked conviction.

"I want you the hell out of my house," Wanda Nell said, her temper getting out of control. "You got some kinda nerve, showing up here like this. Since when did you care a flipping thing about your family?" She was going to find something to hit him with in a minute, and then all hell would break loose. At the moment, she didn't care. Everything just came boiling up. She wanted the bastard out of her life, once and for all. And if that meant a fight, then she was ready for it.

"You are such a bitch, Wanda Nell," Bobby Ray said, stepping around her and striding to the door. "God knows why I ever married you in the first place, except maybe the fact that you were damn good in bed."

His hand was on the doorknob when a red haze seemed to pass over Wanda Nell's eyes. She glanced wildly around her, trying to find something, anything, to aim at his head. She picked up the footstool in front of the couch and pitched it at him, but by then he had the door open and was halfway out of it. The footstool hit the wall to the right of the door and fell with a thud on the floor.

Wanda Nell ran toward the open door and down the steps. Bobby Ray was beating a fast retreat up the road. "Stay away from here, you bastard!" She was screaming, and she didn't care how many of the neighbors heard her. "Keep the hell out of our lives!"

She stood there, her chest heaving, tears streaming down her face, while Bobby Ray disappeared into the night.

# Two

Wanda Nell let the hot water from the showerhead flow over her neck. She had really lost it with Bobby Ray. No telling what she might have done while her dander was up. That was the trouble with her temper, she reflected sourly. When she got mad, her usual common sense flew out the window.

She shouldn't let the jerk get to her that way, but every time she thought she had him out of her system for good, he'd turn up and get her going all over again. It didn't matter that the last two years of their marriage had been sheer hell for her and for their kids, she had loved the son of a bitch with a passion that still scared her.

If she didn't have some lingering feelings for him, she acknowledged, the sight of him wouldn't send her into such a tizzy. The trouble was, she had never gotten any kind of closure on their relationship. Back before Bobby Ray had left her and the kids for good, she used to watch some of those daytime talk shows, and they were always talking about closure and other stuff like that.

With a deep sigh she turned off the water and began to towel herself dry. She might barely make it on time for her shift at Budget Mart, but after that little set-to with Bobby Ray, she had to have a shower to relax her a bit. Instead she tried to think of something pleasant, like that nice Jack Pemberton. He sure was a welcome change, but he'd probably take one look at her kids and grandson and head off running in the opposite direction. She pushed that depressing thought out of her head.

Dressed once again, Wanda Nell grabbed up her purse and stepped out into the hallway. She opened the door to Juliet's room and sneaked a peek. Juliet was on her side, facing the door, one hand stuck beneath the pillow and the other clutching her favorite stuffed toy, a bear named Alexander, to her chest. Wanda Nell stood for a moment and watched her baby sleeping. *Thank you, Lord, for Juliet,* she thought.

Closing the door, she walked quietly down the hall, past the kitchen, into the living room. Miranda had fallen asleep on the couch. Repressing the urge to pinch the girl, Wanda Nell gazed down at her. She was her father's child in more ways than one. Like her brother, she had Bobby Ray's dark coloring and rosy skin. Juliet was the only one to take after her mother, with sandy blonde hair and a tendency to freckle.

Wanda Nell reached down and gently shook her daughter awake. "Wake up, Miranda," she said, her voice low. "You need to get back there and check on the baby. Come on now, sweetheart."

Miranda whimpered as she came awake. "What? Oh, Mama, it's you." She sat up and rubbed her eyes. "What time is it?"

"I'm leaving for work," Wanda Nell said, exasperated. "That's what time it is. You need to get on to bed. I expect you to do some cleaning up around here tomorrow."

"Aw, Mama," Miranda said, yawning. "With that money Daddy gave me, we can pay ol' Miz Hicks to come in and clean up."

"You better be thinking about spending some of that money on diapers and food for Lavon," Wanda Nell said. "Not to mention the bill you owe the doctor for when Lavon was running that high fever." She paused, not surprised at the mulish look on Miranda's face. "How much did he give you, anyway?"

"Five hundred," Miranda whispered.

Wanda Nell drew in a sharp breath. Where in hell had Bobby Ray gotten that kind of money? She wasn't sure she really wanted to know. "Before you start making all kinds of foolish plans for that money, Miranda, you and me are going shopping tomorrow after I get up. You hear me?"

"Yes'm," Miranda said. She refused to meet her mother's eyes.

"Go to bed," Wanda Nell said. "I'm gonna be late, thanks to your daddy."

Miranda mumbled something under her breath, but for once Wanda Nell didn't call her on it. Her shoulders slumped as she went out the door, locking it behind her. She hated having to be so hard on her own daughter, but Miranda didn't give her much choice.

Where had she gone wrong with Miranda, she wondered as she got in the car. She had drummed into the girl's fool head over and over again how important it was for her to be careful. Wanda Nell knew there was no way she was going to stop a girl as pretty and wild as Miranda from putting out for the boys she dated, but she had at least hoped her daughter would be smart enough not to get pregnant.

*Like mother, like daughter,* Wanda Nell thought, suddenly ashamed. How could she look Miranda in the face and chastise her for doing the same thing she had done? She hadn't set such a good example herself.

Wanda Nell had gone only about half a mile when her cell phone started ringing in her purse. Now who the heck would be calling her at this time of night? Her heart racing, worried that something might be wrong at home, she scrambled in her purse with her right hand, trying to find the phone. The only reason she justified spending the money on the dang thing was that the girls needed to be able to get in touch with her right away if the baby was sick or one of them needed something.

She brought the car to an abrupt halt as she peered at the little screen on the cell phone. "Oh, hell," she said, recognizing the number of the incoming call. "Hello."

"Wanda Nell, is that you?"

"Yes, Miz Culpepper, it's me," Wanda Nell said, trying not to grit her teeth at the sound of her former mother-in-law's voice.

"I called that place you work, and they said I should call this number. What are you doing with a cell phone?"

"It's for emergencies," Wanda Nell said pointedly. "Is there anything I can do for you, Miz Culpepper? I'm on my way to work, and I don't have a lot of time to be chatting with you."

Lucretia Culpepper sniffed into the phone. "I don't know how you can live with yourself, going off and leaving those girls in that trailer at night, all by themselves. No telling who might break in on them."

True to form, the old bat hadn't said a word about her great grandson, whose existence she had yet to acknowledge. Wanda Nell felt like throwing the phone out the window and driving the car back and forth over it, pretending that it was Lucretia Culpepper lying in the road instead.

"Since your beloved son can't be bothered to pay his child support, Miz Culpepper, somebody in the family has to earn a living." She might have added that her children's paternal grandparents had never lifted a finger to help them either, but she wouldn't give the old biddy the satisfaction. It was enough to be nasty about Bobby Ray, because she knew Mrs. Culpepper would get riled up.

"If Bobby Ray had fathered either of those girls of yours," Mrs. Culpepper said, "then he might be expected to do his duty by them."

Wanda Nell refused to be baited this time. She had heard it all before, many times. No matter that Miranda was just like her father, the old witch used any excuse she could think of to ignore her family's responsibilities to Bobby Ray's children.

"What is it you want, Miz Culpepper? Was there some reason you called me?" Wanda Nell put the car back in gear and drove slowly down the road. She hated to talk and drive at the same time, but there was very little traffic on the road this time of night.

"Have you seen Bobby Ray?"

"Unfortunately."

"Did he . . . did he say anything about coming to see me?"

At times Wanda Nell felt almost sorry for the old hellcat. Her only child didn't treat her any better than he treated his own children. Old Man Culpepper had died five years ago, and since then she had lived by herself in her fine, big house on Main Street.

"The subject didn't come up," Wanda Nell said. She had reached the highway, and she turned onto it and sped up. Budget Mart was on the other side of Tullahoma, but at this time of night, she should make it in about seven minutes. She glanced at the clock on the dashboard. She'd be only about five minutes late.

"If you see him again, you be sure and tell him his mother wants to see him."

Wanda Nell winced at the sharpness of Lucretia Culpepper's voice. "I'll surely do that."

"I really need to see him."

Miz Culpepper seemed awful persistent about it, Wanda Nell thought. Downright desperate, in fact. Otherwise she never would have called a woman she despised as much as she did her former daughter-in-law.

"I'll tell him," Wanda Nell said, even as she hoped that she wouldn't have the chance. "Good-bye," she said, before Miz Culpepper could exhort her to do anything else. She disconnected and put the phone back in her purse.

She concentrated on driving the rest of the way to work, but she couldn't help thinking about Bobby Ray and his mother. Bobby Ray treated her like dirt, but she took it and then some. *Like me and Miranda, I guess,* Wanda Nell thought. No matter what your kids do to you, you're still their mama.

Depressed, Wanda Nell pulled into a parking space in the lot at Budget Mart and turned off the car. She sat for a moment, staring blindly out into the night, determined not to cry. Then she got out of the car, locked it, and sprinted for the door.

She apologized to the coworker who let her in, but he waved away her apology. "Who gives a flying flip if you're late once in five years, Wanda Nell?" He grinned at her. "Even Ricky can't get mad at you. No matter what he says."

"Thanks," Wanda Nell said, smiling back. She wasn't so sure Ricky Ratliff, her supervisor, wouldn't be mad. He was always a bit rough on her. He was a crony of Bobby Ray's from way back in high school, and he had never liked her all that much. He blamed her for Bobby Ray's problems, but Wanda Nell had figured he was just jealous.

Before she got to work, she knew she had better face Ricky head on, get it over with right away. She tracked him down in the office, where he was sitting with his feet up, leafing through the kind of magazine he shouldn't be looking at while he was at work.

"Improving your mind, I see," Wanda Nell said before she stopped to think about it. She was really in a mood tonight. Bobby Ray always had that effect on her.

Ricky slapped the magazine down on the desk and shifted some papers on top of it. He scowled at her, his face flushing just slightly. "How come you're late? You're never late to work."

"Sorry about that," Wanda Nell said. "But I had unexpected company when I got home from the Kountry Kitchen."

He shifted his bulk in the chair. Wanda Nell and the rest of the night crew had bets on how long that chair could survive under his weight. The way it groaned every time he moved, it couldn't be much longer, she reckoned.

He didn't ask her who the unexpected guest was. He always knew when Bobby Ray was back in town, took great pride in the fact that he was always the first to see and talk to his good buddy.

"He's looking good, ol' Bobby Ray." Ricky leered at her.

"He still looks like the jackass I divorced," Wanda Nell said, deliberately provocative.

Ricky's face got even redder. "Getting hooked up with you was the biggest mistake he ever made." He muttered something under his breath, words that would shame his mama if she ever heard him talk like that. If he'd had the guts, he would have said it to her face. But Ricky was mostly hot air.

Wanda Nell stared him in the eye. She waited a moment, but he just looked at her, a stupid grin on his face. One of these days she was gonna kick him where his manhood was supposed to be, for the hell of it. No use acting like a lady around Ricky.

"Bobby Ray was flashing around a big wad of cash," Wanda Nell said. "Did he tell you how he got his hands on it?"

"Ain't none of your damn bidness," Ricky said. "Bobby Ray, he's on to something hot, and you ain't getting your hands on it."

Unimpressed, Wanda Nell shook her head at him. "It'll all be gone. He can't hold on to money to save his life."

Ricky laughed. "Plenty more where that came from."

"Next time you see your good ol' buddy Bobby Ray, I want you tell him something for me. You hear me, Ricky?" Wanda Nell had stepped closer to him, looked down at him, at his grubby T-shirt, trying not to breathe in his smell. The man sure didn't spend much money on soap and deodorant.

"What?"

"Tell him to keep away from me and the girls," Wanda Nell said. "He's nothing but trouble, and I'm not gonna have him bringing any of his crap around my house. I'll make sure he regrets it. You hear me?"

Abruptly, Ricky pushed his chair back and stood up. "You better watch your mouth, Wanda Nell. You wanna keep this job, you better not be talking to me like this. Why don't you trot your skinny ass back out on the floor and get to work?"

"You mind what I said, Ricky," Wanda Nell told him, refusing to back down. "You tell him, you hear?"

She turned and stalked out of the office. This time Ricky's insult was more audible, but he still didn't have the guts to say it to her face. She wasn't worried about her job. Ricky might bitch about her to the store supervisor, but Mr. Tompkins knew she was a hard worker and wouldn't fire her just on Ricky's say-so.

For the rest of her shift, Wanda Nell restocked shelves and checked prices with her mind only partially on her work. Mostly she fretted and fumed over the problem of Bobby Ray's turning up again like he had. Every time in recent years he had deigned to grace them with his presence, something unpleasant had happened. Last time, he had gotten T.J. all riled up, and the boy had ended up in jail yet again. Wanda Nell's heart was heavy every time she thought of her firstborn. That boy had packed a whole lot of trouble and hard living into just twenty-two years. She wondered if he would even live to see thirty.

She thought back over that scene in the trailer. For the first time, she wondered how Bobby Ray had gotten to the trailer park. She frowned, remembering. She hadn't seen a car anywhere, at least not a car that didn't belong in the trailer park. Surely Bobby Ray hadn't walked the couple of miles out there from town?

Somebody must have dropped him off, she figured. But had that person come back and picked him up? Maybe he had just gone and hid in the bushes until she was gone, then slunk back to the trailer to talk to Miranda some more.

Well, there wasn't a dang thing she could do about any of it now. She'd better concentrate on her job, or she could goof something up and get in trouble after all.

By the time Wanda Nell was done at seven A.M., she was exhausted, but she wanted to get home as quickly as she could. She hoped she wasn't going to find Bobby Ray there, asleep on the couch. Surely even he couldn't be that brazen.

The sun was just coming up, and Wanda Nell yawned all the way home. As she pulled her car into the trailer park, she scanned the area for unfamiliar vehicles. She breathed more easily when she didn't see any signs of one. Clutching her purse, she got out into the cool morning air and shivered a little. She really was tired, and the sooner she got Juliet off to school, the sooner she'd be able to get some sleep.

As she walked around the car toward the front door of the trailer, she glanced at the flower beds she had planted at that end of the trailer. She stopped and closed her eyes, then opened them again. She counted.

Dammit! One of her pink flamingos was missing. That little brat of Janette Sultan's had taken it again. He thought it was real funny to steal one of her pink flamingos and hide it, and his fool mama let him get away with it. For a moment she was tempted to forget about it because she was so tired, but then it just flew all over her. Her temper flared, and she marched across the gravel road to the Sultans' trailer.

She banged on the door as hard as she could. She didn't care if she woke everybody up, she was good and tired of that little brat playing his jokes on her.

"What is it, Wanda Nell? What's wrong?" Janette Sultan opened the door, blinking nervously in the early morning sun and clutching her threadbare bathrobe to her skinny bosom.

"Wayland's done done it again, that's what," Wanda Nell said furiously. "You get that little brat out here right this minute and tell him I want my flamingo back. I'm sick and tired of him and his pranks."

Janette drew up at this attack on her baby. "I'll have you know Wayland ain't here, Wanda Nell. And he ain't been here for several days. He's staying with his daddy this week, if it's any of your business. Now I'll thank you to get the hell out of my face." Stepping back, she slammed the door.

Stunned, Wanda Nell stood there a moment, trying to take it in. Janette might be too easy on her brat, but she didn't lie about things like this.

Slowly Wanda Nell turned around and stared at her trailer. Where in tarnation could the flamingo be? And who besides Wayland Sultan would have taken it?

She looked slowly up and down the trailer park. Hers was the only one with pink flamingoes, and if someone had taken one to stick in a flower bed, she would spot it easily. She headed down the gravel road that divided the park into two long rows, turning her head back and forth.

She had reached the end of the road without having spotted a single flash of pink. Now madder than ever, she was determined to find the damn thing if it killed her. She stalked back up the gravel and stopped in front of her trailer, considering. Maybe someone had taken it and dumped it in the woods.

She went along the road, looking into the woods. The sun hadn't penetrated very far into the dense growth, but if the flamingo was anywhere nearby she ought to be able to spot it.

Abruptly, she halted. What was that? She peered into the woods. A few yards away stood a clump of bushes beneath a stand of trees. Was that a bit of pink she saw?

Cautiously she made her way toward the bushes. She wasn't too keen on finding a snake in the woods. In the summer they had to be real careful, because the snakes turned up around their trailers all the time, sunning themselves. Wishing she had thought to find a big stick, Wanda Nell drew slowly closer and closer to the bushes.

The closer she came, the more she was sure that someone had stuck her flamingo in there. Why, she had no earthly idea.

She stopped in front of the bushes. Sure enough, there was her flamingo. Its pink head was sticking up about an inch through the foliage. Wanda Nell had no idea what kind of bush it was, she just hoped it wouldn't make her break out. She reached for the flamingo, then stopped.

What was that smell?

Jeez Louise, it stank something awful, like someone had been using these bushes for an outhouse. There was some other smell that seemed familiar, but she couldn't quite place it. Holding her breath, Wanda Nell reached for the flamingo again and tugged.

It didn't give much. That was strange, Wanda Nell thought. She tugged again. This time she could hear and feel something move in the bushes.

With one hand on the flamingo, and the other hand pushing some of the foliage aside, Wanda Nell looked down. Then she wished she hadn't.

She let go of the flamingo and stumbled backwards. She was trying not to vomit, but she couldn't erase that picture from her mind.

Someone had killed Bobby Ray Culpepper, driving the metal legs of her flamingo through his neck, pinning him to the ground.

# Three

Wanda Nell threw up the Nabs and MoonPie she had eaten on her last break of the morning at Budget Mart. She managed not to get any of it on her, but the tree she had leaned against wasn't so lucky.

Light-headed, wiping her mouth with the sleeve of her shirt, she staggered away from the tree, back toward the road. She kept moaning "Ohmigod, ohmigod" over and over. The horror of what she had seen wouldn't leave her. She had seen dead people before, but nothing ever like this.

She made it to the road and ran toward her trailer, thinking she would get inside and call the sheriff's office. But then she realized that wasn't such a good idea. She didn't want to get her girls upset any sooner than she had to. Thank the Lord none of the neighbors seemed to be stirring just yet.

Wanda Nell went on to the trailer next door. Her best friend Mayrene was exactly who she needed right now. She reached the door of the trailer and started knocking on it as loud as she dared.

Moments later, Mayrene swung the door open. "Now what in the hell are you banging . . . Oh, it's you, Wanda Nell. My Lord, girl, what's the matter with you?" Hands on her ample hips, Mayrene stared at her.

As usual, Mayrene had not a hair out of place. Wanda Nell didn't know how her friend did it, but she was immaculate every minute of the day, even in a nightgown and slippers.

"Oh, my God, Mayrene, it's awful," Wanda Nell finally managed to get out. She burst into tears.

Alarmed, Mayrene reached out and pulled Wanda Nell into the trailer. "What is it, honey? Is it the baby? Or one of the girls? What's wrong?"

Through her sobs, Wanda Nell managed to tell Mayrene what she had found in the woods.

"Jesus H., Wanda Nell," Mayrene said, staring blankly at her. "I knew the sonofabitch was useless, but who the hell would do something like this?"

Wanda Nell just stood there, sobbing. Mayrene gathered her into her arms and held her close until she got her crying under control. "Now, come on over here and set yourself down, honey. I'm gonna get you some hot coffee with plenty of sugar, and I want you to drink it, you hear me?"

Having been plopped down on the couch, Wanda Nell nodded up at Mayrene. Moments later, Mayrene was back with a mug of steaming coffee, and Wanda Nell wrapped her cold hands around it. Slowly she sipped at the hot liquid, and color began to seep back into her face. "Thank you," she said, her voice steadier now.

"You just sit there and keep on drinking," Mayrene instructed, "whiles I go and call the sheriff's department." She turned away and went into the kitchen to the phone.

Dimly, Wanda Nell could hear Mayrene's voice as she spoke with the dispatcher. She looked down into the mug of coffee, trying to push away images of what she had found in the woods. She raised the mug to her lips and drank again.

"They'll be here soon, Wanda Nell," Mayrene told her gently. "Now you just sit there for a minute, and I'm gonna go throw on some clothes. I don't wanna be giving those lawmen any thrills they ain't entitled to." She grinned at Wanda Nell.

Smiling faintly, Wanda Nell reached out a hand to her friend, and Mayrene gave it a reassuring squeeze. *Thank you, Lord, for Mayrene,* Wanda Nell thought.

Mayrene was actually back in five minutes. Wanda Nell knew exactly how long it had been, because she had been staring at the Elvis clock on the wall to keep her mind clear and free.

"You finish all that coffee, honey?" Mayrene took the mug from Wanda Nell's hands. "Good. You feeling any better?"

Wanda Nell nodded, not trusting herself to speak.

Mayrene sat on the couch beside her and put an arm around her shoulders. "I know it was horrible for you, honey, and I wish you hadn't seen it. But now we've got to start thinking about those girls of yours. We need to get on over to your trailer and talk to them, before the sheriff's men get here, don't you think? It won't do to have them look out and see all those lawmen here without knowing what's going on."

"You're right," Wanda Nell said, surprised at how clear and strong her voice sounded. "And the school bus is gonna be here any minute." She got to her feet. Her knees were no longer shaking, and she took a step forward. "Oh, Lord, what am I thinking? Juliet can't go to school today." She turned to Mayrene.

"Don't worry about that now, honey," Mayrene said in a firm tone. "All in good time." She pointed Wanda Nell toward the door.

Out the trailer they went, across the yard that separated Mayrene's home from Wanda Nell's. Wanda Nell fumbled for her purse, then realized she didn't have it. She turned an alarmed face to Mayrene. "Oh, my Lord, Mayrene, my purse. I must've dropped it in the woods."

"Don't worry, they'll find it," Mayrene said, still in that firm tone. "We better not go looking for it. We don't wanna be messing up the crime scene anymore'n it's already messed up." Mayrene watched a lot of those cop shows on TV, so Wanda Nell didn't argue with her.

Wanda Nell tried the doorknob, and it twisted open easily. She must have forgotten to lock it on the way out last night, and evidently Miranda had never thought to check it.

She opened the door and stepped inside. The sight that met her eyes almost caused her to faint. Mayrene stepped in behind.

"Lord have mercy!" Mayrene said. "What on earth?"

From the back of the trailer, Wanda Nell could hear Lavon crying. She wondered why he wasn't screaming. She sure wanted to, but she took a deep breath instead.

The trailer looked like a tornado had ripped right through it. Cushions had been tossed off the chairs and the couch, and drawers had been pulled open, their contents thrown around the room. Without even thinking about it, Wanda Nell glanced into the kitchen and saw that the same thing had happened there.

Then the shock began to pass, and all she could think about was the safety of her girls and her grandson. "Go check on Miranda and the baby," she told Mayrene. Without waiting for an answer, she ran down the hall to her right toward the two bedrooms which were hers and Juliet's.

She didn't spare a glance for the bathroom or her own room, intent on getting to her younger daughter as quickly as she could. She burst into Juliet's room, then stopped short.

Lying on her bed, her arms and legs immobilized by duct tape, with more tape on her mouth, Juliet blinked her eyes in relief at the sight of her mother.

"Oh Lord, who could do such a thing," Wanda Nell said as she dropped to her knees beside Juliet's bed. With trembling fingers she reached for the tape covering the girl's mouth. At least the person who had done this had wrapped some cloth around Juliet's head and hands to protect them from the duct tape. He'd used the girl's long nightgown to protect her legs. "I don't want to hurt you, sweetie, but I've got to get this off." Juliet nodded, and as gently as she could, but quickly, Wanda Nell found the edge and pulled off the tape.

"Thank you, Mama," Juliet whispered. "I was so afraid those men got ahold of you, too."

Wanda Nell tore at the tape which bound Juliet's arms and legs in such a way that she couldn't have gotten off the bed without injuring herself badly. The tape was wound so thickly that she didn't bother trying to find the edge to unwrap it.

"I've got some scissors in my desk drawer, Mama," Juliet said.

Wanda Nell scrambled for the scissors, then forced herself to slow down. She didn't want to cut Juliet while she was trying to get the tape off. She couldn't bear to think about what else "those men" might have done to Miranda and Juliet. If they had touched either of her girls, she swore she'd cut their balls off with a butter knife.

Then Juliet's arms were free, and the girl grabbed her mother in a hug. Wanda Nell returned it, then gently disengaged her daughter's arms and began rubbing the two smaller hands between her own. "Are you okay, sweetie? Did they hurt you?" She braced herself for the answer.

"No, Mama," Juliet said. At fourteen she was old enough to know what her mother meant. "They didn't touch me. They just tied me up with the tape."

Offering a silent prayer, Wanda Nell started cutting the tape that bound Juliet's legs. They were soon released from their bondage, and Wanda Nell rubbed her hands up and down Juliet's legs to bring the circulation back.

"Thank you, Mama," Juliet said, "but can you help me up? I've got to pee real bad."

Almost laughing with relief, Wanda Nell nearly lifted Juliet off the bed. With a supporting arm around the girl's shoulders, she guided her to the bathroom.

"What about Miranda?" Juliet asked as she sank down on the toilet seat.

"Mayrene is with her," Wanda Nell said. "I'll go check on her, if you'll be okay."

"I'm okay, Mama," Juliet said.

Wanda Nell turned and headed toward the other end of the trailer, afraid of what she might find. She met Mayrene, carrying a diaper, in the hall just outside the door of Miranda's bedroom. Her eyes asked a silent question of her friend.

"She's okay, honey," Mayrene said, reaching out a hand to give Wanda Nell's shoulder a reassuring squeeze. "And so is Lavon. They're just scared. Nobody hurt them. You go on in there, and I'm going to fix that baby a bottle soon as I get rid of this here smelly diaper. He'll settle down when he's had something to eat."

Wanda Nell stepped past Mayrene and into the bedroom. Miranda had Lavon in her lap, rocking him back and forth, crooning to him. On shaky legs, Wanda Nell went forward, then sank down to her knees on the floor in front of Miranda.

Before she could say a word, Miranda said, "I heard the car drive up like fifteen minutes ago, Mama. Where were you?" Her eyes filled with tears. "What took you so long?"

Guilt stabbed through Wanda Nell immediately. "Oh, honey," she said, reaching out for her elder daughter. Miranda, still holding her son, sat stiff in her mother's embrace.

Wanda Nell sat back on her heels. "Miranda, I'm sorry. I wish I'd gotten here sooner, but something happened." She broke off.

The sound of a siren came closer and closer. Miranda's eyes grew wide with surprise. "How'd you know to call the sheriff, Mama?"

"We had to call them about something else, honey," Wanda Nell said, desperately trying to find the words to break the news to Miranda. Of her three children, Miranda was the one who had always idolized her father.

"What happened?" Miranda said. Lavon had grown quiet now, sucking his thumb and watching his grandmother through his dark lashes.

Wanda Nell reached out a hand to her daughter. "Oh, sweetie, something awful's happened." She paused. "It's your daddy."

"What happened to my daddy?" Miranda's voice rose with each syllable.

From behind Wanda Nell, Juliet, now dressed in jeans and a polo shirt, interrupted them. "Mama, the sheriff's men are here. When did you call them?"

Before Wanda Nell could answer either of her daughters, they all heard a loud knock at the door of the trailer.

Reaching behind her to draw Juliet forward, Wanda Nell sat her younger daughter down beside her sister on the bed.

"Girls, I'm afraid I have some bad news about your

daddy." Miranda's eyes were already filling with tears, while Juliet merely gazed at her mother with curiosity. "Your daddy's dead. I found him out in the woods. Somebody killed him."

Miranda burst into noisy sobs, frightening her son, who began wailing just as loud as she was. Juliet frowned. "How, Mama? Was it those men who tied up me and Miranda?"

Wanda Nell drew in a deep, steadying breath. "How they did it don't matter right now, sweetie. And I guess it could've been those men who tied you up and trashed this place. But I just don't know." She stood up. "Did either of you recognize any of them? How many men were there?"

Juliet opened her mouth to speak, but then she clamped it shut and jerked her head sideways at her mother.

Wanda Nell turned at the sound of a throat being cleared behind her.

"If you don't mind, Miz Culpepper," said a man in uniform, "I reckon I'd better be the one asking questions for a while."

*Well, damn!* Wanda Nell thought. *I might've guessed.*

## Four

"Hello, Elmer Lee," Wanda Nell said, feeling like she was going to vomit again. Elmer Lee Johnson was another old buddy of Bobby Ray's, and he despised her, as he made plain anytime he ate at the Kountry Kitchen. He delighted in trying to make her feel like dirt.

"If you don't mind, Miz Culpepper," he drawled, "you better remember to call me Lieutenant Johnson. This here's an official investigation, and we have to keep things on a formal basis, you might say."

"Sure, Lieutenant Johnson," Wanda Nell said, wanting to scratch his eyes out.

"Now, Miz Lancaster here," Elmer Lee said, jerking his head in Mayrene's direction, "called in to the sheriff's department to report that somebody found a body in the woods here."

Wanda Nell nodded.

"If it was you that found the body, Miz Culpepper," he continued, "then I guess I'm gonna have to ask you to show me and my men just where you found it." He stood there, arrogant as a peacock, with his hands resting on the gun belt around his waist while he eyed her up and down.

"Go on, Wanda Nell," Mayrene said, "I'll stay here with the girls while you show Lieutenant Johnson here what you found." Her eyes urged Wanda Nell to be strong and not to let her temper get her in trouble, even if Elmer Lee was acting like a jackass and doing his best to rile her.

"Thank you, Mayrene," Wanda Nell said. She stood up, and Mayrene came forward to take her place on the bed between Miranda and Juliet. Lavon, sensing the tension in the room, had begun to whimper again, and Mayrene took him from his mother and cushioned him against her ample bosom, rocking him gently to calm him.

"Come on, then, Lieutenant Johnson," Wanda Nell said, stalking out of Miranda's bedroom and into the hall. She didn't wait to see if Elmer Lee was following her.

"I guess it's the maid's day off today," Elmer Lee said as he walked behind her through the trailer's living room.

Wanda Nell stopped and whirled around—so quickly that Elmer Lee almost walked right into her. "That ain't a bit funny, Elmer Lee," she hissed at him. "Some men broke in here last night and did this. And they frightened my girls and tied them up."

"Whoa, Wanda Nell," Elmer Lee said, throwing up a hand. "Now just cool off a minute. Are you serious?"

"Yes, I'm serious," Wanda Nell replied. "Serious as a heart attack."

"What the hell is going on here?" Elmer Lee asked, his eyes narrowing in suspicion. "What have you got yourself into, woman?"

"It's not me, Elmer Lee, that's got into anything," Wanda Nell said, working hard to keep a hold on her temper. "It's your good ol' buddy Bobby Ray Culpepper who's responsible for this."

"Is it Bobby Ray's body you found?" he asked, reaching out and taking hold of her arm. His grasp was so tight she winced from the pain.

Wanda Nell jerked her arm away from him. "Yes, Elmer Lee. It's Bobby Ray out there in the woods."

"Then come on, woman, and show me." Without apology he brushed past her and slammed out the front door of the trailer.

Wanda Nell stood still for a moment, taking a couple of deep breaths to steady herself. If she didn't watch it, she was going to end up in jail for assaulting an officer of the law.

She followed Elmer Lee outside, and the sunlight had her blinking for a few seconds. Elmer Lee was talking to a young woman in uniform.

". . . in there and talk to those girls, Taylor," he said. "Find out what happened to them, and take a look around the trailer."

"Wait a minute, Lieutenant Johnson," Wanda Nell said. Elmer Lee turned to face her. "I don't want nobody talking to my girls without me being in the room with them." She knew Mayrene would do her best to look after the girls until she was back with them.

Elmer Lee stared at her for a moment. "Well, you heard Miz Culpepper, Deputy. No talking to the girls unless she's present. But I still want you in that room."

Deputy Taylor said, "Yes, sir," then moved around him to approach the front door of the trailer. She cast Wanda Nell a sympathetic glance as she strode by her.

Elmer Lee made an impatient gesture, telling Wanda Nell to get moving.

Wanda Nell squared her shoulders. She had to face this. It was obvious that Elmer Lee intended to make this as hard on her as he possibly could. She was not going to let him get to her.

Somehow she got her feet and legs to working, and she led the way to the woods where she had found Bobby Ray's body. Elmer Lee and three of his men followed right behind her. The blanket of pine needles and fallen leaves muffled their footsteps. The sun, now higher in the sky, peeked its way farther into the woods, but as she walked into the coolness of the shaded areas, Wanda Nell shivered. She tried to breathe shallowly to avoid the stench she knew was not far away.

She came within about ten feet of where Bobby Ray lay behind the bushes, then stopped. With a hand that quivered only slightly, she pointed to the pink flamingo.

"There," she said, "behind those bushes."

"What the hell?" Elmer Lee muttered. He moved forward cautiously, eyes on the ground, making a circle around to the other side of the bushes.

Wanda Nell turned her back. She wasn't going to watch, and Elmer Lee couldn't make her. She walked a few steps away, back toward the edge of the woods and closer to the sunlight. Shivering again, she rubbed her hands up and down her arms to warm herself. She tried to focus her thoughts on something, on anything other than the horror behind her in the bushes, but it was no use. Now that she was close again, she kept seeing Bobby Ray's dead body in her mind.

She heard Elmer Lee mutter an oath. By now he could see how Bobby Ray had died, pinned there by her plastic flamingo. As soon as the police would let her, she vowed, she was going to get rid of the damn things. After this, she couldn't ever bear the sight of one of them in her yard.

Dimly she could hear Elmer Lee issuing orders to his men. Memories she had tried to suppress came rushing back to her. Memories of a young, tender, and loving Bobby Ray, the one she had been so desperate to marry. She remembered the look in his eyes when their son T.J. was born, how proud he had been of their little boy, how much love there was between them. When had it begun to go wrong?

"Oh, Bobby Ray," she whispered into the cool air. "I did love you, and I know you loved me, at least for a little while." The tears had started streaming down her face, and she fumbled in her pocket for a Kleenex.

"Feeling sorry?" Elmer Lee asked, circling around to stand in front of her. She'd been so lost in her memories that she never heard him approach. "It's too damn late now, Wanda Nell. You shoulda thought about it before you stuck that damn flamingo through his neck."

Stunned, Wanda Nell could only stare up at Elmer Lee. His face twisted into a mask of hatred, and suddenly she was afraid. Surely he wouldn't strike her, right here in front of witnesses. He looked like he wanted to kill her.

"You're crazy, Elmer Lee," Wanda Nell finally managed to say, taking a step back from him. "You're damn crazy if you think I did that."

"You hated him, Wanda Nell," Elmer Lee said, his voice calm and reasonable. He stepped close to her again. "Everybody knows that, and nobody's gonna be surprised you did this to him."

"I didn't," Wanda Nell said, her anger building. This time she held her ground. "I didn't do this, Elmer Lee. I couldn't have. Do you seriously think I could get Bobby Ray to lie there on the ground and be still while I stuck that flamingo's legs through his neck?" She laughed bitterly. "That's about the stupidest thing I ever heard, and coming from you, that's saying a lot."

"You watch your tongue, woman," Elmer Lee said, his voice rough with hatred. "I don't know how you lured Bobby Ray out here in the woods, but you did it somehow, and then you knocked him on the head with something."

"You're crazy, Elmer Lee," Wanda Nell said. She couldn't believe this was happening to her. She knew Elmer Lee despised her, but to believe she was capable of killing Bobby Ray like this, well, that was downright nuts.

"You knocked him on the head, Wanda Nell," Elmer Lee said, bending his head down so that he was almost breathing in her face, "and then you took that flamingo and drove it into his neck. He probably bled to death, Wanda Nell. Did it make you feel good to do that to him? Did you stand there and watch?"

"What's going on here?" A deep voice barked out the question from somewhere behind Elmer Lee, and Wanda Nell was so relieved she could have screamed.

"I'm just interviewing the witness who found the body, Sheriff," Elmer Lee said, taking two steps back, then turning to face his boss.

A florid-faced, heavyset man in his early sixties, Jesse Stanford had run the Tullahoma County Sheriff's department for nearly twenty years. There had been occasional whispers that he wasn't as honest as he claimed to be, but Wanda Nell had known him all her life. He and her daddy had once been good friends, though they'd had a falling-out when Wanda Nell was about sixteen. She never knew what it was about, because her daddy had died less than a year later. He would never speak about it. Still, she reckoned, the sheriff would be fairer to her than Elmer Lee ever dared to be.

"Didn't sound much like an interview to me," Stanford replied. "Sounded more like an accusation, Lieutenant."

Elmer Lee didn't say anything, but his cheeks reddened, Wanda Nell noticed with vicious satisfaction.

"Miz Culpepper," the sheriff said, his voice formal, "is there anything you'd like to tell me about this so-called interview?"

Wanda Nell hesitated. She could get Elmer Lee in a lot of trouble if she told Sheriff Stanford just how rough he had been with her. He might even take Elmer Lee off the case and investigate it himself. But maybe just knowing the sheriff was looking over his shoulder would make Elmer Lee toe the line.

She caught Elmer Lee's eye. He was daring her to say something.

"I was explaining to Elmer Lee here, Sheriff," she said, "that I had nothing to do with this. Except that I found the body, of course."

"I'm sure sorry you had to go through that, Miz Culpepper," Stanford said. "And I know Lieutenant Johnson here appreciates everything you're doing to cooperate with my department. Isn't that right, Lieutenant?"

"Yes, sir," Elmer Lee said, his voice toneless.

"You have an ID on the victim?" The sheriff watched his subordinate closely.

"Yes, sir," Elmer Lee responded, not looking at Wanda Nell. "Bobby Ray Culpepper. Miz Culpepper's ex-husband."

Sheriff Stanford drew in a deep breath. "As I recall, Lieutenant, Mr. Culpepper was a good friend of yours. Maybe I should assign someone else to this investigation, you being so close to the victim and all."

"If you think that's the best thing to do, sir," Elmer Lee said, his face becoming animated again, "but I promise you I can handle this."

The sheriff stared at Elmer Lee for a long moment, while Wanda Nell watched in fascination.

"Okay, then, Lieutenant," Stanford finally said. "You're in charge, but I'm going to keep a close eye on this, you understand me?"

"Yes, sir," Elmer Lee said. "Now, if you don't mind, sir, I'm going to take Miz Culpepper back to her trailer and continue interviewing her there."

The sheriff nodded, and Elmer Lee gestured for Wanda Nell to precede him. While the sheriff walked around them to inspect the crime scene, Wanda Nell gratefully headed out of the woods. Elmer Lee was right behind her.

She had gone only a few steps before she halted, remembering her purse, which she had dropped somewhere in the woods.

"What is it?" Elmer Lee asked.

"My purse," Wanda Nell said. "I dropped it here somewhere when I found the body."

Elmer Lee muttered something under his breath. "Hold on a minute, then." He stalked back to talk to his men.

While Wanda Nell waited for him, she wondered why he hadn't said anything to the sheriff about what had happened at the trailer. Didn't he believe her?

He'd better not try to say that she and the girls had made the whole thing up, Wanda Nell decided angrily. He'd have a fight on his hands if he did.

Surely there had to be enough evidence to convince him. Somebody in the trailer park must have seen something.

"Come on, Wanda Nell," Elmer Lee said, startling her.

"Where's my purse?" Wanda Nell demanded.

Elmer Lee sighed heavily as he took her arm to guide her out of the woods and back to the trailer. "Surely even you realize I can't let you have that purse back, Wanda Nell. You dropped it at the crime scene, and it's evidence now."

Wanda Nell gritted her teeth to try to keep from shouting

at him, or jerking her arm loose from his grip. "Well, then, Elmer Lee, when do you think I might get it back? My driver's license is in there. My credit cards, my cash, and everything. How am I supposed to drive to work if I don't have my license?"

"We'll get it back to you as soon as we can, Wanda Nell," Elmer Lee said. They had reached the yard in front of her trailer, and he dropped her arm.

Wanda Nell rubbed the spot where he had been holding her. "Look here, Elmer Lee. You just better get it through your head, right here, right now, I did not kill Bobby Ray. And every minute you spend trying to prove I did, well, the real killer is making a jackass out of you."

"We'll see about that, Wanda Nell," Elmer Lee said. His whole body had tensed, and once again Wanda Nell had the feeling that it took all he had not to let loose and slap the pee-waddin' out of her.

Someone coughed from behind them. Both Wanda Nell and Elmer Lee spun around. Deputy Taylor stood there, her face solemn.

"I just wanted to tell you, Lieutenant," she said, her voice stiff and official, "that Miz Lancaster wanted to move the young ladies and the baby over to her trailer. I didn't think that would be a problem, sir."

*Thank the Lord for Mayrene,* Wanda Nell thought. Always looking out for her and her girls.

"Is that so, Deputy?" Elmer Lee said. "You're taking a lot on yourself, Deputy, and next time you might want to clear something like that with me first. You got that?"

"Yes, sir," Deputy Taylor said. Her face slowly reddened, and Wanda Nell sympathized with her. Trust Elmer Lee to be pig enough to humiliate her in front of someone, instead of waiting to reprimand her when no one else was around.

"Come on, then," Elmer Lee said. "I need to talk to those girls and find out what *allegedly* happened in that trailer there." He jerked his head sideways to indicate Wanda Nell's place.

Wanda Nell stepped in front of him and mounted the steps to Mayrene's front door. She opened it and walked in. The two deputies came right behind her, and one of them shut the door quietly. All Wanda Nell could focus on was the sight of her two daughters, sitting on the couch with Mayrene. The older woman had an arm around each one. Juliet was quiet, seemingly asleep, but Miranda was crying, sobs wracking her body.

"I put the baby down to sleep in my bedroom," Mayrene said. "He's fine, don't you worry about him." She rubbed her head against Miranda's. "Now, honey, don't keep crying like that. You're just gonna make yourself sick."

Miranda just wailed louder. Wanda Nell knew the girl was upset because she had loved her daddy best of all. Even so, she wanted to jerk a knot in the girl's tail. She was too tired to cope with all this drama.

"Miranda," Wanda Nell said, her voice coming out way too sharp. "Miranda." She spoke her daughter's name again, only this time more gently, as she approached the sofa. "Honey, look at me. I know you're upset. This was something awful, and I'm sorry all of it happened. But you've got to calm down, honey, and talk to these officers here. We've got to help them find out who did this to you and your sister." *And to your daddy,* she added silently.

"Oh, Mama," Miranda blubbered. "I'm scared."

Wanda Nell sat on the edge of the sofa beside her older daughter and wrapped her arms around her. Juliet, awake again, watched in wide-eyed curiosity.

"Honey, it's going to be okay," Wanda Nell said, trying

to soothe Miranda enough so they could get some sense out of her. "I know you're scared, but nobody's going to hurt you now."

"Yes, they will, Mama," Miranda said, almost screaming in her ear. "I saw them, Mama, and they know I saw them. They're gonna come back and kill me!"

# Five

"All right now, little lady," Elmer Lee said. He came over to the sofa and squatted down in front of Wanda Nell and Miranda. "You just get ahold of yourself, now, and don't you be worrying about anybody coming back to get you. We ain't about to let anything happen to you."

As Wanda Nell stroked Miranda's hair, the girl made an effort to get control of herself. "Good girl," Wanda Nell whispered into her ear. In a normal tone, she said, "That's right, Miranda. The sheriff's department isn't going to let anybody come and hurt you or any of us."

"Okay," Miranda said, her voice finally calm and at its normal pitch. "Can I have some Coke?"

Wanda Nell looked over her daughter's head at Mayrene.

"Sure you can, honey," Mayrene said. "You just sit right there, and I'll get you some. Juliet, you want some, too?"

Juliet nodded shyly, then as Mayrene pushed herself up

off the sofa, she scooted over next to Miranda and her mother. Wanda Nell reached out to stroke Juliet's hair, and her younger daughter offered her a tremulous smile.

*Oh, dear Lord,* Wanda Nell thought, *please keep my girls safe. Please!*

Exhaustion hit her then, and she wanted to go climb in a hole somewhere and sleep for a week. Her eyes stung with fatigue, and her whole body had turned to lead. The effort it took for her to turn and speak to Elmer Lee drained her further. "Go on, now, and ask your questions. We're all worn out, and the girls and I need some rest." She leaned back and watched the deputy tiredly.

Elmer Lee flashed her a hostile look, but Wanda Nell only blinked at him.

"Right, then," Elmer Lee said, getting up off his haunches and pulling a chair close. He sat down in it and studied Miranda and Juliet for a moment.

"Now, girls, I want y'all to think real careful about what happened to you, and any little detail you can think of, you tell me. Don't matter how small or unimportant you reckon it may be, you just tell me anyway. Okay?"

Both girls nodded, and Elmer Lee leaned back in the chair. "Good. Who wants to go first?"

Miranda didn't say anything, and Juliet watched her for a moment. "I guess I will, sir," she said, her voice so thin Wanda Nell thought Elmer Lee would have trouble hearing her.

Mayrene came back with a tray and several glasses of Coke. She set coasters depicting Graceland on the coffee table in front of each of the girls and Wanda Nell, then placed glasses on the coasters. She offered the remaining two glasses to the deputies. Elmer Lee waved her away irritably. Mayrene glared at the back of his head before moving away.

"It's okay, honey," Wanda Nell said gently, trying to ignore all this byplay. "Take your time."

"Yes, Mama," Juliet said dutifully, after taking a sip of her Coke. "Well, I was asleep, and the first thing I knew, there was this man in my room. The light was on, and I could hardly see. I started to scream, but . . ." She paused, shuddering.

"It's okay, little lady," Elmer Lee said, and Wanda Nell marveled that he could speak so kindly to her daughter. "Just take it slow."

Juliet drew in a deep breath. "He put his hand over my mouth, and he said for me not to make any noise. If I didn't make any noise he said he wouldn't hurt me."

Wanda Nell wanted to throw up. The thought of some man putting his hands on her daughter sickened her even more than what she had found in the woods. Her hand trembled as she reached out to reassure Juliet with a touch.

"I'm okay, Mama," Juliet said, her voice gaining strength. "He really didn't hurt me. He just tied me up with that tape and warned me again not to make any noise before he put that nasty tape across my mouth. He said he would hurt me and Miranda and the baby if I caused any commotion."

Startled, Wanda Nell glanced at Elmer Lee. His eyes had narrowed in quick comprehension. These men had been pretty well prepared, if they knew ahead of time there was a baby in the trailer along with the two girls.

"What did he do after he tied you up with the tape?" That was all Elmer Lee asked.

Juliet sipped at her Coke again before continuing. "He started looking through everything in my room. He was real fast about it, just like he'd done it before somewhere."

"I'll just bet he had." Mayrene offered a tart comment, but Elmer Lee ignored her.

"Did he take anything out of your room?"

"No, sir," Juliet said. "After he was done searching through everything and making a mess, he told me one more time to stay quiet. Then he turned off the light and left me there."

"Do you have any idea what time this was?" Elmer Lee asked.

Juliet nodded. "Yes, sir. It was about two-fifteen when he left my room. I know, because the way he left me tied up, I could see the digital clock by the side of my bed." She shrugged. "I laid there a long time and watched the clock, and then I finally fell asleep."

"Could you hear what was going on outside your room?"

"I heard him, or I guess maybe it was them, searching in the living room and the kitchen for a few minutes. And in Mama's room and the bathroom. It took 'em about fifteen minutes, I guess. It was about two-thirty-five when I heard 'em leave the trailer."

"Thank you, Miss Juliet," Elmer Lee said, and he smiled at her.

"Yes, sir," Juliet said, dipping her head shyly. "You're welcome."

"Now, Miss Miranda," Elmer Lee said, focusing his attention on the older girl. "How's about you tell me your story."

Miranda tensed. Wanda Nell, her hand resting on Miranda's leg, felt the girl's whole body tighten. "It's okay, honey," Wanda Nell said, puzzled. "Just take it slow, and tell the deputy what happened."

"Yes, Mama," Miranda said, mechanically. "Well, it happened to me, just like it did to Juliet. I woke up, and there was this man in my room. He was pretty quiet, but I could tell he meant business. He had a real mean look in his eyes, and I wasn't gonna do nothing to make him mad."

"What did he look like?" Elmer Lee asked.

Miranda frowned. "Well, I could see his eyes, but that was all. He had on one of them ski masks. Oh, and I could see his mouth." She closed her eyes for a moment, remembering. "I think maybe he had a moustache or a beard or something."

"Okay," Elmer Lee said. "How could you tell?"

"Well," Miranda said, "that ski-mask thing he wore was red, and around his mouth it looked like maybe some dark hair was poking out. So I figured maybe he had a beard or something."

"That's good, little lady," Elmer Lee said approvingly, and Miranda preened a little.

Wanda Nell glanced beyond Elmer Lee to where Deputy Taylor sat. She was noting things down on a pad, her mouth twisted in a frown of concentration. Would any of this, Wanda Nell had to wonder, help catch these men?

"Miss Juliet," Elmer Lee continued, "how about you? Did you notice anything special about the man in your room? Was it the same man?"

"No, sir," Juliet said. "The man in my room had on a black mask." She frowned. "But there was one thing that was kinda odd."

Elmer Lee nodded encouragingly.

"I noticed that his mask didn't come down to but about here," Juliet said, indicating with a finger to her throat where a man's Adam's apple would be. "And below that, there was a lot of color. I couldn't see real clearly, because the light hurt my eyes. He was either wearing a real colorful T-shirt under his black shirt, or he had some tattoos."

"That's good, little lady, that's good," Elmer Lee said. "So was he wearing all black?"

"Yes, sir," Juliet said. "And he was kinda short, too. He was just about as tall as the bookshelf in my room. I could see when he was standing in front of it, searching."

"That's excellent," Elmer Lee said. "Very helpful information."

"The man in my room," Miranda said, her voice a bit petulant, "was wearing all black, too, except for that ski mask thing. But he was real tall. There's a shelf in my room, too, and his head and shoulders stuck up over it."

"That's very helpful, too, Miss Miranda," Elmer Lee said. "You girls did real well, keeping a cool head to notice things like that."

"I watch a lot of those cop shows on TV," Miranda said proudly.

"Did either of these men ever say anything that gave you an idea what it was they were looking for?" Elmer Lee asked.

"No, sir," Juliet said.

Wanda Nell, nearly asleep but with a hand still on Miranda's leg, felt her older daughter go rigid for an instant. Then, with a shaky sigh, she relaxed. "No, sir," she said.

Wanda Nell opened her eyes slightly and peered at Miranda. The girl sure was tense, and Wanda Nell didn't think it was just because of what the girls had been through. Miranda had never been able to lie very well, though the good Lord knew she sure got enough practice. What was she holding back?

Deciding that she wouldn't tackle Miranda about it right now, Wanda Nell closed her eyes again. She'd get it out of the girl later, after she'd had time to rest and think about it.

"The man in my room didn't talk that much," Miranda added. "He had a kinda deep voice, though."

"Would either of you recognize their voices if you heard them again?" Elmer Lee looked at each of the girls in turn. Miranda nodded firmly, while Juliet shrugged. "Maybe," she said.

"Thank you, young ladies," Elmer Lee said. "This was a terrible experience for you, but you've been a real big help. We're gonna try to find these guys, but in the meantime, we're gonna keep an eye on y'all. You don't have to worry anymore, Miss Miranda, about what they said to you. They ain't coming back anytime soon."

"Yes, sir," the girls said in unison. "Thank you, sir," Miranda added.

Elmer Lee stood up. "Now, ladies, if y'all would sit tight for a little while, Deputy Taylor and me are gonna go take a good long look next door. Then I might have a few more questions, so y'all don't go anywhere, all right?"

"They're all too tired to go anywhere, Deputy," Mayrene said, her voice just this side of sarcastic. "You just go on and do what you gotta do, and I'm gonna be looking after them."

"I'm sure you will, Miz Lancaster," Elmer Lee said sourly. "Come on, Taylor."

Wanda Nell, through the fog of encroaching sleep, heard the trailer door close and Mayrene mutter a few choice words under her breath. Elmer Lee had better be careful, because if he got Mayrene riled up, there was no telling what she would do. Smiling at that thought, Wanda Nell slipped into a sound sleep.

Some time later, she surfaced from a dream to feel someone shaking her gently. "Wanda Nell," Mayrene was saying in a low voice, "wake up, honey. Come on, now, girl, wake up."

Yawning, her eyes blinking, Wanda Nell tried to focus. Her eyes sure were tired, and her whole body felt stiff and achy. "What is it, Mayrene? What are you doing here?" She tried to sit up in bed, then realized she wasn't in bed, but on a couch, and Mayrene's couch at that.

"Sorry to disturb you, honey," Mayrene said, "but you gotta wake up for a little while."

Wanda Nell stared up into her friend's face, seeing the concern there. Then the memories came back, and Wanda Nell shuddered.

"I know, honey, I know," Mayrene said, sitting on the couch beside her and throwing an arm around her shoulders. "It's just about the most godawful mess I've ever seen, but you got to be strong, for your sake and for your girls."

"I know," Wanda Nell said, leaning against Mayrene for a moment. "How long was I asleep?"

"About half an hour," Mayrene said. "The deputies came out of your trailer a couple minutes ago, and I figured you'd better be awake in case they come back in here to talk to you."

"Yeah, I guess so," Wanda Nell said. The brief nap hadn't done much to refresh her. She was still dog-tired, and she had no idea how she would manage to work her shift at the Kountry Kitchen and her shift at Budget Mart if she didn't get some sleep.

"I called the school and told 'em Juliet was sick and wouldn't be in today," Mayrene said, her arm still around Wanda Nell's shoulders. "And then I called Melvin at the Kountry Kitchen and told him you couldn't work tonight." She frowned. "I probably should've asked you first, honey, before I did that, but after what you been through, you need some rest."

"Thanks," Wanda Nell said, yawning. "I don't mind a bit, Mayrene. I appreciate you being so concerned and all, and if I can get some more sleep, I can still make my shift at Budget Mart tonight." She yawned again. "What did Melvin say, though?"

"He cussed a bit," Mayrene said, "but when I explained why you couldn't work, it was all I could do to keep him from rushing right over here." She chuckled. "That man sure has got a thing for you, girl. He was gonna come over here, but I told him I was gonna see that you got in bed as soon as you could and got some sleep."

Wanda Nell yawned again. The last thing she needed right now was Melvin Arbuckle acting like some kinda white knight in the middle of all this mess. She appreciated his concern, but if he came running over here now, Elmer Lee might get the wrong idea. He sure didn't need any more wrong ideas to complicate the situation.

There was a knock at the door, and before Mayrene could get up to answer it, the door swung open. Elmer Lee stuck his head in.

"Could I speak with you, Miz Culpepper?" he asked.

"Sure," Wanda Nell said, sitting there and staring at him.

"I mean outside here," Elmer Lee said, his impatience all too obvious.

"Hold on there, Deputy," Mayrene said sharply. "Give her a minute, okay?"

Elmer Lee rolled his eyes. "Alright, but I ain't got all day." His head disappeared, and the door slammed shut.

Mayrene cursed. "Honey, do you think you maybe need a lawyer? You know my cousin Blanche works for one, Hamilton Tucker. Blanche reckons he's about the sharpest lawyer in Tullahoma County, and I bet he'd be willing to look after your interests."

Wanda Nell drew away in alarm. "I don't want a lawyer, Mayrene. I didn't do anything."

Mayrene laughed. "Ain't nobody said you had, sugar. But just because you didn't do a damn thing don't mean you don't need someone who knows what he's doing looking out for you."

"Well," Wanda Nell said doubtfully, "I don't know. You really think I might need a lawyer?"

"It can't hurt," Mayrene said. "Now, how's about this? I'll call Blanche and fill her in a little on what's going on here and see what she thinks. She's pretty sharp herself, and she's been working for this lawyer for about two years now."

"Okay," Wanda Nell said, though she still wasn't convinced it was a good idea. What if Elmer Lee thought it meant she had something to hide? He was going to be ruthless anyway, Wanda Nell reasoned, because of the way he hated her. That convinced her. "Yeah, you know, a lawyer might not be such a bad idea. You go ahead and call your cousin."

"Good," Mayrene said, nodding approvingly. "I'm glad to see you showing some spunk, sugar. Don't let that jerk out there bulldoze you into anything."

Wanda Nell stood up. "I guess I better get out there and see what it is he wants." She frowned. "Where are the girls? Are they asleep?"

"Yeah, they're sound sleep. Miranda's with the baby in my room, and I put Juliet in the other bedroom."

"Thank you, Mayrene," Wanda Nell said, her eyes suddenly tearing up. "I honestly don't know what I'd've done without you this morning."

Mayrene grinned. "You dry those eyes and get out there and let that Deputy Jackass see he ain't gonna intimidate you."

Wanda Nell laughed, resisting the urge to salute. "Yes, ma'am." Still tired, but feeling stronger, she went outside to see what else Elmer Lee wanted.

She found him conferring with Deputy Taylor and several men in uniform. Deputy Taylor coughed to alert him to Wanda Nell's presence, and he broke off what he was saying to turn and face her.

"Miz Culpepper," he said.

"Yes, Deputy," she answered. "Is there something else you wanted?" With all these witnesses around, Elmer Lee was being awfully formal with her. She did her best not to smile and tick him off.

"Yes'm," he said. "I know it's going to be an inconvenience for you, but we need to have access to your trailer for another hour or two. Just until we finish our investigation."

"But then we'll be able to go back in?" Wanda Nell asked.

"Yes."

Wanda Nell shrugged. "Then I guess it's fine with me. In the meantime, me and my daughters will be next door with Miz Lancaster." Thinking Elmer Lee was finished with her, she turned to go back to Mayrene's trailer.

"Miz Culpepper." Elmer Lee's voice came out pretty sharp. "Miz Culpepper," he repeated in a softer tone as Wanda Nell turned back to face him. "One more thing."

"Yes, Deputy?" Wanda Nell inquired.

"Somebody needs to notify the victim's mother," Elmer Lee responded. "We can take care of that, but if you want to be the one to tell her, I'd suggest that you need to do so pretty quickly."

Wanda Nell could feel the bile rising in her throat at the thought of having to tell Lucretia Culpepper that her only son was dead. And murdered, no less. Wanda Nell knew who the old battle-ax would blame.

Taking a deep breath to steady herself, Wanda Nell said, "If it's alright with you, Deputy, I think it would be better if someone from the sheriff's department spoke with Miz Culpepper."

"That's fine," Elmer Lee said. "We'll take care of it, then. That's all for now, Miz Culpepper. We'll let you know when you can get back in your trailer."

Wanda Nell nodded before turning away. She didn't trust Elmer Lee when he was being all polite like this, but she figured he couldn't afford to show his true colors right now. Later on she might not be so lucky.

Mayrene, who had obviously been listening with the trailer door slightly ajar, swung it open to usher Wanda Nell back inside.

"Now you come on in here and get some rest," Mayrene said. "Why don't you tip on back there to the guest room and slip into bed with Juliet? I bet that girl's so sound asleep you won't wake her up."

"In a minute," Wanda Nell said, suppressing a yawn. "I'm so tired I feel like I could sleep for a week. But I don't like the idea of sleeping while the sheriff's department is over there rooting through my trailer."

"I know, honey," Mayrene said, "but by now it's a little bit late to worry too much. You don't think your buddy the deputy is going to try to plant some kind of evidence over there, do you?"

"I wouldn't put it past him," Wanda Nell said. "But what kind of evidence would he plant? He's already got one of my plastic flamingoes as the murder weapon." She shuddered as the image of Bobby Ray, pinned to the ground, came unbidden to her mind.

"Stop thinking about that," Mayrene ordered. "It ain't gonna do anybody a bit of good, and you need to try to get some rest."

"Aren't you going to work today?" Wanda Nell asked, frowning as she remembered that, ordinarily, Mayrene would have left for the beauty shop long before now.

"No, honey," Mayrene laughed. "I called in and told 'em I was sick. I'm not going to leave you in the lurch. You need somebody looking after you and the girls."

"You're a good friend, Mayrene," Wanda Nell said, "and I sure do appreciate you being here."

Mayrene gave her a quick hug, then pushed her in the direction of the guest room. "Go on now, get some sleep. I'll

keep an eye out, and I'll let you know if something happens
you need to know about."

Consumed by a jawbreaking yawn, Wanda Nell could
only nod as she moved down the hall toward the bedroom.
She opened the door to see Juliet sound asleep on one side of
the bed. Moving as quietly as she could, she stepped around
to the other side. Pausing only long enough to take off her
shoes, she lay down on the bed without even undressing.

The bedroom was cool and dim, and the bed comfortable. Wanda Nell nestled her head on the pillow and waited
for sleep to come.

Drowsily, she thought about the events of the morning.
Did she really need a lawyer? She guessed Mayrene was
right, but she wondered how on earth she could afford to
pay a lawyer. Maybe he would let her pay him over time.

Sleep edged nearer as Wanda Nell's thoughts wandered.
She was going to have to talk to Miranda about something.
What was it? She tried to remember, but she was just too
tired. Something Miranda had said, or maybe didn't say.
Wanda Nell tried to concentrate, but the effort was too
much for her. She drifted off to sleep.

# *Six*

Dimly, Wanda Nell became aware of a commotion going on somewhere nearby. Loud voices had brought her out of a sound sleep, and she wanted to resist, to drop back into blessed oblivion. But the voices came nearer and nearer.

The door of the bedroom flew open and thudded against the wall. Wanda Nell jerked fully awake and sat up in the bed. Beside her Juliet whimpered in fright and huddled close. She wrapped a comforting arm around her daughter.

"What the hell is going on here?" Wanda Nell demanded crossly. It took a moment for her eyes to focus, and then she wished she could crawl back in bed and pull the covers over her head.

"That's what I came to ask *you,* Wanda Nell." Lucretia Culpepper, hands on hips and eyes blazing with hate, stood at the foot of the bed. "You get on up out of that bed and face me. I'm going to see your sorry rear end in jail before this day is over."

Mayrene had followed right behind her unwelcome visitor, and she made a vain attempt to pull the older woman away. Shaking off the hand that grasped at her, Mrs. Culpepper turned and said, "I swear I'll slap you six ways to Sunday if you touch me again. I don't know who you are, but you've got some nerve sheltering the woman who killed my son in cold blood."

This was just the reaction Wanda Nell had expected from her former mother-in-law, but she'd hoped to postpone having to face her until she'd had some time to rest. She opened her mouth to protest, but not a sound came out.

Mayrene moved closer until she was face-to-face with Mrs. Culpepper. Taller by several inches, Mayrene also outweighed her opponent by about fifty pounds. Wide-eyed with curiosity and unable to say anything, Wanda Nell waited for Mayrene to lower the boom.

"Now, listen here, you old witch," Mayrene said, and her tone would have made even the sheriff back down, "you don't bust in here like some gorilla on a rampage and start insulting my friends. Wanda Nell and her girls are welcome here, and you, old woman, are not. I'll thank you to take your scrawny carcass out of my house right this minute. Or I might be just tempted to pick you up and throw you out myself."

Lucretia Culpepper wilted for a moment under Mayrene's fierce attack, but then she fought right back. "Who do you think *you* are? You're nothing but a vulgar piece of trailer trash. Do you know who *I* am?" She held up her head proudly while trying to look down her nose at Mayrene.

Wanda Nell had to admire the old woman for even attempting to answer Mayrene back. She would have turned tail and run if it had been her who Mayrene went after.

"I don't give a rat's ass *who* you think you are," Mayrene said, not in the least cowed by Mrs. Culpepper's grande-dame act. "All I know is, somebody who claims to be a well-bred lady wouldn't push her way uninvited into somebody's home and act like a no-account streetwalker."

"Well!" Lucretia Culpepper drew herself up, attempting to gather the shreds of her dignity. "I'm not the one who's a streetwalker."

"And just what do you mean by that?" Mayrene asked, her tone growing even more menacing.

Wanda Nell was mortified by the whole scene, but at the same time she found herself wanting to giggle. Just plain nerves and exhaustion, she decided, clapping a hand over her mouth. Or maybe it's just some kind of bad dream. She pinched herself, then winced. No, it wasn't a dream.

Evidently Lucretia Culpepper decided she'd better not push Mayrene any further. She stepped back, then quickly scooted around Mayrene and made for the door, faster than Wanda Nell had figured a woman nearly seventy could move.

Mrs. Culpepper paused in the doorway for a moment. "Just you wait and see, Wanda Nell. You're going to be in jail before the day is over, and I hope to God you rot in there!" She threw Mayrene one last defiant glare, then dis-appeared. Moments later, they heard the front door of the trailer slam.

In Mayrene's bedroom next door, the baby began to wail.

Juliet was crying, too, and Wanda Nell patted her absent-mindedly. "Hush, now, honey, it's gonna be alright. Don't let your grandmother upset you. She's just all torn up about your daddy."

"She doesn't have to be so nasty, Mama," Juliet said, sniffling.

"Honey, that old woman don't know any other way to be," Mayrene said in disgust. "Now, y'all just calm down a minute, and I'll go see about Lavon, since Miranda can't seem to manage."

Flashing a grateful look at her friend, Wanda Nell drew Juliet into her arms. "Come on, now, baby," she said. "Don't let her upset you like this. You just have to learn not to pay her no mind."

"But, Mama," Juliet said, her tears finally under control, "why does she hate us all so? She won't even speak to Miranda and me, and she's never even sent Lavon a present."

"I know," Wanda Nell said, sighing heavily. "It's me she blames for everything, baby. And you and your sister and poor little Lavon just get caught in the crossfire. She's a lonely, bitter old woman. Deep in her heart, she knows it's your daddy she should be mad at, the way he treated us all like dirt. But he's her only child, and she just can't let herself be mad at him. So she takes it out on us."

"And now she doesn't even have my daddy anymore," Juliet said sadly. "Why can't she be like everybody else's grandmother?"

Wanda Nell's heart just about broke over the forlorn sound of that question. Her own mother had died before Juliet was born, and Lucretia Culpepper had never paid any attention to her, so the poor girl had no idea what it was like to have a loving, gentle, caring grandmother.

"I know, honey," Wanda Nell said, feeling completely inadequate to offer Juliet the comfort she needed. "Maybe someday she'll get tired of being so lonely, and if she does, you and Miranda will just have to be ready to forgive her like the Good Book says, if you can."

"Forgive who?" Miranda demanded from the doorway. "You mean that old witch who's supposed to be my sweet and loving grandma?" She made a gagging sound.

Wanda Nell was too tired to fuss with Miranda over Mrs. Culpepper. "Let's forget about her for now, okay?"

"But, Mama," Juliet protested. "You can't forget about what she said. You know, about getting you put in jail?"

Miranda dropped down heavily on the end of the bed. "What do you mean, getting Mama put in jail? How the hell is she gonna do that?" Her fingers plucked at the bedspread, and she kept her face turned away from Wanda Nell.

"I don't know," Juliet said crossly. "I reckon she thinks Mama had something to do with what happened to Daddy."

"Well, that's about the craziest thing I ever heard," Miranda said. "Mama couldn't have killed Daddy. She was already at work." Her body tensed, and she focused more intently on playing with the bedspread.

Wanda Nell regarded her older daughter with curious eyes. "I do appreciate you sticking up for me, Miranda," she said slowly, "but how do you know I was at work when your daddy was killed? How do you know when he died?"

Miranda, her head still down, turned slightly and cut her eyes over at her mother, then quickly looked away again. "I just know," she said, her voice low. "Mama wouldn't ever kill Daddy. Anyway, you went right on to work after Daddy left last night. Didn't you?"

"Yes, I did," Wanda Nell said.

"Well, see," Miranda said triumphantly, risking a glance at her mother.

"Now, Miranda," Wanda Nell began.

"Lord, I need to feed Lavon," Miranda said, getting off the bed faster than Wanda Nell had seen her move in years. "My poor little baby. All this noise's done upset him real bad," she added piously. Before Wanda Nell could stop her, she scuttled out the door.

Wanda Nell glanced at Juliet, and Juliet was frowning down at her hands.

"What is it, honey?" Wanda Nell asked gently.

Juliet looked up at her mother, her eyes wide with innocence. "Nothing, Mama."

Wanda Nell didn't believe her. Ordinarily, Juliet didn't lie to her, but she was loyal to her sister. It looked to Wanda Nell like Miranda was hiding something, and Juliet knew it. She wasn't prepared, at least not yet, to give her sister the lie. Wanda Nell decided she would tackle both girls later. Right now she was still too tired to force the issue.

Mayrene appeared in the doorway. "Miranda's looking after Lavon now," she said. "Now, why don't y'all lie back down and try to get some sleep?"

"I sure am tired," Wanda Nell said, "but I don't think I can go back to sleep now. What time is it?" She glanced around the room for a clock.

Mayrene pointed to the bedside table behind where Wanda Nell at on the bed. "Nigh on to one o'clock. You managed to sleep for a little over three hours."

Wanda Nell yawned and stretched. "That's something, anyway. But I guess I better get on up and do something about cleaning up next door. Is the sheriff's department gone yet?"

"Yeah," Mayrene said. "They left a couple hours ago, but I didn't want to wake you up. And then that hellcat showed up." She snorted.

Wanda Nell giggled. "I think you settled her hash, Mayrene. I wish I could stand up to her like that."

"I've had better than her try to talk down to me," Mayrene said. "Ain't nobody gonna treat me like trash. That old biddy thinks she's better than the rest of us just because she was married to old Judge Culpepper." She grinned wickedly. "The way he ran around on her, she's got no call to stick her nose in the air."

"Mayrene!" Wanda Nell said, slightly scandalized. She indicated Juliet with a quick tilt of the head.

Mayrene just rolled her eyes. "Oh, come on, Wanda Nell. It ain't gonna hurt your girls to know their high-and-mighty grandparents were just as screwed-up as everybody else."

Juliet giggled, and Wanda Nell couldn't help joining in. After all the horrible things they'd been through that day, the laughter was a welcome release. Mayrene guffawed right along with her. It took a minute or two for the laughter to run its course, but Wanda Nell felt a lot better for it.

"That's enough of that," she said, getting off the bed. "Now I really gotta get over there and start straightening up."

"I'll come and help," Mayrene said. "But first I think everybody could use a little something to eat. I whipped up some chicken salad, so y'all come on and have some."

"What are y'all doing?" Miranda, standing in the doorway with her son in her arms, stared at the other three women.

"I was just saying we all need to eat some lunch," Mayrene told her.

"And then we're going to start cleaning up next door," Wanda Nell said.

Following Mayrene, they all trooped into the kitchen. Mayrene already had the table set with paper plates, napkins, and silverware. As Wanda Nell and the girls sat down at the table, Lavon perched in his mother's lap, Mayrene pulled a large bowl from the refrigerator and put it on the table.

"Who wants a sandwich?" Mayrene asked. "I got some loaf bread, or if you want crackers, I got them, too."

Juliet and Miranda made themselves chicken salad sandwiches, while Mayrene and Wanda Nell ate theirs with crackers. Lavon entertained himself by smearing chicken salad on his face, occasionally eating a bit of it.

"This sure is good chicken salad, Aunt Mayrene," Juliet said, wiping her mouth with a napkin. "It's even better than Mama's." She grinned.

"Thank you, honey," Mayrene said. She cut her eyes over at Wanda Nell. "I'm glad y'all enjoyed it. I just like to cook more'n your mama does, but she's pretty good at it when she wants to be."

Wanda Nell grimaced. "If I was as good at it as you are, Mayrene, I wouldn't mind it so much." She stood up and began clearing away the paper plates. "It always tastes better when somebody else makes it, that's for sure."

Juliet jumped up and helped her mother clear the table. When they were done, Wanda Nell said, "Now I guess we'd better go home and get to work."

"Let's get to it." Mayrene pushed away from the table and stood up.

"I'll help, too, Mama," Juliet said.

"No, I'll help." Miranda thrust Lavon into Juliet's arms. "You stay here, Sissy, and watch after Lavon. I'll help Mama."

Surprised, Wanda Nell stared hard at Miranda for a moment. It wasn't like the girl to offer to lift a finger to anything, but she wasn't going to say anything to risk getting Miranda's back up.

"That sounds like a good idea," Wanda Nell said. "You and Lavon can watch TV, honey, and the three of us'll have the place cleaned up in no time."

"Okay, Mama," Juliet said, bouncing Lavon up and down on her knee. He giggled in pleasure and grabbed at his aunt's long blonde hair. Juliet rubbed her nose against his, and he giggled again.

Mayrene led the way out of her trailer. The sun was bright and warm, and Wanda Nell squinted as she looked around, pausing at the foot of Mayrene's steps. The sheriff's department, or someone, had trampled some of the flowers in the beds around the trailer. She shook her head in disgust. She'd see to them later.

Grasping the knob, Wanda Nell opened the door and stepped inside. It was all as horrible as she remembered. She couldn't stand the thought that strangers had come into her home and done this and assaulted her daughters. She'd like to kill the bastards for violating them all in this way.

Miranda pushed past her. "I'll start in my room," she said. "When I'm done there, I'll come help you in here, Mama."

"That's fine," Wanda Nell said absently. She was still staring at the mess. What on earth had those men been looking for?

As soon as Miranda was out of the room, Mayrene gave Wanda Nell a little push. "Come on, girl, let's start in your bedroom."

"Okay," Wanda Nell said. She followed her friend down the hall to her room.

"This is some ungodly mess," Mayrene announced, and Wanda Nell, surveying the damage, had to agree. Listlessly she began to pick things up and put them in their accustomed places, while Mayrene went to work on folding her clothes and putting them back in the drawers of the bureau, or hanging them back in the closet.

"What the hell were they looking for?"

Wanda Nell wasn't aware that she had spoken aloud until Mayrene answered her. "Hanged if I know," she said. "But I reckon it must've been something they thought Bobby Ray left here."

"Yeah," Wanda Nell said. "I sure can't imagine I had anything they'd want. But what could Bobby Ray have left here?"

Even as she spoke the words, a picture formed in her mind. She saw Bobby Ray flashing that big wad of money and peeling off hundred-dollar bills like they were ones. She sank down on her bed.

"What is it, honey?" Mayrene asked.

Tersely, Wanda Nell explained. Mayrene whistled. "How much money you reckon he had?"

Shrugging, Wanda Nell said, "God knows. If they were all hundreds, he could've had six or seven thousand dollars on him."

"Where the hell did Bobby Ray come by that kind of money?"

"I have no idea," Wanda Nell said slowly, "but you can be damn sure it wasn't anything legal." She got up from the bed and went back to work.

Mayrene had hung the last of the clothes back in the closet and had finished with the bureau when she turned to Wanda Nell with a hesitant look on her face. Wanda Nell was staring down at a smashed picture frame on the floor. Someone had stepped on it and shattered the glass. The picture inside, a picture of Wanda Nell and her three children, taken when Juliet was about a year old, had been scratched and torn.

"Damn them!" Wanda Nell said, dashing angry tears from her face with the back of her hand.

"I know, honey," Mayrene said in sympathy. "I hope they catch those bastards and nail their balls to the wall."

Wanda Nell gave a shaky laugh. "Only if they let me have the hammer."

"That's the spirit!" Mayrene stepped forward and laid a hand on Wanda Nell's arm. "Wanda Nell, I got something I need to ask you."

"What is it?" Wanda Nell was surprised by the look of discomfort on her friend's face.

"Well, honey," she said, "I guess I just oughta come right out and say it." She paused, then plunged ahead, "Do you think maybe Miranda's lying about something?"

Troubled, Wanda Nell turned away. "Why do you ask that?"

"I hate to say it, Wanda Nell, but that girl acts like she's got something to hide. While y'all were all asleep, I was working in the kitchen. I guess Miranda thought I was off somewhere taking a nap myself. She came sneaking into the living room and was about to head out the door when I poked my head out of the kitchen, and she about jumped out of her skin." Mayrene frowned. "When I asked her where she was going, she said she just wanted to get some air."

"Did she go out?"

Mayrene shook her head. "No, she just slunk on back to the bedroom, and that was the last I saw of her, till that old biddy showed up and started her shenanigans."

All the time Mayrene had been talking, Wanda Nell was remembering Elmer Lee Johnson's interview with Miranda and Juliet. At the time, she had thought Miranda was lying about something. She hadn't wanted to question her daughter about it then, but maybe now was the time.

"I'm not sure," Wanda Nell said, "but I think Miranda knows something she's not telling."

"Like what?"

Wanda Nell stared at her friend while her stomach commenced to doing flip-flops. "Like maybe," she whispered, "Bobby Ray came back last night after I went to work. And maybe he left something here, with her, and that's what those men were looking for."

## Seven

That night, during her shift at Budget Mart, Wanda Nell tried very hard to keep her mind focused on her work. The story of Bobby Ray Culpepper's murder had spread all over Tullahoma by evening, and Wanda Nell had to spend the first few minutes of her shift answering ghoulish questions from her coworkers. Finally one of them, a large black man named KeShawn, told the others to leave her alone. Wanda Nell flashed him a grateful glance. As big as he was, nobody would bother her after he told them to shut up. KeShawn just grinned at her when she tried to thank him.

"Ain't none of their bidness," he said. "And you don't need all of them butting their heads in, just 'cause they's curious. If any of 'em pester you, you just tell me."

"I will," Wanda Nell promised, relieved that she had at least one ally at work.

That brought Ricky Ratliff to mind. She hadn't seen him when she'd clocked in, well on time tonight. She hoped he'd stay skulking upstairs in the office and leave her alone, but she wasn't betting on it. Before the night was over, he was bound to call her up there. Maybe she'd take KeShawn up there with her. The thought made her grin.

The familiarity of her job soothed her as she worked steadily, restocking the various kinds of soaps and detergents Budget Mart sold. Her mind was able to wander as her hands did what they had done hundreds of times before. So much had happened this day, it was going to take her a long time to sort it all out.

After she and Mayrene straightened up her bedroom and Juliet's, Wanda Nell had left Mayrene working in the living room and gone to talk to Miranda. She was sure her older daughter was hiding something, and she did her best to stay patient and try to get it out of her.

But Miranda played innocent, no matter what Wanda Nell said, and finally she gave up trying to get the girl to come clean. She wouldn't admit that her daddy had come back last night after Wanda Nell had gone to work. The more she played innocent, the more her mother knew she was lying. By now, Wanda Nell was convinced Bobby Ray had returned, and she suspected he'd left his wad of cash with Miranda. He thought it would be temporary, of course. Bobby Ray never thought he'd get caught, but of course he always did.

Only this time, he paid with his life.

Wanda Nell shook her head at the waste of it all. Bobby Ray had been pretty sharp, at least about some things. He was a good-looking man, he could charm the hind legs off a billy goat, and he could make a woman feel like she was the most wonderful person on the face of this earth. Wanda Nell remembered those times with regret.

The problem was, there was something bent in Bobby Ray. He just couldn't take to holding down a regular, respectable job. His daddy would have sent him to college, would have done just about anything for his only son, but Bobby Ray simply couldn't keep to a straight line to save his life.

Wanda Nell had tried to save it for him, but she soon learned that no matter what she did, it wouldn't be enough. Bobby Ray was hell-bent on his own way, and finally she just had to walk away, to try to save herself and her children. That hadn't done her son, T.J., much good, and she wasn't sure it had done much for Miranda, either. Both of them took after their father, always looking for the easy way out of something.

Thinking of T.J. made her heart ache all over again. Where was that boy? Probably in jail somewhere, she figured. She had to find out, though. He needed to know about his daddy. Maybe that lawyer Mayrene's cousin worked for could help her find him. Or, if worse came to worst, she'd just have to ask the sheriff's department to track him down.

She'd been surprised when Deputy Taylor returned to her trailer about eight-thirty. The young woman, who looked barely old enough to be out of high school, had come bringing Wanda Nell her purse. That saved her from having to ask Mayrene to take her to work at Budget Mart, and then begging a ride home from one of her coworkers.

"If you wouldn't mind, Miz Culpepper," the deputy said, "I need you to check through your purse to make sure everything's there."

"Sure," Wanda Nell said, taking the purse. She sat down on the couch in the living room and began pulling things out of it. After a minute of searching through it, she glanced up at the deputy. "Looks like it's all here."

"Good," the deputy said. "Deputy Johnson wanted you to know he made a special effort to make sure you got this back today."

Wanda Nell eyed the young woman, trying to figure out if she was being sarcastic. "Oh, he did, did he? Well, I guess I'll just have to give him a big ol' 'thank you', won't I? I'm sure that'll make him real happy."

Caught off guard, the deputy grinned slightly. After what Wanda Nell had witnessed earlier in the day, this young woman certainly had no cause to love Elmer Lee any more than she did herself. "I guess you can pass that message along for me, Deputy. Seeing as I don't really have the urge to call up Elmer Lee myself anytime soon."

"I'll surely do that," Deputy Taylor responded, keeping a straight face. She paused for a moment, then reached into her front uniform pocket and pulled out a card. She took a pen from another pocket, scribbled something on the card, then handed it to Wanda Nell. "If you think of anything, Miz Culpepper, anything you think might help, you can call me. That's my cell number, and I have it on most of the time, even when I'm not on duty."

"Thank you, Deputy," Wanda Nell said, fingering the card. What was this young woman trying to tell her? That she had an ally in the sheriff's department? Or maybe she was just ambitious, wanting to pull one over on Elmer Lee if she got the chance. Either way, it was fine with Wanda Nell. She wouldn't mind seeing Elmer Lee eat a big helping of crow sometime. "I'll call you if anything comes up."

"Yes'm," the deputy said. "Deputy Johnson also told me the department is gonna keep a man on duty outside until we run down those guys that broke in here. Something happens, you just stick your head out the door and yell."

"That's fine with me," Wanda Nell said fervently. Having a guard on call was the only way she'd feel like she could sleep in her own home.

"Good night, ma'am," Deputy Taylor said, tipping her hat.

Having grown a bit careless while her thoughts wandered, Wanda Nell nearly dropped a heavy box of washing powder on her toe. She caught in just in time and got it on the shelf, fussing at herself for not paying better attention to what she was doing. She yawned, then checked her watch. Almost three A.M. Lord, but she was tired. Time for a break.

She let one of the others know where she was going, then headed for the bathroom. After that, she settled down in the break room with a cold Coke and some Nabs, and tried to ignore her craving for a cigarette.

She sure wanted one. What she had been through today was enough to make anybody fall off the wagon, Wanda Nell reasoned. But she had fought hard to quit, and she damn sure wasn't going to let Bobby Ray be the cause of her breaking down and lighting up again.

She had just thrown away her empty can and wrapper, preparing to head back down to the floor, when Ricky Ratliff appeared in the break room.

"Here you are, Wanda Nell," he said. He stopped awkwardly inside the door and just stood there, staring at her.

"Yeah, here I am, Ricky," she replied. "Was there something you wanted?" She was surprised he wasn't already ripping into her about Bobby Ray's death.

"Um, yeah," Ricky said. "Um, why don't you come on back to the office with me?"

"My break is over," she said pointedly. "I got to get back to work."

"And I'm telling you I want to see you in the office," Ricky said, his face flushing in anger. He whirled around and stomped off, and Wanda Nell followed slowly.

By the time she got to the office, Ricky was already sitting in his chair. He scowled at her when she came in, but at first he didn't say anything.

Wanda Nell stood there for a moment, wondering if he was ever going to get to the point. Then she figured, *What the hell*. "What did you want to see me for, Ricky?" She sat down in the chair across the desk from him and tried to look relaxed. "What you got on your mind?"

"What the hell do you think, Wanda Nell?"

She shrugged. The office was small and dark, and all of a sudden, she was aware that Ricky was sweating. The room stank. Wanda Nell wondered what Ricky was so scared of. Surely it couldn't be her.

"What did Bobby Ray say to you?" Ricky demanded.

"About what?" Wanda Nell asked, puzzled.

"I don't know, Wanda Nell, anything."

"I don't see what business it is of yours, Ricky." She shrugged again. "But if you must know, we didn't talk all that long. I didn't have much to say to him, and he didn't have much to say to me."

Ricky was fishing for something, but what it was, Wanda Nell wasn't sure. Maybe he knew something about what deal Bobby Ray had been running, where all that money came from. She might as well play him along, see what he could tell her.

"You musta talked about something," Ricky said, desperation in his voice. "Surely Bobby Ray told you what he'd been up to lately."

"Nope," Wanda Nell replied. "He didn't say a dadgum thing to me, and frankly, I didn't want to know. Whatever it was, I doubt it was anything honest."

"God, what a little goody two-shoes you are, Wanda Nell," Ricky sneered. "Acting like your shit don't stink, just like the rest of us. I bet you didn't turn down the money Bobby Ray offered."

"How do you know he offered me any money?" Wanda Nell asked, trying to remain cool and casual.

"Bobby Ray and me was always tight," Ricky boasted. "He always talked to me."

"So I guess he told you how much money he was gonna give me?"

Ricky's eyes narrowed in suspicion. "Didn't he give you any?"

Wanda Nell cussed herself mentally for underestimating Ricky. Time to shift gears a little.

"He may have," she said, grinning. "Then again, he may not have. I still don't see what business it is of yours, Ricky."

"Come on, now, Wanda Nell," Ricky said, half-rising out of his chair. "Don't play no games with me. You don't know what you're messing with, girl."

"You?" Wanda Nell invested that word with as much sarcasm as she could manage, and Ricky's face turned deep red, he was so mad. Wanda Nell began to think maybe she had pushed him just a little too far.

"I ain't talking about me, you dumbass," Ricky said, making an obvious effort to get hold of his temper.

Wanda Nell decided to gamble a little. "Tell me, Ricky, who were those guys that broke into my trailer last night after I came to work? Surely you heard about that. The guys that tied up my girls and turned my home upside down. You know who they were?"

Ricky paled. He didn't say anything.

"Come on, Ricky," Wanda Nell said, taunting him. "Mr. Bigshot. Who were those guys?"

"I don't know, Wanda Nell. I don't know nothing about anybody breaking into your trailer," Ricky said, twisting in his chair like his bottom was itchy. "Are your girls okay?"

"Yeah, they were just scared to death, that's all," Wanda Nell said, not holding back on the sarcasm.

"What were they after?" Ricky asked.

"Now, Ricky," Wanda Nell laughed. "And here I was, figuring *you* were gonna tell *me*. You and Bobby Ray being so tight, that is."

"I know plenty, Wanda Nell," Ricky said hotly. "More'n you do, anyways."

"Then I expect you better get on that phone and start talking to the sheriff's department, Ricky. I bet it's those guys that killed Bobby Ray, and they don't mess around."

"Maybe," Ricky said. He looked away for a moment, seemed to come to some sort of decision. "You sure Bobby Ray didn't give you anything?"

Wanda Nell shook her head.

"Damn!" Ricky said. "Well, you better get on back to work, Wanda Nell, and you just forget about this little conversation. You hear?"

Getting to her feet, Wanda Nell looked at Ricky. "I don't know what the hell you're playing at, Ricky. But you damn sure better leave me out of it."

Ricky didn't respond to that, so Wanda Nell left the office. She took one last look from the doorway, and Ricky had reached for the phone. His fingers trembled as he punched in a number.

Glancing up, Ricky caught sight of Wanda Nell lurking, and he slammed the phone down. "Get back to work!"

It wouldn't do her any good to try to eavesdrop after that, Wanda Nell reckoned, so she scooted on down the stairs and back to work.

What was Ricky up to? She kept coming back to that question, no matter how hard she concentrated on her job. What did he know about Bobby Ray? Did he know who killed his buddy? And what was it he thought Bobby Ray had given her, or told her? He sure as hell was scared to death about something.

Frustrated with not being able to come up with a satisfactory answer, Wanda Nell worked on.

Just how deep was Ricky involved in whatever Bobby Ray had been up to? He always claimed to be in on Bobby Ray's plans, but she knew for a fact that Bobby Ray didn't trust him all that much. Ricky wasn't the sharpest knife in the drawer, and Bobby Ray had known that as well as she did.

But maybe this time he had trusted Ricky, and now Ricky was in over his head in something way too dangerous, without Bobby Ray there to ride herd on him.

These questions and more kept Wanda Nell preoccupied through the rest of her shift, and she was still in a fog when she left the store at six A.M. The dimly lit parking lot was almost deserted by the time she went out to her car, and she paid no attention to an old Cadillac parked a few spaces away from her Cavalier.

She was fumbling in her purse for her keys, and the next thing she knew, something whomped her upside the head.

# Eight

Wanda Nell dropped her purse and went down on her knees. She cried out as her kneecaps came into contact with the hard surface of the parking lot.

More blows came at her, and as she threw up her hands to ward them off, she heard a voice screaming at her.

"You murdering bitch! I'll kill you! I'll kill you!"

The voice went on and on, repeating the same words, even as the blows continued. Wanda Nell staggered to her feet, then thrust out her arms, pushing Lucretia Culpepper away from her as hard as she could.

Though she really couldn't see where she was aiming, trying to keep her face protected from the heavy handbag striking at her, Wanda Nell somehow connected with the older woman's chest. One strong push sent Mrs. Culpepper teetering a few steps backward. She lost her balance and sat down hard on her skinny rear end.

Panting hard, Wanda Nell stared down in horror at her former mother-in-law. The old biddy was close to foaming at the mouth, and she had a wild look in her eyes that scared Wanda Nell. Her hair hadn't been brushed properly, and she was wearing a wrinkled, stained housecoat. She stank of whisky.

Mrs. Culpepper struggled to get to her feet, and the whole time she kept cussing at Wanda Nell, calling her all kinds of ugly names. Wildly, Wanda Nell looked around for her purse. Finding it, she scooped it up, hoping to find her keys and get in her car before Mrs. Culpepper came after her again. *Lord, please don't let her have a gun,* Wanda Nell prayed.

"Hey! What's going on here?"

Wanda Nell was so happy to see KeShawn she could have kissed him. He came striding toward her, covering the ground very quickly with his long legs.

Mrs. Culpepper was on her feet again now, and she scowled at KeShawn, standing next to Wanda Nell.

"Boy, this isn't any of your business." Spittle dribbled out of Mrs. Culpepper's mouth, but she paid it no mind.

"Ma'am," KeShawn said, "I seen you hitting at Wanda Nell here. You was sneaking up behind her, and she never seen you coming. That don't seem right to me."

"She killed my son!" Mrs. Culpepper screamed the words, then all of a sudden she broke into loud, wailing sobs. Her purse slipped out of her hands and dropped to the pavement.

Wanda Nell almost felt sorry for her, though she was sure angry over the way Mrs. Culpepper had attacked her. "I did not kill Bobby Ray." She almost had to shout to make herself heard over the noise Mrs. Culpepper was making.

Wanda Nell kept repeating the words until finally Lucretia Culpepper started to calm down. KeShawn stood there, his brawny arms folded over his broad chest, and Wanda Nell felt much safer for his presence.

"Look, Mrs. Culpepper," Wanda Nell said, "I know you're upset. I'm sorry about what happened to Bobby Ray, but you got to understand, I did not kill him. No matter what you think, it wasn't me."

Lucretia Culpepper's eyes narrowed, and if she could have struck Wanda Nell dead right then and there, she would have. Wanda Nell's words did nothing to soften the hatred in that face.

"My husband's name still stands for something in this town," Mrs. Culpepper announced, "and I'm going to see you rot in jail for what you've done."

"Listen, lady," KeShawn said, stooping to pick up Mrs. Culpepper's purse. "Why don't you go back on home now, and leave Wanda Nell alone. She didn't have nothing to do with any murder. She was here all night long, working. And she's got plenty of witnesses."

Mrs. Culpepper snatched her purse away from him. "Boy, you're just plain stupid. I wouldn't put anything past this piece of trailer trash, and you better watch out you don't end up in jail for lying."

Wanda Nell watched uneasily as Mrs. Culpepper turned and stomped off to her big old Cadillac. The engine roared to life, and with a jerk, the car started forward. For a moment, Wanda Nell feared the old witch was going to try to run her and KeShawn down, but the car turned away from them and sped off through the parking lot, narrowly missing a shopping-cart rack.

"Wanda Nell, you okay?" KeShawn asked. "That sure is some crazy old woman."

"Thank the Lord you were here," Wanda Nell said with a shaky smile. "I don't know what the old biddy might've done if you hadn't'a been here. She *is* crazy, and she hates me so bad she can't see straight."

KeShawn shook his head. "Then you better watch out. She that crazy, she gonna do something to hurt you."

Wanda Nell shuddered. "Thank the Lord she didn't have a gun with her."

"You better tell the police about her," KeShawn advised. "Maybe get one of them restraining orders, something like that."

"Wouldn't do no good," Wanda Nell said. "The high-and-mighty widow of high-and-mighty old Judge Culpepper. Who do you think they're gonna believe, if I go accusing her of attacking me?" She shook her head. "Ain't nobody gonna believe me, even with a witness."

KeShawn grinned ruefully. "And especially that witness being me. That the way it is in this little town."

"Yeah," Wanda Nell said, disgusted by the thought. "But thank you for sticking up for me. I really don't know what mighta happened if you hadn't been here."

"Don't worry about that," KeShawn said. "I'll be keeping an eye out for you, least while you're here. We ain't gonna let that old woman hurt you round here."

"God bless you, KeShawn," Wanda Nell said fervently, shaking his big hand.

KeShawn grinned again, then walked on to his car. Wanda Nell retrieved her purse and her keys, unlocked her car, then sat there staring into the distance while KeShawn drove off.

Out of habit, she locked the doors and turned the key in the ignition. The engine purred, but she sat there, lost in thought. Mrs. Culpepper hadn't really hurt her with that big purse, mostly just startled her. She had taken the blows on the back of her head, and her thick blonde hair had cushioned her. Plus the fact that the old woman had been too drunk to hit her very hard. Her knees ached from contact with the asphalt, and she would have to take care of them when she got home.

A wave of rage hit her. *Damn you, Bobby Ray,* she thought fiercely. Even dead, he was still making trouble for her. It didn't matter how much she had loved him, he had messed up their marriage and helped screw up their kids. And now, getting himself killed, he had made things even worse.

For a moment, Wanda Nell wondered what would happen if she just started driving. Where she'd go, she had no idea, as long as it was somewhere besides Tullahoma, Mississippi. She could be in Memphis in less than two hours, and maybe she could lose herself in the big city.

Then she laughed bitterly at her own crazy notions. No way she was gonna run off and leave her children and her grandson. Her mama and daddy, God rest their souls, had raised her to be responsible, even when being responsible hurt like hell. Even when it meant feeling like your life was being sucked away from you every second and you couldn't ever get it back.

Wanda Nell wiped away angry tears with the back of one hand. Nope, she wasn't going anywhere. Stand and fight, that was what her daddy had always said.

And the good Lord knew that's what she was gonna do.

She put the car in gear and drove home, squinting into the rapidly rising sun.

Ten minutes later, turning in at the entrance to the trailer park, she raised a hand in greeting, waving at whoever sat in the sheriff's department car parked discreetly near her trailer.

Wanda Nell had barely stepped out of her car when she heard her neighbor across the way, Janette Sultan, calling out her name. *Just what I need right now,* Wanda Nell thought sourly.

"Wanda Nell," Janette said, coming towards her, hands clutching her housecoat around her. "You okay?"

Wanda Nell did her best to put on a pleasant face for Janette, but she was too tired to make much of an effort. "About as well as could be expected, I guess." She took a couple of steps toward the door of her trailer. She never had had much use for Janette and her whiny ways, and a little show of sympathy now wasn't going to change that.

Janette came right along with her, her face alight with curiosity.

"How long is the sheriff's department gonna be sitting there?" With a jerk of her head she indicated the nearby official car.

"I don't know, Janette," Wanda Nell said. "Long as it takes to catch whoever broke into my trailer."

"That sure was awful, Wanda Nell." Janette shivered. "And to think I never heard a dadblamed thing. I slept right through it all."

"Yeah, that's too bad," Wanda Nell replied. "It's a shame you had to miss it all."

"Now look here, Wanda Nell," Janette said, "I can't help but be worried about something like that going on here. What if those men had broke in on me, and me all alone?"

Wanda Nell had to bite her tongue to say what she really wanted to say. "Those men weren't after you or anything you had to offer," she finally managed to get out. "And it wasn't your ex-husband they killed, either. So I don't think you got too much to be worrying about, Janette."

Janette took that like Wanda Nell had slapped her face. Red with anger, she whirled around and stalked back to her trailer. Wanda Nell heard her door slam as she opened her own door.

Wanda Nell was too tired to care whether she had made

an enemy of Janette Sultan. At the moment she had other concerns on her mind.

Juliet was in the kitchen, packing her lunch for school. Wanda Nell glanced at the clock. "Morning, sweetie pie. I'm sorry I forgot to get your lunch ready last night."

Juliet grinned. "That's okay, Mama. I don't mind." She stuffed her lunch into her backpack and came out of the kitchen to give her mother a hug and a kiss on the cheek. "I better go wait for the bus."

"Yeah," Wanda Nell said. "It oughta be along in a few minutes. Now, you sure you want to go to school today?" She examined Juliet with concern.

"I'm fine, Mama," she said, "really I am. Don't you be worrying about me. I'll be better off at school. You get some rest, okay?"

With that, she was gone. Wanda Nell went to the door and watched until Juliet was out of sight. She wasn't too worried about her daughter's safety. The spot where Juliet waited for the bus was only a few feet from where the man from the sheriff's department was parked.

Wanda Nell gave a brief thought to having a piece or two of toast, but she decided she needed sleep more. There was not a sound coming out of the room at the other end of the trailer where Miranda and the baby slept. Miranda was lucky Lavon was such a good baby. He would play quietly in his crib while his mama slept on. She would get up about nine o'clock, and Lavon would be ready for some breakfast.

For a moment, Wanda Nell was tempted to tiptoe down the hall and sneak Lavon from his crib. She had a longing to hold him in her arms, make sure he was safe. She loved him fiercely, even though she was still angry at Miranda for getting herself pregnant before she finished eleventh grade.

Right now, she needed sleep. If Lavon was hungry, he'd let his mother know, and Miranda could shift her lazy self out of bed and feed him. Wanda Nell turned and went to her own bedroom.

She set the alarm for two P.M. and hoped she really could get almost seven hours of sleep. She had to show up for her shift at the Kountry Kitchen tonight. Melvin wouldn't take it too kindly if she begged off again.

Her body aching with tiredness, she took off her clothes and slipped on a nightgown. She examined her knees. They weren't as bad as she thought. A little red, and maybe a bruise or two, but nothing worse, thank goodness.

The bed felt cool and welcoming as she slid between the sheets. Making herself comfortable, she closed her eyes and tried to relax.

A pounding on the door awakened her sometime later. Groggily she stared at the clock. One-thirty. She lay back on the bed. Who on earth could be at the door?

Wanda Nell sat bolt upright. What if it was old lady Culpepper? Scrambling out of bed, she reached for a robe and pulled it on as she almost ran down the hall toward the door.

There was no sign of Miranda anywhere as Wanda Nell paused before the door. The pounding resumed, and Wanda Nell peeked through the peephole.

It was Elmer Lee Johnson.

Wanda Nell unlocked the door and snatched it open.

"What do you mean, pounding on my door like that, Elmer Lee?" she demanded. "You about scared the daylights out of me. What is it you want?"

"I need to talk to you, Wanda Nell," Elmer Lee said, pushing his way past her into the trailer. Deputy Taylor, just behind him, offered Wanda Nell an apologetic shrug as she entered the trailer.

"Then what is so damn urgent that you come around here banging on my door like a wild man?" Wanda Nell said, her hands crossed over her chest. She was very conscious of standing in front of a man she despised wearing only a light robe over her nightgown. "Have you caught those men who busted in here?"

Elmer Lee laughed. "That's what I wanna talk to you about, Wanda Nell. We ain't found no trace of any men like those girls of yours described, and I wanna be damn sure y'all aren't just making the whole thing up."

# Nine

Wanda Nell stared at Elmer Lee like he had stepped right off a spaceship from Mars.

"You are out of your ever-lovin' mind, Elmer Lee Johnson," she said when she could finally get her tongue and lips working. "I sure am glad there's a witness to hear me say you are plumb crazy, there ain't no two ways about it."

Deputy Taylor coughed, maybe in warning, but Wanda Nell was too angry to care.

"How dare you come into my home," Wanda Nell went on, "and accuse me of lying like that, Elmer Lee? I know you hate me, but this is just too damn ridiculous!"

She tried to get ahold of her temper before she made the situation any worse. Clamping her mouth shut, she stood there and stared at Elmer Lee.

He was glaring right back at her, and she figured the only

thing keeping him from slapping her up one side and down the other was Deputy Taylor being in the room.

"Now, Wanda Nell, don't you go getting hysterical on me," Elmer Lee said. "I swear, woman, you been on the rag ever since high school. No wonder Bobby Ray . . ." He broke off as Deputy Taylor coughed again, a good bit louder this time. "Now let's just calm down here, okay? I need to talk to you, and it won't do nobody any good you getting all riled up with me."

Wanda Nell had to do something or she was going to scratch his eyes out. "I'm gonna make some coffee. Either of you want some?"

The two deputies shook their heads. "Then sit down somewhere, and I'll be right back," Wanda Nell instructed as she walked into the kitchen.

While she poured water into the coffeemaker and measured out the coffee, Wanda Nell kept telling herself she needed to watch her temper around Elmer Lee. It didn't do her one bit of good popping off at him like she'd done, and if she didn't watch it, she'd find herself sitting in jail.

Back in the living room, she found the two deputies sitting on the couch. Wanda Nell perched on the edge of a chair and faced Elmer Lee. "Okay, now, what is it you wanted to talk to me about?"

"I wanna talk to you about this story you and your girls told me, about some men breaking in here and so on." Elmer Lee held up a hand to warn Wanda Nell not to interrupt. "I'm trying to believe you, Wanda Nell, but it ain't easy. See, the way I reckon it, you coulda got those girls of yours to go along with you. You put together this story about these men breaking in here, and it looks like they musta killed Bobby Ray, too. Isn't that what you think? I mean, those guys are the killers?"

Reluctantly, Wanda Nell nodded.

"Well, I'll tell you, Wanda Nell," Elmer Lee said, using a tone like she was a retarded child, "me and my men have been talking to all your neighbors here, and you wanna know something real interesting?"

He paused, obviously waiting for Wanda Nell to speak. She refused to give in. She stared back at him, not saying a word.

Elmer Lee let the silence lengthen, then finally he started talking again. "What's really interesting, Wanda Nell, is that we talked till we was blue in the face to every single person in this here trailer park, and you know what? Not a damn one of 'em heard a thing that night."

Still Wanda Nell refused to speak.

"Oh, I almost forgot," Elmer Lee said, giving her an evil grin, "one of your neighbors did hear one thing. Seems like that gal across the row heard you screaming at Bobby Ray out there in the road at some point."

It had to be Janette Sultan, Wanda Nell figured. How she musta loved being able to dish some dirt.

The welcome scent of fresh-brewed coffee caught her attention. Without excusing herself, Wanda Nell got up from her chair and went to the kitchen. *Take it easy,* she told herself. *Don't let him get to you. Don't be stupid.* She poured herself some coffee, added cream and sugar, and stirred it for a moment. She took a couple of sips, enjoying the warmth.

Slowly Wanda Nell walked back into the living room with her mug and sat down again. Before Elmer Lee could say anything, she spoke, "Yes, Elmer Lee, I did yell at Bobby Ray. I told him I wanted him out of this trailer, and I told him I didn't want him ever coming back. And that was the last time I saw him."

"Alive, you mean," Elmer Lee said nastily.

"Yeah," Wanda Nell acknowledged, trying hard not to see Bobby Ray's dead body in her mind.

"How do you account for the fact that not a single person in this trailer park heard or saw anything, other than you yelling at the victim?"

"I don't know, Elmer Lee," Wanda Nell said. She drank from her coffee cup before continuing. "Everybody in this trailer park works hard for a living, just like me. They all come home tired at the end of the day, and they go to bed. Most of 'em got to get up early, and they can't stay up all night waiting and watching for something to happen."

"'Specially if there ain't nothing to see," Elmer Lee said.

"I can't help it if nobody but my girls saw those men, Elmer Lee," Wanda Nell said, wrapping her hands around her mug of coffee. The heat of it helped her focus on keeping her temper. "Those men came here and broke into my house, and they tied up my girls. And I bet you they were the ones killed Bobby Ray. No way are you gonna pin this on me. You need to get out there and do your job and stop harassing me."

"Soon's I can find one reliable witness," Elmer Lee said, "one witness who saw those strange men here in this trailer park, or even somewhere around town, then I guess I'll start believing you. Until then, Wanda Nell, I'm gonna do my job as I damn well see fit."

"Fine," Wanda Nell said, hanging on to her mug instead of throwing the hot coffee into his face like she really wanted to, "you do your job. But I ain't gonna just sit here and let you stomp all over me, Elmer Lee. My mama didn't raise no fool, and I got rights. You for damn sure ain't gonna take those away from me." Maybe she ought to take Mayrene's advice after all and call that lawyer.

Deputy Taylor coughed again, and both Elmer Lee and Wanda Nell glared at her. "Sorry," she said, still sputtering.

"It's my allergies acting up." She got up from the couch. "You mind, Miz Culpepper, if I use your bathroom?"

Wanda Nell just pointed. She was still too angry with Elmer Lee to risk opening her mouth.

As soon as Deputy Taylor left the room, Elmer Lee stood up and moved over in front of Wanda Nell's chair. He stared down at her, his eyes sparkling with malice. "If you killed Bobby Ray," he said, his voice low, "I'm gonna see you on death row, Wanda Nell. You just better count on that."

Without missing a beat, Wanda Nell responded. "And you just better count on being disappointed, Elmer Lee. I didn't kill him, and there ain't no way you're gonna prove I did. Now get out of my house." She stood up.

Elmer Lee watched her a moment longer, then stepped past her toward the front door. "Tell Taylor I'm waiting outside." Then he was out the door, letting it close none too gently behind him.

Her hands trembling, Wanda Nell walked back into the kitchen for more coffee. As she tried to steady herself, she heard footsteps behind her. She turned around.

Deputy Taylor stood there, a concerned look on her face. "Miz Culpepper," she said, "you just hang in there, you hear? I know this is real rough on you, but not everybody thinks like Elmer Lee. You know?"

Wanda Nell smiled faintly. She had no idea why this young woman was so determined to be friendly to her, but right now, she could use all the help she could get.

"Thank you, Deputy," she said. "I appreciate that. And I'll keep that to myself."

Deputy Taylor nodded.

"Elmer Lee said he'd be waiting for you outside," Wanda Nell continued.

"Yes, ma'am," the deputy said. She touched her fingers to the brim of her hat, turned, and left. Wanda Nell heard the door open and close, and a few moments later a car engine revved up. The sound receded as she stood in the kitchen and slowly sipped at her coffee.

*What am I gonna do?* Wanda Nell wondered as she drank the last of her coffee. She moved to the sink to rinse out her mug, and she stared out the window over the sink, which looked out on her little carport. Her car was gone, which meant Miranda had taken the baby and gone off somewhere while she was asleep.

Probably gone to see that no-account girlfriend of hers, the same age as Miranda with two kids. Wanda Nell shook her head, thinking about it. She tried to keep Miranda away from that Paulette, but anytime she said something, Miranda just got mad. She kept praying that Paulette wouldn't encourage Miranda to get herself into any more trouble, but there wasn't much she could do about it.

Sighing, Wanda Nell turned away from the window. Thinking about Miranda only depressed her, and right now she needed to concentrate on this mess. Surely, she reflected, once they knew when Bobby Ray died, she'd be off the hook. She figured he had to have been killed after she was safely at work, with a number of witnesses to say she hadn't left work, but she had no idea how long it would take before the sheriff's department had that information. Until then, she was going to have to put up with Elmer Lee and his bullying. She would call that lawyer only when she had no other choice, she decided.

There was one thing she could do, though. She doubted Elmer Lee was looking all that hard for those men who broke into her trailer, and she could at least ask some questions, here at the trailer park, and later on at the Kountry Kitchen. Maybe somebody had seen them somewhere.

Wanda Nell went to the phone and punched in a familiar number. "Hey, there, Roberta, it's Wanda Nell," she said, after the voice on the other end had announced cheerfully, "Lucille's Style Shop. How may I help you?"

"Hey, girl, how you doing?" Roberta's voice revealed her concern. She and Wanda Nell had been in the same grade in school, and though they had never been real close, they had always liked each other. "Mayrene was telling us what an awful time you been having. Anything I can do for you?"

Wanda Nell's eyes puddled suddenly from the unexpected offer. "Thank you, Roberta," she said, trying not to choke up further. "Just hearing you say that means an awful lot to me."

"Well, you know I mean it, honey," Roberta said. "You tell me, and I'll do anything to help out. I made you one of my chicken casseroles, and Mayrene's gonna bring it to you. Now, listen, honey, you holding up all right?"

"I'm doing okay, I guess," Wanda Nell said. "Hanging in there. And thanks for that casserole. I sure do appreciate it, and I know my girls will be glad, too." She paused. "Listen, is Mayrene busy? I need to talk to her a minute."

"Sure, honey, hang on, and I'll get her. She just put ol' Miz Beecham under the dryer." The phone clanked as Roberta set it down on the counter, and Wanda Nell could hear a number of female voices clattering in the background.

A few moments later, Mayrene's voice boomed into her ear. "Hey, girl. You okay? Roberta said you sounded a little shaky."

Wanda Nell gripped the receiver hard, trying not to give way to tears. All of it was suddenly piling up on her, and she had to get hold of herself. "I'm okay," she said, her voice husky. She cleared her throat. "Listen, Mayrene. I need help. Elmer Lee is bound and determined to prove I killed Bobby Ray, and he ain't doing much to find those guys that broke in here."

Mayrene snorted into the phone. "Now why ain't I surprised by that? I've known fence posts smarter'n ol' Elmer
Lee."

Wanda Nell chuckled. "Yeah, well, this particular fence
post is gonna cause me as much trouble as he can. Unless I
can figure a way to get round him."

"What you want me to do?" Mayrene asked. "You know
I'll do anything I can to help, honey."

"Thanks, Mayrene," Wanda Nell said. "I been counting
on that, but I don't know how I can ever repay you."

Mayrene snorted again. "Don't be foolish, Wanda Nell.
Now what is it you want me to do?"

"I want you to talk to all the ladies at the beauty parlor,"
Wanda Nell said. "Tell 'em about what happened to me and
my girls, and see if anybody noticed some strange men in
town that day or that night." She thought a moment, trying to
remember how Juliet and Miranda had described the men.
"Here's what they looked like, best as I can recall." She repeated everything she could remember.

"I can surely do that," Mayrene promised. "And if anybody saw those guys, we'll know it. What are you gonna
do? Talk it up at the Kountry Kitchen?"

"Yeah," Wanda Nell said. "And I'm gonna go round this
trailer park knocking on doors. You can't tell me that Elmer
Lee and his crew really worked that hard at it."

"You got that right!" Mayrene laughed. Then she sobered
quickly. "But, honey, you need to be careful. If Elmer Lee
catches on to what we're doing, he ain't gonna like it too
much."

"I don't care," Wanda Nell said. "He ain't gonna think
any worse of me than he already does, that's for damn sure."

"Okay, then," Mayrene answered. "Look, I gotta go. Miz
Beecham's wiggling around under the dryer." The phone
clicked in Wanda Nell's ear.

She put the receiver back in its cradle and stood staring at it for a couple of minutes. She had been putting something off, but she couldn't much longer. She had to try.

Sighing, she opened a drawer in the cabinet and pulled out a ragged address book. She thumbed the pages until she got to the *C*'s, then scanned down the entries, looking at the numerous strings of digits she had listed under her son's name. The Lord only knew if she could find T.J. using one of these numbers. The last time she had talked to him, nearly two years ago, he had been in jail down in Pearl River County, near the Gulf Coast. She hadn't had the heart to ask what the charges were, just asked how he was doing and how long he was in for, and let it go at that.

She hadn't heard from him since, though she had tried calling him a couple of times, trying various friends he often stayed with. He wasn't still in jail in Pearl River County, that much she knew. She'd simply have to start calling his friends, see if one of them knew where he was.

As she punched in the first number, her stomach knotted. She hated feeling this way about her only son, but he was a puzzle to her. She didn't know how to handle him, what it was he needed from her to try to straighten out his life.

The phone rang and rang. Wanda Nell disconnected, waited a moment, then tried a different number. This time she got an answer.

"T.J.?" The voice on the other end sounded like she had interrupted something. "No'm, I ain't seen nor heard from him in months."

Wanda Nell thanked the woman on the other end and disconnected once again. She got the same response from two other numbers, one a male friend and the other another of T.J.'s former girlfriends. At least they were halfway friendly, Wanda Nell thought. With other women, at least, T.J. somehow managed to part on good terms. Just not with his mother.

Wanda Nell had two numbers left, and with one of them she finally got some results. "Yes, ma'am," the man said when Wanda Nell had identified herself and explained that she was looking for her son.

"Yes, ma'am," he said again. "I saw T.J. 'bout a week ago, I guess, over in Greenville, and he was talking like he was gonna be headin' over your way. Said he had family in Tullahoma, and he was gonna go check on his mama."

"Just a week ago?" Wanda Nell asked.

"Yes'm," he said. "That's the last time I seen him."

Wanda Nell thanked him and put down the phone. So T.J. had been as near as Greenville, about ninety miles away, just a week ago.

Then where the heck was he now? Wanda Nell suddenly had a bad feeling she really didn't want to have.

## Ten

Could T.J. be in Tullahoma and her not know it? Wanda Nell didn't like to think so. In the past he'd always made a beeline for his mama and sisters when he hit town, no matter what. He adored Juliet, she was always his favorite. Miranda he tolerated, but she was too much like him for them to get on well.

When he did turn up, he sure was going to be surprised when he saw his little nephew. Wanda Nell shook her head at that thought. Unless he had changed a lot, T.J. wasn't going to like finding out Lavon's daddy was a black man. A light-skinned black man, to be sure, but still black.

If he was in Tullahoma now, where could he be? Wanda Nell thought about some of the boys he used to hang around with. Maybe one of them had heard from him recently. She checked the phone book for a number, then punched it in.

After three rings, a gruff voice answered. "Yeah?"

Wanda Nell identified herself, then asked, "Is this Jackie Pinnix?"

"Yes'm," he said. "Anything I can help you with, Miz Culpepper?"

"I heard T.J. might be in town, Jackie," she said. "Have you seen him? Or heard from him lately?"

In the pause that followed, Wanda Nell could hear the flick of a lighter and the sound of exhaled smoke. "No'm, I hadn't heard from ol' Teej in a while. But if 'n I spot him somewhere, I'll tell him you're looking for him."

"I'd appreciate that, Jackie," Wanda Nell said. "There's some bad news he needs to know."

Jackie didn't ask what the bad news was. Either he'd already heard it around town, Wanda Nell reckoned, or he just plain wasn't interested. She set the receiver on its cradle with a frown. If T.J. was somewhere in Tullahoma, Jackie Pinnix was more likely to find him than she was. He and T.J. had been real good friends at one point, until they'd had some kind of falling out.

A knock on the door startled her. She went to the door and peered out the window. Two neighbor ladies stood there, each with a covered dish in her hands. Sighing, Wanda Nell opened the door.

"Good afternoon, Miz Hyde, Miz Kennington. How are y'all today?" She stood back to let them enter.

"Afternoon, Miz Culpepper," the older of the two, Mrs. Hyde, said. "How are you and your girls doing? We heard about the terrible thing that happened to their daddy."

Wanda Nell stared at them for a moment. Neither of them had ever made much effort to be friendly before, and from the way they were looking at her now, curiosity had got the better of them.

"They're doing about as good as can be expected," Wanda Nell said. "I appreciate y'all's concern, but I really don't feel much like talking about it, if you don't mind."

Their faces fell, though they tried hard not to let Wanda Nell see their disappointment.

"That's alright, Miz Culpepper," Mrs. Kennington said. "We just wanted you to know we been thinking about you and praying for you in this terrible time." She thrust the dish she was carrying toward Wanda Nell. "I made you a little something, my green bean casserole. It's my own special recipe."

"Thank you," Wanda Nell said. "That's real kind of you." She stood there, holding the dish, waiting for Mrs. Hyde to say her piece.

"And I made y'all some of my fried chicken," Mrs. Hyde said. "The recipe's been in my family for years. I hope y'all like it."

Wanda Nell accepted her dish, too, and carried them both to the kitchen and put them in the refrigerator. Returning, she thanked them again. "Ladies, can I ask y'all a question, if you don't mind?"

"Why, sure, Miz Culpepper," Mrs. Hyde said, her eyes glowing with anticipation.

"Well, I was just wondering," Wanda Nell began slowly. "Did y'all hear or see anything strange last night?"

The two women looked at each other for a moment, then slowly each one turned back to Wanda Nell and shook her head. "Not a thing, dear," Mrs. Kennington said. "I wish we had. Maybe we could help. But once I go to sleep, even Gabriel's horn won't wake me up."

"Me, neither," Mrs. Hyde said. "Sorry."

"Well, thank you, anyway," Wanda Nell said.

"Our pleasure," Mrs. Kennington assured her.

Wanda Nell gently shepherded them to the door. "I'm

sorry I can't talk longer," she said, "but I've got to start getting ready for work soon. I'm sure y'all understand."

Both women nodded before they said good-bye. Wanda Nell watched them for a moment from the window as they walked back down toward the other end of the trailer park, where their trailers stood across from each other. Their heads were together, and Wanda Nell could just imagine what they were busy whispering to each other. She turned away.

Glancing at the clock, Wanda Nell figured she'd better get a move on. She had time to do a little cleaning before she had to get ready for work. She found her rubber gloves and her bucket of cleaning supplies and went to Miranda's end of the trailer. No matter how much she fussed at Miranda, the girl simply would not clean her bathroom the way Wanda Nell wanted her to.

So Wanda Nell just scrubbed it down herself. She couldn't abide a dirty bathroom, and Miranda and the baby would wallow in filth if Wanda Nell didn't take a hand.

Shaking her head in disgust at the state of the bathtub, Wanda Nell switched on the portable CD player Miranda kept in the bathroom and set to work. At least scrubbing at the soap scum allowed her to burn off some of her irritation and uncertainty. As she sang along with Reba McEntire, she was able to think about other things for at least a while.

After she had finished the bathtub and the sink, Wanda Nell reluctantly opened the lid of the diaper pail. She refused to have those disposable diapers in her house, and Miranda wasn't too good about making sure the cloth diapers were washed before Lavon ran out. The pail was almost full, and the smell just about knocked her back when she lifted the lid.

Wanda Nell hastily dropped the lid back down, then grabbed the handle and toted the large pail into the small utility room off the kitchen. A check of the clock told her she didn't have time to run a load of diapers and then let the hot water build up for her own shower, so she left the pail on top of the washing machine.

As she was stripping off her gloves in the kitchen, Wanda Nell heard her car. She looked out the window to see Miranda getting Lavon out of his car seat. Wanda Nell put away her cleaning supplies and went into the living room to greet her daughter and grandson.

"Hi, Mama," Miranda said, pulling the door shut behind her and the baby. "You get some sleep?"

"I did," Wanda Nell said, "no thanks to the sheriff's department."

"What happened?" Miranda asked, shifting Lavon from one hip to the other.

"Oh, that fool Elmer Lee came back, trying to make out like you girls and I been lying about those men that broke in here."

"That's stupid," Miranda protested. "Why'd we make up something like that?"

"Because," Wanda Nell said grimly, "Elmer Lee thinks I killed your daddy, and you girls are helping me cover it up by making up a story about those men."

Lavon held his arms out to her, and she took him from Miranda. She kissed his forehead, then frowned at Miranda. "Miranda, this baby's hot. I think he may be running a fever."

"Oh, he's okay, Mama," Miranda said, not looking at Wanda Nell. "We was just sitting out in the sun for a while, that's all."

"You know better'n to keep this baby out in the sun too long," Wanda Nell said as mildly as she could. "Come on, sugar, let's go get you some water, okay?"

Lavon mumbled something, and Wanda Nell took him into the kitchen for a drink while Miranda disappeared in the direction of her bedroom. Moments later she was back, her face now slightly flushed just like her son's.

"Mama," she said, "where's the diaper pail? It's gone from the bathroom, and I got a couple messy diapers to put in it."

"It's in there on the washing machine," Wanda Nell said. "Yeah, that's Grandma's good boy, Lavon, drink up that water." She turned to look at Miranda, fidgeting in the doorway.

"You really need to run a load of diapers soon's I get done with my shower, honey," Wanda Nell said. "Why'd you let it go this long?"

"I guess I just forgot about it, Mama," Miranda replied, looking relieved about something. "But I promise I'll wash ever' single one of 'em today, after you've gone to work."

"You do that," Wanda Nell said. She turned back to her grandson and checked his forehead. "He's cooling off. He just needed some water. You got to be careful, Miranda, about letting this baby get dehydrated."

But she was talking to the air. Miranda had disappeared. Shaking her head, Wanda Nell carried Lavon with her into the utility room, where she found Miranda peering into the diaper pail.

"They're all still there," Wanda Nell said, "just as stinky as they were when I found them."

Miranda had started at the sound of her mother's voice. "Yes, Mama," she said meekly. "I know, and I'll get all of 'em cleaned up, and I won't let Lavon get too warm again. I promise."

"Good," was all Wanda Nell said as she handed her grandson to his mother after one final hug and kiss. She left the two of them in the utility room.

By the time Wanda Nell had showered, dressed in her uniform, put on her makeup, and done her hair, Juliet was hopping down off the bus. Wanda Nell could see her through the window of the bathroom she shared with her younger daughter. Checking her watch, she saw that it was three-forty-five. As soon as she greeted Juliet and heard a little bit about her day at school, she'd have to head on to her shift at the Kountry Kitchen.

She found Juliet in the kitchen pouring herself a glass of milk. "Hey, honey, how was your day at school?" She stroked her daughter's long blonde hair.

Juliet smiled at her. "It was fine, Mama. Of course, a lot of people heard about what happened to my daddy, and they wanted to know about it."

"Did it bother you, them asking you questions like that?" Wanda Nell asked. "You want me to call your teachers? Ask them to keep the other kids from pestering you?"

"No, Mama," Juliet said, examining her milk, "it's okay, really. I can handle it." Then she looked up at her mother and grinned. "But there's one teacher you can call, if you want to. 'Cause he sure was asking about you today."

Wanda Nell got a fluttery feeling in her stomach. "What are you talking about, honey?"

"Oh, my English teacher," Juliet said airily, "Mr. Pemberton. He asked how I was doing, said he'd heard all about what happened, and he sure seemed interested. Especially in how you're doing, Mama." She watched her mother with a knowing look in her eyes.

"Well, I'm sure he's just being a concerned teacher," Wanda Nell said, trying to sound offhand. "I seem to remember he's a nice man."

"Uh-huh," Juliet said, "like when you waited on him the other night at the Kountry Kitchen. He mentioned that, too."

Wanda Nell turned away, hoping Juliet wouldn't see her blushing. She opened the refrigerator door and stuck her head inside, pretending to look for something. After a moment, when she thought the blush had subsided, she withdrew her head and shut the door. "I guess I need to put Cokes on the grocery list."

Juliet giggled. "Mama, there's a whole bunch in the cabinet over there."

"Oh," Wanda Nell said, feeling stupid. "Oh, well, then. I guess I better be getting on in to work. You girls gonna be okay here by yourselves tonight?"

Juliet's grin faded, but her chin took on a determined cast. "We're going to be fine, Mama, don't you worry about us. That man from the sheriff's department's going to be out there, isn't he?

"Supposed to be," Wanda Nell replied. "So if anything happens and you get scared, you just yell, you hear?"

Juliet nodded. "Don't worry, Mama."

Wanda Nell leaned forward and kissed her on the forehead. "Y'all be good, and call me if you need anything. And you better be in bed and sound asleep when I get home."

"Even on a Friday night?" Juliet asked.

"Even on a Friday night," Wanda Nell said, smiling. "We all need some rest." She grabbed her purse and car keys and headed for the door. "Tell Miranda and Lavon I said 'bye'."

Juliet's "Bye, Mama," floated out the door after her.

Wanda Nell rolled her eyes in annoyance when she saw the inside of her car. Every time Miranda used it, she left it a mess. Sighing, Wanda Nell pushed aside candy bar wrappers and empty Coke cans and set her purse on the passenger seat. She'd make Miranda clean the car out tomorrow.

Ten minutes later she parked her car at the Kountry Kitchen. She wasn't looking forward to working there tonight. A lot of folks ate there on Friday night, and most of them would be curious. She was hoping she could keep from having to answer a lot of questions, because she didn't want to discuss her business with customers any more than she had to.

Steeling herself, she grabbed her purse and her clothes for her shift later at Budget Mart, locked her car, then headed for the front door of the restaurant. No point in sneaking in the back way. She might as well go right on in the front and get it over with.

At four-fifteen in the afternoon, the Kountry Kitchen wasn't very busy, but when Wanda Nell stepped inside and let the door swing shut behind her, every head in the place turned to look at her.

For a moment, nobody said a word. Fayetta Sutton stood behind the counter, coffeepot in hand, staring at Wanda Nell like somebody had dropped dog poop on the floor. Wanda Nell paid her no mind. She could handle Fayetta. It was the customers she was worried about. What if they didn't want her waiting on their tables?

"Hey, Wanda Nell," called one of her regulars, a guy named Pete Jones who worked out at the John Deere place on the highway. "How you doin'?"

The buzz of conversation started again, and Wanda Nell walked over to Pete with a grateful smile. "Thanks for asking, Pete," she said, pausing by the table. "I'm doing okay, I guess."

Pete grinned up at her, his chubby, genial face showing his concern. "Don't let any of these old buzzards give you a hard time. Anybody's known you for more than five minutes knows you didn't have nothing to do with what happened to Bobby Ray." He raised his voice slightly. "And there isn't nobody here who can make me believe you did."

Wanda Nell smiled her thanks at him as several other voices called out greetings. Acknowledging each of them briefly, Wanda Nell made her way around the counter and into the kitchen. She waved at the cook and the dishwasher as she went by, on her way to the small room where the staff kept their personal belongings during their shifts.

Back in the kitchen, she ran into her boss, Melvin Arbuckle, an unlit cigarette dangling from his lip. "Hey, Wanda Nell, how you doing?" He took her arm. "Come on with me while I have a smoke. Fayetta can handle it for a minute."

"Okay, Melvin," she said as she followed him down the hall. "I'm doing okay. I'm sorry about having to miss my shift last night."

Melvin opened the back door and stepped outside. He finished lighting his cigarette before he spoke again. "It was pretty quiet here last night, and Fayetta made plenty extra without you here. So she wasn't too mad, I guess." Smoke streamed from his mouth as he spoke.

Wanda Nell didn't say anything. She didn't care whether Fayetta had been mad or not.

"Anything you need, Wanda Nell?" Melvin asked. "I mean, are you gonna need a lawyer? You know somebody you can call?" He tapped ash from his cigarette onto the ground.

"I'm fine right now, Melvin," she said. "I don't think I need a lawyer, but if I do, my friend Mayrene has a cousin who works for one." For the moment, she couldn't remember the man's name. "According to her—Blanche, I mean—Mayrene's cousin, he's pretty sharp."

"That's good," Melvin said. "But if you don't need no lawyer, then stay away from 'em long as you can." He laughed bitterly. "I don't know one I'd recommend, but if you need any help, you let me know, you hear?"

"Thanks, Melvin," she said, touched by his concern. "I appreciate that. But as soon as that fool Elmer Lee Johnson gets over his idea I killed Bobby Ray, I'll be okay."

Melvin shook his head. "Elmer Lee is one stubborn sumbitch. You be careful about getting crossways of him."

He frowned. "But wasn't your daddy and the sheriff good buddies once upon a time?"

"Yeah, they were," Wanda Nell said. "And I guess the sheriff'll keep Elmer Lee from getting too carried away." It was her turn to laugh bitterly. "I got a good alibi for practically the whole dang night, but Elmer Lee don't want to believe me. But he'll have to, in the end."

"Yeah, I guess so," Melvin said. He took one last drag from his cigarette, then flipped the butt onto the pavement. "Come on, then, let's get to work."

"Okay," Wanda Nell said. "Lemme make a quick phone call, and I'll be right out."

Melvin nodded. "Just make it snappy." He grinned. "You don't want Fayetta getting any meaner'n she already is."

Wanda Nell grimaced. "She better watch her mouth tonight, that's all I got to say."

Melvin laughed as he strode down the hall away from her. Wanda Nell stepped into the storeroom and retrieved her cell phone from her purse. She turned it on and waited. When it was ready, she punched the speed dial.

After a couple of rings, Roberta at the beauty salon answered. "Hey, Roberta," Wanda Nell said, "it's Wanda Nell again. Mayrene busy?"

"Hey, girl," Roberta said. "No, she's just about done and ready to leave. Hang on."

Moments later, Mayrene's voice came on the line. "I was just about to call you, Wanda Nell."

"Yeah, I was gonna ask you if you'd mind keeping an eye on the girls and Lavon tonight," Wanda Nell said. "That sheriff's department man'll be outside, but I'd feel better if I knew you was watching out for 'em, too."

Mayrene chuckled. "Then I guess it's a good thing I'm not planning on going out tonight. Don't you worry, honey.

I'll go over and keep 'em company for a while tonight. And I'll take my shotgun with me."

"I don't know if you need a shotgun," Wanda Nell said. Mayrene and her love of guns made Wanda Nell uneasy sometimes.

Mayrene laughed again. "Don't worry, honey. I ain't gonna shoot anybody, not unless it's one of them jerks that broke into your trailer. Now, listen, don't you wanna know why I was gonna call you?"

"Oh, yeah," Wanda Nell said. She'd been in such a hurry she hadn't really paid attention to Mayrene. "What was it?"

"I can't swear to it, mind," Mayrene said, her voice dropping lower, like she didn't want anyone at the salon to overhear her, "but I think I saw T.J. this afternoon."

# *Eleven*

"Where?" Wanda Nell demanded. "Where'd you see him?" Her chest tightened as she waited for an answer. Something surely must be wrong, otherwise T.J. would've come to see her by now.

"It was about lunchtime, or thereabouts," Mayrene said. "I stepped out for a minute, I was gonna go 'cross the street to the Stop 'n Rob for a Coca-Cola. Durn machine here is broke, and they're taking their own sweet time a'comin' to fix it." She gave a disgusted snort into the phone, and Wanda Nell was about ready to speak up and tell her to forget the dang Coke machine, when Mayrene continued.

"Anyways, I was coming back across the street, just minding my own business, I'll have you know, and this durn fool in an ol' pickup near about knocked me on my you-know-what."

"Were you hurt?" Wanda Nell asked quickly.

"Naw, honey, not a scratch on me." Mayrene laughed. "Lucky I saw 'em coming just in time, and I hopped back outta the way. And I tell you I was so mad, I started hollering and a' shaking my fist after the fool driving that ol' pile of junk, not that he ever even turned his head. But durned if the other guy in the truck didn't turn around and look at me through the back window for a second."

"And you think that was T.J.?" Wanda Nell asked.

"Sure looked like him," Mayrene replied. "Though you know I ain't seen much of him for a couple years, at least." She sighed into the phone. "It was only a quick look, mind you, 'cause they was gone real fast. That ol' boy driving that truck, he wasn't gonna hang around and let *me* give 'im what for."

"Did you know the truck?"

"Looked kinda familiar," Mayrene said, after a moment's thought. "But then it was a Ford like every guy in Tullahoma County drives. Mud all over it, and what wasn't covered in mud was gray."

Wanda Nell sighed into the phone. "I don't know. Could've been T.J., I guess, with one of his old friends. You know Jackie Pinnix?"

"Yeah," Mayrene said. "One of my cousins married his oldest sister. It mighta been Jackie. I don't know what he drives."

Wanda Nell became aware that someone was standing behind her, patting a foot on the concrete floor. And that foot didn't sound too happy. She turned around.

Fayetta Sutton glared at her. "What're you doing back here gabbing away on the phone, Wanda Nell? I been here since eleven o'clock this morning without no break, and I'm tired of waiting for you to get your sorry self in there and get to work. I need to be getting on home."

"I gotta go," Wanda Nell said quickly into the phone, then shut it off and stuck it in her purse. "Just hang on a dang minute, Fayetta. That was important, and I sure don't appreciate you coming up on me like that."

Fayetta drew herself up all haughty and glared at Wanda Nell. *If she don't watch it,* Wanda Nell thought, *that makeup's gonna crack and fall off right here on the floor.*

"Well, Miss Wanda Nell High-and-Mighty, don't you be using that tone of voice with *me*. I was the one covering for you last night down here, and seems to me like you oughta be thanking me."

Wanda Nell held on to her temper hard as she could. "I reckon you made out okay, Fayetta, without me here to get all the big tips."

Fayetta made a growling sound low in her throat, like a cat about to lash out. Wanda Nell took a step back, then could've kicked herself, the way Fayetta grinned at her.

"I reckon I'll be getting lots of tips when they haul you off to jail for killing Bobby Ray," Fayetta said, smirking. "You ain't gonna look too good behind bars."

"Go to hell," Wanda Nell said, then pushed her way past the still-gloating Fayetta. If she didn't walk away now, she'd either say something or, worse, do something she'd have cause to regret.

Fayetta's laugh followed her down the short hall to the kitchen, and Wanda Nell's face was set in grim lines when she pushed through the door into the front of the restaurant.

"Whoa, there, Wanda Nell," Pete Jones said. He stood near the cash register where Melvin was making change out of the drawer. "Who got ahold of you? You look like you're ready to chew up a tree and spit out toothpicks."

Wanda Nell forced herself to laugh and relax. "I'm okay, Pete," she said. "Just thinking too hard about everything, I guess."

Pete grinned at her, and Wanda Nell flashed him a big smile. Pete's eyes widened slightly, and Wanda Nell turned quickly away. Last thing she needed right now was Pete Jones thinking she was interested in him. He'd already been married three times.

For the next couple of hours Wanda Nell did her best to smile and chat and serve her customers like nothing was wrong. Thoughts of T.J. and what he could be doing lay heavy on her mind as she worked. She had to dodge a few questions that were downright nosy, but she turned them off in a way she hoped wouldn't cause too much offense. Though, for being as danged insensitive as some of them were, she ought to have told several of them where to get off. Melvin wouldn't take too kindly to that, so she kept her comments to herself.

She hated being rude, unless there was no other way out, and, besides, she needed good tips. The good Lord only knew whether she was going to have to hire a lawyer at some point, and she didn't want to be beholden to Melvin or anybody else if she could help it.

Fayetta had run home for two hours to get her kids settled in for the night with her mother, and Wanda Nell enjoyed the break. Fayetta was like a little black cloud following her around, and she was sick of rain.

At six, the other weekend waitress came on, and Wanda Nell was glad to see her. Ruby Garner was a tall, plain girl about twenty years old, with a sunny disposition that never wavered. She paid no mind at all to Fayetta and her always trying to start some kind of mess. Wanda Nell enjoyed working with Ruby.

"Hey, Wanda Nell," Ruby said, pausing to give Wanda Nell a big hug. "How're you doing? I heard about what happened."

"I'm doing fine, Ruby," Wanda Nell said, touched by the real concern in Ruby's face. "Don't you worry about me, but I sure appreciate you asking." She smiled, and Ruby smiled back. "Now, how's school?"

Ruby was taking classes at the local junior college. She wanted to be a nurse, and since she didn't have any family to speak of, she was working two jobs to pay her way through school. Wanda Nell always did her best to encourage Ruby, and the younger woman seemed to appreciate Wanda Nell's interest.

"Okay," Ruby said, "though I got a coupla big tests coming up that are just eating my lunch." She shook her head dolefully.

Far as Wanda Nell knew, Ruby hadn't made anything but A's ever since she started junior college, but Ruby was always acting like she was going to fail. "Yeah, I just bet they are," Wanda Nell said, laughing. "Like you've ever failed a test in your whole life."

Ruby dimpled. "Well, I guess they aren't going to be that bad." She was looking over Wanda Nell's shoulder, and her eyes widened slightly. "Now, don't turn around, Wanda Nell," she said, dropping her voice a little, "but there's a real nice-looking man just come in, and he sure is trying hard not to stare at you."

Wanda Nell felt the back of her neck prickle. "Oh, really?" she said. "You ever seen this guy before?"

"I don't think so," Ruby said, "but I sure wouldn't mind seeing him more often. He's cute, even if he is a bit too old for me." She dimpled again, then turned away to take an order.

As casually as she could Wanda Nell turned around. Jack Pemberton was about three feet away from her. Startled, she took a step back.

"Evening, Mrs. Culpepper," Jack Pemberton said, halting suddenly. "How are you?" He watched her for a moment, then his gaze dropped to his shoes.

"Evening, Mr. Pemberton," Wanda Nell said, trying to keep her voice from squeaking. "I'm just fine. Can I get you a table?"

Pemberton looked up at her again, a shy smile coming and going on his face. "Yes, ma'am," he said, "as long as it's one of your tables."

"I think I can arrange that," Wanda Nell said, smiling briefly back at him. "Come on with me."

She led him into the back dining room and got him situated. At the moment, he was the only person seated back there, but before long the restaurant would start filling up. "Can I get you something to drink?

"Some water and ice tea, please," Pemberton responded.

"Be right back," Wanda Nell promised.

In the front room, she prepared the glasses of tea and water, then grabbed a menu. She glanced at the board over the cash register to see what specials Melvin had decided on for tonight. Nodding at one table, who indicated their glasses needed refilling, she hurried back to Jack Pemberton.

"Here you go," she said, setting down his two glasses and offering him a menu. She rattled off the specials, and Jack Pemberton regarded her solemnly.

"How's the chicken fried steak?" he asked.

"Best in the county," Wanda Nell promised.

"Then I'll have that, with the cream gravy, mashed potatoes, and green beans. And cornbread."

"Coming right up." Wanda Nell jotted his order on her pad, took back the menu, and started to walk away.

"Mrs. Culpepper," Pemberton said, his voice hesitant.

Wanda Nell turned back to look at him.

"Um, I'm glad you're doing okay," he said, then his eyes fell, as if something on the table was really fascinating.

"Thank you," Wanda Nell said. "I appreciate that." She cleared her throat. "I'll be back soon with your food."

She didn't wait for a response. She was trying to figure Jack Pemberton out. Was he interested in her? Or was he just showing concern for the mother of one of his students?

He was a bit on the shy side, Wanda Nell decided as she handed in his order to the kitchen. That sure made a pleasant change from the last couple of guys Wanda Nell had gone out with. Roaming hands and wandering eyes, the both of them. Kept on trying to feel her up, and at the same time looking over any other woman that walked by. Wanda Nell had had enough of that when she was married. And that was the end of them.

But Jack Pemberton was a different kettle of fish, Wanda Nell figured. She was willing to bet he wasn't that type, and she could sure enjoy going out with a man who acted like a gentleman.

Then she stopped herself. *You are getting way ahead of yourself, girl,* she scolded herself. *Acting like some man-hungry woman that ain't had a man in way too long.* Which was partly the truth, she decided ruefully. It *had* been way too long, but that particular itch could just wait a while longer to get scratched. She had no business thinking about dating anybody, with the mess she was in right now.

She'd better start paying attention to her tables, or she wasn't going to be getting any tips tonight. The restaurant was filling up with the usual Friday night crowd, and soon she was too busy to think much about Jack Pemberton.

She did check on him several times after bringing him his food, and once he asked for more tea. She paused for a moment at the table after filling up his glass, and he asked her how Juliet was doing.

"Fine, far's I can tell," Wanda Nell said. "Did the kids at school bother her today? You know, asking her about her daddy and everything?"

"Maybe a little," Pemberton said with a frown, "but Juliet seemed to be handling it pretty well. She's sharp, Mrs. Culpepper, and she knows when to ask for help."

"That's good," Wanda Nell said. "I don't want those kids pestering her."

"We won't let them," Pemberton promised.

"Thanks," Wanda Nell said. She left him glancing through the notebook he'd had with him two nights ago. Maybe he was writing a book, she decided, then forgot about it as she got busy again with her other tables.

The next time Wanda Nell caught sight of a clock, it was almost eight. Two more hours to go, and then it would be time to change clothes and head for her shift at Budget Mart. She went to the back dining room to make another check of her tables there, where Jack Pemberton still sat, staring off into space. There was a momentary lull as the crowd thinned out a bit, and Wanda Nell grabbed a tea pitcher and approached Pemberton's table.

"How about some more tea?"

Startled, Pemberton glanced up at her. "Sure. One more, and that's my limit."

"Yeah, you gotta be careful about hitting the hard stuff," Wanda Nell joked as she topped up the glass.

Pemberton laughed, a deep rumble which Wanda Nell found very attractive.

"Mrs. Culpepper," he said, as she started to turn away.

"Yes," Wanda Nell prompted when he didn't say anything.

"Um, I was wondering," he said, fidgeting with his notebook and not looking directly at her, "if there's anything I can do to help. I mean, if you need . . ." His voice trailed off. He stood up abruptly. "What I mean to say is, could I call you sometime? Maybe you'd like to go out for dinner or a movie sometime?"

His eyes held hope, but at the same time, the way he was standing, he was ready for rejection. Wanda Nell was touched by his sweetness and uncertainty.

"I'd like that," she said, and his face lit up.

"Great. Um, well, I guess I'd better be going." He grabbed his notebook from the table. "When is a good time to call?"

"Afternoons," Wanda Nell said. "And I'm in the phone book."

"Right," Pemberton replied, offering her his shy smile once more. "Guess I'd better be going, then. Good night."

"Good night," Wanda Nell said, then busied herself with his table so she wouldn't stand there like an idiot, watching him walk away.

She hummed a little as she cleared the table and pocketed the nice tip he had left her. Maybe the sun was peeking around that old black cloud a little bit after all.

# Twelve

After Jack Pemberton left the Kountry Kitchen, Wanda Nell began to get busy again, as the final wave of evening customers came in. She was in a much better mood than she had been, and she stayed out of Fayetta's way as much as possible. She wanted to avoid any more ugliness if she could manage it, and Ruby Garner, bless her heart, helped keep her and Fayetta from having to speak directly to each other.

A little after nine Wanda Nell came back from the kitchen to find a young woman sitting alone at one of her tables. Wanda Nell thought she looked awfully familiar, but she couldn't place her at first. It was only when she handed the young woman a menu and looked directly into her face that she realized she knew her.

"Evening, Deputy Taylor," Wanda Nell said. "I didn't recognize you for a minute there, you not being in your uniform."

Deputy Taylor grimaced. "Yeah, I know. It always takes people a minute when they're not used to seeing me dressed like normal people." She laughed.

Wanda Nell smiled. "What can I get you to drink?"

"Got any decaf coffee?"

"Sure," Wanda Nell said. "Be right back with it."

"And lots of cream," Deputy Taylor called after her.

When Wanda Nell came back to the table with the coffee and a small pitcher of cream, Deputy Taylor put down her menu and stared up at Wanda Nell. In a normal tone of voice, she said, "I'll have a cheeseburger, well done, everything on it, with French fries." Then, while Wanda Nell was jotting down the order, she continued in a much lower tone, "Can I talk to you, Miz Culpepper? I mean, in private?"

*What on earth does she want?* Wanda Nell wondered. "That'll be right out," she said. Matching the deputy's lowered voice, she went on, "There's a door around back, where I used to go to smoke. I'll meet you there after you've eaten."

Deputy Taylor nodded very slightly, and Wanda Nell went to the kitchen to turn in the order. As she worked, Wanda Nell kept on puzzling over what the deputy wanted to talk to her about in private like that. It felt like something out of a spy novel, Wanda Nell decided. The question was, whose side was the deputy on? Was she playing some game Elmer Lee had put her on to, like maybe trying to catch his chief suspect in some lie? Or was she simply trying to help Wanda Nell because she despised Elmer Lee as much as Wanda Nell did?

Wanda Nell puzzled over it a while longer, then decided she wasn't doing any good, letting herself being distracted from her work. She kept an eye on the deputy, and when the young woman had finished her food and picked up her check, she walked by.

"I'll meet you around back in about five minutes," Wanda Nell said quietly.

Deputy Taylor nodded once, then said, "I enjoyed that. Y'all make great cheeseburgers here." She headed off for the cash register.

Wanda Nell made a quick circuit of her tables, and it looked like they could all manage for a few minutes without her. She caught Ruby in the back dining room and said, "Can you cover for me for a few minutes? I won't be long."

"Sure, Wanda Nell," Ruby said. "Things are slowing down anyway. Take your time."

Wanda Nell flashed her a smile of thanks. She ignored Fayetta, standing at the counter and jawing away with some greasy old guy she flirted with every Friday night, and went through the kitchen and down the hall. If she was lucky, Melvin would stay out by the cash register long enough for her to have her little talk with the deputy.

When she got to the back door, she peered outside. The light was dim back here, and at first she thought the deputy hadn't found the door. But suddenly the young woman appeared out of the darkness, and Wanda Nell stepped back, startled.

"Sorry," the deputy said. "I was just trying to keep out of the light till I saw you."

"That's okay," Wanda Nell said, leaning tiredly against the door frame. As she watched, her little stray feline friend appeared from around the Dumpster and came meowing his way toward her.

"Sorry, buddy," Wanda Nell said, reaching down to rub his head. "I don't have anything for you right this minute, but I'll get you something soon." The cat kept purring as he stretched out on the pavement near her. Wanda Nell shook her head at him. Sooner or later she was going to end up taking him home, she just knew it.

Deputy Taylor had been watching all this a bit impatiently. "Miz Culpepper, I want to talk to you, and I need to talk fast." She hesitated. "I really shouldn't be doing this, but, well, I guess I'm doing it anyway."

"Exactly what is it you're doing?" Wanda Nell asked, folding her arms across her chest.

"Talking to you like this, informally. I could get in trouble if Deputy Johnson found out about this."

"I don't expect I'm going to tell him, if that's what you're worried about," Wanda Nell replied. Why wouldn't the girl get to the point?

Some of her irritation must have communicated itself to the deputy. Taylor shrugged, then said, "So be it, I guess. Look, I don't think you killed your husband, but Deputy Johnson is convinced you did. He's doing everything he can to find the evidence to arrest you with, and if someone don't come up with something else, another suspect, then he's going to try to pin this on you."

Wanda Nell wasn't surprised. She knew what Elmer Lee was capable of, and she hadn't expected anything less. "I know. But I do have an alibi for that night, and surely even Elmer Lee is going to have to see that, at some point."

"You do have an alibi, up to a point, Miz Culpepper," Deputy Taylor responded. "You're covered most of the night. "We checked with the folks at Budget Mart, and they can account for you from the time you signed in till the time you left the next morning."

"Isn't that enough?"

Deputy Taylor shrugged. "It's enough for me, certainly. But there's just enough gap in the time from when you said you last saw your husband alive until you arrived at Budget Mart. That's the time the Deputy Johnson is concentrating on. He thinks that's when you killed your husband."

Wanda Nell sagged against the door frame. "There's got to be something to show I didn't kill him." She thought for a moment. "Do y'all know yet when he died? Surely it had to be some time after I saw him, when I would've been at work already."

Deputy Taylor shrugged. "We're not gonna have results back from the state crime lab for at least a week, if not longer. And the doctor we got out there to look at the body seemed to think he had been dead anywhere from five to twelve hours."

Wanda Nell thought about that for a moment, figuring out the times. "Damn it. No wonder Elmer Lee thinks I did it."

"Yeah, you see the problem. Until we get those results from the state lab, you're pretty much going to remain the chief suspect."

"Then why are you so convinced I didn't do it?" Wanda Nell demanded harshly. "Why aren't you helping Elmer Lee haul me off to jail?"

A smile passed briefly across the deputy's face, then disappeared. "Coupla reasons, I guess. For one thing, I just don't think you *could* do it. Physically, I mean." She frowned. "You'd either've had to knock him on the head and drag his body out into the woods—which we know you didn't do, because there aren't any traces of that. Or you'd've had to lure him out in the woods, knock him on the head with something, and then thrust that flamingo through his neck."

Hearing the deputy speak so plainly about something so awful made Wanda Nell's stomach turn. She stared at the younger woman.

"Sorry," Deputy Taylor muttered. "Anyway, physically, that murder took a fair amount of strength. I'll bet you're pretty strong, but I just don't think you're strong enough. And I can't see your ex-husband letting you lure him out into the woods. That part just don't make much sense to me."

"You got that right," Wanda Nell said. "Bobby Ray knew me well enough, he wouldn't have fallen for some kind of come-on from me to get him out in those woods. Elmer Lee oughta know better."

"Yeah, he oughta," the deputy agreed. "Trouble is, he's got a one-track mind, and he don't like anybody trying to derail it. He's got you lined up for this murder, and he's probably gonna arrest you tomorrow, if nothing else turns up."

"Why hasn't he arrested me already?"

"The sheriff," Deputy Taylor said. "Something to do, from what I've overheard, with your daddy and the sheriff being friends some time ago."

"Yeah," Wanda Nell said faintly. "They used to be real good buddies, once. I'm glad the sheriff still remembers that."

"You're sure lucky he does," the deputy said, "or you'd probably be in jail right this minute. But he don't believe you did it, and neither do I." She paused for a moment. "Trouble is, who else is there? We need somebody else to be looking for."

"What about those men that broke into my home and terrified my girls?" Wanda Nell demanded. "Why aren't y'all looking for them?"

"We are, Miz Culpepper, but so far we haven't found a trace of them anywhere."

"Then y'all aren't looking hard enough. Y'all need to be looking into what Bobby Ray was doing before he came back to Tullahoma. It's got to have something to do with that." In her mind, she saw again that big wad of cash Bobby Ray had been flashing around. And she remembered her conversation with Ricky Ratliff about Bobby Ray and his money.

"What is it?" the deputy asked, who was watching her closely. "You've thought of something."

Wanda Nell regarded her for a moment. Could she really trust her? She didn't have much choice, she decided.

"Another one of my ex's old buddies," Wanda Nell said, "Ricky Ratliff. He's the night supervisor at Budget Mart. You need to talk to him. He knows something about what Bobby Ray'd been up to, and I bet you anything he knows something about those men y'all can't seem to find."

Deputy Taylor exhaled a loud breath. "Then that's something to go on. We'll be talking to this Ratliff, I can promise you that." Abruptly she faded into the darkness.

"Who you talking to, Wanda Nell?"

Melvin Arbuckle had come up behind her, and she'd never even heard him. She just hoped he hadn't heard any of her conversation with the deputy.

Wanda Nell pointed down at the cat, still purring at her feet. "Just this little guy. I been promising him I'd go back in the kitchen and fetch him something good to eat." She smiled at Melvin. "I guess I'm just gonna have to give in and take him home with me."

"Lucky cat if you do," Melvin said. He moved past her and flicked open his lighter. The flame sparked, and he exhaled a cloud of smoke.

"Maybe," Wanda Nell said. "I'll be right back."

In the kitchen she found some scraps of chicken for the cat and dumped them into a napkin. When she returned to the back door, she found Melvin squatting beside the cat, scratching him between the ears.

"And here I thought you didn't like cats," Wanda Nell said, dropping the bits of chicken onto the pavement.

The cat leapt up and greedily began to eat. Melvin stood up and took a couple of steps away. "There's a lot about me you don't know," he said. "But if you ever wanna know, I'll be happy to let you in on it all."

"I'll keep that in mind," Wanda Nell said in a neutral tone. She watched the cat for a moment. "Okay, boy, that's it for now. You hang around another day or two, and I might adopt you."

The cat sat licking its whiskers for a moment, then he trotted off behind the Dumpster and disappeared.

"I'd better be getting back to work," Wanda Nell said as she turned to go. "It's just about time to start closing up."

"Wanda Nell," Melvin said.

She stopped and turned back to look at him.

"Remember what I said." Melvin stared hard at her. "If you need help with something, you let me know."

"I will. Thank you." She smiled briefly before turning away again.

Back in the dining room Wanda Nell helped Ruby and Fayetta clear tables as the last customers departed. Then they all spent a few minutes doing some of the necessary side work so that the morning crew would be ready to open at six the next morning.

At last they were done. All the tables were clean, everything set up for the next day, and Wanda Nell quickly changed into her clothes for her shift at Budget Mart.

When she drove into the parking lot at Budget Mart, she parked underneath one of the big lights near the door. Keeping a careful eye out for anyone who might try to come up on her, especially old women in big Cadillacs, she scurried for the door.

She concentrated on her work, refusing to let herself get sidetracked by worries about what Elmer Lee was planning to do. If he arrested her, she'd figure out something. But no use borrowing trouble before she had to. Maybe she was being foolish, but that was just the way it was going to be. She still had a hard time believing Elmer Lee would actually arrest her.

When the time came for her to clock out, she was ready to head home and fall into bed. She hadn't seen hide nor hair of Ricky all night, and that was fine by her. Now that she'd put the deputy on to him, she was going to stay out of his way. Let Deputy Taylor see what she could get out of him. Wanda Nell had to smile at the thought of Ricky trying to pull some of his good ol' boy sexist crap with the young deputy.

KeShawn saw her safely to her car, and she patted him gratefully on the arm. Thank the Lord old Mrs. Culpepper hadn't shown up again, though Wanda Nell wouldn't have been the least bit surprised if she had been out there waiting in the parking lot.

The road was quiet as Wanda Nell drove homeward. Not too many people out yet in Tullahoma this early on a Saturday morning. As she turned off the highway onto the road leading to the trailer park, she squinted into the sun. She thought she recognized a truck headed in her direction.

Wanda Nell stopped her car, rolled down the window, and waved frantically to stop the approaching truck. She waited, and the truck rolled to a stop beside her. The driver rolled down his window, stuck his head out, and said, "Hey there, Wanda Nell. What's going on? You having car trouble?"

Wanda Nell smiled up at her friendly neighbor. "No, Jim Ed. The car's fine. I just need to talk to you, if you got a minute."

"Sure," Jim Ed Woods said. "I got a minute. What's on your mind?"

"I guess you heard about what happened?"

Jim Ed frowned. "You mean about that dead body they

found in the woods out by the trailer park? Yeah, I just heard about it last night. I was on a run down to New Orleans and back yesterday, and my wife told me about it when I got back."

"So the sheriff's department didn't talk to you yesterday?"

"Nope," Jim Ed replied. "Not yet."

Wanda Nell crossed her fingers. Maybe Jim Ed was the one neighbor who might have seen something the night Bobby Ray was killed.

"Were you at home Wednesday night?" Wanda Nell asked.

"Yeah, I got back from a run about two A.M. or thereabouts," Jim Ed answered after thinking about it a moment.

"When you got back home, did you see anything strange? I mean, like a car or truck you didn't recognize, anything like that?"

Jim Ed frowned, deep lines creasing his forehead. "Yeah, come to think of it, I did see something."

Wanda Nell hardly dared breathe, waiting for him to continue. Maybe he'd seen the guys who'd broken into her trailer.

"Just as I was coming down the road into the trailer park," Jim Ed said, "I passed another truck. I think there was a coupla guys in it, maybe three." He shrugged, his fingers beating a tattoo against the steering wheel. "I don't recall seeing that particular truck at the trailer park before."

"Would you recognize it if you saw it again?"

Jim Ed nodded. "Yeah, I sure would. I mean, I seen it around town often enough."

"What'd it look like?"

"It's all black," Jim Ed replied, "'cept for a streak of yellow lightning down the side. Only one like that in Tullahoma that I seen."

Stunned, Wanda Nell stared back at Jim Ed. She knew that truck, too. Ricky Ratliff sure as hell had some explaining to do. He'd just better hope the sheriff's department got to him before she did.

# Thirteen

When Wanda Nell walked into the trailer, she found Mayrene sound asleep on the couch, snoring, her shotgun on the coffee table within easy reach. Smiling, Wanda Nell shook her head at the picture. When Mayrene had first told her she was going to bring the shotgun with her, Wanda Nell had been a little worried. But when she saw there was nobody from the sheriff's department posted at the trailer park this morning to keep watch, Wanda Nell was all the more grateful for her friend's presence. Elmer Lee had obviously discontinued the watch because he believed it wasn't necessary. And that told Wanda Nell that Deputy Taylor was right. Elmer Lee was planning to arrest her.

Thanks to her neighbor Jim Ed Woods, though, she now had something solid to wave in front of Elmer Lee. He couldn't ignore a witness like Jim Ed.

Wanda Nell stepped carefully closer to Mayrene, still snoring away on the couch. She was about to poke Mayrene gently on the shoulder when Mayrene's eyes popped open.

"Good morning, Wanda Nell."

Startled, Wanda Nell jumped back a little. "Good Lord, Mayrene, you about gave me a heart attack. I thought for sure you were so sound asleep I'd have to shake you to get you awake."

Laughing, Mayrene sat up on the couch. She patted her hair into place. "I do sleep pretty sound sometimes," she admitted. "But I can feel it when there's somebody near me. That's what woke me up."

"Well, I'm glad you spent the night," Wanda Nell said, sinking down on the couch beside her friend. "There was somebody from the sheriff's department out there when I left for work last night, but there ain't a sign of 'em this morning."

"Yeah, I heard him drive off about midnight," Mayrene said. She reached out to pat her shotgun. "But me and Ol' Reliable here's on the job. Anybody'd tried to come through that door had no business here, they'd've ended up with a big hole through 'em."

Wanda Nell did her best not to imagine that. "I got some news," she said, and she proceeded to fill Mayrene in on her conversation with Deputy Taylor.

Mayrene shook her head when Wanda Nell had finished. "Looks like ol' Elmer Lee'd better be watching his back. That girl is sure ambitious, and if he don't watch out, he's gonna have her bootprints all over him." She laughed. "More power to her, that's what I say. That girl has balls, and then some."

"Maybe," Wanda Nell said, "and I sure don't care much what happens to Elmer Lee, but there's something about her I can't quite figure out."

"Well, honey," Mayrene said, standing up and stretching, "she ain't aiming to be your best friend, but I guess you know that. You're her ticket to pulling one over on that jackass commonly known as Elmer Lee Johnson." She laughed again. "You may not wanna trust her far's you can throw her, but usin's a two-way street. You can both get what you want, you play your cards just right."

"Maybe so," Wanda Nell said. "But I found out something else." She motioned for Mayrene to sit down again.

"Okay," Mayrene said as she complied, "but make it snappy. I got a little errand ain't gonna wait much longer."

Wanda Nell grinned. Mayrene's "errand" was the way she always said she had to go to the bathroom. "I saw Jim Ed Woods on the way in this morning," she said. "And he told me he saw a pickup here the night those men broke in. A pickup that didn't belong here."

"And?" Mayrene said when Wanda Nell paused.

"He described it," Wanda Nell went on, "and I knew whose it was right away. There's only one in town I know of."

"Well, whose is it?" Mayrene said, getting twitchy.

"Ricky Ratliff's."

"Why, that little sonofabitch," Mayrene said, her eyes widening. She hopped up from the couch. "Be right back."

While she waited for Mayrene to return, Wanda Nell fished around in her purse for the card Deputy Taylor had given her. When she found it, she sat staring at it until Mayrene came back.

"What's that?" Mayrene asked.

Wanda Nell handed it to her.

"You gonna call her instead of Elmer Lee?" Mayrene asked.

Wanda Nell shrugged. "That's what I'm trying to decide. Jim Ed said he was going to the Kountry Kitchen for breakfast, and I told him I was gonna let somebody from the sheriff's department know about what he saw. I guess I could call her, and she could go over there and talk to him."

"Yeah," Mayrene said, "and you could always say you called her first 'cause you couldn't get Elmer Lee on the phone."

"Yeah, like Elmer Lee'd believe that." Wanda Nell snorted in derision.

"Honey, it don't matter at this point what Elmer Lee thinks about it. He's gonna have to believe Jim Ed and follow up on that lead. And soon's they talk to that human snotball Ricky, they're gonna convince him to come clean."

"And then Elmer Lee'll have to start thinking somebody else killed Bobby Ray," Wanda Nell said. "But I tell you, I could just about kill Ricky myself. He knew damn well when I was talking to him those men used his truck, and he knew they probably killed Bobby Ray. Why didn't he go to Elmer Lee himself?"

"'Cause he's probably mixed up in it, too," Mayrene pointed out, very reasonably. "Honey, you know that little jerkwad'd do anything Bobby Ray wanted him to. And I bet you anything Bobby Ray got him so mixed up in whatever the hell it was, Ricky's deep in the doodoo now. Just depends on who he's scaredest of. The sheriff's department or those men."

"Looks like it was those men," Wanda Nell said. "But I'm about to fix it so he hadn't got much choice." She got up and went to the phone in the kitchen.

Wanda Nell punched in the number on Deputy Taylor's business card and waited. The phone rang four times before someone answered. "Taylor, here."

"Morning, Deputy," Wanda Nell said, then identified herself. "I got some information you oughta hear."

There was a pause, and Wanda Nell thought maybe she'd somehow been disconnected. Then, when she was about to hang up and dial again, Taylor's voice came through, low but clear.

"Look, I can't talk much right now," the deputy said. "We're in the middle of something here. What is it?"

"I found you a witness," Wanda Nell said quickly. "I got somebody who saw a strange pickup here the night those men broke into my trailer. And that pickup belongs to Ricky Ratliff. You need to talk to him soon's you can."

Again there was silence. "Okay," Taylor said, "I'll take care of that when I can. You just hold tight, all right?"

"Sure," Wanda Nell said, puzzled. She had expected more of a reaction, but maybe Elmer Lee was close by, and Taylor didn't want to give anything away. "I'll be here at home the rest of the day."

"Got you," Taylor said, and the line went dead.

Wanda Nell came back into the living room. She told Mayrene about the strange conversation, and Mayrene agreed that Elmer Lee had probably been right there. "That girl's sharp," Mayrene commented. "She's not going to give anything away." She stood up and collected her shotgun. "Time for you to get some sleep, honey. You need me for anything, you just holler."

Wanda Nell gave her a big hug, being careful not to bump the shotgun, then followed her to the door and locked it behind her. She leaned against the door and closed her eyes for a moment. She was so tired she felt like she could sleep for a week. The girls probably wouldn't stir for another hour at least, although Lavon would be ready to get up soon. For once, Wanda Nell decided, Miranda would just have to cope with him. She was going to bed.

In her bedroom she wearily stripped off her clothes, laid

them across a chair, then put on a nightgown. After setting her alarm, she climbed into bed and made herself comfortable under the covers. Sleep came quickly.

When the alarm went off at three that afternoon, Wanda Nell surfaced slowly from a sad dream about Bobby Ray. He had been trying to tell her something, but she couldn't hear him. A loud noise blocked out his voice. As she became more alert, she realized the loud sound was her alarm going off.

She sat up in the bed and turned the buzzer off. Yawning, she stretched, then rolled her head around on her shoulders to ease some of the stiffness there. She found her house shoes and robe and, still yawning, made her way into the kitchen.

Juliet met her with a glass of cold Coke in her hands. "Here, Mama," she said. "I heard your alarm go off."

"Thanks, baby," Wanda Nell said before she sipped at the drink. The caffeine would get her going.

Wanda Nell sat down at the kitchen table and blinked at the sunshine streaming in the window. Juliet sat down across from her.

"Did you sleep well?"

Wanda Nell nodded. "Yeah, thank the Lord. I was so worn out, I sure needed it." She yawned again and quickly covered her mouth. "Guess it'll take me a little while to wake up."

Juliet laughed. "Take your time. You don't have to be at work till six tonight, right?"

"Yeah, just a short shift tonight, and that's it. I can actually come home and go to bed like a real human being."

"I wish you didn't have to work so much, Mama." Juliet's face puckered in a frown.

Wanda Nell stretched a hand across the table to her daughter. "Now, honey, don't you worry about that. I don't really mind, most of the time."

"I'm going to get a job this summer," Juliet announced, "and I'll be able to help out some."

"We'll see," Wanda Nell said. She wanted Juliet to wait until she was sixteen before she got some kind of job, but Juliet was as stubborn as her mother. Wanda Nell really didn't want to argue with her about it now.

As she came more awake, Wanda Nell remembered her odd phone conversation with Deputy Taylor. She wondered why she hadn't heard from the younger woman yet.

"Baby, did anybody call while I was asleep?" When Juliet was home, she would try to answer the phone quickly to keep it from disturbing her mother.

Miranda, with Lavon on her hip, ambled into the kitchen in time to hear her mother's question. "Yeah, you sure did get a phone call, Mama. Why didn't you tell us you had a new boyfriend?" The stormy look in Miranda's eyes warned Wanda Nell to expect fireworks.

Wanda Nell blushed. "I don't have a boyfriend," she said, "and I don't like your tone, Miranda."

"Don't pay any attention to Miranda, Mama," Juliet said indignantly. "She's just being mean." Then she giggled. "But Mr. Pemberton did call to talk to you, Mama."

Wanda Nell felt oddly breathless for a moment. Then she forced herself to speak. "Oh, he did, did he?"

"Yes, Mama, he did," Juliet answered.

"And what did he have to say?"

"Oh, he said he'd call back," Juliet responded airily. "I told him to try back around four. That you'd be up and able to talk coherently by then."

"Juliet!" Wanda Nell protested. "Surely you didn't say something like that to him."

Juliet giggled. "Well, not exactly, Mama," she said.

Miranda had poured some juice in a sippy cup for Lavon, and now she sat down at the table with the baby in her lap.

Lavon pounded the cup up and down on the table and smiled happily at his grandmother.

Wanda Nell reached out and tousled his brown curls. "Your aunt thinks she's awful smart, doesn't she, sweetie? Yes, she does, but she's being real silly, and I'm gonna smack her bottom if she keeps it up." Juliet made a funny face at her mother. Miranda just sat there, glowering at both of them.

Wanda Nell got up to pour herself some more Coke from the bottle in the fridge. With her back to the girls, she said, "Then I guess Mr. Pemberton might be calling back. Do y'all mind?" She closed the door of the fridge and waited a moment before turning around.

"I can't believe you, Mama," Miranda said. "How can you act like this, and Daddy dead. It's not right." She burst into tears, and Lavon, startled by his mother's outburst, started crying, too.

Wanda Nell, stricken, stared at Miranda for a moment. She should have given this more thought. Juliet hardly knew her father, but Miranda had idolized him. She and Bobby Ray had been divorced for a long time, but evidently that didn't matter much to Miranda right now.

Wanda Nell sat down at the table again and reached out her hands to Miranda. "I'm sorry, Miranda. I know how much you loved your daddy. I loved him, too, honey, but it's been a long time since him and me was married. We both moved on."

Miranda regarded her mother balefully. "I don't care, Mama. It just don't seem right. Daddy not even buried yet, and you going out with somebody you barely know."

"Oh, Miranda, stop being so mean to Mama," Juliet said. "How can you be so selfish?"

Miranda stood up from the table, Lavon still crying in her arms. "That's right, Mama loves you best anyway. Take her side, I don't care. Neither one of you cares a bit about me and my baby. Daddy loved me, even if you didn't." She started to walk away.

"Miranda! Don't you walk away from me." When Wanda Nell used that tone, Miranda knew better than to disobey. "Turn around and look at me."

Miranda turned, and the misery in her eyes made Wanda Nell feel even more guilty than she already did. "Honey," she said softly, going around the table to hold out her arms. Miranda stood there, unmoving.

"Honey, don't be like this," Wanda Nell pleaded. "You know I love you, that's just ridiculous. Your daddy loved you, too, but you're making too much out of this."

Miranda began sobbing again, and Wanda Nell stepped closer and wrapped her arms around her daughter and grandson. They all cried for a moment, then Miranda pulled back.

"I'm sorry, Mama," she said. "But it just seems like nobody cares that Daddy is dead."

"I'm sorry, too, honey," Wanda Nell said. "I'm sorry your daddy's dead, believe me." She grinned suddenly. "I can't fuss at him and call him names now like I used to."

Miranda laughed. "He sure could get you riled up."

"Yeah, he could," Wanda Nell said. "That was because I loved him, too, Miranda. Never forget that. I finally got to the point where I just couldn't live with him anymore, so I did what I thought I had to do. Your daddy was the most aggravating man on the face of the earth sometimes, but even then, you couldn't help loving him."

"I know, Mama," Miranda said softly. "I know."

"I promise you, if it really upsets you, I won't go out with anybody for a while."

Miranda shook her head. "No, Mama, it's okay. Don't mind me."

"Well, we'll see," Wanda Nell said. She turned to her younger daughter, who had been sitting very still, watching the scene between her mother and sister. "Juliet, honey, would it make you feel funny if I ever went out with one of your teachers?"

Juliet shook her head. "No, Mama, I wouldn't mind at all. He seems like an awfully nice man. Everybody at school likes him. You deserve to go out and have a good time."

Wanda Nell blinked back tears. "Thank you, honey," she said, her voice husky. She cleared her throat. "Then maybe one of these days, if he does ask me out, I'll say 'yes.'"

Miranda came back to the table and sat down. Lavon had stopped crying, and Wanda Nell rubbed his head. He smiled up at her.

"Tell me something," Wanda Nell said, trying to keep her tone casual, "I noticed that Mr. Pemberton carries this notebook with him. He was scribbling away in it both times he came to the Kountry Kitchen." She watched Juliet covertly as she took another sip of her Coke.

Juliet smiled. "He's a writer, Mama, and it's really exciting," she said eagerly. "He told us all about it a few weeks ago. He's actually sold a book. Can you believe that?"

Wanda Nell was impressed. "That is something! I don't think I've ever known a real writer before. What does he write?"

"He writes true-crime books," Juliet answered, almost bouncing up and down in her chair, she was so excited. "You know, like that Ann Rule writes, Mama? You've read some of her books, haven't you?"

Her hand shaking, Wanda Nell set down her glass. "Uh, yeah, I've read some of her books." Suddenly, the Coke felt like acid in her stomach.

*A true-crime writer,* she thought dully. *So that's why he's interested in me. He wants to write a book about Bobby Ray's murder.*

Dimly, she could hear her daughters' voices. "Mama, are you okay?"

"I'm fine," Wanda Nell said mechanically. She started to take another sip of her drink, then set the glass down on the table with a thump. She stood up. "I'm going to go take a shower."

If the girls said anything in answer to this announcement, she didn't hear it. She was still trying to cope with what Juliet had told her.

Before she had gone more than a few steps, Wanda Nell heard someone knocking at the door. She stumbled toward it, still not totally focusing on anything other than her inward confusion, and opened the door.

Elmer Lee Johnson stood there, his hand raised to knock again. Deputy Taylor was right behind him.

Elmer Lee didn't wait for an invitation, just pushed his way into the trailer.

"What do you want?" Wanda Nell demanded, snapping out of her fog. "Why are you here?"

Elmer Lee regarded her grimly as Deputy Taylor carefully shut the door. Wanda Nell looked past Elmer Lee and appealed to the woman. "What's going on? Did y'all talk to Ricky Ratliff?"

Deputy Taylor's eyes widened, and she shook her head slightly at Wanda Nell.

"Why are you asking about Ricky Ratliff, Wanda Nell?" Elmer Lee demanded gruffly. "What do you know about him? Have you talked to him lately?"

Wanda Nell stared back at him uncertainly. "Not since the other night at work." She clutched her housecoat nervously. "Didn't your deputy tell you I called?"

"Yeah," Elmer Lee said. "We'll get to that in a minute. First you tell me when you last saw Ricky Ratliff."

"I told you," Wanda Nell said, getting angry. "Night be-fore last, at Budget Mart. Now you tell me what the hell is going on here?"

Elmer Lee watched her carefully for a moment before he spoke. "Ricky Ratliff is dead, Wanda Lee. What do you know about that?"

# Fourteen

Wanda Nell couldn't speak. Her mouth wouldn't work, though she tried to say something. She felt an arm slip around her waist, and she turned to see Juliet beside her. Eyes wide with horror, Miranda stood a step or two beyond Juliet, Lavon clutched to her chest.

"My mother doesn't know anything about that man's death," Juliet said bravely. "It was probably the same men that killed my daddy."

"I didn't say he was killed, little lady," Elmer Lee remarked mildly, "just that he was dead."

Wanda Nell found her tongue. "And I reckon you just expect us to think he had a heart attack or something? Come on, Elmer Lee, why else'd you be here, if somebody didn't kill him?"

"Somebody did kill him, Wanda Nell," Elmer Lee said,

his face set in grim lines. "And I'm gonna ask you again, when was the last time you seen him, or talked to him?"

"Mama," Juliet whispered urgently in Wanda Nell's ear.

"Not now, baby," Wanda Nell said.

"But, Mama," Juliet persisted, tugging on her mother's arm.

"What is it?" Wanda Nell bent her head slightly as Juliet beckoned with her finger.

"Maybe you better call a lawyer," Juliet whispered. "Before you say anything else."

Wanda Nell patted her daughter's arm. "No, it's okay, sweetie," she whispered back. Turning to Elmer Lee, she said, "I already told you, Elmer Lee. Last time I saw him was night before last, at Budget Mart."

"You didn't see him or talk to him after that?" Elmer Lee's tone was skeptical.

"No, I did not," Wanda Nell said evenly. She had to keep her temper. Elmer Lee wanted her riled up, and she was determined not to let him do it.

"When you saw him night before last," Elmer Lee said, "what'd you talk about?"

Wanda Nell thought for a moment, trying to recall the conversation. "Mainly I was trying to find out what he knew about Bobby Ray. What Bobby Ray'd been up to, where the money he was flashing around came from." She shrugged. "He liked to carry on like he was still real tight with Bobby Ray, and I figured he might know something."

"Did he tell you anything?"

"Not really," Wanda Nell said. "Basically he just told me to mind my own business, and keep outta his way. I tried to get him to admit he knew something about those guys that broke in here, but he wouldn't." She shook her head. "Guess I was right after all, if they was using his truck to come here in."

Elmer Lee didn't comment on that. Instead he ordered, "Tell me what you did from yesterday afternoon till this morning."

"Same as I always do on a Friday," Wanda Nell answered, as patiently as if she were talking to a backward child. "I got ready for my shift at the Kountry Kitchen, and I got there on time, at six o'clock. I left a little after ten and drove to Budget Mart. I worked my shift, like I always do, then I came home this morning when I got off work."

"And someone at Budget Mart can say you was there the whole time, I guess," Elmer Lee said. "You didn't see Ricky Ratliff there last night?"

"No, I didn't," Wanda Nell replied.

"And he didn't come by the Kountry Kitchen, either?"

"No, he hardly ever did. I didn't see him anywhere last night."

Elmer Lee studied her for a moment. Wanda Nell wished she wasn't wearing her housecoat. The way Elmer Lee was looking at her, she felt real funny.

"You didn't see or hear anything odd at the Kountry Kitchen last night?"

Wanda Nell's gaze flicked uncertainly to Deputy Taylor, who still stood behind Elmer Lee. Taylor shook her head slightly, and Wanda Nell understood she wasn't to say anything to Elmer Lee about Taylor's visit to the restaurant.

"No, I didn't," Wanda Nell said. She tried to act like she'd been thinking about it, to cover up the awkward pause. "It was just a regular Friday night."

Elmer Lee motioned toward the chairs and couch. "Let's sit down," he said, his voice softer.

Wanda Nell stood right where she was for a moment, wondering at the sudden change in him. Then she walked over to a chair, her legs stiff and uncertain, and sat down.

Juliet came and stood behind her, placing a hand on her mother's shoulder. Miranda stayed where she was, whispering softly to the baby to keep him quiet. Elmer Lee sat down on the couch, facing her. Deputy Taylor remained standing, her arms crossed behind her back. Wanda Nell glanced at her, but the deputy's expression told her nothing.

"Wanda Nell," Elmer Lee said, and Wanda Nell's attention focused on him. "Ricky Ratliff's body was found this morning. Somebody'd dumped it in the Dumpster behind the Kountry Kitchen."

"Oh, my Lord," Wanda Nell said. Her stomach lurched. "Who . . . who found him? Was it Melvin? Melvin Arbuckle?"

Elmer Lee nodded. "Yep. Seems Melvin was out back, about five-thirty this morning, having a smoke. He flicked the butt into the Dumpster and lit himself another one. While he was smoking the second one, he smelled smoke. Something in the Dumpster caught fire."

Wanda Nell smiled faintly. "I warned him about that, time after time. I told him he was gonna set something on fire."

"Yeah, well, he sure did," Elmer Lee said grimly. "He ran and got a bucket of water to put out the fire, and when he reached in to dump the water, he got a real big shock."

Swallowing hard, Wanda Nell asked, "Ricky?"

"Yeah, Ricky Ratliff," Elmer Lee replied. "Fortunately, the body was on the other side of the Dumpster from what Melvin set on fire, but it still didn't help nothing, all that water in the Dumpster." His nostrils flared in disgust, and Wanda Nell kept her eyes wide open. She didn't want to see the image of Ricky's dead body that was trying to press itself into her mind.

Realization hit her, and Wanda Nell glanced at Deputy Taylor. Her eyes asked a question, and the deputy answered with a quick nod. When Wanda Nell had called her to pass along the information about Ricky's truck, Deputy Taylor knew right where Ricky was.

Wanda Nell moved her eyes back to Elmer Lee. He was regarding her suspiciously, and suddenly his head whirled, and he was looking at Taylor. After a moment, he turned back to Wanda Nell. "What's going on between you two?"

Not knowing what to say, Wanda Nell kept quiet, keeping her eyes down. She heard Deputy Taylor step forward.

"I can explain, sir," she said. Wanda Nell looked up.

"Then you damn sure better do it," Elmer Lee snapped.

"Yes, sir." Deputy Taylor gazed straight ahead. "This morning, Miz Culpepper called me on my cell phone. She wanted to report that she had spoken with a witness who saw a strange pickup truck at the trailer park the night of the alleged break-in here. According to Miz Culpepper, that pickup belonged to the victim, Ricky Ratliff."

Elmer Lee stood up, his hands clenching and unclenching at his sides. "And do you wanna explain to me why you're just now telling me this?"

Deputy Taylor didn't flinch. "At the time Miz Culpepper called me, sir, you were busy talking to the sheriff and the coroner. Upon thinking about it, I decided it was better to wait and let Miz Culpepper tell you about it herself."

"That's what you thought, was it?" Elmer Lee's voice could have cut through steel. "Next time somebody calls you with information regarding a case, Deputy, you damn sure better let me know ASAP. You don't think about it, you just do it, if you expect to remain employed by the Tullahoma County Sheriff's Department. You got that?"

"Yes, sir," Deputy Taylor said. Her chest heaved once, like she was trying to hold something back. Wanda Nell hoped she wasn't going to break down and cry.

Elmer Lee turned his back on his junior officer, and Wanda Nell watched him warily. "Supposin' you tell me about this witness of yours, Wanda Nell." His tone had mellowed again. Wanda Nell didn't know what to think about Elmer Lee sounding almost friendly.

"His name is Jim Ed Woods," Wanda Nell answered slowly. "He's a truck driver, and he and his wife live in the next-to-last trailer on this side of the trailer park."

"We'll check it out," Elmer Lee said, nodding. "But you tell me what he said to you."

"Jim Ed said he saw a strange pickup here the night those men broke into my trailer," Wanda Nell replied. "He reckons it was about two in the morning. He was just coming back from a run. He'd never seen the pickup at the trailer park before, but he'd seen it around town. Only one like it, as far as he knew."

"He describe this truck to you?"

Wanda Nell nodded. "Yeah, black with a streak of lightning down the side. And when he said that, I recognized the truck myself. Only one like it I ever seen around here was Ricky Ratliff's truck."

Elmer Lee sucked in his breath. "Yeah, that's Ricky's truck all right. And now Ricky's dead, too, just like Bobby Ray." He slammed his right fist into his left hand. "Goddammit, what's goin' on here?"

"I don't know," Wanda Nell whispered. "But now you gotta believe me, Elmer Lee. I didn't kill Bobby Ray, and I sure didn't kill Ricky. You gotta try to find those men that broke in here. Ricky must've known 'em, else they wouldn't have been using his truck that night."

Elmer Lee's eyes bored a hole right through her. Wanda Nell shifted uneasily in her chair. She wished she could tell what he was thinking right then.

Abruptly, Elmer Lee stood up. "Come on, Taylor," he said. "We need to find that goddamn truck."

"You mean Ricky's truck is missing?" Wanda Nell asked quickly.

Elmer Lee scowled at her. "Yeah." He motioned for Taylor to precede him to the door. "And we're gonna be looking for it."

"I'll bet if you find that truck," Juliet said, surprising her mother, "you'll find the men that killed my daddy and Mr. Ratliff."

"Maybe so, little lady," Elmer Lee said. Then he and Taylor were out the door.

"Thank the Lord," Wanda Nell murmured.

"What, Mama?" Miranda asked. She came and sat down on the couch, Lavon in her lap.

"I said, 'thank the Lord,'" Wanda Nell repeated. "Thank the Lord, Elmer Lee finally stopped thinking I killed your daddy."

Juliet sat on the arm of the chair beside her mother. "Maybe they'll find that truck real quick, and those men, too, and this will all be over."

Wanda Nell patted her daughter's leg. "I sure hope so, baby."

"Mama," Miranda said, her head down as she watched Lavon squirm around in her lap, "if they find that money Daddy had with him, what do you reckon they'll do with it?"

Frowning, Wanda Nell regarded her older daughter. "Why, honey, I don't know. Guess it depends on whether it was really your daddy's money."

Miranda flushed. "Mama, why do you always have to think so bad about Daddy? Maybe he earned that money, and if 'n he did, then it ought to come to us. Isn't that right, Juliet?"

Juliet stopped swinging her leg against the side of the chair. "Well, I guess so, Miranda. If Daddy came by it honestly, then it was his. And we're his next of kin, so I guess we'd get it. Unless Daddy made a will somewhere and left it to somebody else."

Wanda Nell snorted. "I can just see Bobby Ray making a will, of all things."

Miranda cut her eyes over at her mother. "Then I guess if we find that money, Mama, we just oughta keep our mouths shut and not tell anybody. Just in case. That way we could keep it, couldn't we?"

"You seem awful concerned about that money," Wanda Nell observed. "If your daddy'd still had it with him, the police would've found it. They hadn't said anything to me about it, but I can ask." Then a thought struck her, and she stared hard at Miranda.

"You sure you don't know something about that money, Miranda? Is that why you're asking all these questions about it?"

Miranda's eyes widened. "Uh, no, Mama, I don't know nothing about it, I swear. I just remembered it, and I got to wondering. You know. It sure would come in handy, wouldn't it?"

"Yeah, it would," Wanda Nell said shortly. "In the meantime, what did you do with the money I saw your daddy give you?"

Miranda got shifty-eyed, a look Wanda Nell knew only too well from years of experience. "Aw, Miranda, don't tell me you done spent all of it already? On what, for heaven's sake?"

Not meeting her mother's gaze, Miranda mumbled, "I kinda loaned it to somebody."

"What?" Wanda Nell said. "What d'you mean, you loaned it to somebody?" She shook her head. "Tell me you didn't give the money to that sorry friend of yours Chanelle. You'll never get it back."

"No, Mama," Miranda said, "I didn't loan it to Chanelle."

"Then who?" Wanda Nell demanded. "Tell me who!"

"She loaned it to me, Mama," a deep voice spoke from behind Wanda Nell, nearly scaring the life out of her.

"T.J.!" Wanda Nell couldn't believe her eyes. "Where'd you come from?"

## Fifteen

Wanda Nell couldn't get over the change in her son. The shoulder-length hair was gone, replaced by a short cut that made his handsome face easier to notice. Gone also was the scraggly beard he used to wear, though he still sported an earring—a small gold hoop—in his left ear. His jeans were neat and clean, his shirt didn't sport some obscene picture, and his cowboy boots, though worn, shone with a high polish.

Her eyes filling with tears, Wanda Nell stared up into his face as he stepped closer to her. Uncertain of his welcome, T.J. hung back a little at the last minute, until Wanda Nell opened her arms. T.J. pulled his mother close to him.

Sobbing against his shoulder, Wanda Nell clutched T.J. hard against her. T.J.'s big hand caressed her hair lightly as he rested his chin on the top of her head. "It's okay, Mama. I'm glad to see you, too."

Pulling back a little, Wanda Nell tilted her head and met his gaze. He was crying, too. She hugged him fiercely again. "I'm so glad you're home, honey," she said, her voice muffled against his broad chest.

"So'm I, Mama, so'm I."

Sniffling, Wanda Nell stepped back. "I just can't get over the way you look, honey. It's so different."

T.J. grinned, and Wanda Nell's heart turned over. He was the spitting image of his daddy at that age, except for the earring, and Wanda Nell had to shut her eyes for a moment to let the wave of emotion pass through.

"And clean, too, huh, Mama?" T.J. was laughing through his tears.

"Yeah, you clean up real good," Juliet said, alternately laughing and crying. T.J. reached out to tousle her hair.

"Thanks, Bug," he said, grinning happily, and Juliet simply laughed at the nickname she used to hate.

Wanda Nell collapsed into her chair. "How long've you been here, honey?" She fixed accusing glares on her daughters in turn. "And how come y'all didn't tell me he was here?"

"We wanted it to be a surprise, Mama," Miranda said, wiping away a few tears of her own, "and we woulda told you soon's you woke up, but we couldn't with those cops here."

"Have you been hiding in Miranda's room all this time?" Wanda Nell asked.

"I got here about two hours ago," T.J. replied, sitting next to Miranda on the couch, "so it wasn't too bad." He made a face. "And I could see real quick Miranda still ain't much on cleaning up her room."

Miranda punched her brother lightly on the arm, and Lavon squealed and almost fell off her lap. T.J. reached for him and pulled the baby onto his own lap. "Come here, little guy, before your mama drops you on your head. We can't let that happen to you, or you'll be just like your silly old mama." T.J. held his face close to Lavon's and grinned while the baby explored his uncle's face with small fingers. "Your mama got dropped on her head an awful lot when she was a baby, and that's why she's the way she is."

Wanda Nell sat speechless while Miranda sputtered in outrage and Juliet howled with laughter. She had expected an entirely different reaction from T.J. when he caught sight of the color of his nephew's skin. T.J. met her eyes as he gently pulled Lavon's probing fingers away from his earring.

"I've learned a few things since the last time I saw you, Mama," he said. He bent his head and kissed Lavon on the cheek. Lavon chattered away in the language that they were all still struggling to understand.

"I guess so," Wanda Nell said slowly. It looked like the change in her son wasn't just on the outside. Her heart lifted. Maybe her boy had finally grown up into a man.

"How long've you been in town, T.J.?" Wanda Nell asked.

For the first time, he wouldn't look at her when he answered. "A few days, I guess. I had some things I wanted to take care of before I came to see you, Mama."

Deciding not to press him for the moment, Wanda Nell merely responded, "Well, I'm just glad to see you, honey." She hesitated. "I guess the girls told you about your daddy."

A shadow passed over T.J.'s face. Abruptly, he stood up and deposited Lavon in Miranda's lap. "Randa, Bug, I need to talk to Mama alone for a little while. Y'all go on back to your rooms, okay?"

Both girls started to protest, but T.J. just looked at them, his face stern. Once again Wanda Nell couldn't help but think of Bobby Ray. The few times he'd ever disciplined the children, he'd had that same look on his face. She tried not to cry.

"It won't be long," T.J. said. He grinned slightly when Juliet stuck out her tongue at him. "Go on, Pesterbug, or I'm gonna pinch your head off."

T.J. waited until his sisters had disappeared into opposite ends of the trailer before he sat down again on the couch. He regarded his mother solemnly.

"What is it, T.J.?" Wanda Nell asked quickly. "What is it you didn't want your sisters to hear?" Her stomach had drawn up into a tight knot. She wasn't really sure she wanted to hear his answer.

T.J. leaned back on the couch and propped one booted foot across the edge of the coffee table. Wanda Nell frowned, but she didn't insist that he move his leg.

"I got to talk to you about Daddy, Mama," he said. His eyes held sorrow and regret. "I don't want to scare you, Mama, but I reckon you oughta know, especially now with Daddy dead like that."

Her chest constricted, and Wanda Nell found it hard to get her breath. *Oh, dear Lord,* she prayed, *don't let T.J. be mixed up in whatever mess his daddy cooked up. Please, please, please!* If those men were gonna come after her son, too, she didn't know what she'd do.

"No, it's not like that," T.J. said, smiling faintly as he seemed to read his mother's mind. "I wasn't mixed up in nothing with Daddy. I promise, Mama. I'm different now, Mama, and I'm not going to let you down ever again. I promise you that, too."

"Oh, honey," Wanda Nell whispered. She desperately wanted to believe her son, believe that he truly had changed and finally grown up, ready to take responsibility for himself. She had to be willing to give him the chance to show her. "I truly hope so, T.J. You'll make me the proudest mother in the world."

He grinned at that, but quickly sobered. "I'm sorry for all the things I done in the past, Mama. I know I can't really make any of it up to you now." Anticipating her question, he went on quickly, "I'll tell you all about it later, Mama. It's kind of a long story."

Wanda Nell nodded acceptance.

"About Daddy," T.J. said, "I don't know everything, but I know a little bit of it." He paused. "Just enough to be kinda scared, Mama."

Wanda Nell's stomach knotted up again. "What is it?" she was finally able to whisper.

"I been out in Houston, Texas, awhile," T.J. said, "and then I decided it was time to come home. Took me a while to get back here. I didn't have a lot of money, but I worked for every bit I had. I saved it up, and I ended up over in Greenville awhile. I thought I might try to get me a job at one of them riverboat casinos. Figured that was as good a place as any to start."

Wanda Nell nodded encouragement. She didn't much approve of gambling, but that was something they could talk about later.

"Anyway, I was hunting for a job there, and one day I ran into Daddy on one of the boats. Last I heard, he was down on the coast, Biloxi, I guess, working with a guy running fishing trips out in the Gulf."

"He was gambling, wasn't he?" Wanda Nell asked, disgusted. "He was always convinced he was gonna hit it big with some jackpot."

"Nope," T.J. answered. "Actually, he was working there. Security guard, if you can believe that." He laughed. "I don't know who he conned into that one, but he said he'd been working there awhile. Told me he thought he could get me on there, too. Said to give him a couple days, then come back, and he'd have it all set up."

The amusement had disappeared from T.J.'s voice, and Wanda Nell anticipated what was coming. "When you went back, he wasn't there anymore, was he?"

T.J. shook his head. "I was a bit surprised, Mama, 'cause Daddy said he was on to a good thing, and he really liked it there. Made good money, and, well . . . " T.J. wouldn't look at her as his voice trailed away.

"And he had some idiot woman waitin' on him hand and foot," Wanda Nell finished the sentence for him.

"Yeah, some girl he'd hooked up with, he really liked her, he told me," T.J. said. "He sounded like he really meant it, Mama, and I thought I was gonna have a job. But I guess I shoulda remembered who I was talking to."

The bitterness in his voice made his mother ache for him. His daddy had disappointed him, time after time. Bobby Ray had had a chance to do something decent for his son, and he'd screwed it up again.

"So what happened?" Wanda Nell asked gently.

"When I went back and asked for him, they looked at me real funny. Wanted to know who I was and what I wanted him for. 'Course, all they had to do was take one look at me, and they knew who I was. One of 'em even said something about it." He scratched his chin. "The way they kept push-ing at me, asking one question after another, I knew Daddy'd done something."

"What?" Wanda Nell asked, though she had a horrible feeling she knew.

"Well, they never would come right out and tell me," T.J. said, "but he had to've ripped 'em off. I just wonder how much he made off with. Must've been a bundle, the way they was grilling me."

"They didn't try to hurt you, did they?"

"Naw, but they sure looked like they wanted to hurt someone. I asked 'em why they wasn't talking to the police if they was so concerned about finding my daddy, and they just said they wanted to handle it privately."

"And I bet they did," Wanda Nell said. "Did your sisters tell you about what happened to them? How those men broke in here and tore this place up looking for something?"

"Yeah," T.J. said, his eyes gleaming with anger. "I wish I could get my hands on those guys for a few minutes." That sounded like the T.J. she knew best. He had her temper, and he'd get into a fight faster than he could spit.

"You better leave those guys alone if for some reason they ever turn up again," Wanda Nell said, "and I mean it. If they killed your daddy, they won't think twice about doing the same to you."

T.J. nodded. "I know, Mama, and I was just talking. I ain't crazy enough to take on two guys like that. At least, not anymore I'm not."

"Good." Wanda Nell hoped he was telling the truth. "Did your sisters tell you anything about those men?"

"Yeah," T.J. said, "and I think one of 'em, the short one, was in the room when they was questioning me at the casino. It sure sounded like him."

"I can't figure out why they just didn't call the police and have them look for Bobby Ray," Wanda Nell said.

T.J. laughed. "Oh, come on, Mama. You can't be that naïve."

Wanda Nell bristled. "What do you mean?"

He pulled his leg off the table and onto the floor, then leaned forward. "Mama, surely you don't think those places are pure as the driven snow?" He laughed again. "Anytime that kind of money's involved, you know there's something crooked going on, too. And knowing Daddy, he was in on it somehow. He just thought he could rip 'em off and get away with it, like he always did."

"I guess you're right," Wanda Nell said slowly. "And if that's the case, they ain't gonna stop looking for that money. We won't be safe until they find it."

"Maybe not," T.J. said. "But they kinda screwed up when they killed Daddy. Now they've got the cops involved, and that wasn't too smart."

"Lord, what a nightmare," Wanda Nell said, sighing.

"Yeah, thanks to my fine, upstanding father," T.J. said. Then he looked ashamed. "I wadn't much better than him, I guess, the mess I made of my life."

Wanda Nell leaned forward and patted his knee. "But, honey, you don't have to repeat all your daddy's mistakes. Anyway, sounds to me like you've made some big changes. Some important changes."

T.J. nodded. "I sure wanna think so, Mama. And at least I've got time to do things different, not like Daddy."

They sat in silence for a moment, then Wanda Nell asked again, "Those men at the casino, they didn't try to hurt you or threaten you, did they?"

"Not really," T.J. said. "They told me to tell Daddy to get in touch with them, if I talked to him. I said I would. Then they let me go."

"Thank the Lord for that."

"Yeah, I have to tell you, I was sweating a bit before they turned me loose. After that, I thought about getting the hell outta Dodge, as they say, but I decided I'd better stick around Greenville a day or two and see if I could track Daddy down."

"Did you?"

T.J. shook his head. "Naw. He didn't tell me where he was living, or anything like that, but I did find a bar near the casinos where they knew him." He shrugged. "But nobody'd seen him for a couple days. One of the guys there told me where he thought Daddy was living, and I went there, too. But his landlady said he'd cleared out. Can you believe, he didn't owe her any money? I was expectin' her to ask me to pay what he owed, but she said his rent was paid up."

"She was probably the girlfriend he told you about," Wanda Nell said.

"Nope," T.J. said around a big grin. "She was about seventy-five, Mama. Too old for Daddy." He thought a moment. "She had a funny name, kinda like a plant. What was it? Turnipseed, that was it."

Wanda Nell laughed. "Yeah, she's about fifty years too old for your daddy."

T.J. just rolled his eyes. "Only thing she could tell me was she thought he might've been heading for Tullahoma. She overheard him talking to somebody on the phone, and he was saying something about Tullahoma."

"Nosy little old lady," Wanda Nell said, "but she was right."

"Daddy didn't have a phone in his room," T.J. explained, "and he asked to use hers, she said."

"Sounds like he treated her better than he treated his own mama," Wanda Nell observed. "Can't say as I blame him, though, that old witch. Wait till I tell you what she done to me." She was about to launch into the story when the phone rang.

"Now, Mama," T.J. was saying. He was the only one of her grandchildren that Mrs. Culpepper had ever had anything to do with, and he had a soft spot for the old battle-ax.

"Let me get that," Wanda Nell said, rising from her chair, "and I'll tell you all about it."

Halfway to the phone, she remembered that Jack Pemberton was supposed to be calling her back. She wasn't sure she wanted to talk to him, after what Juliet had told her about him writing true-crime books. She could always tell him she was busy visiting with her son and put him off, she decided. She walked into the kitchen and picked up the phone. "Hello," she said, preparing herself to get Pemberton off the phone quickly.

"We're watching you," a voice said, low and hard. "If you don't want something nasty to happen to that pretty little girl of yours, you better give us that money back."

## Sixteen

Wanda Nell's hand tightened on the phone. Her temper ignited. "Listen here, you asshole. You keep away from me and my family. I don't have that goddamn money, and if I did, I'd give it to the sheriff's department."

Heavy breathing came back to her over the wire. "*You* listen, bitch. We know you're lyin', and you better hand over that money." He kept on talking, getting more and more explicit about what he was going to do to Wanda Nell and her daughters if the money didn't turn up soon. Sickened, Wanda Nell screamed an obscenity back at him, then slammed the receiver down on the base.

Trembling violently, Wanda Nell stumbled to the sink. Hanging her head over it, she threw up. She felt a hand on her shoulder.

"Mama! What's wrong?" T.J.'s hand tightened. "Are you sick?"

Wanda Nell groped for some paper towels to wipe her mouth. Still a bit shaky, she straightened up and turned on the water with one hand as she wiped her mouth with the other. T.J. spoke again, urgently. "Mama, what's wrong?"

Shutting the water off, Wanda Nell looked up into her son's eyes. "That was one of the assholes who broke in here. He said he'd hurt Juliet if we didn't turn the money over to him." She burst into tears.

"My God, Mama," T.J. said. He drew her into his arms and held her tight. "But y'all don't have the money, do you?"

"Course not," Wanda Nell replied, her voice muffled against his chest. "Why the hell do they think I've got it?"

T.J. rubbed her back with his big hand, and Wanda Nell could feel the calluses on it through her gown and robe. "If those guys don't have it," T.J. said, his voice calm, "then it's still gotta be out there somewhere, don't you think, Mama?"

Wanda Nell pulled back from him. "I guess I wasn't really thinking too hard about that, son. But you're right."

"Okay, then," T.J. said. "What could Daddy've done with it?"

Wanda Nell thought for a moment. "I'd'a thought he might give it to Ricky Ratliff, but since Ricky's been killed, too, I guess he didn't." She shivered. "But if he didn't give it to Ricky, then who?"

T.J. stood watching her, and as she thought about it, several things came together in her mind. Wanda Nell turned away from her son and took several steps from the kitchen into the hall. "Miranda! Get in here."

"What's going on, Mama?" T.J. asked.

"I think I just figured out what happened to that money," Wanda Nell said. "Your daddy was here that night when I got home, and he flashed a big wad of cash at me. He gave Miranda some before he left, and I'm just bettin' he gave her more than he let on."

Miranda came trailing in on those last words, and her eyes grew big as she stopped suddenly and stared at her mother. "What is it, Mama?" Her voice came out in a whisper.

Wanda Nell folded her hands across her chest and gave Miranda her no-nonsense look. "Where's the money your daddy gave you?"

"Oh, you mean that five hundred dollars, Mama?" Miranda fluttered a hand in the air. "I loaned it to T.J., Mama, remember? He said he was gonna try to rent him an apartment."

"Not that money, Miranda," Wanda Nell retorted. "You know damn well what I'm talking about. Where's the rest of the money your daddy gave you?" She waited a moment for Miranda to respond, and when she didn't, Wanda Nell continued. "Your daddy came back that night, after I left for work. Didn't he, Miranda? He came back, and he gave you more money."

Miranda frowned, and her mother recognized the mulish set to her face. "I don't know what you're talking about, Mama. Daddy didn't give me no more money than that five hundred dollars."

"Don't lie to me, Miranda," Wanda Nell said. "Or I'm gonna snatch you bald-headed. Do you understand me?"

Miranda just stood and looked at her.

Wanda Nell itched to grab her daughter's hair and give it a good yank. Miranda gazed defiantly back at her.

Stepping around her daughter, Wanda Nell made for the small laundry room. Lavon's diaper pail still sat where Miranda had left it. When she opened it, Wanda Nell wasn't surprised Miranda hadn't washed any of the dirty diapers yet.

Holding her breath, Wanda Nell stuck her hand in and gingerly felt around in the pail. At the bottom, under all the stinky, messy diapers, her hand encountered plastic. She grabbed and pulled, and out came a large plastic bag bulging with cash. Wanda Nell's stomach rumbled, and she thought she was going to throw up again.

T.J. had followed her, and she felt his hand on her shoulder. Mutely, she turned and brandished the bag. T.J. whistled.

"How much you reckon's in there?" he asked.

"I don't know, and I don't wanna know," Wanda Nell said. She pushed past her son and stalked back into the kitchen, where Miranda waited, backed up against the counter.

"Just when the hell were you going to tell me about this?" Wanda Nell demanded. She shook the bag at her daughter.

Miranda didn't say anything.

"You better start talking to me, Miranda," Wanda Nell said. "We're in a whole lotta trouble thanks to this crap, and you better start talking."

Miranda whimpered. "Daddy gave it to me, Mama. He said he was gonna come back for it, and he just wanted me to keep it a little while." She sobbed. "And then he died, and I didn't know what to do with it. I woulda told you, Mama, I swear I would."

Wanda Nell wondered, not for the first time, how she could have raised a daughter as dim-witted as Miranda. When was the girl ever gonna get any sense?

"Didn't it ever dawn on you, Miranda," Wanda Nell said, trying to keep her temper, "that somebody else wants this money? I mean, what do you think those goons who broke in here were after?"

"I know, Mama," Miranda said, "but Daddy said it was his money. I wasn't gonna tell those men where I hid Daddy's money." Suddenly, she laughed. "I reckon I picked a good place to hide it. That guy came into my room, I saw him open the lid of the diaper pail, and he put it back real quick. Didn't even bother to look inside."

Wanda Nell had to admire Miranda's brief spurt of intelligence. "Yeah, I guess it was a good place to hide it," she admitted. "But you should've told me about it, Miranda. We should've told the sheriff's department about it long before now." She sighed. "Don't you realize what kinda trouble we're gonna be in?"

"I think we should keep it, Mama," Miranda said. "Daddy said it was his, and it should be ours. If those men killed Daddy, they shouldn't get his money."

Wanda Nell felt a hand on her shoulder as she started to speak. T.J. squeezed lightly, and she nodded.

"Randa, honey," T.J. said, "I don't think you understand something real important about this money."

Miranda stared at her brother. "You can have some, too, T.J. There's more'n enough for all of us."

T.J. shook his head at her. "Randa, that ain't the point. That money don't belong to us, and it didn't belong to Daddy. Surely you realize that by now?"

Miranda's mouth set in a stubborn line for a moment, then she spoke. "Daddy said he won the money at one of them casinos over in the Delta. I believe him."

T.J. and Wanda Nell exchanged glances. Wanda Nell shrugged. T.J. reached out and clasped his sister's arm. "Come on with me, Randa. We're gonna sit down in the living room, and I'm gonna explain a few things to you." He pulled her toward him.

Miranda appealed to her mother with a wounded look. Wanda Nell nodded. Miranda's shoulders slumped in defeat, and she dragged her heels a bit as her brother led her into the living room.

Sighing heavily, Wanda Nell reached for the phone. It rang, startling her. Her heart pounded as she lifted the receiver.

"Hello," she whispered. She cleared her throat and spoke again more clearly. "Hello."

"Afternoon, Miz Culpepper," Jack Pemberton said. "How are you? I hope I haven't caught you at a bad time, but you did say the afternoon was the best time to call."

He rushed his words, so it took Wanda Nell a moment to figure out what he had just said to her. Then she had to struggle to frame some kind of reply that wouldn't make her sound like a complete lunatic.

"Afternoon, Mr. Pemberton," she finally managed. "Actually, I'm afraid I really can't talk right now. I'm sorry, but something's come up, and, well, I'm sorry."

The confusion she had felt earlier, on hearing that Pemberton was interested in true-crime writing, came rushing back to her. On top of everything else, it was just too much. She wanted to tell him to buzz off, but she couldn't cope with that right now. Maybe he would take the hint and leave her alone.

"Are you all right, Miz Culpepper?" Pemberton's voice was hesitant. "Sounds like there's some trouble. I don't want to intrude, but if I can help in any way, please tell me."

"Why, so you can put it in a book?" Wanda Nell spoke her thoughts aloud.

There was silence on the other end of the phone for a moment. "I guess Juliet must have told you about my writing, then."

"Yeah, she sure did," Wanda Nell said, "and that made things real clear."

"I guess I can see why you might be suspicious," Pemberton said, "but, Miz Culpepper, I promise you, I'm not interested in you because of what happened to your ex-husband. I'm not interested in writing a book about it."

Something in his voice rang sincere to Wanda Nell. She

really wanted to believe him. But could she afford to trust him?

When Wanda Nell didn't reply, Pemberton continued. "Look, I realize you don't know much about me. But you remember that first night at the Kountry Kitchen?"

"Yes," Wanda Nell said. "I remember."

"Well then, you had to realize I found you attractive," Pemberton said, his voice growing fainter.

Wanda Nell could imagine him, that shy face of his and his eyes, blinking behind his glasses. Her face softened in a smile.

"Yeah, I know you did," she said.

"The reason I wanted to ask you out doesn't have anything to do with what happened to your ex-husband," Pemberton said. "But I can understand that, with everything else going on, now might not be a good time."

"Yeah, there's some things going on I got to take care of," Wanda Nell said. "But I'm hoping it's all gonna be over real soon."

"Then maybe I can call you later on?"

"I'd like that."

"Then I will. And in the meantime, I meant what I said earlier. If you need some help, and there's something I can do, you call me. Okay?"

"I will," Wanda Nell said. "And thank you." She reached for a pen and jotted down the number he gave her.

She set the phone back on the cradle and stared at it thoughtfully. Maybe she had misjudged him after all. She'd find out, when the time came.

In the meantime, she wanted to get rid of the money she was still clutching in one hand. She dropped the bag on the counter and picked up the phone again. By now she knew the number by heart.

"I need to speak with Deputy Johnson," Wanda Nell said when the dispatcher answered. "Tell him it's Wanda Nell Culpepper, and I got some real important information for him."

"One moment, please," the voice responded, and Wanda Nell waited with increasing impatience.

Finally Elmer Lee's voice came over the line. "What is it, Wanda Nell? The dispatcher said you had some real important information. This had better be pretty damn good."

"It is," Wanda Nell said, resisting the urge to tell him to stick it where the sun don't shine. "I found what those guys were looking for, and I think you better get over here right now."

"Whadda you mean, Wanda Nell?"

"That's all I'm gonna say for now, Elmer Lee. You just get on over here. This is serious."

He snorted. "We're on the way, then."

Wanda Nell dropped the phone back on the cradle. She stared for a moment at the bag of money. "Bobby Ray, you sonofabitch," she whispered. Reaching out, she grabbed the bag and stuffed it into one of the cabinets.

In the living room, Miranda was sobbing against her brother's shoulder. T.J. patted her on the back even as he rolled his eyes at his mother.

"Miranda," Wanda Nell said. "Pull yourself together. I just called the sheriff's department, and they're on the way here. I'm gonna turn that money over to them."

"Okay, Mama," Miranda said, turning a streaming face to her mother. "I'm sorry, Mama, I didn't mean to cause trouble. I really did think it was Daddy's money."

"That's okay, honey," Wanda Nell said. There was no point in fussing at her anymore than she already had. "I guess T.J. told you everything?"

Miranda nodded. "I never want to see that money again." Her face turned wistful. "But it sure woulda been nice, wouldn't it, Mama?"

Wanda Nell just looked at her. The girl was never going to understand that life didn't work that way. Nothing came that easy, but Miranda probably never would figure it out.

"I'm going to put on some clothes," Wanda Nell said. "The sheriff's department oughta be here soon."

"I better go check on Lavon," Miranda said. "He's gonna be waking up from his nap any minute now."

As Wanda Nell and Miranda disappeared in opposite directions, T.J. headed into the kitchen. Wanda Nell peeked in on Juliet. She was reading a book and listening to country music on the radio and never even noticed her mother at the door. Wanda Nell closed the door softly and went on into her room to change.

She had barely finished pulling on her jeans and an oversized T-shirt when she heard a thumping at the door. She hadn't heard a car drive up, but Elmer Lee had said he wouldn't be long. She padded on bare feet back to the living room in time to see T.J. backing away from the open door, his hands in the air in a gesture of surrender.

"What is it, T.J.?" she asked.

T.J. didn't look at her, just backed up a couple more steps, and Wanda Nell came to a halt.

A tall man, a hood covering his head, stood in the doorway. He had a gun pointed straight at T.J.

# Seventeen

Wanda Nell's heart raced, and she glanced wildly around for something to throw at the man with the gun.

"Hand it over."

Neither Wanda Nell nor T.J. moved, and the hooded man brandished the gun again.

"Hand it over, or I'm gonna fill pretty boy here with a few bits of lead."

Wanda Nell found her voice. "Just hang on a minute, jack-ass. It's in the kitchen. I'll get it for you." Slowly, carefully, she moved in front of T.J. toward the kitchen. The whole time she was praying that Juliet and Miranda stayed in their rooms.

"Just get it," the man said. The gun didn't waver.

Moving faster, Wanda Nell made it into the kitchen. Her hands trembled as she pulled open the drawer where she had stashed the bag of money. She was tempted to grab a butcher knife and try to take it back in the living room with her, just in case. But then the man called out again. "Get in here with it, woman. I ain't gonna wait all day."

Wanda Nell grabbed the bag and scooted back into the living room as fast as she could. She stumbled to a halt in front of him and held the bag up. He snatched it from her and stepped back slowly into the doorway.

"Y'all just turn around and face the wall," he said. "Don't look anywhere but at that wall for the next five minutes, or I'm a'gonna have to shoot you."

Wanda Nell and T.J. did as they were told. Wanda Nell's stomach knotted in fear as she continued to pray that the girls wouldn't suddenly appear and startle the man. And she prayed he wouldn't shoot T.J. just for the hell of it.

The door slammed shut, and Wanda Nell relaxed slightly. T.J. started to move, and Wanda Nell hissed at him. "Don't you move an inch, T.J., and I mean it."

Wonder of wonders, T.J. stopped and stood completely still. Wanda Nell breathed a sigh of relief.

"We need to see where he's going," T.J. whispered, "so you can tell the sheriff's department."

"I don't *care* where he's going," Wanda Nell whispered back. "The sheriff's department can find him. I don't care. I don't want you or me or the girls getting shot, you got that?"

"Yes'm," T.J. said, and from the corner of her eye, Wanda Nell saw his shoulders sag a bit.

They stood that way for a couple minutes more, then T.J. said, "Mama, this is ridiculous. He's long gone by now, and the sheriff's department's gone be here any minute."

"You're right," Wanda Nell said. She turned to her son. "Thank the Lord none of us got hurt. I was afraid that jackass was gonna shoot one of us."

T.J. grinned. "Well, I'm sure he didn't appreciate you calling him a jackass, Mama."

"Oh, my Lord," Wanda Nell gasped. "Did I really say that?"

"You sure did. You know that temper of yours, Mama."

Wanda Nell sagged against T.J. for a moment, and he wrapped an arm around her and hugged her fiercely. "Lord, me and my mouth. I swear I didn't realize I said that to him."

"Can't be helped now," T.J. said. "But listen, Mama. We only got a minute or two."

Frightened by the urgency in her son's voice, Wanda Nell gazed up into his eyes. "What is it?"

"Just stop and think a second. How come that guy knew to show up right then and ask for that money?"

Wanda Nell's mind worked furiously, and one answer came to her quickly. Appalled, she stared at T.J. "Oh my Lord."

T.J. nodded. "Somebody in the sheriff's department is in on this, Mama. I can't figure any other way that guy knew to come just when he did."

Chilled to the bone, Wanda Nell just stood there. "Oh, Lord, T.J., I never thought of that. And that means it's probably Elmer Lee. What are we gonna do?"

"I don't know, Mama," T.J. said, "but do you think you can stand talking to him without me? It might be better if he don't know for a while I'm anywhere around."

Wanda Nell didn't like the sound of that. She wasn't sure what good it would do to pretend she hadn't seen or talked to T.J.

Before she could say anything, they both heard the sound of cars pulling in to the trailer park. A moment later, several doors slammed, and then came another pounding on the front door. T.J. disappeared in the direction of Miranda's room and Wanda Nell stared helplessly after him.

This was exactly the sort of thing his father would have done, and Wanda Nell began to doubt her son had reformed himself as much as he claimed.

The pounding on the door continued. "Wanda Nell, you in there?"

"Just a minute, Elmer Lee," she shouted back.

She flung open the door, and Elmer Lee stood there with a couple of his men. Elmer Lee stared at her, his eyes hard as granite. "What was so all-fired important that I had to get out here so fast?"

He pushed his way past her into the living room, and she stood aside to let the other men come in after him. One of them tipped his hat politely at her. The other ignored her.

Closing the door carefully behind them, Wanda Nell took a moment to try to cool down her temper. Then she walked around in front of Elmer Lee and stared right back at him.

"I called you to come here because I found something I thought you oughta know about—" she began.

"Well, what the hell is it?" Elmer Lee was too impatient to let her finish.

"I'm getting to that, if you'll just hold on a damn minute," Wanda Nell retorted. "I found what those guys were looking for when they broke in here, that's what."

"Oh, yeah. And what was it, pray tell?"

Wanda Nell hated the patronizing note in his voice.

"Probably about thirty or forty thousand dollars in cash." Wanda Nell crossed her arms across her chest and waited for the explosion.

One of the deputies whistled, then reddened as Elmer Lee whirled on him. "I didn't ask for nothing outta you." He turned back to Wanda Nell. "Where was it?"

"Bobby Ray'd given it to Miranda," she explained, "and

Miranda hid it in the bottom of the baby's diaper pail." She watched him closely for any signs of guilt, but his poker face didn't change.

"Pretty damn smart," was all he said.

"Yeah," Wanda Nell agreed. "One of them even looked in the diaper pail, Miranda said, but he wasn't about to stick his hand down there."

Elmer Lee nodded. "Where is it now?"

She started to reply "As if you didn't know," but she clamped her mouth shut. It wouldn't do to say something like that now.

Instead, she took a deep breath before speaking. "Not three minutes after I talked to you on the phone, somebody banged on the door. It was a man with a hood over his face, and he had a gun. He said he was gonna shoot T—um, me, if I didn't hand over the money."

"And so I guess you just handed it over," Elmer Lee said.

Wanda Nell nodded, relieved that he appeared not to have noticed her slip.

Elmer Lee laughed. "Lord, but that's a good one, Wanda Nell. I got to hand it to you."

"What? What are you talking about?"

Elmer Lee kept on laughing, and soon the other two deputies were laughing with him.

"What the hell is so damn funny?" Wanda Nell stamped her foot on the floor in frustration. That only made Elmer Lee and his deputies laugh harder.

"Oh, come on, Wanda Nell," Elmer Lee said, when he could finally get enough breath to speak. "I mean, I believe you found that money. But do you really expect me to believe some masked man came up to your door in broad daylight and made you hand over the money?" He snickered. "What'd he do then? Did he hop on his horse and head for the hills?" That set him off again.

Wanda Nell was so furious with him, she couldn't speak. She just stared at him.

"Okay, Wanda Nell," Elmer Lee said, after wiping his streaming eyes, "where is it? Where's the money? Surely you don't think you can keep it? I mean, if I was dumbass enough to fall for this story of yours, I guess you thought you could just hang on to it. But I wasn't born yesterday." He shook his head. "That dog ain't gonna hunt, no way, no how."

Wanda Nell finally found her tongue. "I swear, Elmer Lee Johnson, I have known some stupid men in my life, but you must be the stupidest man the Lord ever put on this green earth. I am telling you the truth, and you damn well better believe me. You can rip this trailer apart, and you ain't gonna find that money."

Elmer Lee reddened under the onslaught. "You listen here, Wanda Nell, you better be careful how you talk to an officer of the law. I got witnesses here." He jerked his head to indicate his two deputies.

"That dog ain't gonna hunt, either, Elmer Lee." Wanda Nell refused to be intimidated. "That man came in and took that money away from me. And that's that."

"You got any witnesses to that?" Elmer Lee shook his head. "Did those girls of yours see any of this? Not that it matters, of course. They'd say anything you told 'em to."

Wanda Nell caught herself in time. She'd been about to say that her son had been a witness, but she held back. Instead, she stood mute.

"Pretty clever, Wanda Nell," Elmer Lee taunted her. "Pretty damn clever. But it just ain't gonna work."

"Then tell me this, Elmer Lee, and I wanna know what you think." Wanda Nell braced herself. "How come that man turns up on my doorstep not three minutes after I called the sheriff's department and talked to *you*? How come? You answer that one."

"I don't think I like what you're saying, Wanda Nell."
Elmer Lee almost growled at her. "If you're implying what
I think you're implying, then you're not only stupid, you're
plumb crazy, woman." His face reddened with every word
out of his mouth, until Wanda Nell thought he was going to
have a stroke, right then and there.

"I ain't implying nothing, Elmer Lee," Wanda Nell said.
"I'm just telling you the God's honest truth. That's the way
it happened, and I been trying to think of some explanation." She paused for a deep, steadying breath. "But I can't
think of but one explanation."

Elmer Lee stepped forward, his hand raised, but Wanda
Nell stood her ground. Her eyes dared him to strike her.
Elmer Lee faltered, and Wanda Nell's eyes glittered in tri-
umph.

His chest heaving, Elmer Lee didn't speak for a moment.
When he finally did, his voice rasped. "Since I reckon
you're lying about ever' damn thing you just told me,
Wanda Nell, I'm gonna let this pass. You're just trying to
blow smoke so's nobody's gonna figure you got that money
stashed away somewhere." He threw back his head and
laughed. "I got to hand it to you, Wanda Nell. I shoulda just
hauled your ass to jail right off the bat, and then we wouldn'a
had to go through all this shit of yours."

Wanda Nell's hands clenched tightly at her sides. She
was breathing hard, trying to control the urge to reach out
and slap Elmer Lee as hard as she could.

"Come on, Wanda Nell," Elmer Lee cajoled. "Why don't
you confess, right here and now? Then I'll forget all this
other mess. There ain't no money, there ain't no men been
breaking in here, ain't nothing like that. You killed Bobby
Ray 'cause you was jealous or something, and that's all it
was. Right?"

Wanda Nell stared at him. All the while her heart was racing. How on earth was she going to convince him? What would she do if he took her to jail?

"Wanda Nell! Open the door, quick!"

A loud voice from outside the trailer startled them all. Elmer Lee whirled around toward the door. He jerked his head at one of his deputies, who stepped forward to fling open the door.

Wanda Nell stepped forward, pushing around Elmer Lee to find out what Mayrene had been hollering about. Her eyes widened in surprise.

The hooded man stood at the foot of the steps, his hands up in a gesture of surrender. Mayrene, grinning widely, poked him in the back with her shotgun.

# Eighteen

Wanda Nell heard Elmer Lee mutter an obscenity. She glanced swiftly up at his face but could read only confusion there.

"What the hell is going on here?" Elmer Lee demanded, pushing past his deputies to stand right in the doorway.

"I caught this joker sneaking around in Janette's trailer," Mayrene answered. "And seeing as Janette left sometime yesterday to go spend a few days with her mama, I reckon the Lone Ranger here wasn't up to no good." She prodded him again with the shotgun. "Were ya?"

"Tell her to get that damn gun outta my back!" His voice came out higher than Wanda Nell remembered. She almost giggled as she watched the man swallow convulsively several times.

Wanda Nell poked Elmer Lee in the back. "That's the guy that broke in here and took the money."

"No shit," Elmer Lee said. He refused to look at Wanda Nell. He motioned for his deputies to take charge of Mayrene's prisoner, and Mayrene stepped back, though she kept her shotgun ready, just in case. Elmer Lee climbed down the stoop to watch, and Wanda Nell took his place in the doorway.

One of the deputies pushed the hooded man against the side of the trailer, arranged him in position, then began patting him down. He found a pistol tucked in the man's left boot, and he retrieved it gingerly. He handed it to Elmer Lee, who examined it carefully.

Elmer Lee threw back his head and guffawed. Startled, Wanda Nell almost fell out of the door.

"What's so damn funny?"

Elmer Lee turned and pointed the gun up at her, and Wanda Nell stepped back in horror. Surely even he wasn't going to be crazy enough to shoot her in front of Mayrene. From behind Elmer Lee, she could see Mayrene swing her shotgun into position. If Elmer Lee did shoot her, he'd be dead, too.

"It's a water pistol, Wanda Nell," Elmer Lee said. He guffawed again. He squeezed the trigger, and water squirted out onto Wanda Nell's chest.

By now the deputies were laughing, too, and even Mayrene was snickering. Wanda Nell was relieved, but she sure didn't appreciate Elmer Lee getting her wet like that.

"Well, I'm glad y'all find this all so damn funny," she said, "but how was I supposed to know he was pointing a toy at me?"

Elmer Lee ignored her. He gestured at one of the deputies, who pulled the hood from the gunman's face. Wanda Nell stared at him. Was he one of the men who had broken in and scared Miranda and Juliet?

He was just an ordinary-looking guy, Wanda Nell thought. Didn't look much like a criminal type. His face had blushed a deep crimson, and he turned his head away from her.

"Let me get the girls," Wanda Nell said, "and dry off this water you squirted on me." Without waiting for an answer from Elmer Lee, she stomped down the hall to her bathroom. She patted her chest as dry as she could, then went to knock on Juliet's door.

Pushing open the door, she found Juliet sound asleep on her bed, the radio still baring away. Wanda Nell moved over to the bed and reached gently down to waken the girl.

Juliet's eyelids fluttered open, and Wanda Nell marveled at her daughter's capacity to sleep through all the commotion.

"What is it, Mama?" Juliet asked through a yawn.

Wanda Nell quickly told her what had happened and warned her not to mention T.J.'s presence in the trailer. Juliet's eyes widened as she sat up. "Gosh, Mama," she said. "You think he's one of the men who tied up me and Miranda?"

"Could be, honey," Wanda Nell said. "I want y'all both to come take a look at him and see if he is."

Juliet followed her down the hall. "You wait here," Wanda Nell instructed, "and let me go get Miranda."

Wanda Nell pushed open Miranda's bedroom door. T.J. was sprawled out on the bed with Lavon, playing tickle monster. Lavon giggled as his uncle goosed him, and T.J. grinned happily as he watched his nephew.

Miranda sat on a chair nearby, watching the two of them. A nearby radio blasted out country music. "What is it, Mama?" Miranda asked as she reached to turn down the volume on the radio.

"I swear, a tornado could come through here, and you'd never hear it the way you play that radio. It's a wonder you and Lavon don't go deaf." Wanda Nell smiled to take the sting out her words.

Once again she explained what had happened and that she wanted Miranda to come take a look at the man.

"Don't let on that I'm here," T.J. admonished his sister. She just rolled her eyes at him before she followed her mother out of the room.

In the living room, Wanda Nell crooked her finger at Juliet, and the two girls were right behind her as she stepped to the door. The deputies now had the man's hands cuffed together behind him, and at Wanda Nell's hailing them, they turned the man around to face her and her daughters.

"What do you think, girls?" Wanda Nell asked, standing aside. "Could he be one of the men who broke in here?"

Miranda and Juliet stood without speaking as they carefully examined the man from head to foot. Then each began to shake her head.

"I don't think so, Mama," Juliet said. "He just doesn't look right."

"Me, neither, Mama," Miranda said.

"He's too tall to be the man who was in my room," Juliet said. "And I don't think he has a tattoo on his chest." They all glanced at him and the dark shirt, the top three buttons undone. Bare white skin gleamed back at them.

"And he don't have a moustache," Miranda said. "And I don't think he's maybe as tall as the man in my room."

"According to his driver's license," Elmer Lee announced, "his name is David McKenna, and he lives in Greenville. That ring a bell with any of y'all?"

"Never heard of him," Wanda Nell said, and Mayrene agreed. Both the girls shook their heads.

"Well, Mr. David McKenna," Elmer Lee said, "what you got to say for yourself? Did you break in on these girls a coupla nights ago?"

McKenna's eyes widened in alarm. His Adam's apple bobbled up and down as he attempted to speak. Finally he got the words out. "I ain't never broke in on them. Except once, and that was today."

After that, he refused to say anything else. Elmer Lee finally gave up trying to question him and ordered his deputies to put him in the car.

"Ain't you forgetting about something?" Mayrene waved her shotgun in the air, and Elmer Lee ducked.

"What are you talking about?" he demanded, his face slightly red as he resumed an upright position.

"The money, you goober," Mayrene answered, letting the shotgun rest at her side.

"You mean there really is money?" Elmer Lee asked, one eyebrow arching.

Wanda Nell wished she had something she could throw at his head, like a bucket of ice-cold water. Mayrene rolled her eyes at him.

"Yeah, hotshot, there's some money," Mayrene said. "You get on over there to Janette's trailer, and you'll find it in the grass around back. Buddy here dropped it when I sneaked up on him with my shotgun." She laughed.

Elmer Lee stalked off. When he went around back of Janette's trailer, Wanda Nell could no longer see him, but Mayrene moved to where she could keep an eye on him.

About five minutes later he was back, holding a bag full of money gingerly with two fingers. Elmer Lee wiggled it in front of Wanda Nell.

"Yeah, that's it," she said.

"I'll be damned," Elmer Lee said, shaking his head. "I guess I was wrong, Wanda Nell."

Wanda Nell waited for him to apologize, but after a long moment's silence, she reckoned that was all the apology she was going to get.

"I guess you'll work a little harder now," she said, "to figure out who that money belongs to and who broke in here."

Elmer Lee wouldn't meet her eyes.

"Reckon so," was his only response. He turned and marched to the car. The door slammed, the engine roared to life, and the car turned around in the road. Wanda Nell, Mayrene, and the two girls watched as the car disappeared down the road.

"That's a hell of a note." Mayrene shook her head in disgust.

"Y'all come on inside," Wanda Nell said. "No point in standing out here. I don't know about y'all, but I'm ready for something to drink."

The girls and Mayrene followed her inside the trailer, and after Mayrene shut the door, she propped her shotgun in a corner.

In the kitchen, Mayrene gently pushed Wanda Nell into a chair. "You just sit there and relax a minute," she said, and Wanda Nell smiled gratefully. Mayrene opened the refrigerator and pulled out a two-liter bottle of Coke. She set it on the table, then retrieved four glasses from the cabinet. They each took turns pouring for themselves.

Mayrene raised her glass. "Here's to us girls. If we don't take care of things, it don't get done."

Juliet and Miranda giggled as they raised their glasses and clinked them against Mayrene's. Wanda Nell's eyes misted as she raised her glass with a slightly trembling hand.

"Thank the Lord for you, Mayrene," Wanda Nell said, "and that shotgun of yours." She drank from her glass. The cold liquid felt good going down. "How on earth did you find that guy?"

Juliet and Miranda listened avidly as Mayrene told her story. "I was in the bathroom touching up my makeup," she began, "and I thought I heard a bit of commotion over at your place, but when I came and looked out the window, I didn't see a damn thing. Then I went into the front bedroom to look for some old pictures I want to send my cousin, and while I was rooting around in there, I heard Elmer Lee and them deputies drive up. I looked out the window on that side for a second, but it didn't seem like nothing to worry about. I went on back to trying to find those pictures."

She paused for a drink. "I don't rightly know what made me do it, but I happened to look out the window on the end, and I caught sight of somebody moving around in Janette's trailer. I knew there wasn't nobody supposed to be in there, and I got a bit suspicious. While I was watching, I saw that idiot's head in the window. He still had on his mask, and I thought that was mighty peculiar." She chuckled, a deep, comforting sound. "Then I thought I'd better just see what the heck was going on over there. I grabbed Ol' Reliable, and we marched right on over there, just in time to see Bubba creeping around the side of the trailer with that bag of cash in his hand."

"Weren't you worried he might shoot you?" Miranda asked.

Mayrene laughed at that. "Honey, he was so busy trying to tiptoe around, he wasn't paying no attention. It was real obvious to me that he wasn't too bright in the first place. Otherwise, why would he be sneaking outta that trailer with the sheriff 's department right across the street?"

They all laughed along with Mayrene this time.

"I bet he about peed in his pants when you stuck that shotgun in his back." Wanda Nell spoke between giggles.

"I reckon those pants of his were a bit darker in one spot than they was before," Mayrene said, wiggling her eyebrows at the girls. They giggled, right on cue.

"Mayrene, you are something else," Wanda Nell said. She reached out and clasped one of her friend's hands. "I don't know what we'd do without you next door." She squeezed the hand, and Mayrene returned the pressure.

"That's all right, honey," Mayrene said. "I know you'd help me out if I needed it."

"Is it safe to come out now?" T.J. asked from the doorway to the kitchen.

"T.J.!" Mayrene almost knocked her chair over, she was in such a rush to get up and get to T.J. "I knew that was you I saw, boy! Come here and give me a hug, you rascal."

Laughing, T.J. complied. He clamped his arms around Mayrene and lifted her off her feet. That made her laugh, and T.J. set her down, finishing off with a big kiss on the cheek.

"Where the heck've you been, T.J.?" Mayrene demanded. "And how come you just now put in an appearance?"

Wanda Nell regarded her son curiously. That was a question she wanted to have answered herself. Her son had never lacked courage, so why was he hiding? She realized the answer might be something she didn't want to hear, but she needed to know, just the same.

T.J. shrugged. "No good reason, I guess. I'm just not looking for trouble these days."

"Elmer Lee took that guy off to jail," Wanda Nell said, "and it ain't gonna be long before he mentions you, I bet. So Elmer Lee's gonna know pretty soon you're hanging around."

"Then I reckon he'll know," T.J. said, his voice cool. He went to the cabinet to get himself a glass. Mayrene poured him some Coke, and he had a long sip.

"Who was that guy?" T.J. asked. He leaned his long frame against the counter.

"His name is David McKenna," Juliet answered. "We never heard of him, and we don't think he was one of the

men who broke in and tied up me and Miranda." Miranda
shook her head in agreement.

T.J. frowned. "Something about that name sounds familiar."

"Somebody you know?" Wanda Nell asked.

"Uh-uh," T.J. said. "But I think Daddy knew him."

Wanda Nell and Mayrene exchanged glances.

"You think he was in on whatever scam Bobby Ray had
going?" Mayrene asked.

T.J. shrugged. "Maybe. Daddy didn't do it by himself,
probably. He had to have some help, if he was stealing
money from the casino." He snapped his fingers. "That's it!
That's where I heard that guy's name. Daddy mentioned
him when I asked him about getting me a job at the casino."

Wanda Nell breathed a deep sigh of relief. "Then I guess
that's the end of it. This guy probably had a falling out with
Bobby Ray, and Bobby Ray ran off with the money. He
tracked Bobby Ray here and killed him, but Bobby Ray
didn't have the money on him." Satisfied, she leaned back
in her chair and drained the rest of the Coke from her glass.

"If that's so," Mayrene said, "then how do you explain
those goons that broke in here? Were they all working
together?"

Deflated, Wanda Nell sighed. "I don't know. Maybe the
casino sent them."

In the ensuing silence, they all heard car doors slamming
right outside.

"What on earth?" Wanda Nell said, rising from her chair.

A knock sounded at the front door. Wanda Nell went to
answer it.

Deputy Tracy Taylor, with another deputy at her back,
waited patiently on the stoop. Wanda Nell smiled a greeting. "Come on in, Deputy," she invited. "I'm sure y'all have
heard the good news."

"I know Deputy Johnson has a man in custody," Deputy

Taylor acknowledged, "but I'm afraid that's not what I'm here about, Miz Culpepper." She stared straight at Wanda Nell.

"What is it?" Wanda Nell was frightened by the implacable look on the deputy's face.

"I need to speak to your son, Miz Culpepper," the deputy said. She raised a hand, as if Wanda Nell had offered a protest. "And don't tell me he's not here. We know he is, if he hasn't run off in the last ten minutes."

"I'm here," T.J. said as he came into the room from the kitchen. He halted beside his mother and slid a comforting arm around her. "What do you want?"

"T.J. Culpepper," the deputy said, "I'm arresting you for the murder of your father, Bobby Ray Culpepper."

# Nineteen

"No," Wanda Nell said. Too much was happening, and too fast. She couldn't take it all in. But one thing she knew, her son hadn't killed his daddy. "No, you can't do this!"

"I'm sorry, Miz Culpepper," Deputy Taylor said, stone-faced. "But I've got a warrant for your son's arrest."

"I don't care if you have a warrant," Wanda Nell said. "My son didn't do this. Y'all have a man already who probably did it. Why are you coming after T.J.? I don't understand." T.J.'s arm tightened around her, but he wasn't saying anything.

"I'm sorry, Miz Culpepper," Deputy Taylor repeated. "But we have several witnesses who heard and saw a violent argument between your son and the deceased." She hesitated a moment, as if trying to make a decision. "And we also have his fingerprints from inside the truck of the second murder victim, Ricky Ratliff."

T.J.'s arm dropped from his mother's body. Wanda Nell could feel him go tense beside her. Hardly daring to breathe, she turned to stare up into his face. His features had hardened into an expression she knew only too well. Many a time she had confronted him over something bad he'd done, and he'd shown her this very same face.

"Honey," Wanda Nell whispered. "Tell them you didn't kill your daddy, or Ricky Ratliff."

T.J.'s face softened for a moment as he gazed back down at her. "I didn't do it, Mama, I swear."

Wanda Nell wanted desperately to believe him, but there was something in the way he held himself, a tension in him, that kept a bit of doubt in her mind. "Did you fight with your daddy, T.J.?"

T.J. expelled a long breath. He looked away. "Daddy and I had an argument, Mama, that's true. But I didn't kill him."

Deputy Taylor cleared her throat, then began reading T.J. his rights. Wanda Nell stood numbly by her son, barely aware that Mayrene and the girls had sidled into the living room. The sound of Juliet's weeping finally penetrated her fog, and Wanda Nell trembled. Her family was being torn apart, and she couldn't do anything about it.

The officer who had accompanied Deputy Taylor cuffed T.J.'s hands behind his back, and at that sight, Miranda started screaming. She rushed forward and attempted to hit the deputy who had begun to lead T.J. away. Deputy Taylor stepped forward and grabbed Miranda's hands, but Wanda Nell remained rooted to the spot. She knew she should do something, say something, but words failed her.

Mayrene rushed past Wanda Nell and grabbed Miranda, turning the girl's body into hers and wrapping strong arms around her. "Hush, now, Miranda. You ain't doing anybody a bit of good, carrying on like this. You just hush right now."

Wanda Nell felt a hand slip into hers, and her fingers closed convulsively on Juliet's. Juliet still wept, and Wanda Nell wanted to cry right along with her, but her eyes remained dry.

The two deputies hustled T.J. out of the trailer, and once they had him stowed safely in their car, Deputy Taylor came back to speak to Wanda Nell. "I'm sure sorry about this, Miz Culpepper, but we can't ignore the evidence. You might want to think about getting a lawyer for your son." Tipping her hat, she walked back to the car.

Wanda Nell stared helplessly out the door as the car drove away.

"Mama, what are we going to do?" Juliet asked her. "We can't let them keep T.J. in jail. He didn't do it, did he, Mama? Did he?"

Juliet's voice rose in pitch with each word, and finally the near-hysteria penetrated Wanda Nell's inertia. "No, honey," she said, her voice strong and clear, "T.J. didn't kill anybody. I don't care what kind of evidence they say they got, he didn't do it, and we're not gonna let 'em get away with saying he did."

"I'm gonna call my cousin," Mayrene said, pushing a still sniffling Miranda into a chair. "I'm sure she can get her boss to represent T.J."

"But it's Sunday," Miranda said, still sniffling.

"That don't matter, honey," Mayrene said. "Lawyers have to work strange hours, too."

"Thanks, Mayrene," Wanda Nell said. "While you do that, I'm gonna change clothes. We're gonna need some money to pay that lawyer, and since I know I sure don't have enough to pay him, I'm gonna talk to the one person in this family who does."

Leaving the girls with Mayrene, Wanda Nell hurried to her bedroom and changed as quickly as she could into one of her good dresses and the shoes that matched. She combed her hair carefully and applied her makeup with a hand that didn't tremble. If she was going to see the old battle-ax—T.J.'s grandmother—she wanted to look her best.

Checking to be sure her cell phone was in her purse, Wanda Nell hurried back to the living room. Both Miranda and Juliet had stopped crying, she noticed, and Mayrene had put them to work cleaning.

"My cousin's gonna talk to her boss for you," Mayrene told her. "Here's his number. You call him soon as you finish talking to the old harpy. Okay?"

Wanda Nell accepted the piece of paper, then leaned forward and kissed Mayrene's cheek. "Thank you," she said.

"You want me to go with you?"

Wanda Nell shook her head. "No, if you stay here, I'll feel better about leaving the girls right now. There ain't nothing the old woman can do to me or say to me today that's any worse than what's already happened."

"That's the spirit," Mayrene said. "You go tell her what's what."

Smiling briefly, Wanda Nell retrieved her car keys from the kitchen, then headed for the door. "I'll call as soon as I know something."

During the short drive into town and up Main Street toward the old Culpepper house, Wanda Nell did her best to organize her thoughts and figure out what she was going to say to her former mother-in-law. But her mind kept skittering around. T.J. had to be innocent. He just had to be!

But that little worm of doubt kept niggling at her. What had T.J. and Bobby Ray fought about? And how the hell had T.J.'s fingerprints come to be in Ricky Ratliff's truck?

A chilling thought struck her: What if someone in the sheriff's department was trying to frame T.J.? Surely somebody was working with that David McKenna, otherwise he wouldn't have shown up at her door so soon after she called the sheriff's department to report what she had found.

Wanda Nell pulled into the driveway of Mrs. Culpepper's house and shut off the car. She sat there for a moment, trying to collect herself for what she was going to have to go through with the old biddy. She stared up at the house she had visited only a few times during her marriage to Bobby Ray. His parents had never really approved of her, and the elder Mrs. Culpepper had never gone out of her way to invite Wanda Nell and the children there.

At least, Wanda Nell amended mentally, Mrs. Culpepper had never invited her and the girls that often. T.J. had been so obviously his father's son that the elder Culpeppers had doted on him. Wanda Nell was counting on that now, to enlist the old woman's aid.

Wanda Nell got out of the car and strode up the walk to the front door. She put her finger on the bell and held it down for five or six seconds. Both Mrs. Culpepper and Charlesetta, her maid, were hard-of-hearing.

She was just about to ring the bell again when she could see someone approaching through the beveled glass of the door. Slowly the door swung open to reveal Charlesetta's plump black face. She was about the same age as her employer, but Charlesetta looked a good fifteen years younger. Largely, Wanda Nell suspected, because Charlesetta had a kind heart and a sunny disposition. How she had ever stood working for Mrs. Culpepper for over forty years, Wanda Nell had no idea.

"Good morning, Charlesetta," Wanda Nell said. "I need to see Mrs. Culpepper."

Charlesetta frowned. "I'm sorry, Miz Wanda Nell, I'm afraid she ain't up to seeing nobody today." She started to close the door.

Inserting a foot into the doorway, Wanda Nell said, "And I'm sorry, Charlesetta, but I have to see her. I don't care how she's feeling. This is an emergency, and she's gonna talk to me, one way or another."

Charlesetta bridled at Wanda Nell's tone, and Wanda Nell reached out impulsively and clasped the old woman's hand. "I'm sorry, Charlesetta," she said softly. "But it's about T.J. He's in trouble, and I need Mrs. Culpepper's help."

"Oh, Miz Wanda Nell, what has that boy done now?" Charlesetta forgot the affront. T.J. was as much her favorite as he was his grandmother's. "I declare, that boy is such a caution. It's a wonder he ain't put Miz Culpepper in the grave, and on top of his daddy being killed." She shook her head dolefully as she opened the door. "You come on in."

"Thank you," Wanda Nell replied as she stepped inside. "Where is she?"

Charlesetta jerked her head. "In the parlor." She shut the door. "She in a bad way today, and that ain't no lie. You'll see. I been praying to the Lord to help her, but I think He's just too busy right now. She be hurting something awful, and you know what she does when she like that."

Sighing, Wanda Nell nodded. Mrs. Culpepper's solace was Jim Beam. Over the years, and particularly since the judge's death, Mrs. Culpepper had taken to drinking more and more. Finding her sober was a rarity on the few occasions her path crossed with Wanda Nell's.

"I best go be making some coffee. You just call me if you need something." Charlesetta went back down the hall toward the kitchen while Wanda Nell steadied herself with a deep breath. Then, her stomach knotting, she crossed the hall to the parlor and stepped inside.

The smell hit her first. The room reeked of the sour odors of old age and too much whisky. Mrs. Culpepper sprawled across one end of the sofa, her housecoat hiked up over her thighs and her hair in a tangled, sweaty mass around her red face. Wanda Nell glanced away. She knew the old woman would be furious at being caught like this, but she didn't have any choice.

"Miz Culpepper," Wanda Nell said.

The old woman didn't stir.

"Miz Culpepper," Wanda Nell repeated, raising her voice.

The head moved, and Mrs. Culpepper began to blink her eyes and try to focus on the source of the sound.

"Miz Culpepper, I got to talk to you."

Now slightly more alert, Mrs. Culpepper attempted to sit up. After a moment's hesitation, Wanda Nell moved forward to offer a helping hand. At first, Mrs. Culpepper accepted it, but when she realized who her visitor was, she drew back sharply, as if she had been burned.

"What are you doing here?"

The old woman gazed up at her blearily. She patted her hair with one hand and pulled on her housecoat with the other in a vain attempt to make herself look more presentable.

"I don't want you in my house." Mrs. Culpepper's head swiveled as she glanced around the room. "Where's my medicine?"

"I don't know, Miz Culpepper," Wanda Nell said. "I need to talk to you."

"Don't wanna talk to you. Go 'way."

"I'm not going anywhere, Miz Culpepper," Wanda Nell said. "So you better just make up your mind to listen to me." She waited.

"I want my medicine," Mrs. Culpepper whined. "Give me my medicine, and then you go away."

"No." If the old woman drank any more whisky she'd pass out again, and Wanda Nell had to avoid that.

"Charlesetta! Get in here!" Mrs. Culpepper bellowed so loudly that she startled Wanda Nell into taking a couple of steps backward.

"Now listen here, Miz Culpepper," Wanda Nell said, moving forward again. "Charlesetta's in the kitchen making you some coffee, and you're gonna drink it. You hear me? I got to talk to you, and you can't have any more medicine till you listen to me."

Wanda Nell wished Bobby Ray could see what his mother had become. The years of heavy drinking had taken their toll, and Wanda Nell blamed Bobby Ray for it all. He had always treated his mama like dirt, and in turn she treated everyone else the same way. The worse he behaved, the more Mrs. Culpepper retreated into the bottle. Wanda Nell had some sympathy for her, but she didn't excuse what Mrs. Culpepper chose to do to herself and those around her.

"You get out of my house!"

"Screaming at me ain't going to accomplish a damn thing," Wanda Nell said, holding tight to her temper. She sat down on the sofa beside the old woman. "Look at me, Miz Culpepper. You pay attention to what I'm telling you."

Wanda Nell felt the heat of Mrs. Culpepper's hatred of her, but she didn't wilt. "I got to talk to you about T.J."

"What? What about T.J.? What's he done now?" Despite the strident tone of her voice, the old woman softened. Her lips quivered into a smile. "When's he going to come see me? Is he with you?"

"No, he's not, and that's why I'm here. He's in jail, Miz Culpepper, and he needs your help."

Mrs. Culpepper turned away from her. "Only thing he wants from me is money. All the time, that's all anybody wants. Charlesetta is robbing me blind every day, and soon I'm not even going to have a roof over my head."

"Now, don't start in on Charlesetta," Wanda Nell said, "you know she's good to you." *Better than anybody else would be,* she added silently. "She's not stealing from you."

Mrs. Culpepper snorted.

"T.J.'s in bad trouble this time, Miz Culpepper, otherwise I wouldn't be here."

Something in Wanda Nell's tone must have penetrated the fog of alcohol still clouding the older woman's brain. She made an effort to focus.

"What'd he do?"

"He didn't do anything," Wanda Nell said, speaking slowly and clearly. "But the sheriff's department thinks he was the one that killed Bobby Ray."

"That's a lie! There's no way that boy would have killed his daddy." Mrs. Culpepper struggled to get to her feet, but the effort was too much for her.

"I know that," Wanda Nell replied. "And that's why I'm here. T.J. is gonna need a good lawyer, but I don't have that kind of money. Pretty soon they're gonna figure out they're wrong about T.J. Least, I hope they are, but in the meantime, we've got to be sure he's got a good lawyer."

Mrs. Culpepper nodded vigorously as Wanda Nell spoke. Her eyes began clearing, and, as if on cue, Charlesetta came in with a tray. She set the tray down on a nearby table, then handed her employer a steaming cup of black coffee. Mrs. Culpepper grimaced, but she sipped at it.

"Charlesetta, go and run me a hot bath," she said, and the maid nodded.

"Yes'm" was all she said.

Mrs. Culpepper drank more of the coffee. Then she set the cup down on the table beside the sofa. "I'm going to help my grandson. I'm going to do it for his sake. Not for you. You understand that?"

Wanda Nell waited a moment before she spoke. "Yes, I understand that. I know you wouldn't spit on me if I was on fire, but I don't give a damn about that. All I'm concerned about is my son."

Mrs. Culpepper smiled at her, and Wanda Nell felt her skin crawl. The malice in the old woman's eyes frightened her.

"I'm going to help my grandson," Mrs. Culpepper repeated. "But it's going to cost you."

"What . . . what do you mean?"

"I mean you're going to be in my debt," Mrs. Culpepper said. "And when the time comes, I'm going to expect you to pay up and not argue about it."

"If you're talking about the money," Wanda Nell said, struggling to breathe easily, "I'll find some way to pay you back. If the money means that much to you."

"It's not money I want," Mrs. Culpepper said. "I'll find another way for you to pay me back."

"What do you mean?" Wanda Nell had the sudden urge to bolt from the room and not look back, but she couldn't. T.J.'s life might be at stake here. She forced herself to sit still and stare back at the old woman with an unwavering gaze.

"First you have to promise, and then later on, I'll tell you what I want."

"That's insane," Wanda Nell protested.

Mrs. Culpepper laughed, a rusty sound. "But that's your only option, Wanda Nell. Take it or leave it."

Wanda Nell knew she should just get up and walk out. The old woman loved T.J. too much to let him be accused of murder without fighting back. At least she had thought so. But she was also hateful enough to do this simply to spite Wanda Nell.

"I'll take it."

Mrs. Culpepper smiled and hoisted herself to her feet. "Now I want you out of my house. I'll take care of my grandson, but I don't want to see you until I'm ready to take you up on your promise." She shuffled away without looking back once.

Wanda Nell sat unmoving on the sofa until Mrs. Culpepper had disappeared up the stairs. The old house, stuffed with antiques and with the memories of generations of Culpeppers, pressed in on her until she wanted to scream.

# Twenty

"Miz Wanda Nell, you all right?"

Wanda Nell hadn't heard Charlesetta come back in the room, but the sound of the elderly woman's voice pulled her back into the present.

"I'm okay," Wanda Nell said, smiling wanly. "Just a little worried."

"Yes'm," Charlesetta said, frowning doubtfully down at her. "I heard what you told Miz Culpepper 'bout Mister T.J." She shook her head dolefully. "Lord knows that boy done some bad things before, but he ain't never done nothing like killing nobody."

"No, he hasn't," Wanda Nell agreed, getting slowly to her feet. "And he didn't kill his daddy."

"No'm," Charlesetta said, her head bobbing up and down for emphasis. "He be a good boy at heart, that he surely is. And Miz Culpepper gonna get him a fine lawyer, and that lawyer gonna make sure everybody know Mister T.J. didn't kill nobody."

"I almost forgot," Wanda Nell said, opening her purse and reaching inside. Her fingers closed on the scrap of paper Mayrene had given her. She handed it to Charlesetta. "Please give this to Miz Culpepper. It's the number for a lawyer."

"Yes'm," Charlesetta said, accepting the paper. She peered at the name and number. "Hamilton Tucker. Oh, I heard of him. He's a real good lawyer, they say. Miz Culpepper know of him, I'm pretty sure."

"Good," Wanda Nell said. She put her hand briefly on Charlesetta's arm. "Tell me, Charlesetta, is Miz Culpepper . . ." She floundered to a stop. Taking a deep breath, she plunged ahead, "Is she losing her mind?"

Charlesetta's eyes widened. "Oh, Lord, Miz Wanda Nell. What she been saying now?" She drew herself up. "She better not be telling nobody I been stealing from her again. They's limits to what a body can stand."

"When she says something like that, it's just the medicine talking," Wanda Nell prevaricated. "Anybody knows her, they know that. As long as you've worked for her, nobody's gonna believe a word about you stealing from her."

"They better not," Charlesetta said, sniffing. "But what she say to you?"

Shrugging, Wanda Nell said, "Just something about me paying her back for helping T.J., but it's not money she wants. You have any idea what she's talking about?"

"Ain't no telling, Miz Wanda Nell," Charlesetta replied. "I sometimes doubt even the Good Lord Himself know what be going on in that head of hers." She sniffed loudly again. "That old 'medicine' she be drinking just keep her all mixed up. I tries to hide it sometimes, but she get real mad if she think I be keeping it from her."

"Charlesetta, I think the Lord'll have a special place in heaven for you, after all you been through with that old woman." Wanda Nell tried to make light of it, but the grim picture behind Charlesetta's words saddened her deeply. She hadn't realized just how bad Mrs. Culpepper had gotten with her drinking.

"That ain't for me to say, Miz Wanda Nell," Charlesetta replied, "but I can't look after her much longer. I be so tired all the time, it all I can do to go up them stairs once or twice a day." She sighed heavily. "She been real bad ever since they come to tell her about Mister Bobby Ray. She been grieving over him something terrible. It don't matter he treated her worse than a dog, she still his mama."

"Yeah, he didn't treat her any better than he treated anybody else."

"That boy," Charlesetta sighed. "He was an imp of Satan when he was little, and he just got worse." She sighed again. "Always coming home to his mama with his messes and expecting her to clean 'em up for him. And him still bringing his dirty laundry home to his mama, and him all grown." She shook her head dolefully. "No matter what time of night, he come knocking on that door, and I be the one got to get up and answer it. No matter how he put nobody out."

"Yes, I know," Wanda Nell said. "But Miz Culpepper's not going to take comfort from me, the way she feels. I'm sure sorry you have to have it all dumped on you."

"Don't you be worrying about us," Charlesetta said, returning the consoling pat on the arm. "The Lord'll provide, one way or another. I know He will."

"Bless you, Charlesetta," Wanda Nell said. "I better get going." Charlesetta offered her a sweet smile as she escorted her to the front door.

Charlesetta had her hand on the doorknob when old Mrs. Culpepper's voice floated imperiously down the stairs. "Charlesetta! Tell Wanda Nell to wait for me."

"Yes'm," Charlesetta shouted back. She shrugged at Wanda Nell.

"What do you reckon she wants?" Wanda Nell whispered. All of a sudden, she wanted to bolt out the front door.

Charlesetta shrugged again. "Ain't no telling with her, Miz Wanda Nell."

"Charlesetta!"

"Yes'm?" The elderly maid went to the foot of the stairs and looked up. "What you need, Miz Culpepper?"

"I need your help getting dressed, you old fool. Get up here!"

Charlesetta mumbled something under her breath, but she began to make her way slowly up the stairs. Wanda Nell called softly to her. "I'll go wait." Charlesetta paused for a moment, nodded her head in acknowledgment, then continued her slow progress upwards, stopping every three or four steps to rest for a moment.

Wanda Nell walked back into the parlor and resumed her former seat. Glancing around the room, she shuddered. This house needed light and laughter and a good airing. The smell of the drunken old woman who spent too much of her time in this room made Wanda Nell's nose twitch.

She wished she had the courage to tell the old woman to go to hell and walk out of here. But she was afraid she might need Mrs. Culpepper's money, and if putting up with the old hellcat and her insane demands was the only way to save T.J., she'd just have to do it.

Half an hour later, Wanda Nell was on the point of going outside for a few minutes simply in order to breathe some fresh air. Mrs. Culpepper came clumping down the stairs as she walked into the hallway.

Either the bath or Charlesetta, or maybe both, had worked wonders with Mrs. Culpepper. The contrast between the elegant society matron on the stairs now and the drunken wreck on the parlor sofa amazed Wanda Nell.

"Don't stand there gawping at me, Wanda Nell," Mrs. Culpepper said, holding her heavy pocketbook against her scrawny bosom. She came down the last few stairs and brushed past Wanda Nell to open the front door. "Come along, girl."

Wanda Nell trailed outside behind Mrs. Culpepper, who had paused on the porch. "Go park that junk heap of yours on the street, Wanda Nell. I'm ashamed for anyone to see it in my driveway or in front of my house, but I suppose it can't be helped. We'll take my car to see the lawyer, and you will drive. I have a bit of a headache."

Wanda Nell seethed at the old woman's high-handedness, but there was no point in arguing with her. No matter how petty the old witch was, Wanda Nell was determined to hold on to her temper.

Her car moved, Wanda Nell walked back up the driveway to meet Mrs. Culpepper in front of the garage. Mrs. Culpepper punched a button, and the garage door rose. She handed her keys to Wanda Nell and waited until Wanda Nell had backed the Cadillac out. She closed the garage door, then got into the car.

"Well, what are you waiting for?"

"Nothing," Wanda Nell muttered as she continued backing out of the driveway. "Where's the lawyer's office?"

"On the square, in the old Howell Building," Mrs. Culpepper replied. "I spoke with his secretary. She's expecting us."

During the brief drive up Main Street to the town square, Mrs. Culpepper didn't speak again. Wanda Nell found a parking space in front of the building, and Mrs. Culpepper left her to lock the car. By the time Wanda Nell got inside, the old woman was stepping into the elevator.

Wanda Nell stuck out a hand to keep the doors from closing, and Mrs. Culpepper merely said "Third floor" as Wanda Nell stumbled into the elevator. Casting a resentful glance at the old woman, Wanda Nell punched the button.

The doors slid open on the third floor, and Mrs. Culpepper stepped out. Wanda Nell moved around her and peered at a sign on the wall opposite them. "This way," she said, turning to the left.

Halfway down the hall she found the name HAMILTON TUCKER lettered in gold above the words ATTORNEY AT LAW. Opening the door, she strode in, not bothering to let Mrs. Culpepper precede her. The old woman closed the door with an audible thump.

Wanda Nell examined the reception area. The decor was tasteful and understated, exactly what she thought a lawyer's office should look like. Several empty chairs awaited their choice, and magazines lay in neatly stacked piles on a couple of small endtables. Ahead of them, a frosted-glass, sliding window sported a card which read PLEASE RING BELL FOR ASSISTANCE.

Before either of them could ring the bell, the window slid open, and a plump, beaming face greeted them.

"Y'all must be Miz Lucretia Culpepper and Miz Wanda Nell Culpepper," the woman said. "I'm Blanche Tillman, Mr. Tucker's administrative assistant."

"I'm here to see Mr. Tucker," Mrs. Culpepper announced. "Kindly tell him I'm here."

Blanche Tillman's smile tightened a fraction at the old woman's peremptory tone. "I'm afraid, Miz Culpepper," she said, "that Mr. Tucker isn't here right this minute. He's over at the jail, taking care of your grandson. But if y'all don't mind sitting down and making yourselves comfortable for a few minutes, he'll be along real soon."

"I don't suppose I have much choice," Mrs. Culpepper grumbled. She stalked over to a chair and plopped herself down.

Wanda Nell stepped up to the window. In an undertone, she said, "I really appreciate you getting Mr. Tucker to take T.J.'s case, Miz Tillman. And especially on a Sunday, when I'm sure you got plenty of better things to do."

Blanche winked at Wanda Nell. "Honey, just call me Blanche. Anybody's as good a friend of Mayrene's as you are, I'm mighty glad to help. And don't worry about it being Sunday. This is a lot more interesting than listening to my husband snoring on the couch." She tilted her head slightly in the direction of Mrs. Culpepper. "Mayrene told me about that old biddy, Wanda Nell. Don't let her rile you, hear?"

Wanda Nell smiled her thanks. Blanche wasn't going to be bullied by the likes of Mrs. Culpepper. She felt better.

"Now, can I get y'all something?" Blanche asked, raising her voice. "Some coffee, or tea, or maybe a Coke?"

"Nothing for me," Mrs. Culpepper said. She sat with her pocketbook in her lap, her hands folded primly across it.

"I'm fine, thanks," Wanda Nell said.

"Okay, y'all change your mind, you just let me know," Blanche said. She closed the window.

Wanda Nell found a seat across the room from Mrs. Culpepper and glanced idly through the stack of magazines on the table beside her. She didn't particularly want to try to talk to her former mother-in-law, and Mrs. Culpepper had made it clear she didn't have much to say to her.

Glancing at her watch occasionally, Wanda Nell passed the time leafing through magazines. A half hour passed, then another, and Wanda Nell wondered whether Mrs. Culpepper was wanting a nip of Jim Beam, the way she was twitching around in her chair.

The office door opened, and a tall, dark-haired man strode in. He paused in the middle of the room and looked back and forth between Wanda Nell and Mrs. Culpepper. "Good afternoon, ladies," he said, in a deep, pleasant voice.

Wanda Nell examined him curiously. Her heart sank when she saw how young he was. He couldn't be any more than thirty, and she was afraid he didn't have enough experience to help T.J. out of the jam he was in.

"You must be Mrs. Culpepper," he said, bending over the old woman and clasping her outstretched hand.

"Mr. Tucker," she responded, tilting her head coquettishly. "How good of you to see me on such short notice."

"I'm delighted to be of assistance, Mrs. Culpepper," he said. "I must tell you, I had the greatest respect and admiration for your late husband, Judge Culpepper." He patted her hand.

"He was a wonderful man," Mrs. Culpepper simpered. "Thank you."

*Old buzzard was more like it,* Wanda Nell thought. The late judge's capacity for Jim Beam and young, attractive secretaries had been legendary. But he had been a powerful force in Tullahoma, and few in town had ever crossed him successfully.

Hamilton Tucker turned and walked over to Wanda Nell. "And you are T.J.'s mother," he said, extending a hand.

Up close, he appeared slightly older. Wanda Nell noticed a few lines around his deep-set brown eyes. Maybe he was over thirty after all. He clasped her hand warmly, and Wanda Nell gazed up into a handsome face with a determined chin. He smiled warmly at her.

"Don't worry about T.J., Mrs. Culpepper." The confidence in his voice reassured her. "I promise you I'll do my best for him."

"Young man," Mrs. Culpepper said, getting to her feet, "I am the one who is hiring you, not her. If you are ready, I would like to discuss my grandson's case with you."

"Certainly, Mrs. Culpepper." Hamilton Tucker faced the old woman. "Why don't y'all come right on in to my office?" He moved forward to open the door to the inner chambers. He gestured for the two women to precede him. Mrs. Culpepper turned to Wanda Nell and said, "There's no need for you to accompany me, Wanda Nell. I'll take care of everything."

Wanda Nell stared at the old woman.

"I think—," Hamilton Tucker began, but Mrs. Culpepper cut him off.

"As long as I am paying your legal fees, young man, I am perfectly entitled to speak to you alone." With that, Mrs. Culpepper swept into the inner office.

Hamilton Tucker shrugged at Wanda Nell.

"It doesn't matter," Wanda Nell said, sagging back into her chair. "Go ahead and talk to her, and if you need me, I'll be right here."

"Thank you, Mrs. Culpepper," Tucker said. "I would like to talk to you." He smiled, then followed the elder Mrs. Culpepper through the door.

Wanda Nell sat and stared at the closed door, struggling to hold her temper. What was the old biddy up to? Wanda Nell didn't trust her, not one bit. But there wasn't a damn thing she could do about it, because she needed the old witch and her money.

A few minutes later, the door opened again, and out came Blanche Tillman. She came over and sat down by Wanda Nell.

"Honey, I have to tell you, I don't know how you can put up with that old harpy." Blanche patted Wanda Nell's arm. "I'd be about ready to push her in front of a truck by now."

Wanda Nell laughed. "Believe me, I've been tempted, many a time." She sobered. "But right now, I ain't got much choice, Blanche. T.J. needs a lawyer, and she's the only one who can afford one."

"Maybe," Blanche said. "I sure hope your son's gonna appreciate what you're having to put up with for his sake."

Wanda Nell bridled slightly at the implied criticism. "That don't really matter. I'll do whatever I have to. The only thing that's important is getting my son out of jail."

"I know, honey, I know," Blanche said.

The door opened, surprising them both. Hamilton Tucker stood in the doorway, an odd expression on his face.

"Would you join us, Mrs. Culpepper?" He frowned. "There is something I think you should hear."

Wanda Nell got to her feet, her stomach all at once tightening into a knot. "Sure."

Tucker waved her through the door, and she followed him into an inner chamber. The space was large and comfortable, the walls lined with bookshelves full of law books. Mrs. Culpepper sat dwarfed in a big leather chair in front of a massive old desk, and Tucker motioned for Wanda Nell to be seated in its twin. He went around the desk and sat down.

"Mrs. Culpepper," he said, nodding his head in the direction of the old woman, "wants to put a condition on her assistance for her grandson, and I told her that you had to be told what it was."

Wanda Nell couldn't look at her former mother-in-law. "What is it?"

Tucker glanced down at his hands, resting on top of the desk. Then he looked back up at Wanda Nell. "In return for paying all of your son's legal fees, Mrs. Culpepper wants you to give her custody of your daughters and grandson. She wants them to come live with her because, she says, you are an unfit mother."

# Twenty-One

Wanda Nell came up out of her chair, ready to claw the old woman's eyes out. She caught herself in time, though, before she actually laid a hand on Mrs. Culpepper.

The lawyer had jumped up from his chair and moved, lightning-quick, around the desk to get between the two women. Wanda Nell forced herself to take a step backward, and Tucker halted, mere inches away from her. Wanda Nell took another step backward. He eyed the two of them warily, ready to move if he had to.

The blood pounding in her ears, Wanda Nell heard herself say, "You are absolutely out of your mind, old woman! Where the hell do *you* get off, telling anybody I'm not a good mother? I work my tail off to take care of my girls and my grandson. You've never raised a finger to do a damn thing for them. You don't even know when their birthdays are."

Mrs. Culpepper had shrunk back in her chair at first, but when she saw the lawyer ready to keep Wanda Nell away from her, she relaxed. "You see what she's like? Those girls need to be rescued from that coarse environment before it's too late."

"What planet do you live on, old woman?" Chest heaving, Wanda Nell took a step closer to Mrs. Culpepper.

The lawyer tensed and held up a warning hand. "Now, ladies, I think this has gone far enough. We need to sit down and discuss this calmly and rationally."

"How can you stand there and listen to such crap?" Wanda Nell jerked a hand in Mrs. Culpepper's direction. "I think we oughta be talking about having her committed to Whitfield instead."

Mrs. Culpepper didn't like the sound of that. "Nobody is sending me off to any mental hospital. I'm just as sane as the next person, I'll have you know."

"Tell it to Jim Beam," Wanda Nell said, and the old woman actually flinched.

Tucker leaned back against the desk, his legs stretched before him. Wanda Nell would have to step over him to get to the old woman. He nodded politely when she chose to resume her seat.

"Ladies, I want you to listen to me." He folded his arms across his chest and regarded each of them in turn, his gaze stern and unyielding.

"Yes, you just explain it all to her," Mrs. Culpepper said, leaning forward eagerly. "I'm sure you can take care of it quite easily, can't you?" Her hands fumbled with the clasp of her pocketbook. "I've got my checkbook right here. Money is no object, I assure you."

Wanda Nell gripped the arms of her chair. She was so angry she could have ripped the leather right off the frame. She couldn't listen to any more of this craziness.

"Mrs. Culpepper," Tucker said, speaking to the old woman. "I want you to listen to me, and listen very carefully." He waited until her attention was focused on him before continuing. "I cannot do what you ask. No judge is simply going to award you custody of your granddaughters and your great grandson just because you want them to. Furthermore, I will not be a party to the kind of bargain you are suggesting. No judge would uphold such an agreement, especially one made under such obvious duress."

He paused, but Mrs. Culpepper did not respond.

"Do you understand me, Mrs. Culpepper? I cannot, and I will not, do as you ask. But I will agree to act on your grandson's behalf, if you want me to."

Mrs. Culpepper rose unsteadily to her feet. She clutched her pocketbook to her chest. "Young man, I will not be spoken to in those tones. I cannot believe you have the slightest regard for my late husband. If you did, you would do everything in your power to do what I want." She cast a venomous glance at Wanda Nell. "This piece of trash here has no doubt promised you something so that you won't listen to me. I'm not in the least surprised she's reneging on her pledge to me." Before either of them realized what she was going to do, the old woman spat on the floor, just missing Tucker's shoes.

"Mrs. Culpepper!" The lawyer shot up straight, and for a moment, Wanda Nell thought she was going to have to get between him and the old woman.

Mrs. Culpepper ignored them both as she made her way to the door. Her hand on the knob, she turned back to them for a moment. "You leave me no choice. I'll have to seek legal help elsewhere. Fortunately, there are still men in Tullahoma who remember my husband. They'll do their utmost to see that justice prevails. I can promise you that."

She had the door open and was about to leave when Wanda Nell called out to her. "Here, you'll need these." She brandished the car keys in her fist. When she had Mrs. Culpepper's attention, she threw them at her. They hit the wall near the door and dropped to the floor at the old woman's feet. Mrs. Culpepper didn't say a word as she bent down unsteadily and scooped up the keys.

"Give my regards to Jim Beam," Wanda Nell called out. The door slammed shut behind Mrs. Culpepper.

Wanda Nell turned back to find Hamilton Tucker regarding her with a curious smile. "I'm sorry," she said. "You must think I'm awful, acting that way."

"I would say you had plenty of provocation," Tucker responded.

"Yeah, but I shouldn't let her get to me like that. What am I going to do now, Mr. Tucker? Without her money, I can't afford a lawyer for T.J. And I sure can't afford a lawyer to keep her from taking my girls away from me." Reaction began to set in, and Wanda Nell shivered. She rubbed her arms up and down to warm herself.

Tucker walked over to a cabinet and opened a door. He reached for a bottle, took out the stopper, and poured something into a glass. He brought the glass over to Wanda Nell. "Drink this," he commanded.

"What is it?" Wanda Nell eyed the tea-colored liquid suspiciously.

"Brandy," Tucker replied. "A little bit won't hurt you. I think you could use it right about now."

Cautiously, Wanda Nell sipped at it. She wasn't sure she liked the taste, but she let it slide down her throat. In a few seconds, as she continued to sip, her shivers subsided, and she felt warmth spreading through her body.

"That's better," Tucker said. He had resumed his seat behind the desk.

"Thank you," Wanda Nell said. "I never had brandy before."

"It's useful, on occasion." He smiled at her again. "Now, let's talk about your son's case."

"I can't afford to pay you much," Wanda Nell interrupted. "But if you'll let me pay it out over time, I'll pay you whatever it takes, I swear." She'd have to stop making extra payments on the trailer, for one thing. And if she put her mind to it, there were bound to be other ways she could find more money.

"It may not cost as much as you think," Tucker told her kindly. "But don't worry about it. Please. In certain cases, I'm willing to work for less than my usual fee. I think this qualifies as one of those cases."

"Thank you," Wanda Nell mumbled, embarrassed. Any other time she would have argued, but in this situation, she couldn't afford to be too proud to accept help.

She drank down the last of the brandy and set the glass on the edge of Tucker's desk. "Can she really do it?" she asked abruptly. "I mean, can she really get a judge to take my girls away from me?"

"I doubt it," Tucker replied. Leaning back in his chair, he restlessly played with a pen as he regarded her. "At least, not as easily as she seems to think. She certainly has her own ideas about reality, but in this case, she's way off base. You don't need to worry about her, Mrs. Culpepper."

Wanda Nell shuddered again. "I hate that name! Whenever I hear somebody call me that, it makes me think of that old witch. Please, can't you just call me Wanda Nell?"

Tucker grinned boyishly at her, and Wanda Nell couldn't help responding. He sure was good-looking, and she noticed that he wasn't wearing a wedding ring. *Stop that,* she admonished herself. *What are you thinking?*

"I will," he said, "if you'll call me Tuck." He twirled his pen in his fingers, then laid it aside. "Now, down to business. Let's talk about T.J."

"You saw him?" Wanda Nell asked. "Is he okay? Are they treating him decent?"

"He's fine, Wanda Nell. Don't you worry. They're not going to do anything to him." He leaned forward on the desk. "T.J. told me the sheriff and your father were good friends, once upon a time. Is that true?"

Wanda Nell nodded. "Until about a year before my daddy died, they were real close. And the sheriff has always been real good to me, when T.J. was in trouble before."

"That's what T.J. said, and if that's the case, then I don't think you need to worry. Nobody's going to cross the sheriff when he takes a personal interest in someone."

"No, I guess not," Wanda Nell conceded. She felt part of the weight lifting off her heart. "But we still got to prove that he didn't kill his daddy."

"I'll be working on that. I had a long talk with T.J., and what he told me, I believe. I don't think your son is guilty, Wanda Nell, but it's going to take some time to get everything sorted out."

"What's going to happen now? I reckon it's different from the other times when he was in trouble. This being such a serious case."

"Well, first, T.J. has to go before a magistrate. The sheriff's department will tell the magistrate why they think T.J. is guilty and should be charged with the crime, and the magistrate will decide whether T.J. should be bound over to the grand jury for indictment."

"Okay," Wanda Nell said. "When will they do that? And will T.J. be able to get out on bond?"

"They have forty-eight hours to take him before a magistrate, and it's up to the magistrate to set the bond." He hesitated. "Don't get your hopes up, Wanda Nell. The magistrate most likely will set the bond so high that T.J. won't be released. Given his previous record, they'll probably consider him a flight risk."

"Then he'll have to stay in jail," Wanda Nell said. Her head bent, she fumbled in her purse for a Kleenex. She couldn't find one. She looked up to see Tucker leaning across the desk, a box in his hand. "Thank you." She plucked out several and dabbed at her eyes with one.

"Yes, he'll probably have to stay in jail," Tucker replied. "But we're going to do our best to get him out of there. The grand jury isn't scheduled to meet for several months."

"Several months?" Wanda Nell couldn't bear to think about that.

"I know it sounds awful," Tucker said with sympathy. "But unless the district attorney decides that the grand jury needs to be called sooner, I'm afraid that's the way it has to be. But the good thing is that it gives me plenty of time to develop T.J.'s defense, should it be necessary."

"What do you mean by that?"

"I'll know more when T.J. goes before the magistrate. At that point, the sheriff's department will have to say what evidence they have against T.J. Till then I won't really know what kind of case they have against him. But based on what T.J. has told me, I have to say that the case against him has to be pretty shaky. I'm confident that we can prove he's innocent."

"What did he tell you?" Wanda Nell asked.

"I'm afraid I can't really tell you," Tucker said, his face expressing his regret. "That falls under attorney-client privilege. But it doesn't mean that T.J. can't tell you himself, when you see him."

"Okay, I guess." Wanda Nell said. She wondered whether T.J. would really talk to her. She tried to push her doubts away. "When am I going to be able to see him?"

"Normally, the jail has strict visiting hours, two days a week, but in your case, since the sheriff is a friend of the family, I imagine you might be able to get around the rules."

Wanda Nell hated asking anyone for favors, and she felt uncomfortable at the thought of calling the sheriff. Tucker evidently read her discomfort in her face. "I can call the sheriff for you, Wanda Nell. Just leave it to me."

Relieved, Wanda Nell smiled. "Thank you, Tuck." The nickname sounded funny when she finally said it, but she would have to get used to it. She couldn't call him "Mr. Tucker" with him calling her "Wanda Nell."

"Let me get your phone number, Wanda Nell."

She gave it to him, along with her cell phone number and the numbers of the Kountry Kitchen and Budget Mart, just in case.

"Now, if you don't mind, I need to ask you a few questions. T.J. was able to tell me a lot, but I need to hear some of it directly from you."

Wanda Nell nodded. "Sure. What do you want to know?"

Tuck hesitated. "Why don't you start with the last time you saw your ex-husband, and go from there."

"Okay." Wanda Nell took a deep breath, then started talking. Tuck occasionally jotted something down on the pad on the desk, but most of the time he simply sat and listened. She faltered a bit when she came to tell him how she had found Bobby Ray's body.

"We don't have to talk about that right now if it will distress you," Tuck said, but Wanda Nell shook her head, insisting that she was fine.

It took her a while, but she told him everything she could think of. The only thing she left out was the incident with Mrs. Culpepper in the parking lot at Budget Mart. He didn't need any further evidence that the old lazy was crazy as a Betsy bug.

"Thank you, Wanda Nell," Tuck said, putting his pen aside. "I've got a better overall picture of the situation. The next thing is hearing what the sheriff's department has to say about their case when T.J. goes before the magistrate. That might be tomorrow, but possibly not till the next day. In the meantime, don't worry. I've got everything well in hand." He beamed at her.

Wanda Nell took heart from his confidence, but she would have felt better if he'd told her exactly what he was going to do. She figured, though, he knew what he was doing. Best let him get on with it.

She stood up. "You said you'd let me know about seeing T.J. I guess you can just call me when you know something."

Tuck stood also and came around the desk to see her out. "I'll see if I can't get through to the sheriff some time this afternoon, and I'll call you right away." He shook hands with her and escorted her to the door.

"Thank you, Tuck. I really appreciate it," she said, pausing on the threshold. She wanted to say more, since he had been so generous about the subject of his fee, but she couldn't find the words to convey exactly how she felt.

"I'm glad to do it," he said, his eyes twinkling at her. "You just go on and don't worry about a thing." He closed the door.

Blanche greeted her with a smile. "He's something else, isn't he, Wanda Nell? Good-looking, and nice, too. He's a good guy, and if he tells you not to worry, well, you just listen to what he tells you."

"Thanks, Blanche," Wanda Nell said, approaching her desk. "I can't tell you how much I appreciate what he's doing and what you did, too. If it hadn't been for you and Mayrene, I wouldn't've known who to call."

Blanche waved her gratitude away. "All in a day's work. Now, do you need a ride somewheres? That old battle-ax's done gone off and left you, you know."

Wanda Nell smiled ruefully. "I know, and I tell you, I don't mind walking back to where my car is. I couldn't stand the thought of getting back in her car with her."

"You sure?"

"I'm sure. The walk'll do me good," Wanda Nell assured her. "Bye."

She made her way downstairs and out the front door. The afternoon was warm, but there was a pleasant breeze. Wanda Nell walked slowly around the square and down Main Street toward the Culpepper mansion. It took her about fifteen minutes to reach her car. She was surprised the old witch hadn't had it towed.

Before she unlocked the car, Wanda Nell examined the house for signs of life. Just looking at it gave her the willies. Two old women inside, waiting to die, or so it seemed to her. Poor Charlesetta had better get out of there while she could.

Wanda Nell turned up the air-conditioning to cool off the inside of the car, then put it in gear and drove off. Before she had gone three blocks, she heard her cell phone ringing in her purse. Hanging on to the steering wheel with her left hand, she fumbled in her purse with her right.

Her hand closed on the phone, and she snatched it out. She didn't recognize the number on the caller ID "Hello?"

"Wanda Nell, it's Blanche. Mr. Tucker got right through to the sheriff, and he said it was okay for you to come over to the jail right now and talk to your son."

"Thanks, Blanche," Wanda Nell said. She pulled over in front of the funeral home and put the car in park. "Tell him I appreciate it. I'm going right now."

She stowed the phone away in her purse and looked in her rearview mirror. She waited for a truck to pass, then she made a U-turn in the street and headed back in the direction of the jail. Her heart was fluttering at the thought of seeing T.J. She had some hard questions to ask him, and she wanted answers. She just hoped they were answers she could bear to hear.

# Twenty-Two

Wanda Nell spent ten anxious minutes before they ushered her into the room where the visits with prisoners were held. T.J. sat at a desk behind a mesh screen, and a guard stood discreetly in the corner. The air was stale and cold, and Wanda Nell shivered slightly.

As she sat down in a chair on the other side of the desk from T.J., she remembered other scenes like this. Those other times T.J. had been sullen, defiant, even abusive, but now he just looked sad. The drab jumpsuit he wore made his skin sallow.

"Honey, are you doing okay?"

T.J. smiled briefly. "Well, this wasn't where I wanted to be spending any of my time, Mama. But it ain't so bad. This new jail sure is better than the old one."

Wanda Nell didn't want to dwell on any of the past

escapades that had put T.J. behind bars. "I talked to the lawyer, T.J. Mr. Tucker seems real sharp, and he talks like everything's gonna be just fine."

T.J. snorted. "Easy for him to say. He ain't the one sitting here. I just wanna get out of here, Mama." He rubbed his hands up and down his arms. "I swore I wasn't ever gonna be in jail again, and look at me. And this time I didn't do a damn thing."

"We're gonna get you out as soon as we can, honey," Wanda Nell promised him. "But you've got to help me. You've got to tell me the truth, T.J. About everything."

"Like what?"

She had always known when he was lying to her. His eyes gave him away. He couldn't look her straight in the face when he lied. Probably nobody would believe her if she told them that, but she knew it in her gut and in her heart.

"Did you kill your daddy?"

"No." His gaze never wavered.

"Or Ricky Ratliff?"

"No." Still he faced her without shying away.

The constriction in her chest eased. "I believe you."

His face softened for a moment. He swallowed hard. "Thank you, Mama."

Wanda Nell wanted to cry, seeing the tears glistening in his eyes. She took a deep breath to steady herself. "It's okay, honey. Now, you gotta tell me. They said they had a witness seen you arguing with your daddy. You didn't tell me you seen him here in Tullahoma. I thought you didn't see him after Greenville."

She waited for his answer. He watched her face for a moment before replying. "I guess I shoulda told you, Mama, but I didn't think it mattered." He drummed his fingers on the table. "Me and Jackie was out running around that night. I'd just got into town, and I called him up. And first thing he wanted to do was hit a coupla places we always used to hang out."

Wanda Nell frowned. She knew about those places, and she remembered the times T.J. had gotten in trouble at them. He'd never been able to hold his liquor, and he had a mean temper when he drank. Just like his daddy.

T.J. sighed. "I shoulda known better, but I hadn't seen ol' Jackie for two years, I guess, and all he wanted to do was party. Me and him had a lot of catching up to do, and you know how it is, Mama. Before you know it, you done had two or three beers, and after that, it sure is easy just to keep drinking."

"I know, T.J. And that's exactly why you shouldn't drink." Wanda Nell hated that tone in her voice, but she couldn't help herself. This was the way most of her arguments with Bobby Ray had started.

T.J. didn't seem to take offense, the way he would have before. "Yeah, Mama, I realize that now. If I hadn't been drinking that night, I might not be here right now."

"So what happened?"

"I had me a few beers, and Jackie and me were thinking about heading somewhere else, and Daddy walked in. I saw him go swanning up to the bar, and he pulled out a big wad of cash. Other people was noticing it, too. I waited till he had him a drink, and I got up and went over to him." T.J. frowned. "He didn't act like he was too glad to see me, especially when I told him he better be careful about flashing all that money around."

"And knowing Bobby Ray, he didn't like anybody telling him he shouldn't do something."

"Yeah, that just made him mad. He'd already had a snootful, and you know it don't take much to rile him up when he's been drinking." T.J. shook his head. "I shoulda just left him alone, but I wadn't thinking too clear myself. So I grabbed ahold of his arm and started trying to get him over to where Jackie and me was sitting. He didn't like that, neither."

"I guess I know what happened then." Wanda Nell closed her eyes for a moment. The scene was all too clear in her mind.

"Yeah, he took a swing at me," T.J. said. "And he almost hit me. I was a little slow on the uptake, but I managed to duck it in time. He spun around and spilled his drink, and then he started cussing me out like I was somebody off the street he never seen before."

He tried to hide it, but the memory of that scene hurt him, and Wanda Nell wished she could take his hand and hold it.

"And then Jackie came up and got into it, and it just got worse from there. Daddy was trying to get a hand on both of us, but he was too drunk to do much damage."

"What happened then?" Wanda Nell prompted when he fell silent.

"Daddy said some things to me, and I didn't like it. So I told him I was going to beat the crap out of him if he didn't shut up."

Appalled, Wanda Nell stared at her son. This was much worse than she had imagined. What had gotten into Bobby Ray for him to treat his son like this? "What did he say to you, T.J.?"

"Just stupid stuff. I don't even remember exactly what he said." T.J. blinked a couple of times, then looked down at his hands.

Why wouldn't he tell her what Bobby Ray had said? She knew good and well T.J. remembered. He just didn't want to tell her for some reason. What awful things had Bobby Ray said to his son?

"Well, I guess it don't matter, honey," Wanda Nell said gently. "I just hope nobody that heard it says anything to the sheriff's department."

T.J. shifted in his chair, still refusing to meet her eyes. "I can't help that, Mama, but there ain't no telling what somebody might say. It don't really have a thing to do with this mess."

Best then to move on to something else, Wanda Nell decided. "T.J., they said they'd found your fingerprints in Ricky Ratliff's truck. Do you know how that could've happened?"

This time T.J. looked at her. "Me and Jackie hung around for a little while, but I stayed out of Daddy's way. He just kept drinking, and pretty soon he passed out. Ricky was there, but he didn't show his face until Daddy was out on the floor. Me and Jackie got Daddy up and out to Ricky's truck. That's when I would've touched some place inside his truck, I guess."

Wanda Nell nodded. "I don't think they got much to go on, T.J. I bet Mr. Tucker's going to have you out of here real soon."

"I sure hope so, Mama," T.J. said. "But that lawyer seems mighty casual about the whole thing." He paused a moment, then leaned forward. His voice had dropped to almost a whisper. "How're we gonna be able to pay him, Mama? Is Grandmama gonna help?"

"Don't worry about that, honey," Wanda Nell said. The dreadful scene in the lawyer's office replayed itself in her mind, and she squirmed a little in her chair. She was appalled at her own behavior, and she wondered what the lawyer must have thought of her. She forced herself to forget that for the moment and focus on her son. "We'll manage somehow, even if your grandmama is being difficult.

Not that she is," she added hastily. She didn't want to have to tell T.J. the whole tacky story.

T.J. relaxed a bit in his chair, but he still eyed her suspiciously. "If you say so, Mama. But you can tell Grandmama for me that I'll pay her back every penny if she'll help out. As soon as I'm outta here I'll find a job."

"You mean you're going to be staying in Tullahoma for a while?" Wanda Nell tried not to get too hopeful.

"Yeah, Mama, I am," he said. "If that's okay with you."

Wanda Nell had to work to hold back the tears. He sounded so much like a lost little boy who wasn't sure he would be welcome at home. "Of course it's okay with me, honey." She swallowed hard. "I've missed you so much, I just can't tell you."

The guard cleared his throat to signal that their time was up, and T.J. looked grateful. "I guess I gotta go, Mama." He stood up as the guard approached.

"I'll come again as soon as they'll let me, T.J.," Wanda Nell promised. She watched as the guard led him away. T.J. looked back once and offered her a slow smile. For a moment Wanda Nell saw Bobby Ray standing there, a younger and happier Bobby Ray, holding the promise of the world in his eyes. She blinked, and T.J. was gone.

Shaken, Wanda Nell found her way out of the county jail and to her car. The afternoon sun welcomed her with its warmth, after the chill inside. She breathed deeply of the humid air and felt herself becoming calmer.

Inside the car she let it run for a couple of minutes, until the air-conditioning had time to cool things. She debated whether she should approach Miz Culpepper again and try to patch things up, for T.J.'s sake. But she dismissed that thought after a moment. The old woman might be in a better frame of mind if she waited a day or two to talk to her again.

Hell, she might not even remember any of what had happened this afternoon, depending on how much she'd had to drink.

Wanda Nell put the car into gear and drove away from the jail. She hated having to leave T.J. there. It hadn't gotten any easier over the years, but she vowed this would be the last time. Once they got this mess figured out and got ahold of the person who was really responsible, she would make sure that T.J. lived up to his promise that he really had changed.

The lawyer seemed awfully sure of himself, and Wanda Nell reckoned he is pretty smart. So he must know what he is doing. She just wished that they could speed things up a little. She didn't want T.J. to spend any more time in that jail than he had to. But the lawyer seemed content to let things run their course.

Wanda Nell wasn't content to sit by and watch. She wanted to do something, but what? If what she feared was true, then somebody in the sheriff's department was involved up to their eyeballs in the murders. It had to be Elmer Lee, she didn't see any way around that. He and Bobby Ray had always been buddies, with Ricky Ratliff hitching along for the ride. Chances were, if Bobby Ray had been up to something, Elmer Lee knew about it. And he either connived at it, or turned a blind eye to it, because it was Bobby Ray.

But would he have killed Bobby Ray and Ricky over the money? That was the part that Wanda Nell had a hard time buying. Bobby Ray and Elmer Lee had been like brothers, and, sure, brothers killed each other. But what could Bobby Ray have done that made Elmer Lee angry enough to kill him?

Ricky, she discounted, because he probably irritated

Elmer Lee as much he irritated everybody else that spent ten minutes around him. It would've been just like Ricky to try to blackmail Elmer Lee with what he knew, and Elmer Lee would've squashed Ricky like the big bug he was. That she didn't have any trouble buying.

It always came back to Bobby Ray and Elmer Lee. Maybe that was why, though, Elmer Lee had been riding her so hard. He was trying to shift the blame to her, and now, to T.J. He must think he had it made, because T.J. made such a good scapegoat. If T.J. hadn't turned up, he would've found some way to get her in jail. She was just lucky the sheriff and her daddy had been good friends, or she would've been in jail before T.J. showed up.

Wanda Nell drove, completely immersed in her thoughts. By the time she reached the turnoff for the lake, she had no idea how she'd gotten there without hitting someone.

She scolded herself for driving like that, but she couldn't keep her mind off the situation. Tuck Tucker was going to have to do some mighty fancy lawyering to get the goods on Elmer Lee, because Elmer Lee sure wasn't going to go down without a big fight.

But what could she do, she wondered as she pulled her car into its parking place and shut off the engine. There had to be something. There had to be some way to find the proof they needed to link Elmer Lee to Bobby Ray and whatever scam he'd been running.

She'd discuss it with Mayrene, she decided as she got out of the car and locked it. Together they ought to be able to come up with some kind of plan.

The trailer door was locked, she noted approvingly. She unlocked it and stepped inside. Mayrene was sitting on the couch, reading the newspaper.

"I'm glad you're here, Mayrene," Wanda Nell said, dropping her purse on the coffee table. She sat down beside Mayrene on the couch. "And I appreciate you keeping an eye on the girls and the baby like this."

"I'm glad to do it, honey, you know that," Mayrene said, her eyes still focused on the paper.

Wanda Nell was about to ask Mayrene for advice, when Mayrene interrupted her.

"Wanda Nell, just look at this." Mayrene brandished the paper in front of her.

"What is it?" Wanda Nell took the paper from Mayrene and tried to find what Mayrene had been pointing to, but she wasn't sure what she was supposed to be reading.

"Right here." Mayrene stuck a stubby finger on an article.

"Greenville police search for missing dispatcher," Wanda Nell read aloud. She glanced at Mayrene, who nodded.

"Yeah, they think he was helping somebody rip off one of the casinos," Mayrene explained.

Wanda Nell read more, this time silently. "Oh, my Lord," she said, when she came to the name of the man the police were looking for. His name was David McKenna. "The man who tried to take the money away from us."

## Twenty-Three

Wanda Nell read further while Mayrene patted her foot up and down on the floor, waiting. According to the paper, McKenna was alleged to have ignored a call to the sheriff's department from the casinos reporting a robbery. Casino operators, seeing a robbery in progress, had activated a silent alarm that went straight to the sheriff's department. That call had never been answered, and the thief made off with over a hundred thousand dollars. Now McKenna was wanted for questioning.

Wanda Nell let the paper fall into her lap as she turned to Mayrene. "Bobby Ray must've had something to do with this," she said. "You reckon he actually robbed the casino?"

"He was sure dumb enough to try it and think he was gonna get away with it," Mayrene said. "But it don't sound like something he'd do. From what you told me, he'd rather sell snake oil than do something that dangerous."

"Yeah, he wasn't too anxious to risk a bullet hole in that handsome skin of his," Wanda Nell said. "I can see him cheating some old widow woman out of her husband's insurance money, or running some kind of scam, but as far as I know, he never pulled something like this."

Mayrene shrugged. "If he thought he could get away with it, he might've tried it."

"Maybe," Wanda Nell said, staring down at the paper. "If this guy and Bobby Ray was in it together, then he could be the one that killed Bobby Ray."

"Sounds good to me."

Wanda Nell stood up, letting the paper fall to the floor. "I'm gonna to call the lawyer and see if he knows about this." She strode off for the kitchen as Mayrene leaned forward to retrieve the paper.

Digging in her purse for the lawyer's card, Wanda Nell tried not to get her hopes up. She wanted her son out of jail, and if they could prove this McKenna guy had done it, then T.J. would be free. She found the card and punched in Tuck Tucker's cell phone number.

Her heart beat faster as she waited for Tucker to answer.

"Hamilton Tucker." His voice came through strongly.

"Tuck, this is Wanda Nell Culpepper," she said, the words coming out in a rush. "Have you seen the Memphis paper today? Where it tells about this guy they caught here at my place? They say he's wanted for questioning in a casino robbery, and I bet him and Bobby Ray was in it together, and he killed Bobby Ray over the money."

Almost breathless at this point, she paused.

"I did see that article, just a few minutes ago," Tucker responded. "And it certainly does open up some interesting possibilities. I'll be looking at every angle, I assure you, Wanda Nell. But we can't jump to conclusions. Even if this

David McKenna turns out to be guilty, it's still going to take a little time to get T.J. released."

Deflated, Wanda Nell sighed into the phone. "I guess so. I just want my son out of jail so much I was jumping ahead."

Tucker chuckled. "Perfectly understandable, Wanda Nell. I won't let T.J. sit in that jail cell a moment longer than he has to, I promise you. Now you just relax, and let me handle this."

Wanda Nell wasn't sure she liked the way he said that, but she didn't feel like she could argue with him. He was the one who was the expert, after all.

"Okay, Tuck, I will," she said, then said good-bye. She stared at the wall for a minute or so after she had hung up the phone.

When Mayrene tapped her on the shoulder, Wanda Nell was so lost in thought that she jerked and almost banged into the counter.

"Sorry, honey," Mayrene said as Wanda Nell turned to face her. "What did the lawyer say?"

Wanda Nell frowned. "He said not to get too excited and to let him handle it." She shook her head. "I guess he's right, but I just can't stand this sitting around and not doing anything."

"What else can you do?" Mayrene asked practically.

After a moment, Wanda Nell said, "I'm gonna call Elmer Lee. I don't see where it can hurt anything."

"Call him for what?"

"I'm gonna ask him about this guy McKenna."

"What good's that gonna do?"

"I don't know," Wanda Nell snapped. Mayrene frowned at her tone, and Wanda Nell could've slapped herself. "I'm sorry, Mayrene." She held out her hand, and Mayrene took it, smiling.

"It's okay, honey, I know you're under a lot of stress right now," Mayrene said, "and if you wanna call Elmer Lee, you go right ahead."

Wanda Nell turned back to the phone. By now she knew the sheriff's department number by heart. She punched it in. After a couple of rings, the dispatcher answered.

"Hi, I need to speak to Elmer Lee Johnson. Tell him it's Wanda Nell Culpepper, and it's real important I talk to him right away."

Wanda Nell covered the mouthpiece with her hand as she spoke to Mayrene. "She says he's there, and she's gonna transfer me." She took her hand away from the mouthpiece.

"Elmer Lee, it's me, Wanda Nell."

"What is it, Wanda Nell? I ain't got time for any more foolishness from you."

Elmer Lee sounded so bone-weary Wanda Nell almost felt sorry for him. If it wasn't for that condescending tone in his voice, she would be.

"Now you listen here, Elmer Lee, as long as you got my son in that jail, and him being innocent and all, you better pay attention to what I've got to say."

"Yes, ma'am," Elmer Lee drawled, his tone even more offensive. He started to say something else, but Wanda Nell cut him off.

"I was reading in the Memphis paper about how this guy you arrested at my house was wanted by the sheriff's department over in Greenville. About how they think he might be involved in a robbery at the casino."

"Yes, Wanda Nell, we know all that," Elmer Lee said, "and we don't need the Memphis paper telling us anything about it. Stop wasting my time."

"Hold on just a gol-danged minute, Elmer Lee," Wanda Nell said. "You stop getting snippy with me and listen. It seems to me that this guy and Bobby Ray was probably in on that robbery together, and knowing Bobby Ray, he probably suckered that guy over the money. And," she finished triumphantly, "he's the one that killed Bobby Ray."

"Well, thank you, Miz Sherlock Holmes," Elmer Lee said. "I reckon I'll just put in for early retirement, and you can come on over here to the sheriff's department and take my place."

Wanda Nell's hand tightened on the phone. It was all she could do not to scream at Elmer Lee.

"Well, Mr. Blind-as-a-Bat, I may not be some high-and-mighty deputy," Wanda Nell responded, as cuttingly as she could, "but I can for damn sure see what's right under my nose. It's obvious to me this guy is the one. T.J. didn't kill his daddy, or that fool Ricky, either. Stop sitting on your lardass, and prove it."

Mayrene stared at her, aghast. Wanda Nell just rolled her eyes at her friend. She was so mad at Elmer Lee now, she didn't care what she said to him. Mayrene tried to take the phone from her, but Wanda Nell pushed her away.

Elmer Lee was laughing so hard, Wanda Nell wished she could reach through the line and slap him upside the head.

"What the hell is so damn funny, Elmer Lee?"

It took Elmer Lee a moment to stop laughing long enough to answer her.

"You are, Wanda Nell. I just think it's real funny how you know everything." He laughed a little more, then suddenly his voice hardened. "Now you listen here, Wanda Nell. I don't need you telling me how to do my job. For your information, the suspect in question has a pretty solid alibi for both murders. And I reckon that leaves T.J. right where he belongs. He's still my best suspect."

Wanda Nell started to protest, but Elmer Lee had slammed the phone down. Her ear rang slightly as she replaced the receiver on the cradle.

"Well?" Mayrene asked. "What did he say to you?"

Wanda Nell could feel the tears forming in her eyes. "He said the guy has a pretty solid alibi for both murders, and T.J. is still his best suspect."

"Oh, honey," Mayrene said, holding out her arms.

Wanda Nell leaned into her, and Mayrene hugged her close, rocking her a little. Wanda Nell cried on Mayrene's shoulder for a moment, then she pulled away. Wiping her face, she stared at Mayrene.

"You reckon he's lying to me?"

"What do you mean?"

"I mean, about this guy having an alibi," Wanda Nell said. "What if he's just telling me that out of pure meanness?"

"I sure as heck wouldn't put it past him," Mayrene said, after a moment's thought. "He seems to hate you enough to wanna upset you and get back at you for what you said to him."

"Yeah," Wanda Nell said. "But, I don't know, there was just something about his voice when he said it. Even though he was real mad at me, he sounded like he really meant it."

"If that's the case," Mayrene replied, "then I guess there ain't much you can do about it."

Wanda Nell walked over to the kitchen table and slumped into a chair. "No, I guess not."

Mayrene came over and sat down catty-corner from her. She patted Wanda Nell's hand. "You're just gonna have to have some faith in that lawyer, Wanda Nell. He seems like he's real sharp, and Blanche swears by him. I think you need to let him handle this. Let him earn his money."

Wanda Nell got up and went to the cabinet. Grabbing a

couple of glasses, she asked, "Want something to drink? Maybe some caffeine'll help me think better."

"Sure," Mayrene said, "I could do with something cold right about now. But you got any beer?"

"No, sorry," Wanda Nell said. "Just milk and Coke."

Mayrene laughed. "I don't even know why I asked, honey. I know you don't drink. Let me have some Coke, then."

Wanda Nell poured out the Coke and set the glasses down on the table. She searched in another cabinet and pulled out a large, unopened bag of corn chips. "I never did have any lunch, but I don't feel like fixing anything." She opened the bag as she sat down. Scooping out a handful, she then pushed the bag toward Mayrene. "Help yourself."

Mayrene shook her head. "Honey, if I have just one of those, I'll eat the whole bag."

Wanda Nell smiled as she crunched on some chips. After taking a long drink, she munched some more. Mayrene sat quietly, occasionally sipping at her Coke and watching Wanda Nell eat.

After she'd worked her way through about a third of the bag of chips, Wanda Nell pushed them away. "I've got to do something, Mayrene."

"Like what?"

"I was just thinking, if Elmer Lee was telling me the truth, and this McKenna guy really didn't kill Bobby Ray or Ricky, then I've just got to look somewhere else. Like those men that broke in here. Nobody's ever figured out who they were, but you know what? I bet they're from the casino."

Mayrene pondered that for a moment. "That makes sense. They sure wouldn't sit idly by and let somebody rip 'em off like that, without doing something about it." She shifted uncomfortably in her chair. "But, honey, you know they say the people that run those casinos are pretty rough. Don't nobody cross 'em and get away with it. What if it was some kinda professional hit job?"

Wanda Nell shrugged. "I've thought about that. But the way Bobby Ray was killed, I just don't know. It don't seem like the way some professional hit man would kill someone, does it?"

It was Mayrene's turn to shrug. "I can't see them using a plastic flamingo, if that's what you mean."

"Exactly," Wanda Nell said. "Now, you're the one that watches all those crime shows on TV. Don't it seem to you that if it was some hit man that whacked Bobby Ray they would have just made him disappear somewhere? They surely would've been smart enough not to leave his body around here."

Mayrene nodded. "Yeah, you're right. I bet they would've have dumped him in the Mississippi River with some concrete shoes."

"That whole flamingo thing is just too weird," Wanda Nell said. She shuddered. "I'm going to pull every dang one of 'em up, and go dump 'em in the trash. I should've done it before now. I don't think I can ever stand looking at 'em again."

"I don't blame you, honey," Mayrene said. "And I'll help you."

The phone rang, and Wanda Nell half-turned in her chair. Mayrene got up to answer it.

She listened for a moment, then held the phone against her ample bosom. "It's that Deputy Taylor, honey. You wanna talk to her?"

"I guess," Wanda Nell said, starting to rise from her chair.

"Here she is," Mayrene said into the phone. She handed the receiver to Wanda Nell, who sat down again.

"Hello," she said. "What can I do for you, Deputy?"

"There's something I thought you ought to know," Taylor said, her voice low. "I heard about your conversation with Deputy Johnson."

"Yeah, I'll just bet you did," Wanda Nell said. "He was pretty mad by the time it was over."

"Yes, he was," Taylor replied. "But that's not what I'm calling about."

Wanda Nell waited for a moment, but Taylor didn't say anything. "I'm listening."

"I could get in a lot of trouble for telling you this," Taylor said, "but I think you should know that your son is really in trouble."

"What do you mean?"

Again, the deputy hesitated, until Wanda Nell wanted to scream at her.

"I know I was the one that arrested him," Taylor said in a rush, "but it was Deputy Johnson had me do it. I mean, he was the one that told me where to go to find out about the argument your son had with his daddy, and all that. And once I found all that out, he's the one that decided to arrest your son."

"Okay," Wanda Nell said. "I can understand all that, but it don't really surprise me. Is that what you wanted to tell me?"

"That's not all," Taylor said. "You know that money we got from you? That this other fella was after?"

"Yeah."

"That wasn't near all of the money that's missing from that robbery. It was only about ten grand or so."

Wanda Nell drew in her breath sharply. "So you mean the rest of it's still missing?"

"Exactly," Taylor replied. "About ninety grand more. And Deputy Johnson is after it."

"Well, yeah," Wanda Nell said, puzzled. "They've got to find it."

"You don't understand," Taylor said impatiently. "I don't mean he's trying to find it for the sheriff's department. He was in on the whole thing, and he's trying to get his hands on it so nobody else can find it."

## Twenty-Four

Wanda Nell felt cold to the bone. With that much money at stake, Elmer Lee might do anything to get his hands on it.

Like see that her son went to prison for two murders he didn't commit.

"Are . . . are you sure about that?" Wanda Nell asked, her voice faltering over the words. "How do you know that?"

The deputy sighed loudly into the phone. "I've heard some things, and seen some things, too. Things I wasn't supposed to see or hear. And if Deputy Johnson finds out too soon, then I'm going to be in one hell of a mess."

"We all are," Wanda Nell replied flatly. "But how in the devil are we gonna stop him? Elmer Lee's one of the boys, and you know how that goes. Who's gonna believe you and me if we start telling people he's crooked?"

"We can figure that out later," Taylor said impatiently. "I don't have time to worry about it right now. We've got to get the proof, and then it won't matter."

"What kind of proof are you talking about?"

Again, Wanda Nell heard a sigh. "The money, Miz Culpepper, the money. We got to find that money before he does. 'Cause if he finds it first, then your son's going to prison, probably death row. You get me?"

Wanda Nell shivered. She tried to speak, but couldn't. The image of T.J. locked in a cell, waiting to be executed, filled her mind, and she couldn't block it. Seeing her distress, Mayrene reached out and with warm hands started rubbing Wanda Nell's arms.

"Are you still there, Miz Culpepper?"

"Yes," Wanda Nell whispered into the phone. The fit, or whatever the heck it was, had passed, and she was beginning to feel stronger. "Yes, I'm still here. What do you think I should do?"

"Like I said, we got to find that money. If you can think of anywhere your husband might have hidden it, you need to do that."

"I just don't know," Wanda Nell said. "I don't think it's here, but I'll check on that. And if it's not here, then I don't have the foggiest idea where it could be."

"Just keep trying," Taylor said. "I gotta go now. I'll check in with you later." The line went dead.

"What the heck is going on?" Mayrene demanded as Wanda Nell shut off the phone and laid the receiver on the table. "I thought for a minute there you were gonna pass out on me."

Tersely Wanda Nell repeated what Deputy Taylor had said to her, and when she was done, Mayrene whistled. "Hell, Wanda Nell, talk about being between a rock and a hard place."

"Amen," Wanda Nell said. "But this just means I've got to do something, Mayrene. The deputy's right, I've got to try and figure out what Bobby Ray did with the rest of that money."

"All right, but how?"

"First off, I'm going to sit Miranda down and have a good, long talk with her. I've got to make sure Bobby Ray didn't give her the rest of the money and tell her to hide it somewhere."

"Good point." Mayrene nodded several times. "You can't ever tell what that girl might get up to."

"Tell me about it," Wanda Nell said grimly. She got up from the table and stalked down the hall to Miranda's bedroom.

Knocking on the door, Wanda Nell pushed it open. Miranda was sound asleep on her bed, and Lavon was playing quietly in his crib. Wanda Nell went to him and picked him up, checking his diaper. She was relieved to find it dry. Lavon giggled and chattered away, and Wanda Nell hugged and kissed him, telling him what a good boy, what a handsome boy he was.

*Thank the Lord he's such a good child,* Wanda Nell thought. *Otherwise Miranda would've hightailed it out of here, and left me to look after him.* Setting the baby down again, she bent and gave him one final kiss. He went cheerfully back to his toys.

Wanda Nell turned to find Miranda regarding her warily, one eye open. That eye snapped closed, but too late. "I know you're awake," Wanda Nell said softly. "I want you to get up and come into the kitchen with me. Lavon'll be fine in here for a few minutes by himself."

"But, Mama," Miranda started to protest as she propped herself up in the bed on one elbow.

"No buts, Miranda," Wanda Nell said, her voice steely

hard. "You get up and get in that kitchen, or I'll come in here and drag you out. Your choice."

"Yes'm," Miranda said. "Can I at least pee first?"

Wanda Nell tried not to laugh. "Of course, honey." She turned and left the room.

Some five minutes later, Miranda joined her mother and Mayrene in the kitchen. She plopped herself down in the chair opposite Wanda Nell and stared sullenly at her mother.

"I need to talk to you about something, Miranda, and you're gonna have to promise me to tell me the absolute truth, you understand?" Wanda Nell leaned forward, both hands on the table, palms down. She stared hard at her daughter.

Miranda shifted uncomfortably in her chair. "Jeez, Mama, whatta you think I done now?"

"It's not so much what you might've done, Miranda, but what your daddy might've asked you to do." Wanda Nell forced herself to relax in her chair. "I found that money you hid in Lavon's diaper pail. Was that all your daddy gave you to hide?"

"Yeah." Miranda stared back at her mother.

"I want you to understand how serious this is, honey. That money came from a casino in Greenville. Your daddy and somebody else stole that money from the casino, and it belongs to them. And if you have any idea where it is, you need to tell me. Finding that money may help get your brother out of jail."

The longer Wanda Nell spoke, the larger Miranda's eyes got. By now they were fairly popping out of her head.

"Mama, I swear I don't know anything about any other money. You got to believe me. Daddy didn't give me any more than what you already found."

"You swear to me, Miranda?"

Miranda's head bobbed up and down. "I swear, Mama. And you know I wouldn't do anything to hurt T.J. I swear if I knew about any more money, I'd tell you."

Wanda Nell studied her for a moment. Miranda had never been a good liar, and Wanda Nell believed she was telling the truth. For her brother's sake, Miranda would tell her the truth.

"I believe you, honey." Wanda Nell smiled at her, and Miranda smiled back in relief. "But that night your daddy was here"—she didn't say the night he died—"did he say anything about where he'd been or where he might be going?"

Miranda frowned in concentration. "Well, he said he'd been out drinking the night before, and he was still paying for it. He didn't feel too good." She paused a moment. "And he said he was planning to go back to Greenville the next day. Said he was going to get his stuff, 'cause he was moving back to Tullahoma to stay." She burst into tears.

Wanda Nell got up and went around the table to take Miranda in her arms. "I'm sorry, honey. I wish he could've moved back here."

"He was different, Mama, I swear he was. He said he wanted to spend more time with me and Lavon and Juliet. He didn't like not seeing us." Miranda spoke in short bursts, between sobs. "Why did somebody have to kill him?"

"I don't know, honey, I don't know," Wanda Nell whispered to Miranda's hair as she cradled her daughter's head against hers. "I wish it could've been different, sweetie, I surely do."

Wanda Nell held her until the sobs eased. "Go wash your face with cold water, honey," she told Miranda gently.

Miranda kissed her mother's cheek, then left the kitchen.

Wanda Nell sank down into her chair. Mayrene was eyeing her sympathetically.

"What now?"

Shrugging, Wanda Nell reached for the bag of chips. She stuffed a couple in her mouth and chewed while she thought. When she had finished them, she said, "You wanna go with me to Greenville in the morning?"

"For what?"

"I wanna talk to Bobby Ray's landlady. Could be she knows something about all this. It might be a waste of time, but it's better than just sitting here."

Mayrene regarded her for a moment. "I reckon I can get the day off from the shop. But what about you? Don't you have to work at Budget Mart tonight?"

"Yeah," Wanda Nell said. "But I figure I can come home in the morning, get Juliet off to school, catch a couple hours' nap, then we can drive over there. Shouldn't take long, and we can be back by the time Juliet gets out of school."

"Yeah, I guess so," Mayrene said, "but how are you gonna find this landlady?"

"T.J. told me her name, and she don't live too far from the casino," Wanda Nell replied. "She can't be that hard to find."

"Okay," Mayrene said. "I'm game, if you are."

"Good. Let's leave about nine-thirty or ten, how's that? We can be in Greenville before noon, have a couple hours to talk to this lady, then get back here by three-thirty."

"Sounds like a plan to me." Mayrene got up from the table and deposited her empty glass in the sink. "But what about Miranda and Lavon? Do you think they should stay here by themselves tomorrow?"

"No. I don't want them here by themselves. Miranda'll be happy to go and spend the day with one of her friends."

"Good. Well, I guess I'm gonna get along home. You want me to stay with the girls tonight while you're at work?"

Wanda Nell hated to ask Mayrene to do it when she'd done so much already, but she was leery of leaving the girls and the baby alone in the trailer without someone responsible. Mayrene must have read the indecision in her face, because she laughed.

"Honey, it's not a problem. I don't mind, I really don't. Don't you even think twice about it."

"Thank the Lord for friends like you," Wanda Nell said, smiling.

"At the end of the day, honey, that's all that matters," Mayrene said. "It'd be nice to have a big strong man around, but you and me neither ever had much luck with men. So we gotta rely on ourselves." She grinned. "And my shotgun."

Wanda Nell laughed. "Can't argue with that."

"Don't even try." Mayrene waved good-bye as she left the kitchen. A moment later, Wanda Nell heard the front door open and close behind her.

Glancing at her watch, Wanda Nell figured she had time to cook herself and the girls a good supper and still be able to get a couple hours' sleep before work. She went to her bedroom and changed out of her good dress and slipped on an old housecoat.

She checked in on Juliet, who had her nose deep in a book. She talked to her for a few minutes, then headed back to the kitchen to cook.

Cooking wasn't one of Wanda Nell's favorite activities, but she had learned from her mama, who had loved cooking and had done it extremely well. Wanda Nell was more than competent. She just didn't find the joy in it that her mother had done. She set to work making biscuits and getting a chicken ready to fry. They usually had fried chicken, biscuits and cream gravy, rice, and green beans for their Sunday evening meal, and Wanda Nell wanted to keep things as normal as possible.

By the time everything was done, it was a bit early for supper, but Wanda Nell called the girls in anyway. Miranda settled Lavon in his high chair and gave him a biscuit smothered with gravy to poke his fingers into. "Juliet and me'll clean up tonight, Mama," she said as she heaped her plate. "You get you a nap before you have to go to work."

"Thank you, honey," Wanda Nell said. Miranda sometimes offered, but even when she did, she had to be prodded into doing what she had promised.

Over the meal, Wanda Nell explained to the girls what she planned to do the next day. "And I don't want y'all worrying about me and Mayrene, we'll be fine. Juliet'll be safe at school, and you should be fine with one of your friends, Miranda. Who can you and Lavon go and stay with all day?"

"Laquita won't mind if we come over to her house," Miranda said, after a moment's thought. "She don't work on Mondays."

"Good idea," Wanda Nell said. Laquita was a smart, attractive girl, and Wanda Nell wished Miranda would spend more time with her, instead of some of the no-account girls she knew. "We'll drop you off on the way to Greenville, and we can pick you up on the way back."

"Okay, Mama," Miranda said.

"And we'll pick you up at school," Wanda Nell said, turning to Juliet. "So you wait for us there, okay? I don't want you coming home on the bus and nobody being here."

"Okay, Mama." Juliet echoed her sister.

They talked of other things as they finished the meal, and the girls shooed Wanda Nell away to her nap when, without thinking, she started to clear the table.

Wanda Nell hugged each of them before heading for her bedroom. She had just stepped into the room when the phone rang. She scooped up the receiver on the second ring. "Hello."

"Miz Culpepper, it's me, Tracy." The deputy paused briefly. "You thought any more about what we talked about earlier?"

"Yeah," Wanda Nell said, slightly irritated at the younger woman's insistence. "I have, and I can tell you definitely the rest of that money's not here in my trailer."

"Damn!" The deputy said. "It would've made things a lot easier if he'd left it there."

"Well, he didn't," Wanda Nell replied sharply. "So we've got to look somewhere else."

"Like where?" Taylor asked.

Wanda Nell didn't appreciate this badgering attitude the woman had. "If you have to know," she said, not bothering to hide her irritation, "I'm going to Greenville tomorrow to check into something."

"Greenville?" There was an odd note in the deputy's voice. "You think that's safe?"

"Don't you worry about that," Wanda Nell said. "I may find out something there, I may not. But it's worth taking the chance, don't you think?"

"I hope for your sake you're right."

"I appreciate your concern, Deputy," Wanda Nell said, working on keeping her temper. "But you let me worry about this, okay?"

"All right," Taylor responded grudgingly. "But if you run into any trouble, call me. Maybe I can do something to help."

"I will," Wanda Nell said. "Good-bye." She hung up before the deputy could say anything else. *I've had enough of her for a while,* she thought. *I got to get some sleep.* Slipping off her housecoat, Wanda Nell got into bed wearing just her bra and panties. She was bone-tired, but her mind was restless. She couldn't stop thinking about what the deputy had told her earlier, about Elmer Lee being after the money.

Elmer Lee was a dangerous man to cross. She'd always thought so, but for a long time she'd been able to keep out of his way. Now she didn't seem to have any choice. She worried about what the next day would bring, but gradually sleep overtook her, and she drifted off.

# Twenty-Five

Wanda Nell got home from her shift at Budget Mart the next morning just in time to see Juliet off on the school bus.

"Remember, honey, you wait there at school till we come to get you. If we're late, it won't be but a few minutes."

"Yes, Mama, I will," Juliet promised, giving her mother a quick peck on the check before boarding the bus.

Wanda Nell watched for a moment until the bus had rounded a curve in the road, then walked slowly back to her trailer. The early morning air was cool, and there was a hint of rain in the sky. Maybe it would hold off until she and Mayrene got back from Greenville.

Miranda was feeding Lavon when she stepped into the trailer. "Morning, Mama," she said. "How was work?" Lavon waved his hands and gurgled at her as Miranda stuck a spoon in his mouth.

"It was fine," Wanda Nell said, setting her purse down on a table near the door. She yawned. "But I'm plumb worn out, honey. I'm gonna go lie down for a couple hours before we head out." She came over to give Lavon a kiss on one of his sticky cheeks. She narrowly evaded an equally sticky hand intent on wiping mashed bananas in her hair.

"We'll be quiet, Mama," Miranda said, "so you just go on and lay down. You want me to get you up about nine-thirty?"

"That's fine, honey," Wanda Nell said. She touched Miranda's cheek with her hand, and Miranda smiled.

Miranda could be sweet when she wanted to, Wanda Nell reflected as she walked down the hall to her bedroom. Yawning again, she pulled off her clothes and climbed into bed. Problem was, Miranda didn't want to be sweet often enough.

Too tired to think much about the day's plans, Wanda Nell fell asleep soon after her head hit the pillow.

Some time later she felt someone shaking her gently and telling her it was time to get up.

Wanda Nell came slowly awake, blinking at the sunlight streaming through her window. She mumbled something, and Miranda laughed. "Sorry to wake you, Mama, but you wanted me to get you up."

Stretching, Wanda Nell regarded her daughter. "I know, honey," she said, vainly trying to suppress a yawn. "Lord knows I'd rather stay in bed, but I guess we got to do this."

"You really think it'll help get T.J. out of jail?" Miranda asked.

Wanda Nell pushed herself out of the bed and stretched again. "If the Good Lord is willing, it will." She patted her daughter's arm. "Now, you go and get Lavon ready, and all the things you'll need over at Laquita's today, while I jump in the shower. I won't be long."

"I done it all already, Mama," Miranda said proudly.

Touched, Wanda Nell kissed her on the cheek. "Thank you, Miranda. I appreciate all your help."

Dimpling with pleasure, Miranda left the room. Wanda Nell stumbled to the shower. She luxuriated in the hot water for five minutes, then washed herself and got reluctantly out of the shower. *How nice it would be just to stay here for a while*, she thought. But she forced herself to finish dressing in record time.

Mayrene was waiting for her in the living room, and Miranda and Lavon were ready to go. They put Miranda, the baby, and all the stuff they'd need into the backseat of Wanda Nell's car, and then they were off. It was just about nine-forty-five.

Laquita's house was on the way out of town, and after a quick greeting, Wanda Nell and Mayrene were back in the car. They headed out Highway 7 towards Greenwood. From there they'd hit 82 and take it all the way in to Greenville.

Wanda Nell wasn't much in the mood for conversation this morning, and Mayrene for once didn't try to fill the silence with chatter. At one point, when they were nearing Greenwood, Wanda Nell reached over and squeezed Mayrene's hand. "Thanks for being such a good friend."

Mayrene laughed. "Now, honey, don't start all that again. You know I'm glad to help." She laughed again. "Besides, this is a helluva lot more interesting than listening to gossip at the beauty shop."

Wanda Nell had to laugh, too. "You're gonna have a few good stories to tell yourself, once this is all over."

"I reckon so, Wanda Nell, I reckon so." She sighed. "Honey, how about stopping soon? I got to pee, and you must be dying for something to eat. Did you have any breakfast?"

"No, I didn't," Wanda Nell admitted. "Now that you mention it, I sure am hungry." She peered at the fuel gauge. "And I guess I could stand to fill up the car, too."

A few minutes later she pulled into a service station on the outskirts of Greenwood. While Mayrene hurried to the ladies' room, Wanda Nell filled the tank. Inside, she found some halfway fresh-looking doughnuts in a case and bought half a dozen, along with a large cup of hot coffee.

"Want any coffee?" she asked as Mayrene joined her at the counter.

"Sure," Mayrene said, and Wanda Nell paid while Mayrene fixed her coffee.

Back in the car, Wanda Nell finished a doughnut before starting the car. The bag of doughnuts sat on the seat between them, and Wanda Nell motioned for Mayrene to help herself.

"I really shouldn't." Mayrene sighed heavily. "I got to do something to shed a few pounds." Her hand hovered over the bag. "But not today." The hand reached into the bag and came out with a doughnut. She munched happily and sipped at her coffee as Wanda Nell pulled back onto the highway.

Before long they were on 82, headed for Greenville. They made it all the way to Leland before they both needed to stop for the bathroom again.

"That coffee just goes right through me," Mayrene complained as they got out of the car.

On the road once again, Mayrene said, "Now, honey, what's the plan? How are we gonna find this woman?"

"Real simple," Wanda Nell said. "We're gonna look in the phone book, and then try to find her house." She drained the last of her coffee from the cup and set the empty down on the seat beside her. "T.J. told me her name. Can't be too many Miz Turnipseeds in the book."

Mayrene laughed. "No, I guess not. What a name!"

It was about eleven-twenty when they reached Greenville. Wanda Nell watched for a likely place to stop and look at a phone book. A service station seemed as good a place as any,

so she pulled the car into the first clean-looking place she
spotted. Mayrene followed her inside.

Wanda Nell scanned the shelves first for something to
buy. She figured the man behind the counter might be inclined to be more helpful if she was buying something. She
grabbed a couple of Baby Ruth candy bars from a box and
approached the counter.

"That be all for you?" The man smiled brightly at them
both, but his eyes lingered on Mayrene's buxom figure. His
name tag read "Luther."

Wanda Nell didn't have a chance to respond. Taking the
man's interest as her cue, Mayrene leaned forward, resting
her bosom on the high counter, and batted her eyelashes
at him.

"Why, Luther, honey, there is something else you can do
for us. That is, if you don't mind helping two ladies who
don't know their way around this big ol' town very well."

Wanda Nell had to turn her head to hide her grin. The
poor man was practically drooling on the counter at the sight
of Mayrene's chest plopped down on his counter that way.

"Why, I reckon I'd be glad to help." The man's voice
came out a bit higher than before.

"You sure are a gentleman," Mayrene cooed at him. "Do
you mind letting us use your phone book?"

" 'Course not," he said, fumbling blindly around under
the counter. He couldn't even tear his eyes away long
enough to look underneath.

Wanda Nell wanted to giggle when he yelped in pain. He
had poked himself on something sharp, and he stuck the injured finger in his mouth. He goggled foolishly at them for
a moment, then bent down to finish rummaging under the
counter.

He placed the phone book on the counter with a flourish.

"Thank you, Luther, honey," Mayrene said, her voice

husky. She pulled the book toward her, and Wanda Nell leaned over her shoulder as she thumbed through the pages.

Quickly Mayrene found the right place, and her finger skimmed down the page, coming to rest on three entries for Turnipseed. "Well, look at that," she said, "who'd'a thought there'd be more'n one."

Wanda Nell frowned at the entries. There were a David L. Turnipseed, an L.J. Turnipseed, and a T.R. Turnipseed. They all lived on different streets. She turned the book around and pushed it toward the man. Tapping her finger on the spot where the Turnipseeds were listed, she asked, "Can you tell us if any of these addresses are anywhere near the casino?"

"You mean the ones for Turnipseed?"

"Yes," Wanda Nell and Mayrene chorused.

He leaned over and examined them. "I guess this one here," he said. "This L.J. Turnipseed. That's not far from the casino."

Wanda Nell and Mayrene looked at each other. "Might as well try that one first," Wanda Nell said. Reaching into her purse, she copied down the address and the phone number for L.J. Turnipseed. She also jotted down the information on the other two, just in case. Almost stuttering with happiness, the man gave them directions.

Mayrene handed the phone book back to the man, saying in her throatiest tone, "Luther, honey, you sure have been a big help." She breathed deeply. "And we sure do appreciate it."

Wanda Nell barely made it to the car before she burst out laughing. "You are shameless, Mayrene. That little man didn't know what hit him."

Mayrene settled herself into the car. Grinning complacently, she said, "Well, honey, you just got to use whatever the Good Lord gives you." She glanced down at her bosom.

"I reckon I ain't hurting nobody, and it sure did give him a thrill he ain't gonna forget anytime soon."

Still chuckling, Wanda Nell drove off.

It took them about fifteen minutes to find the quiet, slightly shabby street where L.J. Turnipseed lived. "Even numbers on this side," Mayrene said, squinting through the sunlight. "So it's over here. Next block, though."

Wanda Nell drove on and, three houses down from the corner in the next block, pulled the car to a stop in front of a large three-story brick house. The yard, unlike some others on the block, was well-tended. The grass had been mown recently, and the flower beds sported masses of color.

As Wanda Nell got out of the car, she glanced down the street. A large black car was parked, facing them, about four houses down, on the other side of the street. Wanda Nell thought she saw someone sitting inside, but with the sun in her eyes, she couldn't be sure.

Mayrene claimed her attention. "Look at this, Wanda Nell," she said. Wanda Nell's eyes followed the pointing finger to a spot in one of the flower beds near the front door.

"Isn't it just too sweet?" Mayrene said. "Maybe you should get something like this to take the place of your flamingoes."

Wanda Nell regarded the figures with interest. Two stone frogs, one male and the other female, sat facing each other on a love seat. An open stone umbrella shaded them as they gazed lovingly into each other's eyes. The whole thing stood about two feet tall.

"It is cute," Wanda Nell said. "I'll have to think about it." She wasn't too fond of frogs, ever since her little brother Rusty used to shove them down her dress.

She stepped past Mayrene, still lost in admiration, to ring the doorbell. As soon as the bell sounded, dogs began barking somewhere inside the house. Big dogs, too, Wanda Nell thought uneasily. She didn't like big dogs, either.

The door began to open, and Wanda Nell heard a childish voice scolding the dogs.

"Now you just hush, boys," the voice said. "Company's here, and y'all don't be rude."

The small figure at the door stood slightly in the shadow, and Wanda Nell couldn't see her clearly. She looked and sounded like she was about eight years old. Then she stepped into the light, and Wanda Nell almost gasped.

An elderly, wrinkled face beamed up at her. "Good morning, honey, what can I do for you?"

Wanda Nell stared down at her. She wasn't even five feet tall. Realizing she was being rude, Wanda Nell spoke hastily. "Good morning. I'm sorry to trouble you like this, but my name is Wanda Nell Culpepper, and—"

That was as far as she got. "Oh, I do declare, you must be Bobby Ray's wife," the little old woman said. "Now, you just come right on in here, and tell me what that scallywag has been up to." She stepped back and motioned for Wanda Nell and Mayrene to come inside.

Wanda Nell stopped in alarm before she had taken three steps into the house. Three very large, very black dogs sat at the foot of the stairs, tongues hanging out. They were all big enough that their little hostess could ride them like horses.

After shutting the door, the woman moved around in front of her visitors. "Now, y'all just don't pay my boys any attention at all. They are sweet, sweet boys, and I know they look ferocious. But they're just Mama's little lambs, aren't they?" Still cooing, she approached the dogs and rubbed their heads, one after the other.

Neither Wanda Nell nor Mayrene had advanced any farther into the hall.

"You're sure they won't bite?" Mayrene asked.

"Oh, honey, I'm sure. Now, if you was somebody trying to break in here, why then they might just eat you up. But they know you're friendly, and as long as you're friendly, they won't bother you."

Wanda Nell understood the threat in that gentle sentence, and she was sure Mayrene did, too.

Wanda Nell made an effort to smile. "Oh, we're friendly, ma'am. You don't have to worry about that."

"No, ma'am," Mayrene said.

"Good, then y'all just come on into my parlor. Boys, you stay here." Their hostess tottered across the hall and through a door.

Casting uneasy glances over their shoulders, Wanda Nell and Mayrene followed the little woman.

Using a step stool, their hostess climbed onto a chair. Waving a hand, she indicated that Wanda Nell and Mayrene should seat themselves on a sofa.

"Now, Miz Culpepper, what can I do for you and your friend, before you tell me all about what Bobby Ray's been doing?"

"This is Mayrene Lancaster, ma'am," Wanda Nell said. "And you must be Miz Turnipseed."

"That's Miss Turnipseed," she corrected smilingly. "Miss Lucinda Jane Turnipseed, dear. Pleased to meet you, Miz Lancaster."

"Likewise, I'm sure," Mayrene said.

Wanda Nell glanced around the room. Every inch of it was crammed with things. Pictures, little figurines, cushions, just about every knickknack you could imagine perched on every available surface. The room was spotless, however. Wanda Nell figured the poor dear must spend every minute of her day dusting and cleaning, even though she must be eighty.

"About Bobby Ray," Wanda Nell began.

"Oh, isn't he just the handsomest thing," Miss Turnipseed said, clapping her hands together. "And such a smooth talker, too. I can't imagine how you could bear to let him live over here and work in Greenville, and you over there in Tullahoma with your children." She sighed. "And he misses those children dreadfully."

Wanda Nell and Mayrene exchanged startled glances.

"Is that what he told you?" Wanda Nell asked finally.

"Oh, my, yes," Miss Turnipseed said. "You should see all the pictures he has in his room. He told me all about T.J., and Miranda, and little Juliet." She beamed at them. "Such a proud father."

"Um, I suppose so," Wanda Nell said. She shouldn't be surprised that Bobby Ray had fed this old lady such a line of crap. He sure wouldn't have told her the truth. And no telling how old and out-of-date those pictures of the kids were.

"When he gets back from his trip," Miss Turnipseed was saying as Wanda Nell tuned in again, "he said he would be moving back to Tullahoma permanently. I sure hate to lose him, he's been such a good lodger. But a man's place is with his family, after all."

"Where did he tell you he was going, Miss Turnipseed?" Mayrene asked.

"Why, to Texas, of course," Miss Turnipseed said, puzzled. "To claim his lottery prize. But surely you know all about that."

# Twenty-Six

"A lottery ticket?" Mayrene's voice rose on each syllable. "You have gotta be kidding me."

"Why, yes, Miz Lancaster," Miss Turnipseed replied. "A friend in Texas sent it to him, Bobby Ray said. It was a birthday present, I believe." She smiled. "And what a lovely present, too. Winning all that money, and him so down on his luck before that. He so wants to be able to do things for you and the children."

Wanda Nell stared at her, unable to respond.

"Oh, yes," Miss Turnipseed went on, "the three months he's been here in Greenville have been just torture to him, the poor boy. He just can't stand being away from you and the children. He surely doesn't like working at that casino, being around all that gambling and drinking and Lord-knows-what kind of carrying on."

"Oh, really," Mayrene said. "Now hold on just a minute."

Quickly, Wanda Nell jabbed an elbow into her friend's side, none too gently. Mayrene subsided with a grunt.

"Miss Turnipseed," Wanda Nell said slowly, "I'm afraid I have some bad news for you. I don't know how to tell you this, but Bobby Ray is dead."

"Oh, my," Miss Turnipseed said before she fainted.

Alarmed, Wanda Nell jumped up from the sofa and scurried over to Miss Turnipseed. Kneeling on the floor, Wanda Nell clasped one of her tiny hands in her own and rubbed it gently. "Try to find her some water or something," she instructed Mayrene.

While Mayrene went looking for some kind of restorative, Wanda Nell continued chafing those small hands. Slowly, Miss Turnipseed showed signs of stirring.

"Oh, my," she said, her voice barely above a whisper. Freeing one of her hands from Wanda Nell, she fumbled in the bosom of her dress and withdrew a small bottle. She handed it to Wanda Nell. "Could you open it for me, please?"

Wanda Nell took the bottle, opened it, and spilled some very tiny pills out into the palm of her hand. Shakily Miss Turnipseed grasped one of the pills and stuck it under her tongue.

"Nitroglycerin," she whispered after a moment. "For my heart."

"Oh, my goodness," Wanda Nell said, feeling like fainting herself. What had she almost done? "I'm so sorry, Miss Turnipseed. I shouldn't have told you that way. I'm so sorry."

The small hand stroked hers. It felt like a butterfly fluttering on Wanda Nell's skin. "Don't blame yourself, dear. You couldn't know about my bad heart. Just one of my tiresome spells." Miss Turnipseed closed her eyes and rested for a moment.

"Here," Mayrene said, thrusting a glass of water into Wanda Nell's free hand.

"Try to drink some of this," Wanda Nell said, holding the glass close to Miss Turnipseed's mouth.

Miss Turnipseed sipped delicately. "Thank you, dear," she said. Her voice was stronger, and she made an effort to sit up. Wanda Nell helped her. The little body seemed so frail under her big, work-roughened hands.

"I'm better, dear, thank you." Miss Turnipseed's color had come back, and she did indeed look much better than she had minutes before.

Wanda Nell and Mayrene sat back down on the sofa. Wanda Nell's stomach ached. She had almost given the poor little thing a heart attack. Mayrene patted her hand soothingly.

"Now, don't you worry, dear," Miss Turnipseed said. "I'll be just fine. But tell me, dear, about poor Bobby Ray. What happened? Was it an accident?" Tears began slowly trickling down her face. She reached again into her bosom and extracted a lacy handkerchief to dry the tears.

"Well, no," Wanda Nell said, hating to have to tell her the truth. "I'm afraid, Miss Turnipseed, that somebody killed Bobby Ray."

"Oh, how dreadful," Miss Turnipseed said. The handkerchief fluttered as she dabbed at her face.

Wanda Nell feared she was about to have another spell, as she called it.

"That poor boy," Miss Turnipseed said. "All he wanted was to take care of his family, and somebody hurt him like that."

Wanda Nell exchanged glances helplessly with Mayrene, who shrugged.

"It's pretty complicated," Wanda Nell said, choosing her words with care, "but I guess what it boils down to is, somebody was after Bobby Ray's money."

Beside her on the sofa, Mayrene coughed. Wanda Nell figured it couldn't hurt to gild over the truth a little bit. She couldn't bear to cause this elderly woman any more grief than she had to. She glared at Mayrene, warning her not to say anything.

"People can be so greedy, and so vicious. What a world we live in nowadays." Miss Turnipseed shook her head dolefully. "What are we coming to?"

"I know, it's sure terrible," Wanda Nell agreed. "And the police are trying to track down who did it, and what became of Bobby Ray's money." *Please Lord,* she thought, *let the police leave this poor woman alone so she never finds out the truth about Bobby Ray.*

Miss Turnipseed had been staring off into space, and Wanda Nell could see her lips were moving, even though they couldn't hear her saying anything.

After a moment, Miss Turnipseed's gaze focused on them again. "When did it happen?"

"Three days ago," Wanda Nell said.

"Oh, dear," Miss Turnipseed sighed. "A few nights ago, I reckon it must have been the night before he died, when he'd already left for Tullahoma, somebody was prowling around outside the house."

"What happened?" Mayrene asked.

"It was about two in the morning," Miss Turnipseed said. "The boys woke me up, they were making such a racket. And whoever it was must've heard them and took off." She smiled proudly. "My boys look after me. Don't you, boys?"

Hearing themselves summoned, the dogs padded into the room and settled on the floor around Miss Turnipseed's chair. Wanda Nell and Mayrene regarded them warily.

"Whoever it was must have been after Bobby Ray's winning lottery ticket. Did he even have time to go to Texas to collect it?" Her eyes fixed brightly on Wanda Nell, Miss Turnipseed waited for an answer.

"No, ma'am," Wanda Nell said, trying to think what to tell her. "He didn't make it to Texas, after all."

"And the ticket?"

Mayrene snorted. "That ticket's gone, Miss Turnipseed. No point in pining over it now."

"You mean whoever killed Bobby Ray got away with the ticket?" Miss Turnipseed said, dabbing at her eyes again. "That's just wicked, that surely is."

This conversation just kept getting weirder by the second, and Wanda Nell wasn't sure what to say next to Miss Turnipseed. By not telling her the truth from the get-go, she'd gotten them bogged down in all these lies. She decided she'd better come clean, at least part of the way.

"I'm afraid, Miss Turnipseed, that there wasn't no winning lottery ticket," Wanda Nell said, watching their hostess for signs of an impending spell.

"Oh, dear," Miss Turnipseed whispered in response. "I was mighty afraid of that." She fixed Wanda Nell with a stern gaze. "I didn't want to say this, dear, because he was your husband, and he was a dear, sweet boy who was very kind to me, but I knew Bobby Ray wasn't always as honest as he should be."

Wanda Nell breathed a sigh of relief. This little old lady wasn't as naïve as she first appeared. "No, ma'am, Bobby Ray was known to stretch the truth on occasion. I know that all too well."

"Tell me, then, did he have some money unexpectedly?" Miss Turnipseed folded her hands in her lap and watched Wanda Nell like a hungry little bird.

"Yes, ma'am, he did," Wanda Nell answered, wondering how much more she should say.

"Then that's where he got his rent money," Miss Turnipseed said, almost to herself.

"He didn't owe you any money?" Mayrene asked, squirming on the sofa. "I'm sitting on a bad spring or something," she whispered to Wanda Nell.

"No, the day he left, he paid me everything he owed me, plus for two more weeks," Miss Turnipseed said. "I'll be happy to refund that extra part, dear."

"No, no," Wanda Nell said, "you keep that money. I promise you, I don't need it."

"That's very kind of you," Miss Turnipseed said, "and I won't argue with you, prices being what they are these days."

Wanda Nell stood up. "Miss Turnipseed, would you mind if I saw Bobby Ray's room? If he left any personal things behind, well, I guess I ought to take 'em back with me."

"Why of course, dear," Miss Turnipseed said. "You'll forgive me, I know, if I don't accompany you. Just go up the stairs, and it's the first door on your left. The two rooms on that side were Bobby Ray's." She fumbled in a pocket of her dress for a set of keys. She handed them to Wanda Nell and indicated the correct key.

"My maid hasn't cleaned in there this week," Miss Turnipseed called after Wanda Nell and Mayrene. "So please forgive the mess."

Upstairs, her hand trembling slightly, Wanda Nell inserted the key in the lock and opened it. She pushed open the door and stepped into the room.

Despite what Miss Turnipseed had said, the room was very clean. There was a faint odor of Bobby Ray's aftershave, and Wanda Nell found herself tearing up unexpectedly as she smelled it. The furnishings were all antiques in good repair, and Bobby Ray had left little imprint on the room. Wanda Nell did find the pictures Miss Turnipseed had mentioned. She examined them one by one and wasn't surprised to see that they all dated from nearly ten years before.

"Oh, Bobby Ray," she whispered, wiping the tears away with the back of her hand. It was all so pathetic. The best he could do was ten-year-old pictures of his children.

"I'll go ask Miss Turnipseed for a box," Mayrene said.

Wanda Nell nodded. She peered into the closet, but there was nothing inside except a uniform. His work clothes for the casino, she guessed. She found little else, just a few pieces of ragged underwear in a drawer and a few dirty magazines in the nightstand drawer.

Could Bobby Ray have hidden any of the money here? she wondered. She didn't have the heart to do a thorough search, and after thinking about it, she decided Bobby Ray wouldn't have left the money behind. The money was in Tullahoma.

She stared again at the dirty magazines. Bobby Ray would always buy them when they were still together, and he would try to hide them from her. But she always found them. He'd been buying them since he was a teenager and had to hide them from his mother and Charlesetta.

That reminded her. Charlesetta had said something to her, something that might be important. She'd have to think about all this for a while.

Mayrene came back then with a couple of small boxes, and together they packed the pitiful remains of Bobby Ray's life in Greenville. Mayrene wrinkled her nose in disgust over the dirty magazines, but Wanda Nell just shrugged. They were no surprise to her.

"What you wanna do with this uniform?"

"We'll take it with us," Wanda Nell said, "but I don't have any hankering to take it to the casino. Do you think we should?"

"I don't think it matters all that much," Mayrene said. "They ain't gonna go broke over one uniform."

Downstairs again, they checked on Miss Turnipseed. She sat where they had left her, in her chair guarded by her boys.

"Thank you, Miss Turnipseed," Wanda Nell said. "I'm sorry to have to tell you such bad news."

"Don't worry, dear," the old lady assured her. "I'll get on with things, never fear. You just take care of yourself and those precious children." She paused for a moment. "And say good-bye to Bobby Ray for me." She turned her head away.

That almost made Wanda Nell break down completely. She clutched the box she held to her chest and tried to hold on to her composure. Mayrene moved closer to Miss Turnipseed, blocking Wanda Nell from view.

"Is there anyone we can call to sit with you?" Mayrene asked.

"No, dear, I'll be fine," Miss Turnipseed said. "My maid will be back soon from her errands, and she'll look after me. Y'all just let yourselves out."

Wanda Nell had herself under control again, and she said good-bye to Miss Turnipseed. She and Mayrene made their way out of the house and into the sunshine.

"Lord," Wanda Nell said. "I feel about a hundred years old now."

"I know what you mean," Mayrene said, following Wanda Nell down the walk to the car.

Wanda Nell got her keys out of her pocket and went back to the trunk. "Let's put that stuff in here." She balanced her box on her hip while she opened the trunk with her free hand.

The trunk popped open, and Wanda Nell moved some junk aside to set the box down. She moved over to let

Mayrene put her box in, and as she did so, she caught sight of a black car coming slowly up the street toward them.

Wanda Nell was about to open her door and get inside, when the black car came to a stop beside them. The driver's window slid down.

"Howdy, Miz Culpepper," said the driver. "We want to talk to you." The back door opened, and a hand motioned for her to come closer.

"I don't know who the hell you are," Wanda Nell said, her heart racing, "but I'm not getting in any strange car."

"Yes, you are," the driver said, pointing a gun straight at her.

# Twenty-Seven

Wanda Nell stared blankly at the gun for a moment. Surely this couldn't be happening, right out here in the daylight.

The driver waggled the gun at her again. "Stop messing around, Miz Culpepper, and get in the car."

Wanda Nell stood her ground. She wasn't going to get in that car. Surely they wouldn't shoot her, right out here in the street. "I'm not getting in your car, mister. You can flash that gun at me all you want." Her voice came out a lot stronger and more defiant than she thought it would.

"You'd best be moving on, Bubba," Mayrene said from behind her.

The driver's eyes widened, and the hand holding the gun faltered for a moment. Wanda Nell turned her head slightly, and she could see Mayrene, leaning across the hood of the car with her shotgun pointed straight at the driver's head.

Wanda Nell looked back at the driver. Smirking, he said, "Come on, honey, you don't even know how to use that big ol' gun. I can put a hole through Miz Culpepper's head, and you can't do nothing about it."

"I reckon you could," Mayrene drawled back at him, "but then you ain't gonna have a face left if you do. It's pretty damn ugly anyway, so it wouldn't be much of a loss." She laughed. "Your call, Bubba."

The driver's face reddened, and Wanda Nell feared for a moment that he was going to shoot her anyway. Then the hand went down, and the gun disappeared. He brought his empty hand back up and put it on the steering wheel.

"That's better, Bubba," Mayrene said. "Now why don't y'all just move on along, and leave us alone."

"If I might have a word with you first." A voice with clipped northern tones came from the backseat. A moment later a head emerged, shining in the sunlight, followed by a tall, lean body. He was completely bald and about fifty years old, Wanda Nell figured. He wore a suit that looked real expensive and a bit hot in the early afternoon sunlight.

"I apologize for my associate's rather rash behavior, ladies," he said. "It was not my intention to frighten you, but I do need to talk to Mrs. Culpepper."

"Go right ahead," Mayrene said. "Ain't no reason you can't talk right here, mister. I'm real comfortable." She held the shotgun steadily on the driver.

"Yeah, say what you have to say," Wanda Nell told him, taking a couple of steps backward to make sure Mayrene had a clear shot if she needed one.

The bald man spread his hands in a gesture of surrender. "Very well, ladies." He sighed deeply. "This is all terribly uncivilized, but if this is what you want. We could just as easily discuss this over a nice, leisurely lunch at one of this lovely city's finest restaurants. My treat. What do you say?"

"I say, talk or get the hell out of here. My trigger finger's getting real itchy," Mayrene said.

Wanda Nell nodded in agreement. Her heart rate had slowed down to almost normal. These guys must be from the casino, and she was curious what the bald man wanted from her.

"As you wish," he said. He leaned against the car. "Mrs. Culpepper, first let me convey my sympathies on the death of your husband."

"Ex-husband," Wanda Nell corrected.

The bald man inclined his head slightly. "Whatever. The main point is, Mrs. Culpepper, your ex-husband took something that didn't belong to him. It's my job to see that it is returned to its proper owners. With your husband—pardon me, your ex-husband—sadly out of the picture, it's now your responsibility to help me."

"I don't have your damn money," Wanda Nell said, getting madder by the second, "and I don't have any flippin' idea where it is. Frankly, I could give a rat's ass. It ain't my problem."

"Oh, but it is" the bald man began to say smoothly.

Wanda Nell interrupted him before he could say anything else. "Now you just listen here, bud. You can threaten me all you want, but I ain't got your damn money. You already had the nerve to send some of your goons to search my home and terrify my daughters and my grandson. What kind of men are you, to do something like that to children? Did your mama raise you to treat people like that? Where I come from, people who do things like that ain't nothing but trash."

The bald man reddened slightly under the onslaught, but the expression on his face never changed. "If you've had your say, Mrs. Culpepper, I'll continue. You can say what you like about me, but I could give a rat's ass, to borrow your own colorful phrase. I want that money back, and I expect you to hand it over."

"Well, Bubba, I guess you're just going to be disappointed. Santa Claus ain't gonna leave nothing but coal in your stocking this year." Wanda Nell was so mad, she could feel the veins in her head throbbing. "I don't have your damn money, I never did. And if I do find it, I'm gonna turn it over to the police. You can get it back from them."

"Now that's a pity," he said coolly. "I might be inclined to offer a reward if the money is returned without the police getting involved. But if they are, well, no reward."

Wanda Nell told him just what he could do with his reward. His expression changed, finally, and Wanda Nell didn't like what she saw.

"Very well, Mrs. Culpepper. This could have been much easier, but you chose to make it difficult. I trust you understand that." He got back in the car and slammed his door.

"Hold on a minute," Wanda Nell said as the driver started to put the car into gear. "I do have one thing that belongs to you."

She went around to the trunk and pulled the casino security uniform out the box. Wadding it into a ball, she walked back to the black car and thrust it into the driver's face. Scowling, he snatched it and dumped it in the lap of the man in the passenger seat.

The wail of an approaching siren startled Wanda Nell. The driver heard it, slammed his foot on the accelerator, and the black car sped off.

Wanda Nell leaned weakly against the car. "Oh, Lord, I'm glad that's over." She pushed away from the car and turned to face Mayrene. "And, honey, you were something else. I didn't even know you brought that shotgun with you."

Mayrene grinned. "Told you it'd come in handy, didn't I?"

"Amen. But would you really have shot him?"

"I shot plenty of snakes in my time, Wanda Nell. He just woulda been one more, that's all." Mayrene stowed the shotgun in the backseat.

Just in time, too, Wanda Nell saw. A Greenville police car was coming up the street. She hoped they hadn't seen what Mayrene was doing.

"Y'all all right, ma'am?" The police car had come to a halt, and the officer driving poked his head out the window. "We had a report there was some kind of disturbance going on in the street here."

Wanda Nell smiled at him. "Everything's fine now, officer. Just some men bothering me and my friend. Didn't seem to want to take 'no' for an answer, but we finally convinced them just about the time they heard your siren."

"You sure?"

"I'm sure. We'll be fine now. Those men won't be bothering us again." Wanda Nell sounded more confident than she felt.

"Okay, ma'am. Y'all have a nice day now, you hear?"

Wanda Nell and Mayrene waved as the police car slowly drove out of sight.

"Let's get the heck out of here," Wanda Nell said, sliding into the car.

"Amen," Mayrene said, slamming her door shut. "We oughta thank whoever called the police, but they probably wanna see the back of us by now."

Wanda Nell made a U-turn right there and headed the car back the way they had come. She was surprised to note, when she glanced at her watch, that it was barely one o'clock. So much had happened, surely it ought to be later than that.

"I don't know about you, honey," Mayrene said, "but I wouldn't mind a little something to eat. All that excitement's made me hungry." She laughed.

Wanda Nell laughed with her. She felt very tired now and wanted nothing more than to crawl in a bed somewhere and sleep. But she couldn't do that. Maybe something to eat, and something with caffeine in it to drink, would perk her up.

"We got time, I guess," Wanda Nell said. On their way back out to Highway 82, she spotted a small restaurant that didn't appear to be too busy. "How about there?"

Mayrene followed her pointing finger. "Looks just fine to me, honey."

The place wasn't much more than a hole-in-the-wall kind of diner, but the food turned out to be very good and very cheap. They both ordered the day's special, country fried steak with mashed potatoes, cream gravy, and corn on the cob. Dessert was lemon icebox pie.

Neither Wanda Nell nor Mayrene said much as they ate. Mayrene asked for a second slice of the pie. Wanda Nell grinned at her.

"It sure was good," she said.

"Uh-huh," Mayrene said, savoring the last bite of her pie.

"I sure would like a cigarette about now," Wanda Nell said, sighing. She missed them most after eating. Somehow a meal just didn't seem complete without a cigarette.

"I know, honey," Mayrene said, "but you're better off not smoking. You notice you don't cough the way you used to."

"Yeah," Wanda Nell agreed. "Even so."

"I'll be back in a minute," Mayrene said. "Watch my purse for me."

Wanda Nell nodded. She glanced at her watch as Mayrene departed for the ladies' room. One thirty-five. They'd better get a move on. The drive back to Tullahoma would take about ninety minutes, and they had stop to pick up Miranda and Lavon before they picked up Juliet at school. They'd be a little late, but Juliet could wait inside for a few minutes. There'd still be plenty of teachers around.

Wanda Nell grabbed up Mayrene's purse and her own and took them to the ladies' room with her. Mayrene was washing her hands. "It's getting late," Wanda Nell said. "We need to get going."

"I'll pay and meet you outside," Mayrene said. She waved away the money Wanda Nell tried to give her. "Next one's on you, honey."

A few minutes later they were on the road again. After what had happened to them today, Wanda Nell felt a sense of urgency to see her daughters again. She wanted to be sure they were safe. She didn't trust that bald man not to do something to her kids. She kept looking in her rearview mirror, just in case, but far as she could tell, nobody was following them.

Wanda Nell pushed the accelerator up to seventy out on the highway, and the little car buzzed along. Traffic was fairly light, and Wanda Nell said a short prayer that they wouldn't run into a highway patrolman. "High-tailers" was what T.J. had called them when he was a little boy. She smiled, thinking about that. She wanted her baby out of jail, and soon.

"Where do you think that money is, Wanda Nell?"

Mayrene's question broke through her thoughts.

"I've been thinking a lot about that," Wanda Nell said. "I sure don't think it's anywhere in my trailer, and the only other place I can think of that Bobby Ray might've hid it would be at his mama's house."

"Did he even go see his mama before he was killed?" Mayrene snorted in disgust. "I thought he stayed pretty far away from that ole biddy."

"Usually," Wanda Nell said. "She even called me that night, asking me to tell him to come see her when I saw him. And you know she had to be pretty desperate to do that."

"Do you think he did?"

"I think maybe he did," Wanda Nell said. "Yesterday, when I went to see her about helping T.J. with the lawyer, Charlesetta said something about Bobby Ray. I didn't pay it too much attention at the time, but now I'm thinking maybe she was referring to Bobby Ray visiting his mama that night. It would've been pretty late, but he never paid much mind to the time."

"And did he have the money with him, you think?"

"Probably."

"How was he getting around, all over the place like that? He sure wasn't walking everywhere."

"No, he wasn't," Wanda Nell said. "I figure he must've had Ricky Ratliff's truck at least part of the time. Ricky was in on it somehow, else he wouldn't've got killed like that. But Bobby Ray wouldn't have trusted him too much, because Ricky couldn't keep his mouth shut to save his life."

"I reckon not," Mayrene said dryly.

"Nope." Wanda Nell felt a twinge of regret for Ricky. Poor, dumb, slob Ricky, whose only excitement in life came through whatever stunt Bobby Ray was pulling.

"So, what you gonna do? Just march right up to the door and ask for the money?"

"Yeah, right." Wanda Nell laughed. "That old witch has no idea all that money's right under her nose. I'll just have to go there and look. And maybe I'll take you and your shotgun, just in case." She laughed again.

"Did you see the look on that asshole's face?" Mayrene guffawed. "Honey, I bet he like to wet all over himself. Some man, waving a gun at women like that. Who the hell's he think he is?"

"You showed him," Wanda Nell said. "But the whole thing was like a nightmare. What am I gonna do if they come after me again?"

"All we got to do is find that money, and there ain't gonna be a next time. You find it and turn it over to the sheriff's department. End of story."

Wanda Nell sighed. "I sure as hell hope so."

They drove on in silence. They made good time to just beyond Greenwood, where they left 82 and headed northeast on highway 7 toward Tullahoma.

At five minutes to three they pulled into the driveway at Laquita's house. Miranda had seen them and came hurrying out with Lavon on her hip.

"I thought y'all'd be back way before now," she said. "We're gonna be late picking up Juliet." She handed Lavon to her mother, who'd gotten out of the car to help her. Not waiting for any answer, Miranda ran back to the house and got the baby's diaper bag and other things. Wanda Nell had Lavon fastened in his car seat by the time Miranda returned.

"I appreciate you hurrying like that, Miranda, but we won't be but a few minutes late picking up Juliet," Wanda Nell said.

"I know, Mama," Miranda said, "but I just been feeling anxious all day. I don't like this."

"I know, honey," Wanda Nell said. She wasn't going to add to the girl's distress by telling her what had happened in Greenville. "Let's just go get your sister and get on home."

They drove up to the front of the high school at eleven minutes past three. Wanda Nell waited a moment for Juliet to appear. A number of students and teachers were still milling about, and she thought maybe Juliet hadn't spotted them yet.

They waited a few more minutes as the crowd continued to thin, but still no Juliet.

Frowning, Wanda Nell got out of the car. She walked up the steps into the front door of the school. No sign of Juliet anywhere in the hallway.

A sick feeling settling in the pit of her stomach, Wanda Nell hurried down the hall to the school office. A woman looked up as Wanda Nell stumbled to a halt in front of her desk.

"Can I help you?"

"I'm looking for my daughter, Juliet Culpepper," Wanda Nell said, trying to catch her breath and talk at the same time. "I was supposed to pick her up, and now I can't find her."

"There must be some mistake," the woman said, staring at Wanda Nell suspiciously.

"What do you mean?" Wanda Nell demanded. "What kind of mistake?"

"We had a call about fifteen minutes ago from someone in the sheriff's department that you'd been injured in a car accident," the woman said. "And that a deputy would be coming to pick up your daughter and take her to the hospital."

# Twenty-Eight

Wanda Nell gripped the counter in front of her to keep from fainting. "Somebody's lying," she managed to say.

"I assure you, Miz Culpepper," the woman said in frosty tones, "I am not making this up. We summoned Juliet from her class to tell her, and one of the secretaries waited with her until the sheriff's department car arrived to pick her up. That was about ten minutes ago. And I assure you everything was in order, or Miss Belson wouldn't have let Juliet leave."

"I wanna talk to this secretary, this Miss Belson," Wanda Nell said. "Somebody lied about an accident, and I wanna know who took my daughter off."

"She's already gone home," the woman said. "I'm sorry, Miz Culpepper, I'm sure there's just been some kind of misunderstanding. If it wasn't you that had the accident, could it've been somebody else in the family?"

Wanda Nell wanted to scream in frustration, because none of this was helping. Then she realized what the woman had asked.

"Oh, my Lord," Wanda Nell gasped as the implication hit her. "Maybe it was Juliet's grandmother." She frowned. "But that don't make no sense. Why would they come get Juliet? She hardly knows her grandmother."

"Maybe she was the only member of the family they knew where to find?"

Wanda Nell stared at the woman. What should she do?

"I need to use a phone," she said.

The woman pointed to one on a nearby desk. "Just dial nine first, then dial your number. It's not long distance, is it?"

"No, it's not," Wanda Nell said shortly. She moved over to the desk and punched in the number for the sheriff's department.

"I need to speak to Elmer Lee Johnson. This is an emergency."

The dispatcher's voice squawked in her ear.

"Then where the hell is he?"

More squawking.

"Then is Deputy Taylor anywhere around?" Wanda Nell listened for a moment. "All right, then. Maybe you can tell me something. My name is Wanda Nell Culpepper, and I'm here at the high school to pick up my daughter Juliet. But they tell me somebody from the sheriff's department called and told 'em that I was in an accident, and they'd be coming to pick up my daughter. Do you know anything about that?"

The voice disclaimed all knowledge of such a call.

"Then where the hell is my daughter?" Wanda Nell shouted at the dispatcher. Without waiting for an answer, she slammed the receiver down so hard her arm tingled.

"Miz Culpepper!" The woman stood up from her desk. "Please. That's school property."

Wanda Nell turned to glare at her, and the woman backed away. "You got more than school property to worry about, lady. If something happens to my daughter on account of this, I'm gonna sue your ass up one side and down the other. Why didn't somebody call the sheriff's department and check out this story? They say they never made any such call."

The woman paled and sat down abruptly, almost missing her chair. "Oh, my Lord."

"I ain't got time for this," Wanda Nell said. She ran out of the office and back down the hall. She burst out through the doors, almost knocking down a man.

"Sorry," she muttered, "but I'm in a hurry."

"Mrs. Culpepper, are you okay?" He laid a hand on her arm.

When Wanda Nell finally saw him clearly, she realized it was Jack Pemberton.

"I've got to find Juliet," she told him. "I don't have time to talk."

"Juliet? What's happened?"

Wanda Nell read the real concern in his face, and despite her impatience to be on her way, she explained briefly.

"Let me come with you," Pemberton said impulsively. "You may need help."

"Thank you," Wanda Nell said, "but—"

"Wanda Nell," Mayrene called, interrupting her. "Your cell phone's ringing."

Wanda Nell ran down the steps to the car and plucked the cell phone from Mayrene's hand. She was trembling so much that she almost dropped it and didn't take time to read the caller ID. "Hello?"

"Mama, it's me," Juliet said faintly. "I'm here at Grandmama Culpepper's. You need to get here right away."

"I'm on the way, baby. Are you all right?"

"Just hurry, Mama." The line went dead.

"Oh, my Lord," Wanda Nell said. She thrust the cell phone back at Mayrene and ran around to get in the car.

"Wait up, I'm coming with you," Jack Pemberton said as he hurried down the steps toward them.

"Well, get in the car, honey," Mayrene said.

Pemberton opened the back door on the passenger side and stuffed himself in. Miranda and the baby's car seat took up a lot of the room.

Wanda Nell didn't waste time arguing. She floored the accelerator, and the Cavalier surged past a couple of cars moving down the driveway toward the street. If it was Elmer Lee that pulled a stunt like this, she vowed she'd serve his balls to him on a plate and make him like it.

"Careful, honey," Mayrene said. "It's not gonna do us any good to run over somebody."

"Sorry," Wanda Nell muttered, "but we gotta get to ol' Miz Culpepper's house."

"What's going on, Mama?" Miranda demanded. "And who is this guy?"

"Jack Pemberton," he said. "I'm Juliet's English teacher."

"Oh, him," Miranda said, her voice cool.

"Yes," he said. "And you must be Miranda."

"Pleased to meet you, Jack Pemberton," Mayrene said, twisting around to look at him. "I live next door to Wanda Nell and the girls. I'm Mayrene Lancaster."

"My pleasure, Miz Lancaster," he said. "I apologize for barging in like this, but I thought maybe I could be of some use."

"Maybe so, if somebody would just explain what the heck is going on here," Mayrene said, "and why we're in such an all-fired hurry."

Tersely, Wanda Nell recounted what she had learned in the school office.

"Something smells pretty fishy to me," Mayrene said.

"Mama, you think somebody kidnapped Juliet?" Miranda bounced up and down on the seat in her excitement. Lavon, startled by his mother's actions, began to cry.

"Everybody just shut up," Wanda Nell said. "Please. I can't even think. We got to get to Miz Culpepper's house and see what's going on. Maybe something happened to her, and they got Juliet to come. Maybe that's all there is to it."

Wanda Nell wanted desperately to believe that herself. It didn't take much imagination to see the old woman falling down the stairs and hurting herself, not the way she drank. Or maybe she ran over somebody in her car or smashed herself into a tree. Wanda Nell didn't really care, as long as Juliet was safe and unhurt.

Miranda quieted Lavon, and no one else said anything as Wanda Nell maneuvered through the afterschool traffic. The high school wasn't all that far from Main Street, just on the other side of the highway.

Wanda Nell turned onto Main two blocks from the old Culpepper house. Looking up the street, she didn't see any signs of an ambulance, police cars, or anyone from the sheriff's department.

When she pulled into the driveway, she saw a small, beat-up Toyota parked to one side of the concrete apron by the garage. Whose car was that?

"Something seems mighty strange about all this," Mayrene observed as they all got out of the car.

"Maybe y'all had better stay here," Wanda Nell said, "and let me go in."

"Nope," Mayrene said. "Miranda and Lavon can stay out here." She pointed to a nearby tree with a wooden bench beneath it. "They can sit over there in the shade. You just pop open the trunk, honey, and let me get my insurance policy."

Jack Pemberton eyed her curiously, but Wanda Nell ignored him. "Mayrene's right, Miranda," she said. "Why don't you take the baby over there, and y'all sit out in the shade." She tossed the keys to Mayrene. "Help yourself."

Miranda had a mulish look on her face, but for once she didn't argue. She took Lavon over to the bench and flopped down.

Wanda Nell strode up the walk to the front door, ignoring Mayrene's instructions to wait for her. Jack Pemberton was only a step or two behind her.

Wanda Nell stuck her finger on the doorbell and held it down. She could hear the strident ring through the door. Peering through the beveled glass, she saw a shadow approaching them. She took her finger from the bell.

Slowly the door swung open, and Charlesetta's dark face brightened when she saw Wanda Nell. "Thank the Lord, you here," she said. "Y'all come on in."

"What's going on here, Charlesetta?" Wanda Nell demanded. "Where's Juliet?"

Charlesetta didn't reply. Her eyes were fixed on Mayrene and her shotgun. Wanda Nell tapped Charlesetta on the arm. The old woman's eyes focused on her.

"What you say, Miz Wanda Nell? Oh, Miss Juliet, she be in the parlor with her grandmama and that other lady."

"Other lady?" Wanda Nell pushed past Charlesetta and ran for the parlor. So it wasn't Elmer Lee.

"I'm so glad you're here, Miz Culpepper," Tracy Taylor greeted her. She sat with Juliet to her right on the sofa, and old Mrs. Culpepper stared with bleary eyes from a chair to the left of her.

"But who are all these people?" The deputy's hand slid to the gun in the holster at her waist. "And why does that woman have a shotgun?"

"These are my friends," Wanda Nell said. "Never you mind who they are, or why one of 'em's toting a shotgun. You better start telling me what the hell is going on here."

Juliet, staring fearfully at her mother, started to get up from the sofa, but the deputy placed a restraining hand on her leg. Juliet shrank bank onto the sofa.

Wanda Nell took a step forward. Deputy Taylor held up her hand. "Let's all just relax here," she said. "No need to get all excited. Why don't y'all sit down in those chairs over there." She kept her hand on the holstered gun as she nodded to the chairs.

Warily, Wanda Nell, Mayrene, and Jack Pemberton did as she said. Mayrene kept a grip on her shotgun, making sure the deputy could see it.

"Okay," Wanda Nell said after she sat down. "So what's going on here?"

"I'm trying to save your daughter's life, and yours," Taylor said calmly.

"By scaring us all half to death?" Wanda Nell demanded.

Taylor shrugged. "I had to act fast, or else Deputy Johnson would have got to her first. You oughta be thanking me for what I did."

"Why would Elmer Lee Johnson be after Juliet?" Mayrene's voice dripped scorn. "That don't make no sense whatsoever."

"He was gonna take her and hold her for ransom," Taylor said. "He wants to force Miz Culpepper there to turn over the money, and then he was gonna skedaddle out of here."

"I don't have any money," old Mrs. Culpepper said. "Charlesetta, what's she talking about?" She turned to look up at her housekeeper, who had taken a place next to her employer's chair.

"Now you just hush, Miz Lucretia," Charlesetta said firmly. "They ain't talking to you."

The old lady had a cane resting across her lap. Wanda Nell had never seen her use one before. She glanced down at Mrs. Culpepper's legs. Her left leg sported a bandage around the ankle.

"She's talking to me, Miz Culpepper," Wanda said loudly. "But I don't have the money she's talking about, either."

"But you must know where it is by now," Taylor said, her voice sounding a little desperate. "You've got to find it before Elmer Lee turns up."

"What money are they talking about, Charlesetta?" Mrs. Culpepper moved restlessly in her chair.

"I'm talking about the money your son stole from a casino in Greenville," Taylor said impatiently.

The old woman drew herself up proudly in her chair. "I don't know who you think you are, young woman, barging into my house like this, and bringing all these people with you. But I assure you my son didn't do any such thing. He was a good boy, and he didn't steal."

"Give me a break." Mayrene muttered under her breath to Jack Pemberton, sitting on her left. "The old lady is as crazy as a Betsy bug."

Wanda Nell turned her head and glared at them. Mayrene quieted, and Jack Pemberton winked at her. She grinned back. Despite the tenseness of the situation, she appreciated his steadfast calm.

"You must have some idea where he hid it," Taylor was saying. "If it's not at your trailer, then it's probably here somewhere, in this house."

"It just might be," Wanda Nell said. "But if we find it here, and I'm not saying we will, but if we do, what are you gonna do then?"

"Turn it over to the state police," Taylor said. "I've already called them, and they're on their way here."

"Really? That's good," Wanda Nell said. She wanted to believe the deputy, but this whole situation made her uneasy. She had a good idea where the money might be, but she didn't want to play her hand too soon.

"Yeah, but we got to find that money quick," Taylor said. "Time's running out. Why don't you start looking for it?"

"That's gonna take time," Wanda Nell said. "This is a big house, and there's lots of places to look."

"Then start looking," the deputy snapped at her.

Wanda Nell stood up. "I don't like your tone, Deputy."

"I don't care," Taylor said. "Just do what I say."

The doorbell rang, startling them all. Charlesetta moved toward the door, but Taylor, her gun drawn, motioned for her to stay where she was. "Nobody move," she said. "This could mean trouble."

Wanda Nell looked at Charlesetta, a question in her eyes. Charlesetta understood. "I locked the door when y'all come in."

"Let me go see who it is," Wanda Nell said.

Taylor shook her head.

A voice called out to them from the front porch. "We know you're in there, Taylor. Don't do anything stupid. No need for anybody to get hurt."

It was Elmer Lee Johnson. Wanda Nell stared at Taylor.

"What's going on, Elmer Lee?" Wanda Nell yelled so loud that both Charlesetta and Mrs. Culpepper started.

"I'm here to make an arrest, Wanda Nell," Elmer Lee yelled back. "Taylor's the one that killed Bobby Ray."

"He's lying." Taylor stood up. "Don't believe him."

Wanda Nell took a step toward the door of the parlor.

Taylor pulled her gun. "Don't do it, Wanda Nell. Trust me. He's lying."

Wanda Nell stared at her. Which one of them was she going to believe?

# Twenty-Nine

"She says *you're* lying, Elmer Lee." If she had to keep yelling like this, Wanda Nell figured her voice would give out pretty quick.

"Jesus, Wanda Nell, don't give me that crap." Elmer Lee banged on the front door several times.

"I'm not kidding you, Elmer Lee. Now which one of you am I gonna believe?"

"Come on, Wanda Nell."

"Why should I believe you, Elmer Lee? You're the one who was trying to make out like I killed Bobby Ray. Then you put my son in jail saying he did it. What's it gonna be?"

"He killed your husband, Wanda Nell," Deputy Taylor hissed at her. "No matter what he tells you, he's the one done it."

Wanda Nell stared hard at her. She couldn't make this woman out. She had seemed helpful, almost from the get-go, going behind Elmer Lee's back to tell things she shouldn't. Now she was acting like she was trying to save them all from Elmer Lee.

"I figured out pretty quick you didn't do it," Elmer Lee shouted. "We knew Bobby Ray had to have help, but I didn't really figure it was you. You wouldn't do something like that."

"You keep saying nice things like that, Elmer Lee, and I'll think you like me."

"Don't be funny, Wanda Nell. That little girl in there's the one that killed Bobby Ray. Has she got a gun on you?"

"She's got a gun, and my daughter Juliet's in here, along with Miz Culpepper and a few other folks." Wanda Nell glanced at Mayrene, who had her hand on the shotgun. Deputy Taylor seemed to have forgotten all about it. She had her eyes focused intently on Wanda Nell.

"All right, Wanda Nell. We ain't aiming to do nothing real suddenlike."

Wanda Nell waited for Elmer Lee to say something else, but all she could hear was the scuffling of feet on the porch. How many men did Elmer Lee have out there with him? She wished she could get to a window and look out.

And, dear Lord, Miranda and the baby were out there. Well, there wasn't a blessed thing she could do about that now. They were in the Lord's hands. Right now Wanda Nell had to keep her mind on what was going on in Miz Culpepper's parlor.

Deputy Taylor hadn't moved away from the sofa. She was still too close to Juliet, and Wanda Nell didn't like that. Even if the deputy was telling the truth, Wanda Nell wanted to get her away from Juliet.

"Don't anybody move," Taylor commanded. "Stay still. Don't let 'em hear us moving around. And if I tell you to, hit the ground and stay there."

At that, Charlesetta started singing and praying, just loud enough for the others to catch a bit of the words.

"Oh, hush up with your foolishness, old woman," Mrs. Culpepper snapped at her. "Nobody's interested in your carrying on."

Charlesetta paid her no attention, but Taylor was momentarily distracted. Juliet had never taken her eyes from her mother's face, and Wanda Nell tilted her head slightly. Juliet blinked her eyes several times to indicate she understood.

"Wanda Nell!"

"What is it, Elmer Lee?"

"There's some things I think you oughta know."

"Like what?"

"Like that so-called deputy in there was running around with Bobby Ray. She don't think we know about that, but we do."

Wanda Nell watched Taylor's face carefully. The deputy blinked once, but then her eyes hardened. "He's lying, I tell you. Why would I take up with scum like that?"

"She says you're lying, Elmer Lee."

"We also done figured out," Elmer Lee yelled back, "she was the one helped Bobby Ray get that money out of the casino. You know how they did that?"

"How?" Wanda Nell kept staring at the deputy.

"Miss Deputy in there dressed up like an old lady, and she went in that casino and told 'em she had a remote-control bomb in her purse. If they didn't give her some money, and give her time to get away, then she would let the bomb go off."

Taylor was shaking her head back and forth in denial.

"She's still denying it, Elmer Lee. You know what she told me? She says you want that money for yourself." Wanda Nell's throat was starting to hurt. She wanted some water desperately, plus she had to pee.

She could hear Mayrene and Jack Pemberton near her, their breath coming a little ragged. They were all trying to keep still, and the strain was getting to all of them. Juliet was white as a sheet, and Charlesetta's skin had a gray tinge to it. Wanda Nell was suddenly afraid the elderly woman might have a heart attack.

"I'm not the one after the money, Wanda Nell," Elmer Lee called back. "She is. Get her to tell you about her cousin that worked over in the sheriff's department in Washington County. The one that didn't tell anybody the casino called to report a robbery."

"What's he talking about?" Wanda Nell demanded.

Taylor shrugged.

"He's the one who showed up at your door demanding the money, Wanda Nell. How do you think he got there so fast after you called us?"

"I didn't call him, whoever he is," Taylor said, her voice starting to sound increasingly desperate. "I swear I didn't."

"She's still not budging, Elmer Lee."

As Wanda Nell glanced back at Taylor, she saw something that made her blood run even more cold, if that were possible. There was a window in the wall behind the sofa, about six feet away. A man stood there with a rifle. He had it aimed straight at Taylor.

This couldn't go on much longer, one way or the other. Wanda Nell tried to figure out what she could do to get Juliet out of the line of fire. Elmer Lee could have the damn money, if only she could get them all out of this mess alive.

"Come on out now, Taylor," Elmer Lee yelled into the silence. "Don't hurt those people in there. Don't dig the hole any deeper for yourself."

Wanda Nell watched for a moment. Taylor didn't move. Her eyes appealed to Wanda Nell for belief.

"What's going on in there, Wanda Nell?"

"Nothing, Elmer Lee. We ain't moving."

She could hear him cursing. Then he started yelling loud enough for her to hear again.

"Tell her, Wanda Nell, we got us a witness that saw her car that night at the trailer park."

"Who?" Wanda Nell demanded.

"Your daughter, Miranda."

Wanda Nell took a moment to absorb that. "You got to be kidding me, Elmer Lee."

There was silence for a moment, then loud footsteps on the porch.

"Mama, it's true, I saw her car."

Miranda was frightened, Wanda Nell heard it in her voice. But she wasn't lying. Elmer Lee wasn't forcing her to say that.

Deputy Taylor must have read the situation in Wanda Nell's face. Before Wanda Nell realized what she was doing, Taylor grabbed Juliet by the arm and jerked her upright. She pulled the girl in front of her as a shield.

"Anybody move, and I blast this girl to kingdom come."

Wanda Nell wanted to faint. *Dear Lord,* she prayed, *don't let her hurt my baby. Take me if you have to, but don't let her hurt Juliet.*

Taylor had moved slightly so that her back was turned toward Mrs. Culpepper. The old woman stared hard at Wanda Nell, then slowly she winked.

Wanda Nell couldn't breathe for a moment. What was the old witch trying to tell her?

"She's got a gun on Juliet, Elmer Lee," Mayrene yelled out. "Don't anybody move."

"We won't," Elmer Lee said.

Wanda Nell glanced at the window. The man with the rifle hadn't moved. He was still aiming straight for Taylor.

She took a deep breath. "Why'd you do it, Taylor? Why'd you kill Bobby Ray? What'd he ever done to you?"

"That lying sonofabitch was gonna leave me high and dry," Taylor said, her face reddening in anger. "He thought he was gonna get away with all the money and leave me with nothing. That piece of scum tried to run out on me."

Taylor had loosened her grip just slightly on Juliet. Wanda Nell kept an eye on Mrs. Culpepper. The old lady took her cane like a club, and with a bellow of rage that made them all jump, cracked Taylor right in the middle of her back.

Taylor screamed in pain, while Wanda Nell dove toward Juliet. Jack Pemberton got there before her and grabbed Juliet in his arms. He swung her around, so that his back was toward Taylor, protecting Juliet from her.

Wanda Nell was on her knees when she heard the shot. She saw Jack Pemberton stagger.

From behind her, Wanda Nell heard another shot, and then she saw a bright crimson flower forming on Taylor's chest. The deputy toppled to the ground, and Wanda Nell scrambled back out of the way, almost knocking over the sheriff's deputy who stood there, gun in hand.

Getting shakily to her feet, Wanda Nell held out her arms to her daughter. As she clasped a shivering, crying Juliet in her arms, Wanda Nell watched Jack Pemberton sink to the floor, clutching his leg.

"We need an ambulance," Mayrene shouted. She got down on her knees beside Jack Pemberton. "Honey, where'd she shoot you?"

"Leg" was all Pemberton was able to say before he passed out.

"Ambulances are on the way," Elmer Lee said, laying a hand on Wanda Nell's shoulder. "Is your daughter okay?"

Wanda Nell couldn't say anything. She just nodded and continued stroking Juliet's hair.

Elmer Lee squatted on the floor beside Mayrene, taking a quick look at Jack Pemberton. Then he stood up and went over to check on Mrs. Culpepper and Charlesetta. The elderly housekeeper had stumbled to the sofa and collapsed onto it, and Mrs. Culpepper stood over her, patting her hands and telling her to stop her nonsense.

Wanda Nell couldn't look at the crumpled body of Deputy Taylor on the floor. Shivering, she drew Juliet away and out of the house. Miranda, with Lavon in her arms, awaited them anxiously in the driveway, held back by another deputy. Wanda Nell held out an arm, and Miranda came running.

All three of them were crying now, and Lavon joined in. Slowly they made their way over to the bench under the tree, and Wanda Nell sat down in the middle. She kept an arm around each of the girls.

"Thank the Lord, y'all are okay, Mama," Miranda said. "I was so afraid." She started crying again.

"Mama was so brave, Miranda," Juliet said through her tears. "I was scared to death, but Mama stayed so calm. I swear I would've just died right there on the spot if Mama hadn't come."

"It's over now," Wanda Nell said, "and I'll thank the Lord every day that neither one of you got hurt." She turned to Juliet anxiously. "She didn't hurt you, did she, honey?"

"No, Mama, she just scared me." Juliet wiped her eyes with trembling fingers. "They called from the office for me to come down there, and they told me somebody from the sheriff's department was coming to pick me up. All they would tell me was that you'd been in an accident."

"That school's gonna hear from me," Wanda Nell said. "They should've checked to make sure that was a legitimate call."

"What did she tell you when she came to pick you up?" Miranda had calmed Lavon, and Wanda Nell took him into her lap. He snuggled against her, and she stroked his soft hair.

"She said she needed to take me to my grandmother's house. There'd been an accident, and they needed a member of the family. Then when we got here, she had me call you on your cell phone, Mama, but she wouldn't let me tell you anything."

"I'm sorry she put you through all that, baby," Wanda Nell said.

"I'm just glad it's over, Mama," Juliet said, leaning against her. "Can we go home now?"

"Probably not just yet," Wanda Nell said. "But as soon as we can, I promise."

As they watched, the paramedics brought Jack Pemberton out on a stretcher. "Oh, my Lord, Mama, I forgot all about Mr. Pemberton," Juliet said. "You think he's gonna be all right?"

"I hope so, honey," Wanda Nell said, her eyes filling with tears again. He had risked his life to save Juliet, and she would never be able to thank him enough. He had to be all right, he just had to.

Moments later, another stretcher came out of the house. This time it was Charlesetta, and Wanda Nell prayed for the elderly woman. What had happened inside that house was enough to give anybody a heart attack.

Elmer Lee came out of the house and glanced around. When he saw them, he came down the steps and across the yard and driveway toward them. Wanda Nell watched him. His face was gray with exhaustion, and he walked like an old man.

"Y'all okay?" His voice was gruff, but for once, Wanda Nell read real concern in his eyes.

"Yeah," Wanda Nell said around a sudden lump in her throat. "Thank you, Elmer Lee." She waved a hand in the direction of the departing ambulances. "What about Mr. Pemberton and Charlesetta? Are they going be okay?"

"The old lady may've had a heart attack," Elmer Lee

said, "so they're going to check her out. Pemberton's gonna be okay. Looks like the bullet went clean through his leg. They don't think it even hit the bone."

"I'm glad he'll be okay," Wanda Nell said, "but poor Charlesetta. It was just too much for her."

"I'm sorry y'all had to go through all that, and I hope the old lady'll be just fine," he said. He looked away. "I knew that girl was desperate, but I didn't think she was stupid enough to try something like this."

"She must've had some reason to get spooked enough to try it, though," Wanda Nell said.

"I'm pretty sure she must've overheard me talking to the sheriff," Elmer Lee said. "I thought she was somewhere else, but I reckon she wasn't, after all. I was telling him we'd found a connection between that dispatcher and some-one in our department." He wiped his face with a handker-chief, then stuffed it into his pants pocket.

"So she figured she'd better get the money quick as she could, and get the hell out of Dodge."

"Something like that," Elmer Lee said. "You want the doctor to check this young lady out?"

Wanda Nell turned to Juliet. "You okay, honey?"

"I just want to go home, Mama."

Wanda Nell looked up at Elmer Lee. "Can I take them home now?"

Elmer Lee nodded.

"Wanda Nell!"

Elmer Lee stepped back, and Wanda Nell looked up to see Mayrene hustling toward them. "Wanda Nell, what're we gonna do with the old battle-ax? We can't leave her here alone."

"Oh, Lord," Wanda Nell groaned. "I forgot all about her. And if she hadn't done what she did, no telling what might've happened."

"What did she do?" Elmer Lee asked.

"She whacked that bitch of a deputy in the back with her cane," Mayrene said, laughing. "I bet she durn near broke the woman's spine, too. Hell, I hope I'm that tough when I get to be her age."

"I don't think you have to worry about that," Wanda Nell said dryly, and they all laughed. Even Elmer Lee joined in.

Wanda Nell stood up, handing Lavon to Miranda. "But I guess we need to do something about her. You're right, we can't just leave her here by herself. I don't think she's capable of looking after herself anymore."

"How about I stay the night with her?"

"Mayrene, after all you've done, I can't believe you want to do this."

Mayrene shrugged. "Oh, hell, honey, her and me'll get along just fine. And it'll only be for one night. We'll find something to do with her tomorrow."

Wanda Nell gave her a hug. "You're priceless, you know that." Linking her arm with Mayrene's, she motioned for the girls to follow them.

"Uh, Wanda Nell," Elmer Lee called. "You're forgetting about one thing."

Wanda Nell stopped and turned. "Yeah, what is it?"

"The money," Elmer Lee said. "You have any idea where Bobby Ray hid it?"

Wanda Nell laughed. "Yeah, I think so. I'm not sure, but I bet you'll find it in the closet in his old bedroom. There's a crawl space over the closet ceiling, and you just push a board out of the way to get up there. And it's probably in a laundry bag or something like that."

"Hell, I'd forgotten all about that place," Elmer Lee said, then swore under his breath. He strode past them toward the house.

"When'd you figure that out?" Mayrene asked as they continued their progress back to the house.

"Part of it was Charlesetta saying something to me yesterday about Bobby Ray always bringing home dirty laundry. I didn't realize at the time she meant he really brought his dirty laundry home." She shook her head in disbelief. "The man couldn't even wash his own clothes. Anyway, that was one thing. The other was seeing those dirty magazines of Bobby Ray's that we took from his room at Miss Turnipseed's." Wanda Nell whispered now so the girls wouldn't hear her. "I remember him telling me one time about that crawl space. That's where he hid anything he didn't want his mama to find. Like his dirty magazines."

Mayrene laughed all the way into the house, and Wanda Nell couldn't help laughing right along with her.

# Thirty

Wanda Nell stood in front of her closet, picking out something to wear to Bobby Ray's funeral. The only black dress she had was the one she'd worn to her mother's funeral. She pulled it out of the closet and held it up against her. She'd put on a few pounds in the last six years, so she hoped it would fit.

She slipped the dress off the hanger, unzipped it, and stepped into it. Pulling it up and thrusting her arms through the sleeves, then zipping it as far up as she could, she was pleased to find that it was only a little tight through the waist. She could make it through a few hours in this dress, if she didn't take any real deep breaths.

She took the dress off and laid it across the bed. Padding in to the bathroom, she stood at the mirror and began working on her hair and makeup. She wanted to look right for the funeral. She didn't want old Miz Culpepper making any catty remarks about how she wasn't dressed properly for the occasion.

Wanda Nell grinned at her reflection. She had to admit, the old battle-ax had really surprised her, whomping Deputy Taylor in the back with her cane. Meanness had its uses, and the old lady had saved her granddaughter's life with that vicious blow, maybe even saved all their lives.

"The nerve that little tramp had, standing there bad-mouthing my son," Mrs. Culpepper had fumed. "I would have given her a few more, if I'd had the chance. And her threatening a grandchild of mine with a gun! It's a good thing she's dead."

Though it pained her to be beholden to her former mother-in-law for anything, Wanda Nell had to give her a heartfelt thank-you for what she had done. "Both your granddaughters and your great grandson appreciate it very much," Wanda Nell had said. The old lady scowled, but Wanda Nell could tell she was pleased.

Besides having Juliet come through the ordeal unhurt, the best thing about it all was that T.J. was out of jail. Tuck Tucker had gone to work immediately, and the sheriff's department had cooperated, so that T.J. was released as quickly as possible. The sheriff had also pulled strings to get the autopsy on Bobby Ray rushed through, so they could release the body for the funeral.

The downside was that T.J. was staying with his grandmother. Her maid, Charlesetta, had suffered a heart attack, and the doctor had told her she had to take it easy. He advised her to retire, and Charlesetta was thinking about it. In the meantime, T.J. volunteered to stay with Mrs. Culpepper and keep an eye on her. Wanda Nell wished she could have him with her, but since the old lady had written a check to Tucker without batting an eye, she wasn't going to complain too much. Besides, if anyone could get Mrs. Culpepper to lighten up and treat her granddaughters and great grandson decently, T.J. could.

Hard to believe that three days had passed since that nerve-racking ordeal. Wanda Nell never had made it to her shift at the Kountry Kitchen that evening, but Melvin was being real nice about it. Since then she hadn't missed a minute of work at either the restaurant or at Budget Mart, and she felt like things were finally back to normal.

The only interruption in the routine was Bobby Ray's funeral this morning. Mrs. Culpepper had set it for ten at the funeral home, just down Main Street from her house. Burial would take place at the cemetery a few blocks away where Bobby Ray would rest beside his father.

Wanda Nell gave her makeup one last check, sprayed her hair for the final time, then went back into her bedroom to dress. Panty hose, dress, and low-heeled black pumps—she looked, she decided, like a proper mourner. She reached up into the back of the closet and pulled out a hatbox. Inside lay a black hat with a veil that had once belonged to her mother. An ornate hatpin rested in the box beneath the hat. She'd worn it once before, to her mother's funeral.

Wanda Nell took the hat to the mirror and placed it on her head. She fiddled with it for a moment, getting it set just right, then pulled the veil down to study the effect. Perfect. She slid the hatpin into place and moved her head about a bit. The hat sat firmly on her head.

Pulling the veil up and over the brim, Wanda Nell then grabbed her handbag and went to Juliet's bedroom to check on her. Glancing at her watch, she saw they had a half hour to get to the funeral home.

"Ready, baby?" she asked from the doorway.

Juliet, dressed in a becoming black sheath and black pumps, turned to her mother with a nervous smile. "I guess so, Mama. I don't really want to go, but I guess I have to, don't I?"

"Yes, baby, you do," Wanda Nell said with sympathy. "I know you didn't know him that well, but he was your daddy. And it's proper to go and say good-bye." She held out her arms, and Juliet came to her for a hug.

"You look real nice, Mama," Juliet said, pulling back after a moment.

"You do, too, sweetie," Wanda Nell said. "Remember to thank your grandmother for the dress and the shoes."

Wanda Nell had about fainted from shock when the old woman gave her a check to buy dresses for Miranda and Juliet to wear to the funeral. She had wanted to argue, but Mrs. Culpepper brushed aside any protests.

"Nonsense," Mrs. Culpepper had said. "The girls should be properly dressed for such an occasion." She paused. "It's the least I can do." After that, Wanda Nell kept her mouth shut. Mrs. Culpepper had also taken T.J. shopping herself, to buy him a black suit. He was going to be one of the pallbearers, along with Elmer Lee Johnson and several of Bobby Ray's old buddies from his high school days.

"Let's go check on Miranda," Wanda Nell said. "Bring your sunglasses, baby, you'll need them for the cemetery."

"Yes, Mama," Juliet said.

"Miranda, are you ready?" Wanda Nell called down the hall from the living room.

"Yes, Mama," Miranda answered. "Be there in a minute."

Miranda had asked their neighbor, Janette Sultan, to baby-sit Lavon during the funeral, and Janette had agreed. Still in shock over the fact that someone had broken into her trailer, Janette was being awfully nice to Wanda Nell and the girls. Wanda Nell suspected that Mayrene had sat Janette down and had a long talk with her.

With her dark coloring, Miranda was beautiful in her

black dress. Wanda Nell sighed. The girl was too pretty for her own good, but over the last few days, Miranda had been like a different person. She had helped clean the trailer, did the laundry without complaint, and had even managed to cook dinner twice. Wanda Nell wondered how long it would last, but in the meantime, she made sure Miranda knew how much she appreciated it.

Wanda Nell reminded Miranda about sunglasses, and Miranda patted her purse. A knock sounded at the door, and then the door opened and Mayrene stuck her head in. "Ready?"

"We're ready," Wanda Nell said. The girls followed her outside, and she locked the door.

Mayrene was driving them to the funeral in her stately old Cadillac. It was a lot more comfortable than Wanda Nell's small car, and she appreciated Mayrene's support. This was going to be a difficult morning, and Wanda Nell couldn't wait for it to be over.

"Y'all all look real nice," Mayrene said as they got into the car. She was quite a picture herself in a lacy black dress that did little to hide her ample bosom or her other generous curves. A saucy little hat with a wisp of a veil perched atop her hair, and Wanda Nell couldn't repress a smile. Mayrene had her own way of doing things, no doubt about it.

On the brief drive into town to the funeral home, Mayrene quizzed Juliet about Jack Pemberton. "Has he come back to school yet, honey? I bet everyone's talking about what a hero he is."

"Yesterday was his first day back," Juliet said. "He has to use crutches for a while, and he told us the doctor said he was really lucky. The bullet went right through his leg. It missed the bone, and it also missed the main artery. So he's going to be just fine."

"Thank the Lord for that," Wanda Nell said. She had visited Pemberton in the hospital the day after he had been shot, and she'd had to struggle to find the proper words to thank him for what he'd done.

"No need to thank me, Wanda Nell," he said, blushing. "I'm glad I was there. I'm very fond of Juliet, and I couldn't just stand there and let that awful woman hurt her."

"I'll never forget what you did," Wanda Nell said, her eyes tearing a little. "And here you are, in the hospital, and no telling what it will cost."

"Now, don't you worry about that," Pemberton told her, smiling. "Juliet's grandmother has already been by this morning, and she told me that she would take care of everything."

"Good for her," Wanda Nell finally managed to say. The old witch was full of surprises.

After a couple more minutes of awkward conversation, Wanda Nell stood up to leave. She was nearly out the door when Jack Pemberton called her name.

"Can I do something for you before I go?" she asked, turning back to face him.

He blushed again. "Well, I was just wondering, could I maybe take you out to dinner sometime?"

Wanda Nell smiled. "I'd like that, but maybe let's wait a month or so, okay? Maybe this summer, when school's out?"

Pemberton smiled back. "I'm going to hold you to that."

Wanda Nell had waved good-bye and gone on to her shift at the Kountry Kitchen. Since then, she had gone back and forth over it in her mind, wondering whether he really would call to ask her out, and whether she would really go. He was a very nice man, but he was much better educated than she was. What would they have in common?

Then she told herself firmly that was a bridge she could cross later. In the meantime, she needed to focus on getting her life and the girls' lives back to normal as quickly as possible.

Mayrene drove the car around to the back of the funeral

home, and one of the employees directed her where to park for the procession later to the cemetery.

They entered the funeral home, which had once been one of the old family mansions on Main Street, through the back door. Hector Padget, the funeral director, met them and escorted them personally to the viewing room.

As they came into the room, T.J. moved forward to greet them. He had been sitting with his grandmother on a nearby sofa. He gave Miranda and Juliet quick hugs, then held his mother for a longer embrace.

"Thank you, Mama," he said quietly.

Wanda Nell searched his face. He looked older somehow. The past few days had taken a toll on him, on all of them really, but T.J. had a new set to his shoulders. There was a maturity about him now, Wanda Nell decided, that he'd never had before. Her wayward son had finally grown up. "I love you, honey," she said softly back to him. "And I'm real, real proud of you."

T.J. offered her his arm and led her forward to the casket. Wanda Nell braced herself. She hated this part. Gazing on the dead always made her want to faint, and she was glad of T.J.'s support.

"He looks so peaceful," she said finally. She closed her eyes for a moment as the memories, good and bad, came flooding into her mind. The wave of grief she felt almost brought her to her knees. She had loved him deeply, and some part of her had kept on loving him, no matter what he had done.

Opening her eyes again, she held out a shaking hand and stroked his arm. The tears came, and she didn't resist when T.J. turned her head to his shoulder and wrapped his arms around her. He let her cry, and she could hear him crying quietly with her.

After a moment, she felt two other pairs of arms encircle

her and T.J. The girls lay their heads on her shoulders, and they stood that way until Mayrene came and gently drew them away.

Wanda Nell fumbled in her purse for a handkerchief, and Mayrene led Miranda and Juliet over to a sofa in the next room. After drying her eyes, Wanda Nell followed T.J. to where Mrs. Culpepper sat.

Bobby Ray's mother gazed upon Wanda Nell with red-rimmed eyes. Wanda Nell could see that grief had reddened her eyes, and not liquor, for once. Impulsively, she held out a hand to her former mother-in-law, and Mrs. Culpepper grasped it like a lifeline. She motioned for Wanda Nell to sit beside her. T.J. stood at her other side.

They sat in silence for a few moments. Then Mrs. Culpepper drew a ragged breath. "Burying a child is the hardest thing you can ever do, Wanda Nell."

"Yes'm," Wanda Nell said, patting her hand. "I still can't quite believe it all happened."

"He was such a sweet little boy," Mrs. Culpepper said. "So loving. But he was mischievous. Always getting up to something. But his father and I were so happy that the Lord had finally blessed us with a child, we let him do just about anything he wanted." She sighed heavily.

"And that was our mistake," she continued with a sob. "We brought him to this, Thaddeus and I. Thank the Lord, his father isn't here to see this day." She broke down then, her body shuddering with the force of her grief.

Wanda Nell hesitated for a moment, then reached out and drew Mrs. Culpepper gently to her. They cried together for a while, then gradually Mrs. Culpepper quieted. She squeezed Wanda Nell's hand as she sat back against the sofa.

"Can I get you anything, Granny? How about you, Mama?" T.J. asked.

Mrs. Culpepper smiled up at him through her tears.

"Could you get me some water, T.J.?" He nodded, then glanced at his mother. Wanda Nell shook her head.

T.J. moved off, and Wanda Nell sat there, wondering what to say to Mrs. Culpepper. Before the silence grew too awkward, people began to approach them to offer condolences. For the next fifteen minutes, neither Wanda Nell nor Mrs. Culpepper had time to do anything other than listen and occasionally respond with a thank-you.

Mayrene, Wanda Nell noted at one point, was keeping a close eye on Miranda and Juliet. After bringing his grandmother a cup of water, T.J. circulated among the visitors, and Wanda Nell glimpsed him briefly chatting with the lawyer, Tuck Tucker. Tucker had his hand on T.J.'s arm, and T.J. was smiling down into the lawyer's face.

Then Mr. Padget came to signal them it was time for the services to begin. T.J. escorted his grandmother into the family section of the chapel, and Wanda Nell came behind with Mayrene, Miranda, and Juliet. There was no other family to sit with them.

Afterward, Wanda Nell remembered little of the service. The preacher, a young man who obviously had never known Bobby Ray, spoke at some length, but Wanda Nell could never manage to focus on what he was saying long enough to take in the sense of it. Instead, she let her mind wander over the past. She thought of the good times she and Bobby Ray had spent together, resolutely pushing away any of the bad memories. No point in dwelling on those now.

Eventually the casket was loaded into the hearse, and they all filed outside to get into the cars for the short drive to the cemetery.

The sun beat down on them, and Wanda Nell was glad of the shade provided by the graveside tent as they took their seats. The preacher talked some more, and Wanda Nell looked past him, staring off into the trees on the other side of the cemetery. She didn't want to see the mound of earth nearby, discreetly covered by a large green tarp. She didn't want to believe any of this was happening.

Wanda Nell couldn't cry any more. It was all like some strange dream, and surely she'd wake up any minute now.

Juliet, sitting to one side of her, held on to her hand, and Miranda on the other side did the same. T.J. stood behind his grandmother, his hands bracingly on her shoulders. Mrs. Culpepper cried quietly the whole time the preacher spoke.

At last it was over, and people began to move away. Wanda Nell, an arm around each of her daughters, stood for a moment at the graveside. *Good-bye, Bobby Ray.*

With the girls beside her, she turned and walked slowly toward the entrance to the cemetery. T.J. and Mrs. Culpepper weren't far behind them.

"Wanda Nell."

She turned at the sound of Elmer Lee's voice. The grief in his face almost brought the tears back. Elmer Lee, in his own way, had loved Bobby Ray, too.

Mayrene motioned for the girls to come with her, and Wanda Nell stood aside. Mrs. Culpepper and T.J. walked past as she waited for Elmer Lee to catch up with her.

He held out his hand, and Wanda Nell took it. He led her a few feet away, into the shade of an old oak. She lifted her veil and tucked it on top of the hat.

"What is it, Elmer Lee?" All the animosity she had felt for him had drained away. She could almost forgive him for all that he had put her and her family through.

"I just wanted to say how sorry I am about everything," Elmer Lee said haltingly. His eyes avoided hers.

"It don't really matter now," Wanda Nell said. "We should just let things rest."

"Maybe." Elmer Lee sighed. "But I feel like I owe you

more than that, Wanda Nell. At first I was so mad over what happened to Bobby Ray, all I could think about was getting back at you."

"I know," Wanda Nell said. "You were pretty rough on me."

"I guess I was really mad at Bobby Ray for pulling such a damn-fool stunt," Elmer Lee said, "and I was taking it out on you." He shook his head. "He never learned. I tried my best, but he never would listen to me."

"No, he wouldn't." Wanda Nell leaned against the tree. She was so tired she could go to sleep right here. "But you loved him like a brother. And I still loved him, too. Even after everything, I still loved him."

"I know that," Elmer Lee said. He sounded almost angry, and Wanda Nell regarded him with surprise. "I could never figure it out, Wanda Nell. Why him? He treated you like dirt, almost from day one, and you let him get away with it."

"I guess so," she said, slightly puzzled. "I don't know, Elmer Lee, I guess love just makes you blind. Isn't that what they say? And I was blind for a long time, even though Bobby Ray did his damnedest to make me open my eyes. It took me a while, but finally I did."

Elmer Lee finally looked at her. "I wish you'd opened 'em a lot sooner, Wanda Nell. You never could see anything but him." He leaned forward and kissed her cheek.

Wanda Nell stared at him in surprise.

He turned and walked away.

Wanda Nell watched him go. She stood there under the tree for a moment, shaking her head in disbelief.

Pulling her veil back down over her eyes, she stepped into the sunlight and walked slowly to the car where her family waited for her.

# Wanda Nell's Favorite Recipes

## Wanda Nell's
### Original Thousand Island Salad Dressing

*½ medium onion (red or white)—chopped*

*½ cup sweet pickle relish*

*2 large hard-boiled eggs—chopped*

*Mix all together, add:*

*½ cup ketchup*

*2 cups mayonnaise (light mayonnaise may be substituted for regular)*

Blend all together, refrigerate for 24 hours before using. Makes roughly one quart of dressing.

## Mayrene's Wedges

*½ cup melted butter (4 ounces)*

*1½ cups oatmeal (4 ounces)*

*6 ounces milk chocolate chips*

*6 ounces pecans, coarsely chopped*

*1 can condensed (not evaporated) milk (14 ounces)*

Mix everything together and pour into a 9-inch buttered pie pan. Bake at 350° for 45–60 minutes. Cool; cut into wedges. Serve with a dollop of Cool Whip or unsweetened whipped cream— according to taste.

# GET CLUED IN

*Ever wonder how to find out about all the latest Berkley Prime Crime and Signet mysteries?*

## berkleysignetmysteries.com

- *See what's new*
- *Find author appearances*
- *Win fantastic prizes*
- *Get reading recommendations*
- *Sign up for the mystery newsletter*
- *Chat with authors and other fans*
- *Read interviews with authors you love*

# MYSTERY SOLVED.

berkleysignetmysteries.com

M2G0907

# Penguin Group (USA) Online

*What will you be reading tomorrow?*

Tom Clancy, Patricia Cornwell, W.E.B. Griffin,
Nora Roberts, William Gibson, Robin Cook,
Brian Jacques, Catherine Coulter, Stephen King,
Dean Koontz, Ken Follett, Clive Cussler,
Eric Jerome Dickey, John Sandford,
Terry McMillan, Sue Monk Kidd, Amy Tan,
John Berendt…

You'll find them all at
**penguin.com**

*Read excerpts and newsletters,
find tour schedules and reading group guides,
and enter contests.*

Subscribe to Penguin Group (USA) newsletters
and get an exclusive inside look
at exciting new titles and the authors you love
long before everyone else does.

## PENGUIN GROUP (USA)
us.penguingroup.com